The Forbidden

Three Novels of French Love

David Rehak

ISBN: 978-1-8479-9264-2
Angel Dust Publishing Group

Copyright 2007 by David Rehak
All rights reserved, including the right to reproduce this book or portions thereof in any form whatsoever, except for excerpts used for the purpose of book review.

The Forbidden

CONTENTS

Even An Angel Can Sin   4

From the Peasant Life to Paris   81

Sisters In Love   180

The Forbidden

Even An Angel Can Sin

The Forbidden

Ah, there is no better life than this;
To have known love, how bitter a thing it is,
And afterward be cast out of God's sight;
Yea, these that know not, shall they have such bliss

High up in barren heaven before His face
As we twain in the heavy-hearted place,
Remembering love and all the dead delight,
And all that time was sweet with for a space?

from *Laus Veneris*, Algernon Charles Swinburne

You wake in me each bestial sense, you make me
What I would not be.

You make my creed a barren sham, you wake foul
Dreams of sensual life,
And Atys with his blood-stained knife were better
Than the thing I am.

from *The Sphinx*, Oscar Wilde

The Forbidden

Prologue

It was the summer of 1910. Twenty-two-year-old Theo Bidault lived in metropolitan Paris--a handsome young man with an athlete's body and a scholar's brains. His background was very ordinary, middle-class. His father was a shopkeeper. Theo was far along in his law studies (he was planning to become a lawyer, according to his father's wishes, or rather, his command). Though still very young, Theo was a very precocious and highly promising poet in every sense: passionate, thoughtful, uniquely gifted and serious about his literary talent. A small, close circle of friends and he started a writer's group of their own--a movement, they liked to provocatively call it: The Cult of the Dionysians. However, Theo hated what he viewed as his friends' unhealthy preoccupation with so-called depraved poets like Rimbaud and Baudelaire. He was far more idealistic, pious, and wholesome. All they ever wanted to talk about was whores, fucking, drinking, fighting, and telling dirty jokes. Then when they finally did get around to high-brow intellectual conversations, they usually centered them around things like whether the theory is true that all sexual perversion comes from mental disorder or genetic abnormality.

***

"In a hundred years, people will erect monumental statues to the Marquis de Sade," predicted Theo's best friend, Marcel, at one of their usual meetings. "He will be hailed a genius, a true benefactor to humanity. His works will rival those of Balzac and Hugo; his philosophical ideas will outshine those of Rousseau and Voltaire!"

And the others heartily agreed.

Encouraged, Marcel proceeded: "It's very interesting, reading the intimate case studies of sexual perverts in Krafft-Ebing's masterpiece *Psychopathia Sexualis*. He was wrong about some things, but he was so right about others. It's interesting to imagine what it would be like to be the

The Forbidden

filthiest of sexual deviants, to be in their shoes ... but only for a day! I'm curious." After a brief pause, Marcel added, "I must agree with one of the female patients in that book who says, 'I feel assured in my belief that moral law was created only for normal humans, but is not intended to apply to anomalies.' You won't believe some of this shit. Here, let me read it to you. For example, here's a bit about passive flagellation as practiced by believers to emancipate the soul from sexual temptation. And I quote: "... a daughter with parents of high and respectable standing, she was a Carmelite nun in Florence (about 1580), and she became very celebrated because of her flagellations, especially due to the effects they had on her, and she is even mentioned in the *Annals*. She got the greatest pleasure from having her hands tied behind her back by the mother superior and being whipped by her in front of all the other assembled nuns ... Her thoughts were full of sexual lust while she was being whipped ... and she would cry out with longing: "Enough! Put out this flame which consumes me! I should not desire this! There's too much delight in it!"

A pause. Disbelief all around the room among the Dionysian members.

Marcel grinned and continued: "Case 24. "He dug up the corpses of females between the ages of three and sixty, sucked on their breasts, performed cunnilingus on them, but rarely intercourse or mutilation. One time he took away a woman's head, and another time it was a three-year-old's corpse. After his ghoulish sexual acts, he would put the grave back in order so no one would know it had been desecrated. He lived a private life, alone, was known to be a grim and melancholy person, and never showed any signs of having a heart ... He worked as a grave-digger for a short time in 1892. He later joined the army and became a soldier but then deserted and ran away, going house-to-house as a beggar. He loved eating rats. After he was found and arrested, they sent him back to his regiment, but he deserted again ... Finally dismissed from the army, he went back to grave-digging. When a seventeen-year-old girl with very large breasts was buried, his old passion was re-awakened. At night he dug her back up and used her body in his usual way. From then on, he did this more and more often. He fell in love with the face of one woman, so he took her head back home with him and covered it with kisses, calling it his bride. He was eventually found out after he took home the body of a three-and-a-half-year-old child ... He satisfied his sexual desires on her putrid body even while it was falling to pieces. The stench of her corpse from his house gave

The Forbidden

him away. He admitted everything."

There was now even more stunned silence in the room. Curiosity reigned. To Theo's apparent chagrin, Marcel continued reading aloud: "'Case 87. Miss X., age twenty-six. Mutual cunnilingus at six years of age; then solitary masturbation until age seventeen due to lack of opportunity to do more. After that, cunnilingus with various female friends, sometimes playing the passive role, other times the active role, always making herself come in the end. She practiced coprophilia for years. She loved to lick a beloved friend's anus and it gave her great pleasure. She also loved the effects of flagellation on her naked buttocks by a strong female friend who was good with the whip. The thought of ass-licking with a man was disgusting to her. Satisfaction came only when she imagined a woman was doing it to her. She also didn't like intercourse with a man. Her erotic dreams and fantasies were always of a lesbian nature and were limited to active and passive cunnilingus and analingus. During her bouts of kissing with her companion, it gave her much delight to bite or nibble on her companion, especially on the neck or earlobe ...'

"Case 166. This one's about a woman who dressed up as a man and tricked another woman into marrying her. Her full anatomy is described in minute detail. Listen to this: '... breasts quite well-developed and soft. Thick black hair covering her pubis. Labia majora quite large but normal; labia minora almost touching and under the thicker outer labia majora; completely normal without a trace of hermaphroditic appearance, but appearing no more developed than that of a ten-year-old girl's. Small and very sensitive clitoris; perineum very narrow; hymen lacking (perhaps congenitally) but vagina so narrow that it would be impossible to insert a male penis. It looks certain that she has never had intercourse ...

"'Case 189. Mrs. V., since her youth a sexual maniac for men. Came from good, decent household, very cultured, friendly, even shy, blushing easily, but always causing great worry to her family. Whenever she was alone with a male, it didn't matter whether he was a child, a man, or an elderly person, good-looking or ugly, she would undress herself in front of him and lustfully demand sexual gratification, and if he didn't comply, she responded with violence ... She was in love with her husband, but couldn't stop herself from demanding intercourse from any man, no matter if he was a deviant, a working-man, or a student.

"Every attempt to correct her behavior failed. Even as a grandmother, she still remained as sexually insatiable as the legendary

The Forbidden

Messalina. She enticed a twelve-year-old boy into her bedroom and tried to seduce him. He managed to break free and run away, and his older brother dealt severely with her. But it was no use, she didn't or couldn't change her ways. After being sent to a convent, she was the perfect model of proper behavior and didn't commit any lewd acts. This gave the nuns the mistaken idea that she had reformed, so they sent her back home, and there she continued with her perverse practices. Her family could stand it no more, so they moved her out to her own modest dwelling and put her on a small allowance. She had to work hard to make the money she needed to "buy her lovers". Just by simply looking at the neat, respectable-looking matron of sixty-five years of age, with her good manners and warm disposition, it's difficult for anyone to understand how and why she was so desperately needy in her sex life even at that old age.

"In the end, she was sent to an insane asylum and there she lived until May, 1858 when in her seventy-third year she died of a stroke. Her conduct at the asylum was perfect when under surveillance, but as soon as she was left to herself, she looked for any opportunity to indulge in her old desires, even as late as a few days before she died.'"

A few chuckles came from Marcel's listeners.

"You haven't heard nothin' yet," said Marcel, grinning. "Under Violation of Animals, among other things it says: 'In the big cities, the sexual intercourse of women with animals is limited to dogs. A peculiar example of this moral degeneracy is recorded by Maschka (Handb., iii); it's the case of a Parisian prostitute who allowed herself to be seen in the sexual act with a trained bulldog to a private gathering of roués, at ten francs a head ...'

"Here at the end, there's an even more unusual case reported by a certain Doctor Tardieu: 'A chronic nymphomaniac mother, obviously homosexually inclined, would climb into her young daughter's bed in the middle of the night and masturbate her for hours in vagina and anus. While doing this, she was very excited.'"

Theo was sickened by such accounts. He was interested in God and the wholesome things in life. The writers that moved him were ones who concentrated on beauty and uplifting subject-matter, on the pure and spiritual, not the dirty and carnal. His own poems were about love, nature and visions of a better tomorrow, not sordid sex, city squalor and cynicism.

Theo: "Enough, Marcel. This is really distasteful."

Marcel took the remark personally. "And what would you prefer I

The Forbidden

read? John Bunyan? Or maybe some *Alice In Wonderland*? Ha, ha, ha."

"No," replied Theo, unintimidated. "But I fail to see what good can come of always pondering over misery, immorality and degradation the way we do, without talking or writing about solutions to these problems!"

Marcel's grin disappeared for a moment. He nodded. Then, cheekily: "And what's your all-wise answer, O mighty moralist?"

Theo ignored the mockery and in earnest replied, "What we do need to address is: who's going to fix it, how, and when."

Theo spoke with such conviction that no one, not even Marcel, tried to differ with him. And they changed the subject, as it was depressing everyone.

Marcel was the exact opposite of Theo. He not only wallowed in vice and darkness, he loved it. His love and knowledge of the occult was immense, as he had been dabbling in it for years. And the pleasures of women were everything to him. His idea of the perfect mate was one who is very beautiful, witty, and wicked. The sexual proclivities he liked to see in women were adultery, lesbianism, incest, and whoredom. If by Jekyll-and-Hyde one means opposite personalities, Theo was the good Dr. Jekyll and Marcel was the bad Mr. Hyde. But despite their differences in outlook and beliefs, somehow their personalities really clicked and they enjoyed each other's company, they got along surprisingly well. Their friendship was very tight-knit.

There was a knock on Theo's window. It was Marcel.

"What is it?" Theo opened it.

"You coming to the meeting tonight? Everyone else will be there. Bring some of your poems. I think they're brilliant. Better than any of our stuff."

"I don't know ... I ... I ..."

"Don't worry, we won't dare you to sleep with that whore at the brothel like before. We won't be going anywhere. Just reading our latest creations, that's all. Here, look at this new one I wrote just before coming here."

Theo took it from his grasp. The paper was wrinkled and the ink smudgy. He muttered it aloud to himself:

The Forbidden

The sun gently stroked the nude bathers
As they surfaced from the blue;
These women washing together--
Whatever shall Propriety do!

Bare breasts swaying like apple-burdened trees;
Large, strong, solid thighs and buttocks that please.

And, of course, the hymeneal shrine,
Where phallic incense is burnt--sublime!

O how many bosoms like clusters of fruit!
O how many pink cunts for men's cum to shot!
O how many pretty eyes and prettier smiles!
O if I could fuck them all behind a masked guise!

They're good for takin' cock.
And haven't I one to spare?
My engine runs on libido;
Where there's pussy, I'm there!

The sun gently stroked the nude bathers
As they surfaced from the blue;
These women washing together--
Whatever shall Propriety do!

"Well? I think it's my best one yet. Like it?"

"Marcel, you know I don't like licentious verse. Write something uplifting ... Something from the heart, not the genitals. But who knows. You should send it off to a pornographic magazine. That's what Maupassant did with his dirty poems. He used a pseudonym: 'Guy de Valmont.'"

"Maybe I'll do that ... So, come on. And bring some of your work. Something good. You'll outshine us all."

"Thanks. Sure, all right, I'll come. Just let me get my coat."

Theo grabbed his coat and a sheet of paper with some of his poetry on it, which he folded and put into his pocket.

The Forbidden

The night was a peaceful and fragrant one as they made their way to the secret meeting place.

"So what have you been doing lately?" asked Theo. "You're not still fooling about with the occult, are you?"

"Of course I am. Just last night, I performed a difficult conjuration using Hermetic magick. It's quite new, developed or at least made known by an Englishman named Aleister Crowley, I believe. I summoned a demon named Belial. I let him come into me. I shouldn't have done it."

"You sold your soul!"

"No, I simply gave him entry. But it was quite dangerous. This was a powerful demon. As powerful as any demon from the Necronomicon. I'm afraid that he now has free access and can stay if he wishes."

Theo looked concerned. "I want you to give it up, Marcel. It's not a game. Demonology is a direct link to the supernatural forces of evil."

They walked up the hill towards Montmartre. In a matter of minutes, the secret meeting place was just ahead--a spacious crypt-like room below an old abandoned farmhouse. There was a stair passage down and the area was filled with flickering candles.

"Ah, so you made it," one of the members named Henri said to the both of them as they descended to meet the others. They were seven in all. The Cult of the Dionysians. What a name. Would they make their mark, like the Romanticists, or Symbolists? That remained to be seen. But really, most of them weren't all that serious about writing. It was just for fun, a hobby.

Again, as time went on and the bohemian atmosphere of the meeting sunk into Theo, he began to feel like an outsider. As usual. Like he didn't belong with this "wicked" bunch. He was far from a bohemian. The 'tortured hedonistic writer' routine just didn't appeal to him.

"Try some hashish?"

"No, thanks," replied Theo.

A few chuckles were heard.

"Absinthe?"

"No ... I ... I had some before coming here."

"Sure," they laughed. His companions grumbled amongst themselves and then to Theo: "Smoking hashish and drinking absinthe is the fashionable thing for poets these days to do. Come on, you're a poet, aren't you?"

The Forbidden

"That's right, and a far better one than any of us," said Marcel in his friend's defense.

Auguste, a thickset youth with muscular limbs, was probably the least talented of them all. He looked more like a weight-lifter. But he was very funny and his rude, Rabelaisian poems always entertained their senses, if not so much their intellects. Faking the stern and exaggerated mode of expression popularly used by many of the conventional, academic writers of his day in their public readings, Auguste stood up in front of them all and began:

Herve loved his bloody beans;
They filled his gut and rounded it like the moon.

But what was it that they produced?
Farts more fierce than a hag's foul breath.
Farts more inevitable than a lonely spinster's suicidal death.
Farts so huge they rip the anal canal.
Farts more fragrant than a virgin's dreams of love.

Yes, Herve ate his big brown tasty beans...
They made him fart, but that's a small price to pay!

They laughed.

"Your verse is improving," Marcel said, not without a tinge of sarcasm.

No one was allowed into these secret meetings. The only exceptions were the average slut (every town had at least a dozen well-known ones), and those vain, coquettish, illiterate prostitutes one could pick up any night of the week by the riversides or landing-docks, aside from the red-light district. They were always pleasant, these girls. Always eager to "catch" a customer, to please and to be pleased.

"I got us some whores tonight. Procured them a few hours ago. They'll be arriving at eight. Fresh girls, new to the trade. One's even a virgin."

"How many are coming?" asked Auguste.

"I got us one each, of course," said Marcel.

The Forbidden

"Are you sure they'll know the way here?"

"Of course. The procuress will bring them herself. She knows the way. She always brings our bitches."

Often, on those occasions, the seven young poets would show why they truly and literally were Dionysians in every sense of the word, staging the most elaborate, frenzied and perverse orgies. The warm night was ripe for such an occasion. Theo never took part in these, of course. He would quietly excuse himself. And his friends' boasting afterwards would irritate his sense of moral decency. Also, as usual, he would feel left out. Marcel, who was very fond of him, would defend him and try to cheer him up. But the sense of unease was always there for Theo, along with the secret moral outrage kept under a tight lid.

Theo angrily whispered to Marcel so the others couldn't hear: "You told me no whores tonight."

Marcel: "No, I said we wouldn't force *you* to fuck a whore. You don't have to fuck anyone. I'm sure we'll be too preoccupied with our girls to ever bother about what you're doing. Don't worry."

The group consisted of Marcel, Henri, Jules, Auguste, Robert, Charles, and sometimes, Theo. Marcel was the most sexually daring of the bunch. He was a devilish character with the heart of a libertine. But he had his good qualities, particularly his loyalty to his friends, his intelligence, and his capacity for kindness. Marcel was a tall, slim twenty-one year old. His body gave the impression of being malnourished because of its rather homey thinness, and his arms didn't have much meat on them either. But he had a very appealing and striking face and manner that attracted many young girls his way. He was a charming conversationalist, not at all shy with the ladies. In fact, he held the record--seventy-three--for having sex with the most girls of them all. Theo, who was his best friend, was the only virgin. Then we have the over-sophisticated Henri--always well-dressed, immaculately neat and well-groomed. He was a real gentleman, with the air of an aristocrat that seemed to come so naturally to him (he even wore a monocle). His parents had vague ties to nobility and he would take excessive pride in it. They were wealthy owners of a very successful tobacco company. His verse, as one might expect, was elegant and refined. On the whole, it was not bad. Jules comes to our attention next. He was the smartest one, the one with the highest I.Q. All of the members held a certain reverence towards him, intimidated by him, not that an Einstein was of any use to them. Still, they found his observations on science and

The Forbidden

philosophy enlightening. His poetry, however, didn't shine so well, too full of hidden meanings and obscure references. And because it was neither bawdy nor funny, it found little interest among the group. Auguste's poetry, on the contrary, was just that. He was the 'funny man', the one whose rude jokes everybody looked forward to. He rarely said anything that in some way wasn't meant to be offensive, or humorous, or both. His talents as a poet didn't seem extraordinary because he insisted on writing in an unimaginative and prosaic style, free from a lot of metaphor, imagery, and the like, which he found to be false and 'forced' devices. Well, his poems were the easiest to understand at least. He wanted to find a way, a formula, to combine poetry and prose into one art-form. Robert enters the picture next--he was the quiet one, and also the pessimist. You'd rarely find him in a really good mood. Sadness and apathy revolved around his being like flies around a carcass. He seldom spoke, but he smoked his pipe a whole lot. He was born with a half-gimpy leg so he had been made since the earliest age to walk with a cane. On top of that, his cheek had a nasty scar from when his alcoholic father burned it with a hot iron for his neglecting to carry out a chore. He was only eight years old at the time that it happened. All the group members felt sorry for him, and he hated them for it. His poems were very powerful, emotional and striking, but they were so dark, morbid and violent that they probably wouldn't find a large audience. Charles was the singer and songwriter. Inspiration for writing came very slowly to Charles. He preferred to bring his guitar to the meetings and sing lyrics from poems and songs authored by other people. Although everyone acknowledged he wasn't a real poet, they kept him in the group anyway because of his musical abilities. And last but not least, there's the from-time-to-time member, Theo, the one with the high principles and morals. He was sometimes teased for them, but not maliciously. His fellow Dionysians nicknamed him 'The Angel That Cannot Sin.'

    As they waited for the girls to arrive, they had nothing better to do, so they started a little debate, theological in nature.

    "All religion is an excuse for hatred and violent acts," Henri reasoned in that snobbish manner of his. "And indeed, a bore. I certainly can't be wrong about that."

    "On the contrary, you've been right about things only a precious few times. And this isn't one of those times," Auguste smirked. "I can't call myself a Catholic in the true sense of the word. But I was born a Catholic, I was brought up a Catholic, and I'm sure that superficial, sentimental

The Forbidden

attachment to the church will always be there in me."

"With me," said Theo, "It isn't God or the Bible that I have a problem with, it's church dogma, and the Catholic church's totalitarian control over people's minds. Its reign through guilt. Its tactics of showing God as this judge of humanity, when he's really the creator and lover of humanity, isn't that so? Trying to use the Fear of Hell to fill their pews on Sundays, when love alone is the tool of God."

"Well-said," uttered Marcel, nodding and agreeing whole-heartedly in support of his best friend Theo, even though he himself was an occultist.

There were footsteps. "This way, girls," said the voice of an older woman.

"It's the procuress. She's brought her brood at last," Auguste rubbed his hands together in lascivious anticipation.

"Indeed it is," said Marcel with a smile, as the procuress Madame Touchet and seven young beauties waltzed into the room.

"Here they are, Marcel,' she said. "Now pay up and I'll be on my way, young man, to leave you gentlemen to your ... pleasure."

"It's my treat tonight, boys," Marcel said to his companions, giving the procuress her money. "Be sure you give these girls back their fair share in the end, Madame Touchet. Remember, it's them who'll be earning the whole lot."

Madame Touchet, defensively: "I'll have you know that I look after my ladies very well. It's not easy, Marcel, not easy at all."

Marcel smirked. "That will be all."

When the procuress was gone, each man took his pick. Marcel got a short, plump, bosomy blonde with the prettiest face on earth; Robert chose a tall, slim, vivacious brunette with no hips and very Jewish features as well as a good, medium-sized bosom; Auguste ended up with the bawdiest slut, a girl with long, wavy, raven hair and the nicest ass, whose sense of fun and humor matched his own; Charles liked younger girls and chose a fifteen-year-old, but he didn't let her age fool him--she was a whore right down to her bones, as he was soon to discover; Henri didn't like the cheap, tawdry look, and he wound up with a neat and elegantly dressed whore who actually cared about her appearance at 'work'; Jules chose the least desirable one of the bunch, a very ugly blonde, quite morbid-looking in her skeletal thinness, with pallid skin, acne, and bright-yellow teeth, titless and with a morose temperament. She was also

The Forbidden

malodorous and, by the smell of it, much given over to flatulence. Last but not least, there was a beautiful redhead--virginal, freckle-faced, with lips soft and smooth to kiss, a prominent and dazzling head of hair, and tits as hard and round as fresh apples. Seeing that Theo was alone, she approached him.

The orgy began as a smorgasbord of undressing bodies took to the floor, mingling and sampling body parts.

Marcel was smothering his face in his blonde's large, pillowy breast-flesh, rubbing his palm between her thick thighs.

Robert liked rough sex, and his lively, full-fleshed, gray-eyed, brown-haired partner was glad to see it, as he fucked her with frantic speed and strength, mauling her breasts, biting and scratching like a beast.

Auguste found that he had more than he could handle. His lust was no match for the raven-haired slut, as she demanded to be sodomized, mouth-fucked and whipped all at once!

Charles' whore took the initiative. It was unbelievable. The little bitch ate him alive, drove him over the brink of exhaustion in their fuck frenzy. She knew every position, every trick.

"Let's rest a while," he sighed. In truth, he was feeling disgusted with himself, as he always did after sexual release, no matter who he fucked. He couldn't explain it.

"Just make me cum one more time, then we'll rest. Please?" She masturbated, begging him.

"You truly are a whore by inclination, not necessity."

Insulted, with tears in her eyes: "You better watch it, you hypocrite, or ..."

Charles chuckled. "Or what? What will you do to me, you baby?"

"Go tie your cock between your butt-cheeks and fuck yourself!"

She left, hurt.

"You sure have a way with the ladies," joked Auguste.

Henri wasn't a wild lover. His love-making was very self-conscious and methodical, one is tempted to say dull. It's as though he maintained his gentlemanly self-control even in orgasm. After the long fuck was over, the girl was left feeling vaguely undesired and yet adequately satisfied.

Strangely enough, it appeared that Jules was indeed very happy with his disgusting pick. Her foul-smelling body and mouth were, for him, exciting to kiss. Her every orifice was a veritable refuge for the most

The Forbidden

unspeakable variety of odors.

"Please be a little careful. I'm still a virgin," said the redhead to a just-as-nervous Theo.

"Oh, I'd never force you to do anything against your will ... In fact, you don't have to do anything ... anything at all."

The anxiety in his voice and the silliness of his words made her giggle.

"I like you," she said.

Theo, unresponsive, looked up and got a good look at her for the first time. No, she was not to his taste. She had what some might call an impressive beauty, but beauty is in the eye of the beholder, and what one man finds beautiful, another one finds 'average' or not attractive at all, visa versa.

"Doesn't it disturb you, all this debauchery ... all this sin?" asked Theo as they both looked at the others in the room.

"I don't know, truly," she replied with honesty. "I've never experienced it in a group ... or any way, yet."

"I'll never give myself up to the pleasures of fornication. Never. Never. Even if I were to fall in love. That kind of lust doesn't appeal to me."

"Yes," replied the virgin whore, siding with his position while at the same time secretly delighting in the orgiastic spectacle.

The poetry-reading (or rather, love-making) went on till two in the morning, and might have gone on longer if the candles hadn't burned out for good.

The next day was a mercilessly hot one--the air itself seemed to seethe like in an oven, and you could see it almost as well as you could feel it. Theo was taking a lunch break from all his studious boredom as he usually did, by going to eat at one of the local inns. His favorite place was temporarily shut down for repairs, so he decided to try a new one a little further along towards the beach. It looked like a typical English tavern, perhaps a bit smaller, plain but clean. There, by taking a seat near his fellow bourgeois countrymen and listening in on their often entertaining and lively chatter, he could escape the lonely quiet of being cooped up indoors for half the day, a slave to lessons he felt absolutely no desire to learn. He wanted to

The Forbidden

live the adventurous, carefree, and romanticized life of the poet, not the dull, routine, and difficult desk-bound life of the lawyer. Law was nothing more to him than memorizing an endless series of codes. The only joy in his life was that he was on his own, free and independent, away from the watchful eye of his strict parents. Not that they had any cause for concern with Theo. Still, it was very nice for him to be on his own. It was a sort of freedom within slavery--the unsalaried slavery of law school.

The inn was quite full when he arrived, for you can bet that there were many men eager for beer on such a hellishly hot day as that. He took a seat and ordered soup. While waiting for it, he faced the bar where most of the rowdies sat. They were for the most part muscular, tough, hard-working men, men who got up at the crack of dawn every morning and thought about nothing but the grueling work that burst sweat from their tireless skin ten hours a day. When he saw them, Theo became ashamed for thinking that he had it so bad. He realized how lucky he really was for continuing his studies. As was commonly the case, bar-girls flirted and talked with these rough, dirty, jovial men. Yes, Theo agreed to himself, they were all happy ... but as soon as the last sips of refreshment were swallowed, as soon as the pretty girls' enticing compliments were no more and these men's arms began to toil away as before, those hearty smiles would quickly smudge from their faces.

Theo was struck by one girl in particular. She looked about his age--a cheerful, giggly, affectionate type. She had long, straight, golden hair that appeared even blonder when the sun gleamed on it, and those lips, shaped like a heart as if carved to look that way by the Creator himself, won him over instantly. Her eyes were the kind that simply draw you in--big, bright and crystal-blue. Theo tried not to make his stare appear too obvious, but he couldn't help it. How could he be subtle with the overpowering beauty of Aphrodite in his presence. Unlike Marcel, Theo wasn't at all experienced even with talking to girls, let alone approaching them. Two hungers were eating away at him--his hunger for food and his hunger to know this princess. But how? How would he do it without completely humiliating himself? Besides, she seemed to be paying constant attention to one of the oarsmen standing at the bar. It made Theo nauseous to see his hand almost erotically rubbing the nape of her neck and the small of her back. The filthy brute wasn't even attractive. What was she doing with him? thought Theo. His soup was brought to him and he ate it slowly, still captivated by his seductress, who was the first woman he'd ever felt

The Forbidden

that strongly about.

As he was getting up to leave, Theo didn't see it, but the girl noticed him. Those magnificent eyes of hers that knights in medieval times would have killed for--yes, those eyes!--they examined him momentarily. And again, as he exited the doorway on his way out, she gazed at him, but this time her eyes never left him until he was outside and out of sight.

When Theo got back to his two-room apartment, he found it impossible to work. He clasped his hands behind his head, looking up at the ceiling, and muttered to himself: "My God, I want her."

Thoughts of the girl at the bar ruled over his mind like some ancient Roman tyranny. Theo was confused. Could this really be happening? Such powerful sensual thoughts? He tried to wrestle with them, but each time they pinned him down. He realized how naive he had been for thinking that temptation of that kind, which his friends were always so keen to give themselves up to, could do nothing to a young man of his spiritual strength and piety. The truth of the matter was that he was just as open to romantic and sexual bodily urges, now that he'd deeply felt them for the first time.

By the time evening came, the heat was long gone. A soft breezy coolness had replaced it, which was a relief to those who know the sleeplessness that boiling nights can bring.

There was a knock at the door. It was Marcel. He usually came in the evenings and they would do things together. When Theo opened the door, Marcel could immediately tell something was out of the ordinary.

"What's the matter?" he asked.

"Come inside," Theo's voice muttered, as if in a trance. "I have something that I really have to tell you."

"What? What is it?"

Theo looked at him with a stone seriousness. "I know it sounds like a cliche, but I've met the girl of my dreams today. I can't stop thinking about her."

There was a pause. Marcel's face lit up and his mouth quivered, struggling for what to say.

"You?" he stupidly asked, as if it wasn't humanly possible. "What's her name? Who is she? When did you meet her?"

The Forbidden

Theo's eyes fell and he turned gloomy. "I ... I ... that's the whole problem ... that's what's ripping me apart inside ... She's the girl of my dreams, and she doesn't even have a clue that I exist!"

"Well, where did you see her at least?"

"At the inn on the Boulevard de Quiveau. She was up at the bar ..."

Marcel broke out in laughter. "A bar-slut? You've fallen for a coquette? Our spotlessly sinless Theo has fallen in love with a cheap tart? Ha, ha, ha."

Marcel wouldn't stop laughing. It was like he thought the irony of it was the funniest thing. It hurt Theo to see his closest friend's response. It almost made him shut up and decide to never mention anything about it again. But his desire to talk about her was too great.

"You don't know if she's that kind of girl!"

"Oh, you poor fool," said Marcel, "how little you know ... those types of girls, they're all 'that kind'. They can't help it. It's in their nature. I wouldn't be in the least surprised if I've already had her myself."

Theo was sick of listening to this. He was downright angry. "Will you just leave? Just go!"

These words sobered up Marcel and he got serious. "My God! Don't get upset. I was only joking, I'm sorry. No need to lose one's head."

Theo became gloomy, pensive, silent.

"I've got an idea," said Marcel, after a few straight minutes of unbroken silence. "Why don't we go to the inn right now. Chances are that she's working there now as we speak. I know a lot of girls there."

Theo shifted his position. "But ... what would I say ... She's so beautiful ... I couldn't just walk up to her and start a conversation. It would be too awkward. She'd think I was strange."

"No, not at all. That's how it's done. Women like that--they like when you take the initiative. Besides, I'll be right behind you--it won't be as frightful as all that. And anyway, we don't even know if she's there ... Hey, if you don't take this chance, someone else will."

Those last words made Theo's mind up for him. Quickly, he got up, put on his shoes, and they were off.

The inn was only a short fifteen-minute walk away. The streets were dim and empty as the moon hung high and full-bellied. A combination of excitement and anxiety churned the contents of Theo's stomach until he thought he would feel unwell. He felt like a young student feels before the most important exam of his life.

The Forbidden

When the inn was in sight, Theo stopped dead in his tracks, turning around as if he had just sighted something too horrible to contemplate.

Marcel was puzzled. "What is it now? You haven't changed your mind, have you?"

"No," replied Theo. "It's just that ... it's just that ..."

"What? What?"

"There she is, damn-it! That's what!"

And he nodded to the entrance of the inn. That's where the girl stood, leaning against the wall. She was alone, as if waiting for her lover to arrive. It was noisy and rowdy inside so she had come out for a peaceful cigarette-smoke.

"Have you ever seen her before?" Theo asked.

"Actually, I have. But I don't really *know* her. One of her friends was a girlfriend of mine, but I've only actually talked to her a few times. She never took much interest in me. But yes, we know each other a little."

When Theo heard this, a surge of pleasure raced down his spine. To think! A girl that didn't find the legendary Marcel to her liking! Now that was a first! But he was even more delighted to realize that Marcel couldn't have slept with the girl, which had been a big fear for him initially because it would have ended his feelings for her.

"So you know her. That's splendid. It takes all the pressure off me. You can introduce us yourself."

Marcel nodded. "Yes, I s'ppose I can."

When she saw them coming, the girl called out: "Marcel!"

"Hi, Juliette," he answered, giving her one of his charming winks.

"Where's your fiancee-to-be, Brigette? I haven't seen you together for some time," she said with interest, all the while nervously eyeing Theo.

"It seems that Brigette will have to be somebody else's fiancee-to-be."

"It's over between you two?"

"Well, I wouldn't say that. She's a fine girl. It's just that there are so many other fish in the sea, it makes it hard for a man to--"

"You pig!" She giggled interruptingly.

"At least I'm honest," he chuckled back. "... So why aren't you working?"

"Oh, I'm off today. But I thought I'd keep the other girls company. Mimi and Jeanne are working tables inside. I just felt like

The Forbidden

coming out into the fresh air for a bit."

There was an uncomfortable pause.

Marcel finally blurted out: "Oh, by the way, let me introduce a good friend o' mine--Theo Bidault. He's a student, unlike myself. He'll be a wealthy lawyer one day and make a real name for himself."

"Not if I can help it," Theo joked laughingly. "Hopefully I'll flunk out."

"Why? You don't like studying?" Juliette asked him. "I so wish that I could have gone to school."

And from there began a long and probing conversation that proceeded inside the inn and left the three of them feeling at the end like they'd known each other for centuries. They became instant friends. Juliette turned out to be a witty, clever girl, quick with her tongue and easy to talk to. She could really understand you, that was the impression Theo got. And there was a certain simplicity and innocence underneath the surface, a certain adorable and affectionate side, that Theo found irresistible. This girl was surely no hussy! he assured himself. She behaved like any good, sweet, uneducated peasant-girl. The same simple, casual manner of expression, the same warmth and friendliness.

After four long hours, they said good-bye to Juliette, promising to see her again very soon. On their way back to Theo's apartment, Theo acted as excited as a fish out of water.

"The whole thing feels like a dream, my friend. I can't believe things turned out as well as they did, can you?" he kept asking, repeating it over and over, aware of how silly he was being but not giving a damn.

Marcel was amused, but he also saw the danger in a man becoming so strongly besotted and vulnerable to a woman. To be rejected by a woman one was infatuated with could be a very painful experience. And even if she was interested in him, that too had its drawbacks. Unlike Theo, Marcel was well aware of how dominating, selfish and jealous some women could get. How bitchy they could be. But, at the same time, he didn't want to hamper his friend's euphoria.

Theo was already planning meeting Juliette again soon, and planning it in detail. His mind was elsewhere as they walked along.

"Ah, my job is done," said Marcel, content to leave things as they were.

The Forbidden

Three uneventful days passed. Theo found his studies that much harder to do, with Juliette on his mind all the time. He even started having very intimately erotic dreams about her. Dreams he wouldn't dare tell anyone. He kept racking his brains with questions like: does she feel the same way about me? How can I find out?

When Marcel came to pick him up in the evening to take him to another group meeting, he was quite drunk, which irritated Theo because those were the times that he could hardly talk to him about anything. And Theo had been looking forward to asking when they'd get together with their 'new friend' again. Marcel stumbled in without even knocking, and fell hard on the bed, coughing and chuckling.

"You better not puke all over my sheets, you drunk. I just had them washed today," warned Theo.

"Fuck your sheets. We have to be at the meeting in twenty minutes. C'mon, let's go."

Theo looked disgusted. "I can smell your breath all the way over here. Have you been boozing all day long?"

"Ha, ha, just about. I met these two girls. They were bi-metallic, as they say."

"Bi-metallic? What's that?"

"I mean 'bisexual.' You know. They swing both ways--men and women. I took 'em to my place and ..."

"Yes, yes, I get the picture ... I'm just glad you didn't bring them. I don't want cheap sluts like that coming here, and neither does the owner of this building, I would imagine."

"Yeah, yeah. So, you comin'?"

"Well I have to, don't I ...Who's reading tonight?"

"Robert, Jules and Charles, I think."

"Charles the plagiarist?"

"Just because he recites the words of other poets doesn't make him a plagiarist. Besides, he's a far better singer than any of us will ever be," Marcel said in Charles' defense.

When they arrived, Auguste was missing, so the atmosphere wasn't as jovial and energetic as it normally was.

"We've been waiting for you two," Henri said, with a touch of

The Forbidden

aristocratic displeasure, sporting the dark and polished clothes of a dandy.

"Marcel's drunk as a beggar. I had to practically carry him here," replied Theo with equal displeasure.

"Alright, I'll start," Jules said aloud. "This is a poem I've been struggling with for weeks now, writing and re-writing it, every word, every line, like some obsessive lunatic. In fact, the new psychology of Doctor B. Misset has for some years now been studying such obsessive and compulsive behavior with--"

"Will you please get on with it!" interrupted Robert with an impoliteness all his own.

"Alright, alright, no need to shout. Ah, here it is. I've tried to write something satisfactory to your tastes. I call it 'Levitate The Undead':

Levitate the Undead
Onto the roof o' Night's

Alienation
Like an acephalous lubber fend

Tripping over tombstones.
Maculate Renifieurs

Finding companions
In the gutter.

All the charged rapists
Are by the Law's harsh

Shout eunuchs,
Soon to start a special club,

No doubt.
There's people like

Lord & Lady Sandwich
Having voluntary

The Forbidden

Excerebration with the
Hopes of

Having twice as loony surgeons
Find a cure for

Dementia precox.
A better chance of finding

Demiurge I think
You'd have.

    Robert hissed. "And what's that supposed to be? Most of it doesn't even make sense. Why don't you ever go for clarity in your poems? I mean, what the hell is 'excerebration'? or 'Renifieurs'? Are those psychology words or something? Don't you realize that the average person doesn't know these rare words? Why be a collector of rare words? What's the point of meaningless verbiage? Poetry, if it's to play a part in society, must be clear and comprehensible ... must be inclusive, not exclusive. It must be there for you to grasp and understand with ease and swallow with little chewing. Poetry must be for *all*!"

    Robert wasn't one to hold back. And though his lesson to Jules was blunt, it was just, holding more than an ounce of truth.

    But Jules, elitist to the bone, felt his ego bruised, and took offense: "Ha! This coming from a miserable, scar-faced cripple!"

    Naturally, Robert flew at him with a violence. "Filthy bastard! Stupid, untalented, poxy dog! Go back to your stinking little science lab where you spend half your measly, pathetic life!"

    Theo and Henri had to pull the rough and rugged Robert off of the frail and panicking Jules.

    Then, just when things were starting to cool down, the intoxicated Marcel pulled down his trousers in front of everyone and started to piss, laughing out loud all the while.

    "Marcel, you pig!" shouted Theo.

    Some of the urine sprinkled on Jules. "Shit! Shit! Shit!" he wailed hysterically. "You've ruined my new shirt!"

    Marcel's pissing went on so long that rather than let it continue to

The Forbidden

its bitter end, Robert pushed him sideways to get the yellow stream flowing at a safe distance from the rest of them.

Marcel fell to the ground, laughing even louder than before.

Auguste showed up out of the blue with five girls. They were all familiar to the group. Altogether, they were an attractive bosomy blonde; an ugly blonde; a tall, thin brunette; a gray-eyed, full-fleshed brunette; and a beautiful redhead.

"What in God's name has been going on in here!" Auguste demanded to know, half-smiling and half-confused.

"Don't even ask," Theo sighed.

After a groan or two, Marcel passed out.

"Is he alright?" one of the girls asked, concerned.

"Oh, sure," replied Henri, posing with his usual sophisticated gestures and high-class mannerisms. "If drunkenness were a palace, he'd never leave its golden gates."

Charles, thinking fast, covered a mat over the piss so that the ladies wouldn't be disgusted. They didn't even notice it was there.

Trying to bring some order and sanity back into the proceedings, Charles began playing an old folk tune on his guitar, dazzling all those present with the musical skill of Orpheus--god of melody. To his delight, the girls knew the words to the song and started singing as all of the others looked on--all except Marcel, of course. He was passed out.

It was turning out to be a very pleasant evening from what had started out being anything but. After they were too tired to sing anymore and poor Charles had run out of songs, Robert stood up somberly to recite something he'd written all while the rest of them sang (since he himself couldn't sing, nor had the desire to try).

Without a word of introduction, he began:

Reunion of Lovers

The black, half-decayed breasts
Of my lover exhumed
Upon which star-light rests
And Night's eyes begloomed--

The Forbidden

They, cobwebbed and bad-smelling,
A sordid tale of Disintegration telling,
Grip my attention and my sex,
Biting my libido like a vampire bites necks.

Stench of Death,
How your perfume
Galvanizes my nostrils!

Breasts foul as you are,
Don't refuse to be kissed;
Life from you from now is far
And has your flesh dismissed.

"Wow, that's horrible ... and yet so beautiful," Auguste commented.

One of the girls, the red-haired one, perhaps a little squeamish, said, "how could you write something so ugly? Ugh! A man kissing the breasts of a female corpse. Disgusting!"

"No it isn't," the ugly blonde boldly intervened. "I don't see one thing in it that one can call objectionable or distasteful. It's a poem about a lover who misses his beloved so much, with so much love and longing, that he opens her tomb to be with her again. I, for one, would die for a devotion so great!"

"Yes," agreed Charles enthusiastically. "Baudelaire would have been proud to have written it."

In the meantime, the ugly blonde started to make a few sexual advances on Theo, flirting and petting him with affection. Jules, who had always found her desirable and whose favorite choice she had always been, looked on with some jealousy.

In tune with her characteristic boldness, she asked, "do you find me attractive?"

Theo was a stranger to such situations and he didn't want to offend the girl, especially considering how self-conscious and low on self-esteem he presumed girls like her were. "Yes ... you seem ... nice."

She giggled. "Nice? Is that all?"

As Theo looked around, he noticed everybody else was getting

The Forbidden

quite amorous as well. Marcel and Auguste were simultaneously fucking the blonde with large breasts. She seemed to love it up the ass; but her greatest thrill was to be double-or-triple-fucked. Unlike most women, she liked the taste of men's cum, and when Marcel and Auguste splattered theirs all over her face, she gasped her approval, licking their engorged cockheads clean.

Charles, Henri and especially Robert, cheered, whistled and laughed uncontrollably as the slim brunette whipped the full-fleshed brunette, delighting in her groans of pleasure.

"Now slap me, you weak little shit!" the full-fleshed masochist demanded.

Robert roared with laughter.

The slim girl started slapping the big girl's ass ecstatically, enjoying it every bit as much as her submissive.

"Now my cunt, you shit-fucked, skinny piece of shit," the big brunette said, and knowing exactly what was expected, the little brunette started tapping the woman's rather large clitoris with the palm of her hand, making her writhe and squirm through her teeth as she bit into her lower-lip.

Like an uninhibited voyeur, the redhead watched everything, completely hypnotized and masturbating so desperately that her pussy was damp. Every once in awhile she would stop, as if to rest her hand and put her cunt-juice-covered fingers to her nose to smell and lick before starting up again as before with a new energy.

The ugly blonde started pulling off Theo's pants, all the while staring at him with those half-lidded eyes of spell-binding seduction. When she put her hand on his penis, sliding down the foreskin, a surge of temptation attacked Theo's self-control. Like a cruel and cold she-vampire, she was draining away his power, leaving him weak. She made him lean back on his back, his pants dangling down by his ankles. The ugly blonde was behaving like the foul whore she was, already sweating with sexual anticipation and arousal.

"I'm not the type that needs to be treated gentle. I like it rough, like my friend over there," she said, pointing to the masochistic brunette and breathing with a hot, sexy breath. "I also like it nasty."

Suddenly, Theo's conscience filled his mind with thoughts of Juliette. The guilt made it torture. When he realized the impact of what he was about to do, Theo shoved the ugly blonde aside just as she was

The Forbidden

pulling up her skirts to get on top of him, and he hurried outside.
"Hey! Where are you going!" she hollered like an angry beast. "I don't have the pox!"
"Juliette, I wish *you* were my love," he kept muttering silently like a madman, racing for home. He fled his temptation like Saint Augustine of Hippo, embarrassed though he was. Sure, he heard the others laugh at him when they saw what happened, but that was the last thing on Theo's mind. He alone knew the real reason for what he did, but that was enough.

At noon the following day, Theo went to the inn to have his lunch. He was hoping to run into Juliette. She was there, chatting some sailor's ear off. Theo called her over, to the chagrin of some of her rowdy company. She was very pleased, and even a little surprised, to see him. They hugged and sat down at a table.
"So, what'll you have to eat?" he asked.
"Oh, nothing. I'm trying to keep my figure."
"And an hourglass figure it is." Theo smiled.
"Thanks. I'd like to hope so."
Theo ordered veal, but felt bad about being the only one eating.
"So, where's your friend, Marcel?" she got around to inquiring.
"Well, at the moment, he's probably reaching the final stages of a nasty hang-over."
"Oh, that Marcel," she rolled her eyes, "he never does anything in moderation."
"Yeah. I'm afraid the wine flowed a little too freely in his veins last night. He was already drunk by the time he reached my house. I almost booted him out ... People say that we're French, wine's in our blood, but one of these days this heavy drinking will poison Marcel. Fewer and fewer are the days that I find him perfectly clear-headed and sober. He gives in to sexual excess as well. One of these days he'll catch something he can't get rid of, if you catch my meaning. But it's the price he pays for being Don Juan."
"And you? You're not much of a Don Juan?"
"Me? Are you joking? I don't have time to be frivolous or love-struck. My studies are just such a pain in the you-know-what. They're so hard and time-consuming, and leave little room for anything else."

The Forbidden

"But would you want to be love-struck?" Juliette asked, putting her hand on Theo's. She rubbed his fingers with hers gently and gave him one of those flirty glances which made its meaning clear. "Would you like to see where I live?"

"Very much," Theo nodded.

It was obvious to him--they were on their way, not only to her home, but to romance! To the erotic love of youth! To a beginning for both of them! This situation was the one Theo had only dreamed about for so many nights. And here it was--no dream. Much closer than any fantasy. Though he was a little nervous, the excitement far outweighed the anxiety. He was ready to sacrifice his virginity, to give this woman his all--his body, his soul, everything, in supreme selflessness and vulnerability.

Along the way, Theo said: "Juliette, why do you work at the inn? Don't you hate those dirty men pawing at you and talking all obscene like they'd never dare in front of their wives? It's terribly low-class."

Wanting to make Theo jealous to make him desire her more, she took the opportunity to say, "maybe I like them. What's it to you?" She smiled.

"N-nothing," stuttered Theo. "It's just ... uh ...well ... I don't think it's a good idea, that's all. You never know what those brothel-hounds are capable of."

"Oh yes? As it so happens, I see many of those so-called brothel-hounds every day ... do I ever."

Eager to discontinue this thread of discussion, Theo didn't even bother asking what she meant by that last remark. They arrived at house and went inside.

"Well, this is it. I know it isn't much. But it suits us fine."

"Us?"

"Yes, I forgot to mention. I live with two other women. We rent the place."

"Really? Where are they?"

"They're out somewhere."

"So we're alone," Theo grinned, inching closer to the prize that he hoped would soon be his.

"Yes, even the air is silent." She caressed his cheek with the back of her hand.

A tear leaked from the corner of Theo's eye. "My God. Please don't think me stupid, but ... I think I'm in love with you," he sighed almost

The Forbidden

inaudibly, yet meaningfully.

Hearing him say this urged her lips to his, as the two of them melted into each other, body and soul. There was nothing sentimental about it. Pure magic!--that's what it was. After a long, undisturbed kiss, Theo broke away gasping. He was already hot and beginning to sweat.

"Holy Christ, I want you, Theo. I've never felt so much for anybody ... I've never wanted anybody like I want you; God help me, I'm telling the truth."

"You're my pure angel--perfect," Theo replied.

"I'd love for you to think that."

"I do." He smiled. "Oh, I do!"

"Come here, Theo," she grabbed him by the shirt, tugging him close. "I want your lips."

Theo: "They're burning for you like you wouldn't believe."

Right before he kissed her, Juliette stopped him and said: "I'm gonna make this time together so memorable for you ... I want you to go wild with desire for me."

She led him into her bedroom and what happened behind those closed doors was the awesome union of love and sex linked together into one. To those uninitiated in the rites of true love, this nameless feeling makes no sense. Those who are virginally chaste and those who are brutes of lust don't care for or understand this more special, more spiritual love. Theo and Juliette did. They understood it well. And they reveled in it. They knew it to be the blessed combination which is the very life-source of all love-relationships, when both partners exchange love madly, desperately, blindly, feeling that there is no higher peak than the one upon which they lay. This was more than just lust. Theo had entered the room wrapped in the plain white linen of boyish virginity, and he would leave it hours later gleaming with manly virility and a heart deeply in love.

"Now that I've had you," said Theo, embracing her, "I'll never let you go. You know that, don't you?"

"Theo, you know I'm yours. Nothing will hinder us. Not Death or even the Devil himself can kill my love for you. I've wanted you ever since that day I saw you at the inn," she paused, "eating soup."

"You saw me that time? But my eyes were on you the whole time. I never saw you look my way."

"Oh, I did, out of the corner of my eye. Believe me. And I said to myself, 'will I ever see him again?' I thought of you constantly. And then

The Forbidden

when I saw you with Marcel coming my way, I thought I was going to faint."

With a lot of emotion, Theo clasped her face and said, "But I felt the exact same way! ... I wish so, so very much that I could take you away ... that we could be off on some long voyage ... to a holiday in Greece ...Corsica, anywhere. Just to get away. To a beautiful, exotic land. To be together ... where nobody knows our names. Perfect strangers in a strange paradise. Just think of the adventure! The freedom! I would bring you oranges picked fresh from the trees outside our window in the morning. Can you picture it?"

"Yes ... in my imagination."

"Don't worry, it'll happen some day. I have my studies to finish. But after that, the world is ours!"

"Would you like some coffee?" she asked, getting up and walking to the kitchen.

"Yes, please. By the way, how do you get by on a waitress' wages? How do your friends get by? For a nice place like this so close to the water-front and such a good location, the rent must be something."

"Yeah, something awful. No, actually, we get by quite comfortably." That moment, something gave her the courage to confess: "We're all three of us part-time prostitutes."

"What?" Theo was as shocked as if he had just witnessed a public execution.

"Don't look surprised," she said placid-faced. "Do you know how many girls there are who do this? Besides, don't believe the stereotype. Most of us are every bit as good as the average girl. Only difference is, we get paid for a poke between the thighs. That's all. We get paid for it from strangers, whereas other girls give it free to their boyfriends or husbands ... Don't be such a prude. It's a business like any other. It's an honest trade."

Ironically, Theo's feelings for Juliette appeared to change completely in that split second. The invincible, all-powerful love he had felt was now crushed by one single hard blow that left him wobbling in bewilderment. He didn't know what to think. He was stunned. It was one thing to be a playful, flirty bar-girl by day, and a whole other thing to be a cheap little whore by night.

"Do you still love me? Even after this horrible revelation?" she asked, fearful of what his answer might be.

Theo took his time to answer, and in a shaky voice said, "of course

The Forbidden

I still love you. I'm shocked and disappointed. But my feelings for you are carved in stone. What can erase them? Virgin or prostitute, I love you all the same."

Delighted by his words and terribly relieved, Juliette madly threw her arms around him, smothering his face with warm, quick kisses.

The next evening, Marcel came to Theo's apartment and was met by a hostile Theo.

"Why didn't you tell me she was a prostitute? Damn-it! Didn't you know?"

Marcel knew the game was up, and rather than beat around the bush, he honestly confessed, "yeah, I knew. But just listen!--you seemed so happy, floating on clouds as you were, in love, that I wasn't about to step in and spoil it. Honestly, even if I had told you then, would you have even cared in such a state? I doubt it."

"Ah, maybe you're right. But it still would have been a softer blow coming from you."

"So she told you?"

"Yes, yesterday."

"Yesterday?"

"She took me to her house. We ... we ... Let me put it this way, we proved our feelings for each other."

"You made love? Wonderful! Amazing! She's in love with you as well?"

"Yeah. And all would be perfect paradise, if only..."

"If only what, you fool! This is it! True love! What else do you want!"

"I can't get it out of my mind--her sleeping with all those men! My God! A fallen woman! Such a defiled creature! What should I do? I can't give her up ... and yet it tortures my conscience to have her."

"Theo, listen to me! Will you forget your precious little principles for once? You've got to be realistic! You've got a wonderful girl on your hands. It's not nymphomania that drove her into prostitution. It's necessity! That's all! Don't you know that's the case with most of them?"

"I ... I ... but I can't support her, yet I don't want her selling herself. And ..."

The Forbidden

"But why don't you take her 'in' here? It's two bedrooms," suggested Marcel, rather wisely.

"Yes, that's it. That's what I should do. That's what I have to do."

"Alright, then. Now that that's settled, it's off to another Dionysian meeting."

"No, I can't possibly go," said Theo. "You were in drunken oblivion. You didn't see what a laughingstock they made of me when I refused to fuck one of their town sluts."

"Who cares? I'm sure they've forgotten by now. Everybody was sloshed out of their minds. You can't just not go. You're an initiated member--consider it your solemn duty."

"No, really; not this time."

Marcel laughed like his friend's words meant nothing, and he literally dragged him out the door. "You'll have fun tonight. Give it a chance."

When they got to the meeting, Theo quickly found that all was not forgotten and that the incident was still fresh in everybody's mind. Auguste, especially, had a hayday with his joking: "Oh look, everybody, it's our little altar boy ...Where's the priest who's been making you toss him off since puberty? ha, ha, ha! When will you finally give some girl a poke between the legs?"

Even Marcel got carried away, telling the group of how desperately Theo had wanted to meet Juliette and to be introduced to her.

They teased Theo non-stop.

At one point, Auguste remarked, "just imagine the two of them in bed. Would Theo have enough sense to get hard? And what a pair they'd make--like an angel and a devil making love together, ha, ha, ha."

This drove Theo into such a rage, that both out of a religious need to confess and out of a need to prove his manhood, he shouted: "For your information, I *did* sleep with her! We're lovers! For now! For always! So go fuck yourself!"

Theo spoke with such feeling and strength of sincerity that all his fellow Dionysians were in shock. Were they hearing him right? Was this Theo? Theo the saint? They all knew of Juliette's notorious reputation. They knew she was a 'nymph of the night.' And a much sought-after one at that! But rather than finally get the respect of his peers, a respect he would have so treasured, a respect he thought that a loss of virginity would produce, what they gave him instead was more snickering, with Auguste

The Forbidden

himself characteristically leading the way: "Well, Theo, you always gave us the impression of being an angel who cannot sin. Don't tell me that 'The Angel That Cannot Sin' *can* sin, ha, ha, ha!"

At their next rendezvous, Theo remembered Marcel's advice and offered Juliette to board with him.
"Oh, Theo. Are you sure?"
"As sure as day follows night. That way, we'll never be apart. But won't you get bored of me?"
She giggled. "If anyone will be bored, it's you. But I have a place. I'm comfortable and content where I'm living now."
"But it would be better if we live together," said Theo.
"Yes, alright then, I'll get my things."
It took her a few hours to move her possessions in. Everything was turning out very well. And the initial disgust and righteous indignation Theo had felt over Juliette's prostitution was starting to disappear, through the power of his unconditional love for her. He knew that she didn't love these men, she was simply allowing her body to be used. Theo deceived himself into believing that it was a job like any other, and tried not to be jealous. However, things didn't start off as smoothly as both of them had hoped they would. Gradually, she turned his apartment into a kind of semi-brothel. It got to the point that it was common for Theo to be studying, while in the next room, one of those dirty workmen would be grunting and groaning, fucking the living daylights out of Juliette. Theo would hear the sounds through the wall and they cut him like a daggar to the heart.
One day, it sent him over the edge. Just couldn't take it anymore. This time, Juliette was with the unattractive oarsman who Theo had seen that day up at the bar with her. It was the same man who had been caressing Juliette the first time Theo had ever seen her. Theo remembered him well--he hated him then, and he hated him now.
"Suck it, baby!" screamed the filthy oarsman lewdly, loudly. It gave him great joy to have sex with whores who found him to be as repulsive as he was because it produced in him a strangely erotic and sadistic thrill to know they were disgusted and yet bound to perform to his satisfaction. "Yeah! Suck it, you bitch! Yeah! ... I'll cum in your hair, you frigging bitch! Wrap them gums tight around it! ... Go! Go!

The Forbidden

Faster! Suck hard! Yaaaaaahhhhh, that feels gooooood!!!! Who taught you to suck cock like that, you slut!" And he mocked her: "It was your father, wasn't it, ha, ha!"

Suddenly, Theo flew into the room, slamming the door open. He was absolutely furious.

"Aaaarrrhhh!" he yelled, charging the large, muscular oarsman, who threw Theo across the room with ease after a harmless punch missed him, just brushing the side of his face.

"Sorry little man! but you'll have to wait your turn, she's mine until I've shot my load! Now get out! I'm not done yet!" The oarsman was starting to get furious.

Theo gave him a defiant stare and walked right up to him, only to get a punch in the face that sent him tumbling to the floor holding his face.

Juliette: "Please Theo, he'll kill you. Just do as he says."

Theo was quite afraid and, reluctantly, did as he was told. But as soon as he was safely out of the room and back at his desk with the fear gone, he felt a profound sense of guilt over his cowardice.

Theo got up spontaneously and left the apartment in haste, trying hard to hold back his unmanly tears. Lost in a sea of emotions, he carried on almost aimlessly down the empty, winding streets, and at one point he somehow managed to run into Marcel sitting at a public bench and smoking his tobacco pipe, trying to pick up on another pretty girl as usual.

"Marcel!"

Seeing his friend in the bad shape he was in, an embarrassed Marcel excused himself from her company and rushed over to Theo.

"What the hell's happened? ... Hey, what's that on your face? Did you get into a fight?"

"One of those fucking brothel-hounds struck me ... I'm not gonna take it anymore."

"What do you mean?"

"Doesn't she know what a hell this puts me through?--to see all of these strange men come into *my* home and sleep with *my* woman?" he said to Marcel. "What kind of man would put up with that? I've had enough! It's gotten out of hand. The whoring--it's too hard for me to bear, it's too much. How could I have been so stupid, to even compromise this much?"

Moral and religious outrage began to build up in him. He became troubled by a sense of God's wrath upon him and a personal need to repent. Theo kicked her out.

The Forbidden

"You've got to go," he told her.

"What?" She looked bewildered.

"I'm not content to share you with other men. Maybe you'll find another lover more open-minded. But that isn't me." His tone was so stoical, so unfeeling, so hard, so cold, it crushed and froze her.

"You self-righteous weasel!" she flared. "You call yourself a Christian? What about forgiveness? Mercy? Tolerance? Aren't those Christian virtues? Do you think you're any holier than me? Do you think you're any better? Unlike you, I don't have a father to pay my bills! Unlike you, I don't have the time to sit hunched behind a desk all day!"

"Oh, and you think I do that for fun?" he exclaimed aloud in deep irritation.

He threw his heavy law textbook at Juliette, hitting her on the shoulder.

"Aaaouch!" she gasped, rubbing it. "Alright, you ... you dog. I'll leave. And then don't you dare speak to me or approach me ever again!"

It took her only half the time to pack out as it did to pack in.

It wasn't only the fact that she slept with all those men that led Theo to his drastic decision. Equally so, he found it impossible to deal with the guilt and disgust of letting himself have sex with her even after she was sleeping with all those other men for profit. Also, he looked down on her, which in itself can be fatal to any relationship. Pretending not to care what was going on under his own roof, and pretending to ignore it, could only last for so long before an explosion occurred. Theo felt hate towards her baser self, when he really was so deeply in love with the rest of her at the same time. For him, it was a love-hate combination of emotions, all the way back from the beginning after he first discovered what she was by profession.

"If you truly loved me," she said emotionally on her way out, "you would have found a way to get over this!"

"How could I!" he answered and equaled her depth of emotion. "A good, decent sort like me can only endure so much!"

"Good-bye," Juliette whispered sorrowfully on her way out, her head lowered. She felt so sad and dejected that the weight of the world seemed to be crushing her heart.

The Forbidden

When Marcel came over half a week later, he found Theo at his desk in a state of collapse, his head resting down on his folded arms.

"Didn't you hear me knocking?"

Theo looked up at him blankly. "Sorry, I guess I didn't."

"What's wrong? You look a wreck."

"It's over," he moaned.

"What's over?"

"Me and Juliette, that's what. So much for destiny."

"What happened?"

"What do you think? I got fed up. She turned my apartment into a house of ill repute, for God's sake. Those nights when I came home dying for her embrace, only to hear her in the next room, pleasuring some pitiful bastard who should have been home getting it from his wife instead! Ugh! Never again, I said. Never again."

"Theo, that's insane. The one girl in your life, the one and only girl you've ever loved, and you throw her away like that? If she weren't the one, then I suppose not much harm has come of it. *But*, if she *is* the one, then you've just made the biggest mistake of your life. I envied you, friend."

"You?"

"Oh, yes! Because you found true love. I mean, surely, I've had many women. But do you suppose there was something more than carnal pleasure involved? It's true that in some cases I felt more for a girl than in others. But affection, no matter how great or how generously bestowed, is never love. Deep true love for me was an unattainable dream, and so, you understand how jealous I was when you--the unlikeliest candidate--found it ... and found it so easily, as if it'd been waiting for you. What a blessing; I'm shocked you don't see this. You've treated this blessing with the contempt of a curse!"

"All very well-spoken. Bravo. But keep in mind that you have no idea what I went through. I felt like a laughingstock. And the fact that my name through Juliette was being put to shame, was the least of my concerns. But if my mother were to find out about it, she would have had a stroke. A woman with nerves as bad as hers."

"Didn't you love her?"

The Forbidden

"Well of course! I still do! Why do you think I've been sitting in this same chair for the last few days like a cripple, like I'm on death's doorstep? I haven't eaten for three days, and yet it's for Juliette that I hunger the most."

"My God! Get up, we'll go get a bite to eat!"

"No. Starvation is a fine suicide. Guaranteed. Look, I'm over halfway there already."

"You're mad is what *you* are. Now, I'll get you to eat if I have to stuff it down your throat myself! All right, up you go. The inn is still open. We'll both order leg of lamb ... or some chicken."

"The inn? No, we can't go there, Marcel," Theo said feebly. "Juliette is sure to be there. It's her pick-up place for ... "

"Well then we'll go somewhere else."

"Why don't you just leave me alone! I'm too weak even to stand up at this point! Can't you see I want to die?" he burst out angrily.

"I won't just stand by while my best friend commits a slow and painful, not to mention foolish, suicide. Not if I can help it!"

Just as Marcel said this, Theo started coming over dizzy and after a moment or two he fell from his chair and fainted. He was as pale as the wall. Both his mind and body were terribly weakened and under deep strain.

"Don't worry!" gasped Marcel, picking him up and carrying him over to the bed. "Everything will be alright."

"I'm dying, Marcel," he muttered. "I know it."

"Don't be stupid!"

"I feel so terrible about how things have turned out between Juliette and myself."

"That can all be fixed, just bear with me."

Theo was going delusional, and seemed to be talking to himself, losing a sense of reality in his semi-conscious state.

Marcel tried desperately to revive him in any way he could think of, with minimal success. He even gave him some water to drink.

Theo kept on mumbling all throughout: "I'll never again have the same feelings for another girl that I had for Juliette."

The obvious sincerity with which he spoke those words would have been enough to move anyone's heart. But then apparently without even realizing it, he contradicted himself by adding, "if it had been God's will that I live, I would have become a monk ... to avoid the whole

The Forbidden

complicated business of love forever." He chuckled. But it was a bitter chuckle. Theo was in such a state that he didn't know what he was saying.

"I'm going to fetch a doctor. Don't move. Stay as you are. I'll be back as soon as possible."

"No! No!" Theo shouted. "I hate doctors! Don't you dare leave me in the middle of my death-agony!"

"I'll be back soon!"

"Soon? I'll be dead by then. Dying alone--what horror!"

"You mustn't think dark thoughts. Drink the rest of the water in your glass. It'll help revive your system."

Marcel was gone in a flash and as he hastened away, he could hear Theo's loud shout: "Tell Juliette I was sorry! Tell her! Tell her!"

By some miracle or miraculous stroke of good luck, the doctor arrived just a half-hour later, with Marcel, out of breath, tagging close behind.

Theo looked more hopeless than ever.

"Is it too late?" gasped Marcel.

"We shall soon see," the old doctor replied, giving Theo pills of some kind and an injection. "This should help him ... it's mighty lucky that you called on me when you did. In his state, he wouldn't have made it to morning alive."

Within the hour, Theo saw rapid improvement.

"Your friend will be just fine," said the doctor to a deeply relieved Marcel.

"We're so indebted to you, Doctor Armand. And you'll be paid for your service, you can count on that. My address is 14 rue de la Breton. Stop by tomorrow, say about noon? I'll hand you your fee. Again, I must thank you. If it weren't for your intervention, Theo was a dead duck."

"Yes, well, just let him rest. Don't let him stress himself. But what he needs now more than anything is a warm, wholesome meal. Please see to it that he gets it immediately now. Go to the local restaurant just down the street here and have something brought over. But he must not eat too quickly at first, when the body is this starved. It would cause a shock to the system."

"I understand. Will do, doc."

Shortly afterwards, the doctor left, asking to be called upon if anything happened to go wrong.

The Forbidden

A worried Marcel spent the whole night by the side of his friend, nursing him back to recovery. By morning, Theo was almost back to his old self.

Days later at the Dionysian meeting, the others were not pleased at all when they found out about Theo's 'break-up' with his girlfriend.

"What happened? Was she disappointed by the puny size of your prick? Ha, ha, ha!" Auguste laughed.

"Shut up, you fat shit. The problem went far deeper than that. And don't make me explain it to you--it's something you wouldn't understand."

"Oh, wouldn't I? It seems I understand very well already. Face it-- you were cast aside. Kicked aside! Discarded like a piece of rotting meat! You weren't *man* enough to keep her. If you won't admit it to us, then at least admit it to yourself."

"Pshaw! Why am I even talking to you."

Charles started playing his guitar to defuse the tension. He sang:

There once lived a girl in Normandy
She was sweet as a girl can be
I married her as soon as I could
If only to see what lurked under those skirts

There once lived a girl in Normandy
The prettiest thing I ever did see
We made love in a big soft bed
But only long after the wedding guests were fed...etc

Theo left in the middle of it. He promised himself that he'd never return. They could have their "meetings" for all he cared. But he wasn't about to let himself be made a fool of over and over again.

Back at the apartment, all was calm as ever, which meant that it was too calm. Theo became so bored that he had to stop studying. He lay down in bed and started staring at the ceiling like an idiot without a thought.

Then, there was a knock on the door.

The Forbidden

"Go away, Marcel! I'm not feeling well!" he yelled.

But the knocking didn't stop. He realized that he didn't recognize the knock. It sure wasn't how Marcel usually knocked. This one wasn't as sharp, or as fast.

Then he heard a female voice: "Please, Theo. Let me in."

Theo jumped out of bed. He was startled beyond belief. Was it really? No, it couldn't be ... but it was ... Juliette!

He strolled back and forth, trying feverishly to figure out what to do.

"Please, Theo ... please ... let me in." Her tone sounded somewhat pathetic and urgent. "I need to talk to you ..."

Finally, knowing that she wouldn't leave until he opened the door, and feeling pity, Theo admitted her in. But really, he was just as desperate to see her as she was to see him.

Juliette came crawling back to him: "I'm sorry about everything, Theo. Let's forget about the past. I can't live without you. I feel so miserable!"

When Theo heard her say that, he felt her pain. "I want you back too."

"Do you mean it?"

"Of course. I ... I feel sorry about the whole thing. We can be together again...but only under one condition--that you give up the prostitution! I mean, stop completely."

Enthusiastically, she agreed. "You don't know how relieved I am now that things will be as they were," she said.

When he heard this, Theo let loose his emotions as well. "Juliette, my little jewel, you can't begin to imagine how lost I was with you completely out of my life. Honestly, I was close to suicide. If Marcel hadn't found me in time and put me back together, this would have been my funeral day. I'm not exaggerating."

"Oh, promise me that we'll never again let an argument get the better of us. Never, never, never."

"You can count on that. I'll learn to hold my tongue, dear one. I'm sorry. Do we forgive each other?"

They kissed. A kiss which was the spark that ignited an entire night of red-hot passion and lust. At the end of it, their mutual love was stronger than it had ever been before. And thus resumed their dreamy life as lovers.

The Forbidden

"Promise me once more that your prostitute days are over. Promise me again."

"Yes ... over for good. I won't risk losing you. And now I see what a destructive force it was to our happiness together. It wasn't worth it. I'll get a job sewing somewhere, or working in a shop or factory. Don't you worry, we'll get by somehow. It'll be harder, but we'll find a way."

"That's the spirit. Just you wait. When I start my law practice and secure a stable earning, you won't even need to work outside of the home. I have only a few more months anyhow until I graduate."

"Then we'll get married."

"Yes, married."

Theo waited patiently for Marcel to come the next night, and at eight o'clock in the evening, he did. This time, sober. Theo explained to him everything that had happened between him and Juliette the night before.

Although his first reaction was one of surprise, Marcel was overjoyed to know that they were back together again, and his excitement showed. "See? You and she were just meant to be," he said with conviction. "Yeah, I had a feeling all along--something would happen to change things around and to bring you two back together. I'm happy for you."

"Not as happy as I am. Though, I will admit, I tried not to show it too much. I had to be firm and to make it clear that she had to give up her old lifestyle."

"So she's given it up? Completely?"

"Yes, for certain. She's said it with her own lips. And I trust her. In fact, I wish she wouldn't work at the inn anymore either, that's where she comes in touch with many of her regular 'customers.' I'll just have to trust her. We all deserve a second chance. And I don't want to be her keeper or to dominate her like some slave-master. That wouldn't be right."

"Yes, I agree," said Marcel. "A woman has to have her independence. Must have room to breath. More so than not, it's not infidelity but jealousy that's the obscenity."

"Well we don't have to worry about either."

Marcel: "Yeah, well ... it's time we should be going, eh? The meeting starts soon, and you know how they hate it when we're late."

The Forbidden

"They can stick carrots up each others' asses for all I care. I'm never going back there again."

"But you can't do this. Everybody knows you're the best poet of us all. They all admire you. You can't let a few bad jokes get to you. Besides, what can they say now?--you're with Juliette again." Then an idea struck Marcel: "I got it! I can't believe I never thought of this before!--bring her along. Make all those idiots jealous. Make their eyes green with envy. Make them eat their words. If that doesn't stir up a little respect, nothing will."

"That's actually not a bad idea."

"It's a great idea!" gasped Marcel.

There was a light in Juliette's house when they got there, and just as they came to the door, she opened it.

"Hello boys. I saw you coming. Come in and make yourselves at home."

"To be perfectly honest," started Marcel, "we're in a bit of a hurry. I ... that is, Theo and I, were wondering if you'd like to come to one of our Cult of the Dionysians meetings."

"Oh, Theo's told me all about them."

This made Marcel chuckle. "Has he? And what has he told you?"

"Only what's on the surface," Theo answered for her.

"Did you want me *now*?" she asked.

"Well, yeah. If it's at all convenient," said Marcel.

"Well, sure. It's not as though I'll be 'working' tonight." She smiled.

Theo smiled back. "Or any night."

"Come, my good little Christian," she said to Theo, taking his arm. "And lead the way."

When they arrived, all members were present, including one or two non-members--girls.

"Welcome, welcome," said Henri, ushering them in. "There's enough room." And then he said something in Latin to prove his erudition. But no one paid any attention.

Auguste approached Theo just as he took a seat, and apologized for his insulting and insensitive remarks. "You know me," he added, patting him on the back, "I often get carried away."

They shook hands and all was forgiven.

Marcel explained that Theo and Juliette were lovers again,

The Forbidden

interrupted by Theo, who added, "and marriage is just on the horizon."

There were a few hurrahs and some applause.

"If only I had your courage," Auguste chuckled.

He handed out a glass to everyone, pouring out to each and all the juices of a sweet-tasting and inexpensive white liquor.

"What is this piss?" Henri said nonchalantly, a connoisseur of everything from fine wines to the fine arts. "I prefer it more sour. This is afar too much on the sweet side of things."

The simple peasant-girls there, knowing nothing of sophistication and refined taste, found it quite funny to see Henri in his exaggerated, mannered pose.

"It's getting pretty stuffy in here," Jules was the first to observe. "How about we all take a nice brisk walk. The fields are magnificent at a time like this. I love their evening solitude. The dew feels so fresh against the fog."

Everyone agreed and they were off. Theo and Juliette were the only ones to stay behind.

Just as their burning lips were about to meet, Juliette whispered, with eyes closed: "Recite one of your beautiful poems to me. To this day, I've never even heard one."

"Well then how can you say they're beautiful?"

"I just know."

Theo opened his notebook and began reading aloud:

Romeo and Juliet
Permitt'd Poison's goblet
To mislead them as master
And spill its elixir o' Disast'r.

O this harsh Fate mistak'nly born
Smother'd a love strong'r than Satan's scorn,
One which Death would e'er adorn.

"You're a marvellous poet," she whispered against his cheek. "I had no idea. If more of your poetry reads like this, then your place in French literature is assured."

The Forbidden

Then after a little thought, she giggled, "the name Theo is not far from Romeo. And Juliet? I'm Juliette!"

"Yeah, that is a funny coincidence, isn't it?"

Their kissing soon became so passionate, so instinctual and raw. Animal urges deep within them were released. They fell on a dirty old mattress together and Theo unbuttoned her blouse to put his hands on and squeeze a twin pair of large, long swells of flesh capped by flat, small, brown nipples. He ran the other hand along her black stockings-encased legs, all the way up to the thick tuft of curly hair nestled under her belly. Theo's fingers found the crack that went down and under. He massaged it gingerly, probing along the purplish labia and the tiny pearl at the top of it. This adorable little pearl was somewhat hidden under a hood of skin, but as soon as Theo exposed it to any sensation what-so-ever, Juliette was left squirming, writhing and shrieking in such a way that if someone had walked in on them at that moment, they wouldn't know if she was in pleasure or in pain. Once the muscles of the vulva opening were softened and moistened enough, Theo plunged his instrument of virility in to her hilt with the first stroke, and he managed it with such skill, hitting the G-spot square on the nose, that a fiercely lust-bound Juliette was ejaculating puddles before she'd even found her rhythm! All throughout, they were both at an equal level of arousal--in fact, they came at just about precisely the same instant!

Suddenly, as their last deep breaths died down, Auguste's booming voice could be heard: "Sure you two haven't got it in you to go one more round? That was spectacular!"

The others burst out laughing.

Theo and Juliette were mortified. How humiliating! To be seen by all!

"There, there, don't be shy," Auguste went on. "You have nothing to be ashamed of, that was a wonderful performance! ha, ha, ha. In fact, seeing your bodies bumping and grinding like that, it's put me in a rather randy mood myself. And when my sex is inspired, believe me my friends, only good things flow, ha ha ha!"

The meeting concluded with some light petting and mild love-play with the girls.

The Forbidden

The months that came and went were bliss incarnate. Theo and Juliette were the happiest and the most fulfilled of all lovers. Nothing stood in their way. Neither God nor any devil that tried. But, like all dreams, this one came to its end.

"I'm pregnant," said Juliette one fine morning.

"What? How?"

"What do you mean *how*?"

"I mean, what I mean is ... I wasn't expecting this."

"Well neither was I," Juliette muttered. "I've tried to be careful. I've avoided those days of the month. Never gotten pregnant before. How could this happen."

Theo was scratching the back of his head. "Things happen ... Aren't you pleased?"

"Well, yes ... I mean, I don't know ... I mean, of course I am ... I suppose ... I've just never thought of being a mother."

"You know, this is going to work out really well. I'm only one month away from finishing my studies. It couldn't have come at a more opportune time! How far along are you?"

"I don't know. Maybe two months?" she guessed.

"Two months! Are you sure?"

"As sure as I can feel the little round lump."

"Well, all right, that's fine. We'll marry right after I start work. Don't worry, it'll all turn out well. Nobody will know ... Just to be on the safe side, we won't tell the others. Not even Marcel. Got it?"

"Yes."

After the month had passed, Theo wrote to his parents of his intent to marry Juliette. The portion of the letter referring to it, went as follows:

Mother, I hope you'll be pleased to know that I have, indeed, found the girl I would like to spent the rest of my life with. Her name is Juliette Poulet, and she's the most perfect girl. I'm completely under her spell. We're planning, with your and father's permission, to get married after I start work at one of the firms back home. That way, we'll never be far apart from you. Please reply as soon as you can with your thoughts, and especially, your consent.

The Forbidden

I remain ever your devoted son,

Theo

      Their reply came very quickly indeed. It was in his father's hand.

Theo,

What is this foolishness about marriage in your letter? What makes you think you can marry at your age, boy? You'll need at least three or four years of working your way up the ladder to get to the point where marriage will even be an option. You're still very young. I understand how you feel--being young and in love is enthralling to say the least. Hard as it may be for you to believe, I still remember the liaisons of my twenties. All I'm saying is, this may not be the right girl. Take your time. Don't rush. Marriage can make or break a man's life. That one decision to say 'I do' could be your signature to Misery. Who is this girl anyway? In your letter you never even told us a thing about her. Do you have something to hide? Again, I repeat, marriage is out of the question. I have more than adequately specified why. We want you to know how incredibly proud we are of you now that you've passed your examinations with flying colors. Your future's looking bright, son. I know you'll do well in this life. Since you were born, I've been knocking the obstacles out of your path, putting you in the right schools, bringing you up right, etc, etc ... Now it's paid off at last. Nothing stands in your way. You'll lead a long and prosperous life. Your mother and I will be expecting you in a week, now that your student days are over. That gives you more than enough time to say good-bye to your sweetheart. I feel we're being generous. We welcome you with open arms,

your loving parents

      As soon as he read it, Theo ripped up and crumpled the letter, furiously throwing it at the wall.
      "Shit!" he yelled. "Shit! Shit! Shit!"

The Forbidden

Now that Juliette was living with him again, she couldn't help but hear his outburst, and came rushing to him from the other room.

"Is anything the matter?"

He crushed the sheet of paper with his shoe so she wouldn't notice it.

"No, not at all. Why would it be?"

"What was that you yelled? You sounded upset."

"Oh, it's just something I read in the newspaper just now. Got me a little worked up, that's all. It's nothing. I'm alright."

She didn't make much out of it, shrugging her shoulders before going back to the other room. When she was safely out of sight, Theo took the letter and tossed it out the window. He wanted to spare her what he viewed as his parents' narrow-mindedness.

Instead, what he did tell her, after dinner, was: "Oh, by the way, I got a letter from my father today. Both my parents are overjoyed about the news of our intent to get married ... They say they want nothing more in the world than to meet you in person. I know they'll fall for you just as I have." He smiled.

"Well I'm relieved."

"What, did you ever doubt that this would be their reaction to our wedding plans?"

"Well, I don't know. They've never even met me. Are you sure we won't be imposing by living with them? I mean, will there be enough room?"

"More than enough, I assure you ... If only you wouldn't worry so much. Look at me--I never worry. Especially when there's no reason to. I see only good things ahead."

"Rouen is a beautiful city, I'm sure I'll like it there."

"You will."

"When do they want us to arrive?"

"We're expected in a week's time."

"Wow. I'm already looking forward to it."

"And so are they, I'm sure," he replied, finding it hard to say it naturally.

"I'll wear my finest clothes. They'll be impressed ... won't they?"

"A girl as beautiful as yourself doesn't even need fine clothes to look impressive."

Her pride swallowed the compliment whole-heartedly. "Oh, you

The Forbidden

flatterer ... Still, I want to make a good impression."

"First of all," he said with a smile, "I'm so smitten with you, how can my adoration of you not take the form of flattery in one way or another. You know how in awe I am of you."

"You're making fun of me, you beast," she giggled half-seriously. "Remember, it's not how elaborate a compliment sounds, it's how sincere it is that counts."

Theo was so in love with her that he believed, perhaps naively, that the minute his parents saw her, she would automatically be accepted, or at least in time. What he didn't realize was that he gave little thought to the fact that he would clearly be defying them. But what did he care? A man in love doesn't act on reason. A man deeply in love is in such a 'heightened' state, he's lost touch with reality to a certain degree. He acts on his senses, his emotions, which in that case are steered by amorous love and its selfish ethereal yearnings. His position is that everyone must see things his way or they're blind.

Marcel was the first to hear about their departure soon-to-be.

"When did you decide all this?"

"Almost a week ago. I got a letter from my folks. They want us to come. Besides, I'm finished with school now and quite homesick. I have to find a position now. Shouldn't be too hard, though. I heard they're looking for new lawyers in Rouen. I can't wait to get my start!"

"Yeah, well, the best of luck. I'll miss you. Really will," said Marcel.

"Ah, you're being sentimental," Theo retorted with a chuckle. "You're starting to sound like me."

"I am, aren't I?"

"Yes, Marcel. It's a good thing I'm going. God knows I've been corrupted long enough by you and your kind," Theo added in a joking manner.

"Well, know this: the Dionysians are always here for you. If you're ever in trouble ... if you're ever in need, just remember, we're a brotherhood, and you *are* a member. Always were."

"Thanks, Marcel. You've always been a very loyal friend."

"Oh God, it sounds like we're saying our good-byes already."

The Forbidden

"Yeah, it does, doesn't it?" laughed Theo.

"Juliette and I don't leave until tomorrow, on the ten o'clock morning train."

"I wish I had known sooner. But I've been so busy lately, I couldn't see you till tonight."

"Who cares. We have tonight." Theo looked at his watch. "We've got to hurry if we're gonna make it to the meeting."

Marcel looked surprised.

"What's with the bewildered gaze?" said Theo.

"It's just that I'm shocked you really want to go. Most of the time, I have to practically drag you there."

"I guess I've had a change of heart."

Two people were absent from the group that evening--Henri and Jules. They were good friends and were probably off together somewhere.

"Sad news, friends," Marcel grimly declared, "Theo's leaving the group. His studies are done and there's nothing to keep him here."

Spontaneously, Charles started making a sad song out of it, improvising:

The lovers felt they could not stay
In the city that fools call paradise
The lovers felt they could not stay
So they left its stinky, overcrowded streets

"The melody sounds good enough, but those words wouldn't have one foot to stand on as poetry," Marcel said to Charles.

"I'll never be a real poet like the rest of you. Music is my only Muse," Charles replied.

"What about Juliette?" asked Auguste.

"She's coming too," replied Theo.

"And you plan to marry her."

"Exactly."

"Well, just don't forget about us. To visit on occasion. Will you do that?"

"Sure thing." He meant it. At the end of the evening, Theo recited

The Forbidden

the last poem:

*She wept her sky-color tears
Into a vase of Sadness,
Never to be emptied out.*

*The amber-colored roses
Which were her amorous lips,
Are now marked for always
With a stamp of fading kiss-memories.*

*How sad when lovers say good-bye
And their love is sentenced to die
By a judge and jury named Fate, oh my
And rejected suitors query endlessly, "why?"*

*Love, you capricious occultist,
Hypnotist of hearts young and old!
Lust, that hag spouse of yours,
Eternally, inevitably lags right behind you.*

*She wept her sky-color tears
Into a vase of Sadness,
Never to be emptied out.
Love's gavel cruelly bangs!*

"I wrote this after Juliette and I parted ways. But that's buried in the past. She and I are about to embark on a fantastic journey together, a life journey that I'm sure will have its share of hardships, but far more joys," Theo mused.

When it was time for farewells, even the sullen Robert showed some emotion--a strong indication that Theo would really be missed by him.

"You're a great poet," Robert muttered, which was saying something, since Robert (with the exception of Marcel) was the only other talented poet in the group. "Think of us now and again."

The Forbidden

Marcel: "It's a real pity Henri and Jules aren't here. If they'd known--"

"Oh, it's all the same," Theo interrupted. "I don't care much for good-byes anyhow. But be sure to give them my best."

"Of course," said Marcel, "and give Juliette a warm farewell from us as well, alright?"

"Yeah ... I guess I should go soon. The train does leave in the morning tomorrow. With my luck, we'll probably miss it."

"You wouldn't hear us complain," joked Auguste.

A few more minutes of chatting, and then he left.

The clock went off at eight in the morning, startling Theo as it always did with its loud ring. The train station was over an hour away, so they didn't have an abundance of time to get ready.

"Make sure you don't forget anything," said Theo. "I doubt we'll be seeing this place again anytime soon."

All their things were packed up and ready, and at half past eight their carriage arrived.

"Well, Theo, looks as though we're slowly on our way," Juliette remarked. She looked content.

Upon arriving at the station, they learned they were a good twenty minutes early.

Juliette: "I guess we'll have to wait. I'm so restless, I can't even sit down."

"We came at a good time. Not too early and not too late," said Theo. "These trains can be so unpredictable. Once, I remember, I had a train that never came at all."

"Ah, I might as well sit down then."

The train did come of course, and the ride itself was a long, tiresome one. Tired and miserable, they ordered a cab as soon as the train hit the station where they got off. Juliette slept the whole way on Theo's shoulder, cuddled up in a cotton blanket he'd put over her.

Theo gazed out upon the moonlit landscape. As soon as he started recognizing the natural surroundings, he began to get really uneasy within. Perhaps he hadn't thought this through very well, he thought. Theo argued that he was an adult now and could make his own decisions. He tried to

The Forbidden

reassure himself with the thought that all he had to do was present Juliette to his parents and to prove his love for her to them, to prove that she was much more to him that a passing love interest. If by some evil miracle that didn't work, it would be too late to change things anyway because of the pregnancy. And besides, his parents couldn't be so cruel and impolite as to make 'a scene' or worse yet, to throw a stunned Juliette out of their house! They would simply have to keep their mouths shut and accept the fact, he reasoned. Besides, he didn't care much for their approval. Soon he would be making his own living and no longer in need of any financial support.

The air was a starless midnight black by the time they got to Theo's parents' residence, a quaint and roomy middle-class home. It was a one-story structure, but quite large; painted white; a black, arched roof; massive windows. It was fairly new and well-looked-after.

"Wait in the carriage," he said to her. "I'll be back in a moment. Just stay put."

Juliette was too tired to ask any questions and didn't even watch as Theo entered the house.

Theo was immediately met by the vigorous embrace of his mother and firm handshake and pat on the arm by his father.

"It's a pleasure to have you back, boy," the hoarse voice of his father said aloud. "It's been a lot quieter around here without ya. So quiet, I sometimes feel I'm hearing ghosts, ha, ha, ha."

Theo wanted very much to speak, but they wouldn't keep their mouths shut, over-excited as they were to have their one and only son back home safe and sound--not to mention educated far above the level of the average man. What pride! What achievement! Their son! Something to brag about!

"I'm really happy to see both of you too. And I have a great surprise for you--one that will take your breaths away ..." Theo paused and his voice turned timid: "I've brought Juliette along. We fully intend to be married, so there's nothing you can do or say. I beg you not to get angry. She's in the carriage now. I'll bring her in."

"You will *not*!" his father roared loud enough for even the sleepy-eyed Juliette to have heard outside.

"Father, get a hold of yourself! Can't you see we're in love? Yes, the real thing! Love!"

"Juliette! Juliette! Juliette! If I hear that name once more I'll strangle myself!"

The Forbidden

"What you do is your business. I don't dare barge into it. Why do you have to barge into mine!"

His mother, weeping now not tears of joy, but tears of aggitation: "Please, Theo! Please! We're your mother and father! We love you! Think this over! What you're doing is foolish! You can't support a wife on an apprentice's salary!"

The argument continued, each minute more and more intense.

Finally, Theo was so fed up that he let out the truth: "She's with child! Damn-it! She's carrying my child!"

His mother almost fainted, going weak in the knees and falling back on the couch. She was hyperventilating.

"With child? With child!" hollered his father, almost ripping out his hair in fury.

"I didn't want to tell you so suddenly, but ... Anyway, I think it's time you meet her."

Theo fetched the drowsy but still gorgeous Juliette, leading her into the house.

His parents tried to act civil towards her, but it was very hard. Luckily, poor Juliette was too tired and worn out by the trip to even notice how forced their polite behavior was.

Wanting to talk more about it alone with Theo, they led Juliette to a spare bedroom and left her to her dreams.

"You won't get a franc from us, boy," muttered his father in a low voice, spitting with every word, red-faced. "Do you know what you've done? Now you have to marry this girl. You no longer have the choice, you dolt. Scandal must be avoided at all cost."

"But don't you see? That was always my intent, to marry her, pregnant or not."

"You naive child ... Is this the thanks I get for all the effort I've put into making you--"

"Oh, be quiet, father, please. You're exaggerating, everything will be fine. Besides, you're wasting your breath needlessly. What's done is already done. There's no turning back the clock. You'll have to accept it ..."

"Insolent bugger. I'll kick you out is what I'll do!"

"Please, please, let's be sensible!" cried Theo's mother.

His sentimentally pious and easily excitable mother, Vitalie, was still sobbing. Like her husband, she was a typical bourgeois--narrow-minded, puritan and dull. Her clothing was very modest and she always

The Forbidden

dressed in brown or black. Neighbors would say she was 'stingy as a Jew'. But everyone who knew her swore she was a kind and caring soul, good and decent. Her only real faults were that she would over-react on occasion and was as forgetful as a drunkard. Theo's father, Claude, was a large, burly man, toughened up and used to hard work. He was very proud of the shop he owned, which had taken him his whole life as a field laborer to acquire. Many years of saving money. A fair chunk of that money had also gone towards Theo's education. Whenever Claude spoke, he had the distracting habit of playing with his thick and neatly W-shaped mustache. Unlike Theo's mother, he was a very proud and boastful man and a brawler. It never took much to awaken his violent and aggressive side. But all that aside, he too was a good and upright human being.

"In time, you'll grow to love her just as I do," Theo said with assurance to his upset parents. "Believe me. Please believe me."

Barely a week later, the wedding took place. It was a very informal, joyful and pastoral affair. A typical country wedding. Lots of celebration and excuse for drinking, and all manner of silliness and tomfoolery. All the women, especially the matrons, chattered away like geese, gossiping like people who lead boring lives. Once these meddlers got their tongues wagging, discretion went out the door in a hurry. At the wedding feast and party that followed outside the church, these same sour old gossips couldn't keep their eyes off the newlyweds. They were suspicious of Juliette, since she was a stranger.

"There's something not quite right about this," one of them said. "To be married just *one* week after university graduation?"

"Oh, I don't know," said another, enjoying how happy and in love they appeared to be. "They'd probably wanted to for some time, only they had to wait till now."

"Hmmm, well, say what you will," the other one continued, "but there's something fishy about this whole thing. I know the Bidaults, and they wouldn't have allowed it unless there was more to it than meets the eye. I say, there's something fishy about it and I don't know what."

"Well, it couldn't be that she's wealthy," another woman joined the conversation, after having eavesdropped to that point. "I happen to know she's not brought any sort of dowry to the marriage. Nothing. In fact, if I

The Forbidden

heard correctly, she has only a few worthless belongings. It's all so peasant-like. She has looks, though. I'll give her credit there."

The other one nodded, but couldn't help making this insightful point: "Still, so little is known about her. Such a mysterious character. I dined with the Bidaults only two days ago, and they said absolutely nothing about her. As if they have something to hide. Well, they casually mentioned who she was and that she'd be living with them ... but nothing more. No enthusiasm about her or the wedding to come, nothing. Doesn't that strike you in the least bit odd?"

"Quite odd. We must make a note of it to confront them next Sunday at church."

A new voice joined the conversation: "And here's another observation. Where are the girl's parents? None of her family, relatives or friends are present. Could she have been an orphan? Is that, perhaps, the big secret?"

"No, I don't think so," the other one said. "It has to be something even worse than that."

And as the sour old gossips let their imaginations run wild, Theo and Juliette acted like they couldn't be happier. However, Theo's parents did nothing but mope. Their disapproval, disappointment, or whatever it was, couldn't have been more clearly evident.

"I don't know if you've noticed," Theo whispered cautiously to his new wife, realizing that they were being watched, "but I think they're talking about us."

"Let's get away;" she put her hand in his and ran, leading him into the woods. He could hardly keep up, almost tripping a few times. Juliette had to hold her hat down on her head with the other hand, giggling as she ran.

"Where are you taking me, temptress Eve." Theo laughed.

"To the Garden of Eden ... paradise."

"Ha, ha. Then I'll have to build up my resolve, won't I?"

They came to a high grassy clearing and fell to the ground, exhausted.

Juliette was the first to sit up. "Look, we can see everybody down below from here. They look so far away from this hill."

As she spoke, Theo was subtly caressing and undressing her.

"Such a small, firm waist, and yet such strong, broad, heavy thighs. And those bosoms, white as snow, such chubby creatures. I could

The Forbidden

play with them for hours without the slightest sign of being bored."

Juliette blushed, embarrassed by the shameless frankness of his evaluation of her charms--his lewd praise. Theo had completely changed from the immaculate virgin he first had been, to the earthy, sensual beast he'd become, with Juliette's bedroom expertise certainly having quite a lot to do with it. However, his religious values and beliefs still held a steady influence over his life, and he was more than a little relieved that their lovemaking would now no longer be filthy fornication, but lawful married sex.

"We can't now. Not now." She tried to shrug him off. "What if somebody were to go looking for us? Hmm? To find us copulating like farmyard goats ... A great beginning that would be to our marriage!" She laughed. "Believe me, I know. And rumors like that die slow, if they ever die at all."

"You really sound like you know what you're talking about," said Theo.

"Let's just say that if you've had to grow up as quickly as I did, and have known the people I've known in life, you become very world-wise and a flawless judge of character. There's nothing about human nature that I don't understand."

"Did your family really die in a shipwreck when you were little?"

"Yes. They were headed for England, got caught in the worst storm ... and the rest is history. I should have been with them, but I was notorious for my sea-sickness, so they decided it would be better to leave me behind in the care of my grandmother. When she died in my teenage years, I was lost. Prostitution became the only solution. I was fourteen years of age. Can you believe it? Just fourteen!"

Theo was uncomfortable. "Let's not talk about that. It's all in the past."

"You're right. Oh, but didn't your parents ask about my family?"

"Of course. And I told them about the shipwreck, but nothing about prostitution. I said you spent the rest of your early years in a convent."

Juliette giggled. "You did not!"

"I swear." Theo laughed.

"Where will we go on our honeymoon? Paris?" she asked, daydreaming and brushing a flower over her nose.

"Paris sounds satisfactory I suppose. But we used to live there, we

The Forbidden

know the place, so why would we want to go there? ... No, actually, let's go abroad. I'm sick of this country. Let's try some place different. Something completely new. Let's experience life beyond. Vienna, Rome, Athens ...Whatever you want. What do you think?"

"We couldn't afford that, silly. Paris is probably our only good option. Or then there's Belgium. Brussels?"

"No. I hate small, unimportant countries." He said stupidly and smiled.

"Very well, then it's Paris."

"No, I hate big cities too." He laughed.

"I think we should go back before everybody's started worrying where we've disappeared to."

Theo thought about this for a second, grinning. "Don't you mean, you're afraid they might think we're 'fooling about'?"

"Well that too."

They returned, right when the festivities were at their height. There were games to play, goodies to gobble, songs to sing, etc...

"Where were you?" Theo's mother asked Juliette with curious eyes. She was dressed in black as usual. A very plain and sensible dress. One could see she was just aching for a chance to over-react. "What is a wedding banquet without the bride and groom?"

"We were just taking a walk. That's all." Juliette's nonchalance was natural and effortless. It left the older woman nothing to suspect.

Hours later, the fun was over, and everybody went their separate ways, including two people, united in matrimony under Heaven.

The honeymoon would be a three-day excursion to the capital--the City of Lights, the City That Never Sleeps ... Paris. Theo, at first lacking enthusiasm, started looking forward to it. After all, it *was* the cultural, artistic and intellectual centre of the country, ideal for someone interested in the arts, like himself.

When they got there, the newlyweds were definitely struck by the change of pace, the vitality and vigor of the urban environment. Rouen felt more like a large rustic town, whereas Paris made one feel that they were in a large city. The streets just seemed to swarm and buzz with all kinds of people clothed in colorful and fashionable garments. Parisians certainly

The Forbidden

paid more attention to appearance than people living in rural communities did. The sun was extraordinarily bright and hot, but a refreshing breeze brought relief. This was Paris on any given weekend afternoon. People would wait all week for it.

Theo and his new bride first stopped off at a fairly ordinary hotel, settling into some reasonable accommodations as tourists. The place was somewhat old and rundown, as the cracked and faded paint revealed. But it was clean and the furnishings within were quite new; the interiors were even sort of stylish, in their old-fashioned sort of way. Its location near the most densely populated part of the city was good for business, even if some of the business happened to come from shady and disreputable types.

When they got to their room, Theo unlocked the door and Juliette ran in, falling on the bed and lying on her back. Theo brought their luggage in and lay down beside her. He kissed her.

Theo: "Do you want to stay in tonight, or--"

"Let's have a night out. Paris comes to life at night."

"Whatever you wish. I'm merely a wanton follower." He chuckled.

"What time is it?"

"It's only half past five," replied Theo.

"Oh, it'll still be hours till it's dark out," complained Juliette.

"That's alright. It gives us time to dine first."

They took in a show at one of the cafe-concerts, and the site they first decided on seeing the following morning was the Louvre.

"What a grand building," sighed Juliette when they got to it. "Imagine how many fabulous works of art must be stored inside."

"Yes, absolutely. Are you sure we won't get lost in such a maze of masterpieces?"

"Maybe if we're lucky," she giggled.

As they came in through the grand entrance, Juliette said: "Did you know that this will be the first time I've ever seen any of Renoir's paintings in person?"

They strolled the corridors for hours, and even though Juliette's feet were starting to hurt, she was hardly aware of that fact. She had no concept of time, thoroughly admiring many of the paintings.

After the Louvre, they sat down outside a cafe and ordered some fine champagne.

"Can we afford this?" she asked.

"Does it matter?" Theo winked.

The Forbidden

As they sipped slowly, tranquilly, they watched the world go by in front of their eyes. There was a silent but absolute contentment in both their hearts, that special sort of sweet happiness that comes when it looks like there are no troubles ahead and everything is going well. But it's a very temporary euphoria, lasting only a few precious moments for some, hours or days for others.

The next stop was the Eiffel tower, which Juliette called 'the tallest single man-made thing I've ever seen.'

"Let's climb to the top," suggested Theo.

"Are you crazy? What if there were an earthquake or something," she said stupidly.

Theo laughed. "Oh how likely."

"I don't like it," she said. "It's quite ugly, wouldn't you say? Like a big, black skeleton."

Theo: "I don't know ... It looks like quite an architectural achievement to me. Very original"

Pere Lachaise, the national cemetery where all of the dead celebrities were buried, was next on the menu. Theo wanted to see it especially. To see the monumental tombs of his idols, like Balzac.

Several big names were missing but in time would join their fellow illuminaries. The names of Proust, Lilly Langtry, Sarah Bernhardt, Apollinaire, Colette, and most recently, Jim Morrison, would one day join those of Chopin, Moliere, Rousseau, etc ... Theo fantasized about what it would be like to be buried in the midst of such greats--such immortals. As he studied each grave, he could feel his skin crawl. It was very spiritual. As if the ghosts of those people were haunting his soul. Juliette found it all very morbid, and it wasn't long before she wanted to leave, whereas Theo could have easily stayed for hours. As an uneducated person, her knowledge of those dead legends of the past was limited and superficial, so naturally, she didn't get much out of the experience.

In the evening, they went to see one of George Bernard Shaw's plays translated into French, called *Mrs Warren's Profession*, whose heroine was a prostitute. The curtains were drawn and all went well until quite a way into the drama, when someone hissed aloud in prudish indignation. Theo was uncomfortable about the realism, but because of her past, Juliette found she could really identify with the heroine and her motives, which were driven by her survival instinct rather than sexual licentiousness. When the last act was over, most people chatting amongst

The Forbidden

themselves seemed to have enjoyed it immensely. A few Parisians, used to more lurid entertainment, found it disappointingly harmless, as Theo heard one of them observe: "What a waste of money. I didn't even see a naked ankle, let alone a well-developed chest! Would've been better off goin' to the music-hall!"

Theo was equally dissatisfied, but for a far different reason. "That was disgusting. Like something out of a Zola novel," he said when they'd left the playhouse. He appeared slightly irritated. "Here I thought we were going to an elegant theatre to see a charming play, and we may as well have been in the Folies-Bergere! I wouldn't have known the difference."

"Oh, stop exaggerating. Besides, maybe this Shaw has a reputation for testing the bounds of acceptability and good taste?" she mused.

"Well he should be banned."

"Surely you believe in liberty ... the freedom of expression."

"Sure," said Theo, "but not liberty at the expense of morality. Why throw filth in the face of the public just to prove that it's there? What's the point? People know it's there. They don't need to be buried up to the neck in it to know that."

"Well then, why do we still have slums? Why do we have social problems like prostitution, for example?"

"Because we have lazy, incompetent leaders. That's why. Political leaders who know the problems better than anybody but are less interested in solutions and more interested in partisan bickering. I'm sick of words that amount to nothing. Words, words, words. But no action!"

But regardless of any differences of opinion between these two newlyweds, they truly loved each other. Their nights of passion were very special. A mixture of tender love and fervent lust. The next few days zoomed by, and before they knew it, Theo and his beautiful Juliette were returning to the real world, which in their case happened to be called Rouen.

They started off on a very good and happy life, and it showed. Claude and Vitalie were especially impressed by this new member of their family and gradually started to get along with her. In fact, they even grew to really like her, though it would have been heresy to admit it.

It was an ideal and peaceful Sunday afternoon. Nature was alive

The Forbidden

with colors and sounds intensified by the delightful weather. The mood was one of almost heavenly tranquility. Juliette was enjoying a pleasant conversation with Theo's parents over lunch outside at the table in the garden. Theo had already started his law practices and was off at work.

Suddenly, an open carriage arrived and stopped in front of the house. Juliette recognized the two women in it immediately. They were her old room-mates. They looked somewhat drunk and disheveled. They *were* drunk and disheveled.

Juliette started to panic within, but held it in with incredible poise and grace. She had no choice--she'd have to pretend she didn't know them.

"Juliette!" the short, pudgy one named Emilie yelled out, catching sight of her at the table.

This was not good. The woman knew her name! How could she, then, pretend not to know her!

The other one, a younger, less brazen and more subdued creature, said nothing, only lagging behind. Marie was her name.

When Emilie came up and hugged Juliette with her strong, fleshy, rugged arms, Juliette made no response what-so-ever.

"Excuse me," said Juliette, pretending to be confused. "But I don't believe I know you. You must be mistaking me for somebody else. It's strange that you know my name."

"Good heavens, Juliette, what's gotten into you! It's me--Emilie!--for Christ's sake! And Marie!"

Claude gave the two women a cold stare, knowing by the look of them that they were common tarts, and said: "You heard the lady. You've made a mistake. Now shove off, hussy."

"Is that how you talk to a lady! Your daughter-in-law Juliette is just as much a hussy as I am!"

Vitalie looked at Juliette: "Are you sure you don't know this woman?"

"Yes! Positively sure! I haven't the slightest idea what she wants."

"Don't believe it, madame," said the middle-aged Emilie, adding spitefully, "this so-called 'lady' here boarded with me since the age of fourteen. She's been a whore all her life. Nothing but a filthy whore like the rest of us. And now you shun me in front of these fine people, Juliette? After all I've done for you! And I was only paying you a friendly visit. And to think, I, out of the goodness and charity of my heart, took her in when she would have starved in the streets! Only to be paid back in this

64

The Forbidden

fashion! Outrageous!"

Emilie left Theo's parents asking: "This is true, what she's saying. Isn't it, Juliette?"

Juliette only remained silent, which was as good as admitting her guilt. She had been doing so well, making such a positive impression on her husband's family, and then something unforseen like this had to happen!

"I should have known! This might have been expected!" flared Claude violently, a raging bull, while his wife only swooned in horror, begging for a glass of water.

Marie, who had been quiet throughout, only said, "we just wanted to visit you, Juliette. Just to say hello. To see where you lived now and how you were getting on. That's all. I didn't want it to come out ..." Marie gave her an apologetic glance, knowing it was too late, that the damage was done.

Juliette too felt deeply remorseful. She had completely disrespected Emilie, the only real mother she had ever known.

The two women got back into the carriage and were off. Emilie could be heard cursing even at a distance. She was a vulgar woman, as vulgar as any brothel-keeper.

If only I had expected this! thought Juliette to herself, I could have prepared to avoid it! She wondered how they knew where she was living, but then realized that she had left them the address the night before the departure so that they might write to her and keep in touch.

Though troubled and outraged, Claude was willing to shut up about the whole revelation and ignore the incident. First of all, Juliette was already married to his son. Second of all, she was pregnant and everyone in town knew with whose baby. It was the same old rule all over again: scandal has to be avoided at all cost. The general belief was that hypocrisy was so much less messy than the confession of sins, the idea behind it being that it was nobody's business and that repentance was achieved far easier under the veil of secrecy.

However, the strict puritan blood flowing through Madame Bidault's veins wasn't quite so forgiving. She couldn't turn a blind eye. Not a woman of her solid and overly moralistic character. She ranted and raved continuously, panting all the while: "I won't have it! Did you hear that, Claude? A harlot! A whore! Since age fourteen!" Her weak nerves started acting up again, as her eyes went big with frightful speculation: "She's

The Forbidden

given my boy syphilis, I'll bet! This whore's murdered my son!"

Juliette fled into the house, weeping, as Claude tried to calm his wife down.

"That's nonsense," moaned her husband.

"Well, let's see you brag to the neighbors now about what a good and virtuous girl she is! ... what a wonderful wife for your son!"

They didn't know how lucky they were that nobody had witnessed this scandalous incident. What an orgy of delight the sour old gossips would have had with it!

Theo came home as cheerful as ever. He was already working his way up the ranks and starting to make quite a name for himself representing the government as a prosecutor in the courts of law. He was winning his cases and his efforts consistently met with success. He was also being praised far and wide for putting some of the most infamous criminals behind bars.

When he walked in through the front door, whistling a happy tune, he stopped upon hearing the voice of somebody weeping. He rushed into his wife's room ... and there he found Juliette face-down on the bed, bawling her eyes out.

"What is it?" He embraced her, rocking back and forth. "Has anything happened?"

"They came here," Juliette finally whimpered in a weak, barely audible voice.

Who? Who did?"

"My former room-mates. Emilie was like an adoptive mother to me all my life. I denied knowing her. I did it out of fear. I didn't know what to do. Now she hates me. On top of that, your parents know my wicked, sordid past. It's almost put your mother in an early grave!"

Juliette explained to Theo everything that happened, even exaggerating a bit, she was so hysterical.

"Curse it to hell. Just when things were going so well," he muttered. "But don't worry, it's alright; everything will be alright," Theo tried to calm her, just like his father had tried to calm down his mother.

"Where are they?"

"I don't know ... although I did hear them leave in a carriage. They seemed in quite a hurry," Juliette recalled.

The Forbidden

Theo thought about this. "That's odd. I wonder where they went."

"Theo!" She grabbed him by the collar. "Let's move away," she pleaded. "I can never face your respectable, conservative little bourgeois parents now."

"Oh, who cares that they know! What can they do now! We're married! You're my wife whether they like it or not!" He grinned.

"But it just makes me so mad!--that they know! I'll never be treated equal. Whenever they look at me, they'll say to themselves: 'I'm looking at a prostitute, a slut.' It'll kill me!"

"There, there. You're blowing things all out of proportion."

"Truly, Theo, you can't imagine how bad it was!... If only you had been here." Then, turning to desperate words, she said, "Please, Theo, I'm begging you on hand and knee ... I can never face your mother again! What hell that would be! What torment! Please Theo! Please!"

"My love, you know I would do anything for you ... anything. But we can't move. Not yet. I'd need a few more months. Maybe half a year to save up enough. And even then we couldn't live nearly as well as we do here. You're deciding on this too early. Can't be too hasty. Not until we've ... that is to say, not until I've talked to them. I need to see how they feel, and their side of things. I need to know the extent of this unfortunate mess."

Juliette: "I'd rather die than see your mother's eyes look at me again ... those angry eyes ..."

"Don't worry. This will all be fixed. Juliette, you don't know how well things are going for me back at the firm. I have the highest success rate of all my colleagues, bar one ... and even with him, the gap is closing! My salary was doubled this morning!"

"Doubled? That *is* good news! What a promotion!"

"The best part is, my salary will continue to grow substantially, if I keep it up ... I'm being assigned to some very prominent criminal cases. Very well-publicized ones indeed."

"Are you sure you won't burn out under all the strain and pressure?" asked Juliette.

"I can more than take the heat. I was born for this work. No doubt about that."

They waited and waited, but still, by nightfall, no sign of Theo's parents. This made Theo very uneasy. After a very heartfelt prayer for their safety, Theo went out visiting everyone his parents knew, hoping to find

The Forbidden

them there. No luck. Nobody had seen them all day.

After endless hours of tireless searching, and just as he was returning empty handed, Theo heard a carriage behind him.

"Stop, driver!" a voice said aloud.

Theo automatically recognized it as his father's.

The door flung open.

"Where have you been!" Theo gasped.

"The hospital. It's your mother. You know about her chronically weak heart. Well, something happened today, the shock of which ..."

"Yes, I know all about it! How bad is she? What's exactly the matter with her?"

"Her nerves couldn't take the strain, she had a complete and utter collapse. If only she weren't such a frail and high-strung sort, if only her health weren't always in such a delicate state."

Theo got in the carriage. The ride back was a very restless one. Father and son sat in grim and silent contemplation. There was great distress about their women.

Theo suddenly spoke: "Juliette wants us to move out. She doesn't believe there's any chance for a reconciliation. You were there--where do you stand on this whole thing?"

"To be honest, I can't really say. I can't side with Juliette. I'd be going against your mother, that's how she would see it. I was quite upset at first, but not anymore. What's the fuss? So she *was* a prostitute. So what of it! Back in the '70s when I was a young man, it was far easier to know a whore than a girl who was pure and chaste. I could tell you stories that would make your head spin. It's a wonder I ever ended up with your mother, of all women. That's not to say I regret it. She's the woman I fell in love with in the same way that you're in love with Juliette. She made me experience real love for the first time in my life, and she saved me from the kind of wild, dissipated life that leads nowhere. I owe her everything. If it weren't for her, I don't know where I'd be today."

"Will she be alright?" Theo asked.

"Doctor says she's suffered a great blow to her nervous system ... almost resulting in heart failure. But it's too early to say as yet. I sat by her side all day. She looks pale and weak, I won't deny it. But she'll get through it. Fifty-eight years of age isn't ancient."

"But it isn't young, either," Theo sighed pessimistically.

The Forbidden

Vitalie died very early the next morning in her sleep, before her husband and son even reached the hospital.

"She didn't know what hit her," the doctor said. "I'm deeply sorry for your loss. She wasn't in pain but passed away peacefully."

Claude collapsed into a deep, deep depression and became a complete recluse. Juliette, feeling that it was her fault, was also depressed, sulking all day, spending most of her time in a listless daydream. As for Theo, he was depressed enough even just by seeing them both so depressed!

"Well one thing's for sure," he said to Juliette that evening. "You won't need to be afraid of having to face my mother."

Less than six months later, Claude died. Having to live without his Vitalie proved too hard a test to endure. Theo inherited the house and everything in it. He resisted the temptation to blame Juliette for all the recent events. Instead, he lamented his parents' deaths, holding firm to their memory. He was certain they had gone to a better place. By that time, Juliette had given birth, and the joy of the newborn took away at least some of the sorrow and created a renewed sense of optimism, a feeling that everything was going to be alright from there on. What other tragedy could possibly fall upon them? What was left to possibly go wrong? The baby was a girl. And she grew fast--a pretty, soft-fleshed, fair-haired, playful child with loads of energy and a mind of her own. They named her Celeste. Theo sold his father's shop, which brought in a substantial sum in addition to his already hefty salary, so there weren't going to be any financial worries any time soon. Juliette would stay home and raise Celeste, while Theo took on an ever-increasing number of cases, now that he was esteemed as one of the best up-and-coming lawyers in the province. Unfortunately, he had far less time for his poetry-writing, which was growing less and less precious to him, replaced by his endeavors in the field of law and justice. Juliette, of all people, realized this. She'd known he had enormous talent ever since he recited a poem to her long ago.

Going into Theo's drawers one day, she found a whole bundle of loose and wrinkled pages--the kind of lined paper students use in school. They were filled with his poems, arranged in no particular order. She recognized the writing as Theo's. The poem on top immediately caught her

The Forbidden

attention. It was entitled *To My Beloved Wife* and the opening lines read:

The grace of your every curve
Entices envy from Beauty's eyes.

    That evening while they were relaxing in front of the fire, she confronted him about his work. "Why don't you publish it? You surely have enough material for a book."
    "No, I don't have the time. Maybe when I'm older."
    "Do it. You don't know how good you really are. Your love-poetry is really out of this world."
    Theo blushed. He wasn't one for flattery. He didn't even believe her. "You publish it, then."
    The idea struck Juliette for the first time. "Fine then, I will. Then you'll really thank me for it. Not only will you be a successful lawyer, as you are now, but you'll be a renowned poet as well."
    "As you wish," he chuckled, chucking another piece of wood into the fireplace.

It wasn't difficult for Juliette to find a home for her husband's writing. She personally delivered it to two separate publishing companies, and the second one accepted it after a week of evaluation.
    "We'd be delighted to publish it," the president of the company told her after careful consultation with his editorial staff. "It's splendid ... the best work I've seen in many years. Give your husband my congratulations. We have high hopes for his book."
    Four months later, the book came out. The reviews were many, practically unanimous in their praise. Most of them made such a big fuss, that the book was hailed as the discovery of the decade. Theo began to be lionized by popular society and sought out by all the fashionable salons of the day. He had anticipated none of the attention. It caught him completely by surprise. The most well-known society lady from whom he received a dinner invitation was Madame Genevieve Strauss, a woman who was well-acquainted with all the celebrities and artists of her time.

The Forbidden

"Oh my God!" exclaimed Juliette. "We got an invitation to one of her dinner-parties! Can you believe that? I'm in absolute shock! Only the most prominent people are invited to her mansion. I always read the gossip columns to get the latest scoop on what she's doing, who she's hosting ...We're invited to dine with the woman herself!"
Theo looked indifferent.
"You're not even in the least bit excited?"
"Well, to be perfectly honest ... no."
"But why?"
"I don't know," he said. "Won't it be awkward being in their company? We won't know anybody. How will we know what to say, how to behave, and so on. They'll soon know we're not one of them. Besides, what would you wear?"
"I have my blue evening dress. You know, the one that looks so becoming with my new wide-rimmed black hat."
"Are you sure you want to go through with this?"
"Of course! How could we decline even if we wanted to ... That would be rude!"
They arrived at the party on time. After they'd eaten, the guests, thirteen in all, followed Madame Strauss to her magnificent ballroom, where the dancing commenced to the music of a live orchestra. Juliette enjoyed herself immensely and danced the night away with various men, but Theo sat out most of the dances and found it impossible to elude the so-called charming, if not-so-beautiful Jewess, Madame Strauss, who kept doting on him every chance she got, like a fly that one swats with the back of one's hand only to see it return a moment later, buzzing all the louder.
When it was all over and everybody started leaving, Theo smiled for the first time that whole night, as his wife complained: "We have to go? So soon? But I was having such fun."
It was quite late when they got home.
"I think an apology is in order," Juliette said out of the blue. "Don't think I didn't notice how that Madame Strauss flirted with you all evening. And I wasn't the only one who noticed. Watch out, you crafty devil ... she has a husband."
"Do you think I give a fig about her? Do you think I get any pleasure from her or her kind?"
"But I don't understand," said Juliette, somewhat surprised. "Aren't you at least a little smug? Your name is being compared to the greatest

The Forbidden

literary men of the age ... Don't pretend you're not pleased!"

"I'm sorry. It's just that, you know how I am. I don't like the attention. You don't know what it's like--they treat you like a possession, something to display. That's all you are to these society people. They don't care about your work. All they care about is having you to show off at their parties to impress their rich friends. I don't like it ... actually, I can't stand it. I wish I'd burned all of my literary work before we came to live here."

"I don't understand your attitude," Juliette sighed peevishly, interpreting his reply as ingratitude towards all she'd done. "I thought this is what you always wanted! You hated your law studies, remember?"

"Well that was when I was in school. But now I'm in practice. I'm doing so well too! My older colleagues say they've never seen a man like me accomplish so much in so short a time. In a few short years, we'll be as well-off as any one of those stuffy, empty-headed aristocrats! I'm on a roll, and I can't be stopped!"

"Yes, it's a compulsion, you care more about your job than you do me!"

"I'm sorry, Juliette, but I just don't have time for all this foolishness. Don't you like all the fine things that my money buys? Don't you like living comfortably? Well, fine. But you can't keep on using me and my reputation to break into high-class society. Let's be sensible about this. You have quite a handful raising little Celeste, and I ... I have a very time-consuming profession, one which I studied for God knows how long to get. Now that I have it, and have gotten so far ahead in it, I won't just throw it all out the window for a temporary taste of literary success. The life of a writer is a very risky, unstable profession. You're only as good as your last book, in the eye of the public."

"You want to let all your talent go to waste," Juliette pouted.

"God Almighty! I curse the day I ever read you my verse! If I knew it would come to this ... It was meant to be private. Private. Like a diary. To this day I feel violated for letting you put it in print."

Pretending not to hear, Juliette mused: "Hmm. I wonder what your fellow Dionysians think of all your fame. How proud they must be!"

In time, Celeste grew into a plump, affectionate, and as could be expected, energetic six-year-old. It was 1914, a year that would make its lasting mark

The Forbidden

on the whole century, for it was the year the First World War began, a disastrous conflict that would lead millions--soldiers and even civilians--to death and ruin.

The Bidault family was living very comfortably in their Rouen home. Theo, still only in his late twenties, had amassed a fortune of some size over the last few years through his law practice, and his reputation had not waned. Neither had his fame as an international writer decreased, even though he hadn't once picked up the pen to write since his first book.

All was going well on the surface. But underneath, Juliette was starting to sense that something was very, very wrong. What she didn't know was that Theo was displaying symptoms of the syphilis she had infected him with--a syphilis that she didn't know she had. Unbeknownst to anyone, including himself, Theo was at a serious stage of his illness. The most striking symptoms that Juliette noticed were eye troubles, hair falling out, headaches, and heart trouble. Theo always complained that his eyes were giving him problems and he experienced periods of temporary blindness, which made it so difficult to read and study his cases because as soon as he concentrated on the written page for any length of time, his eyes began to tire. Considerable bits of hair would fall, whether he was bathing or running his hand through his hair. He was pestered by long and intense headaches, night and day. And another visible symptom was a rapid heart beat. His heart would start galloping like a race horse all of a sudden for no apparent reason, pounding hard like a drum. It was uncomfortable and would happen unexpectedly and scare the hell out of him. However, Theo had a fear and dread of doctors and medicines. He became convinced that these symptoms were all stress-related, due to over-work, and that it was only his mother's nervous traits he'd inherited, persuading himself that the condition was only temporary, a passing faze. He did nothing about it, other than trying to improve his diet a little.

One night in bed, Juliette expressed her deep concerns, only to have her husband sneer at her dismissingly, and roll his eyes. "Juliette. I've told you over and over. I look fine. I *am* fine. Don't be such a hysteric. You're starting to remind me of my mother."

"Yes, you do look fine. But looking a certain way and feeling a certain way are two completely different things. Don't you see? I love you too much to let anything terrible happen to you. Why won't you see a doctor. Why?"

"Juliette, stop all this exaggerating. I'm perfectly healthy."

The Forbidden

His stubborn denial was unshakable. Turning the lamp off, he huddled up under the sheets as if hiding from a bogeyman, unwilling to face his worsening condition.

After several more years of the same torment, Theo was blind and paralyzed in parts of the body. He was bedridden, and as for his profession, he had to kiss it good-bye ... forever.

"If only you'd listened to me!" Juliette would shout at him in tears. "If only you'd agreed to get at least some kind of treatment! But no! You admit something's wrong only when it's too late!"

Thinking that he didn't have long to live, he made a request. "I want you to invite all my old friends, the Dionysians. Especially Marcel. Send a telegram. I can't remember the last time we had company."

"Very well," said Juliette. "It will do you good to see them."

All of the members came as soon as they could. They knew nothing of the illness until their arrival, and it was more than a shock to find their friend in his pathetic state.

"You really can't see us?" asked Marcel, gulping.

"No, that's not true. I can see you very well in my mind," the blind Theo retorted. "I can also see the faint traces of your silhouette ..."

"Oh God, Theo," Marcel put his arms around him. "What's happened to you? What's your illness?"

"Damned if I know. I'd have to attribute it all to really bad nerves," he said stupidly. "I've inherited my mother's nervous disposition. Or maybe a mysterious disease of the blood. I don't know. But now, at last, it's come to haunt me. I suppose my successes were too good to last ... Uninterrupted happiness and everlasting success are things the gods do not allow us mere mortals."

The others gathered around his bed, deeply affected and concerned. There wasn't a dry eye. Robert, being handicapped as he was, seemed especially affected.

"Who knows," Theo said expressionlessly, "I suppose I'll die." He was already surrendering to death. "And I thought that when I got to this age, the best years of my life would begin. Ha, ha, ha." His wry chuckle was soon replaced by a frown.

No one else was laughing.

"Tell me," he turned to them all, "are you still meeting regularly? Is The Cult of the Dionysians still alive and well?"

Marcel: "Well, a lot of us have settled down considerably. But,

The Forbidden

yes, we still have our secret meetings."

"I'm glad to hear it."

"You'll also be glad to hear that I've stopped playing around with the black arts--the sexually perverse rituals of Thelemite sorcery. To tell you the truth, it got pretty boring for my taste. Those big, thick old books dealing with esoteric knowledge make for such dull and difficult reading."

Then Marcel went babbling on and on to Theo about the popularity of his poetry, explaining how everybody, from the intellectual to the chimney-sweeper, were *still* reading and raving about his book. And now his writings were being taught in schools.

For the first time in a long time, Theo really paid attention to things said about his work and felt really sorry for abandoning it as pointlessly as he had.

Grabbing Marcel by the arm, he mumbled, "it was always my goal to be a poet," adding a little untruthfully, "this lawyer business never meant anything to me. I should have ... I should have listened to my heart, not my reason."

And so with these words, he again became Theo the poet, rather than Theo the attorney.

Desperately, as if unaware that he was nearly blind, he begged for a pen and paper. "Quick, I have to write something. My last poem. Before it's too late! I must write it for the living--there are no readers among the dead!"

"No, Theo. You first have to see a doctor ... you have to get better."

"No! No doctors!"

"Do you see what I've had to contend with?" gasped Juliette. "He's got one foot in the grave, and he still refuses any medical aid that could save his life."

Marcel was confused. "Why?" he asked. "Remember that time long ago when you were near starvation? You saw a doctor then ... and you were so weak I had to feed you myself, remember? Why not see a doctor now?"

"Don't you see that it just doesn't matter any more? My body's dying. There's your answer. Now I don't want to hear another word about it. Please, make my last hours as pleasant for me as you can."

Seven hours later, Theo called out, "Juliette!" There was nobody else in his bedroom, as they were leaving him to rest.

The Forbidden

"What is it?" she rushed in.

"This is it." He smiled. "Dying young like all Romantic poets."

"What?"

Gazing intently into her eyes, he had just enough strength to run the fingers of his hand once through her hair.

"It wasn't supposed to turn out this way ... It's like Rabelais said at his deathbed: 'I'm off to the Great Perhaps.'"

Having said that, he kissed her hands. Then his eyelids fell and his body went slack. He was dead.

"No! Theo, no! Come back, Theo! Come back!" She raved, shaking him. "Wake up! Oh please wake up ...!" Her tears soaked him. But they didn't revive him.

Marcel ran into the room and had quite a time trying to pry Juliette off of Theo's corpse as she shook him by the neck, then crushing his cold, lifeless lips in a hot kiss of almost erotic grief.

Finally, a physician was brought in. He was a local but very capable and experienced practitioner. He pronounced the body deceased.

"Tell me what he died of! Tell me what he died of!" Juliette repeated. "It's not natural for a man to die this young ..." She threw a fit.

Marcel had to hold her down; he led her out of the room and calmed her down.

After some close physical examination, the doctor came out and replied: "You can tell the lady her husband died of a venereal infection."

Juliette was in shock. "Are you absolutely sure?" she spat.

"Yes, madame. His blood is infected with the disease. It attacked his whole immune system, his spine, muscles and brain, weakening it gradually till it got to the point where his body could no longer cope. If he had lived, his mind would have been the next thing to go. You can consider yourself lucky he died when he did. Insanity is a terrible thing. A terribly embarrassing thing as well, if I may say so, and that's certainly where he was headed ... Please pardon the indelicate question, but do you have any idea how he might have contracted the deadly disease?"

"I have no idea!" she exclaimed. "Are you implying--"

"I'm not implying anything," the good doctor was quick to explain. "But I'm sure you are aware, as most people are, that whoring and adultery are still commonly practiced by some men, married or not. I'm posing this only as a possibility. Do you have any suspicions of adultery?"

"No, none!"

The Forbidden

"Very well, then. Good."

There was a tense pause.

"I can think of only *one* other possibility, then," said the doctor.

Juliette gave him a frightened stare. She knew what he was going to say. It was inevitable.

"Please raise your skirts. I'll need to have a look at you."

"This is ridiculous!" raved Juliette, "I don't see how--"

"Please ... just do it," said Marcel, making her sit down beside the doctor on the bed.

"I'm sorry, madame, but this way we can know immediately whether it was you who infected your hus--"

"Alright, alright!" she cut him off at the last word.

"I assure you, it'll only take a moment."

Marcel waited outside the room. The vaginal examination was brief.

"Ah, just as I thought," said the doctor. "I mean, what I hoped wouldn't be the case, is. You have chancres, otherwise known as syphilitic ulcers. This lesion appears when--"

"It was I who killed him!" Juliette interrupted, "it's all my fault!" Juliette screamed uncontrollably. "This is my punishment for what I used to be ..."

The doctor gave her a sedative; she was clearly in an anxious and disturbed state.

Taking Marcel aside, he said: "This woman's just had the greatest shock of her life. Let's leave her alone."

Just as the doctor was getting ready to leave, Marcel asked: "But what's going to happen to her? Why doesn't she show the same symptoms as he did?"

"It could be any number of reasons. It varies. For some, the symptoms come almost immediately. For others, they go on feeling well for years before it seems to strike them out of nowhere. Sometimes, decline is slow and gradual. It may not be a good idea to tell her yet that she, too, might not have long to live."

"Good, because I would definitely lack the courage with that," Marcel sighed.

The Forbidden

Theo Bidault's death was reported in all the major newspapers the following day. The best article came from a Rouen paper, the Gazette des Beaux-Arts, noted for its conservative bias (although more bohemian or 'Parisian' papers equally emphasized the tragic loss):

DEATH OF A GREAT POET

'Monsieur Theo Bidault, who has been very favorably known for some years now as one of our rising lyricists, died at his home in Rouen yesterday. The cause has not yet been disclosed, and readers should expect further reports. Readers hardly need to be reminded that Bidault had some time ago attracted wide international acclaim for his passionate and exceptionally unique book of verse, 'Talking to Lovers and God.' As this was his only published work, admirers will no doubt be hopeful that a posthumous volume of his writings might be available some time in the future. Apart from its mastery of style and incredible technical dexterity, what made Theo Bidault's poetry so special and vital to our times was its sparkling, yet practical, optimism. In his work, one finds none of the dark, hopeless, or obscene elements which our poets today seem to embrace and glorify so distastefully. There is a purity, innocence and sanity to his work that is a truly rare thing indeed. On this November twenty-third, 1917, France grieves the bitter loss of arguably its best poet.'

Everyone close to Theo lamented his death bitterly. Theo had many friends and associates. The funeral was large. It was declared a national funeral. Both his law partners and admirers of his verse alike showed up in droves. While his law associates praised him for being a man who never compromised on his principles, admirers of his poetry praised his small but lasting contribution to literature.

As he stood before Theo's grave, shaking his head, Marcel couldn't help but thank his lucky stars that Juliette was one of the few whores he actually *didn't* get a chance to sleep with. And he was struck by the cruel irony that Theo, who unlike him had led such a chaste life, met with such

The Forbidden

demonically bad luck.

Juliette too stood there in deep contemplation, and as the coffin was being lowered, she thought about how relieved she was that Theo never lived to know the cause of his death and who was responsible for it.

In the hours and days that followed, she orchestrated a clever cover-up that let nothing about Theo's mysterious death leak out. First, she visited the doctor. He lived in a house in a quieter, less urbanized side of town, as did Juliette.

"Have you spoken to anyone about my husband's death?" she asked.

"Oh no, of course not. All that is strictly confidential. It would be easier for you to get a priest to reveal to you somebody else's confession than for me to reveal to you what's meant for my ears alone."

"But priests are sworn to secrecy."

"That's my point."

"Look, sir, I don't understand you, and I don't have time to chat. Speak plainly. Do you swear you'll keep the cause of my husband's death a secret ... for as long as you live?"

"I won't spill a word of it, my dear madame. You have my full assurance. That's what I'm trying to tell you."

She breathed a sigh of relief and was suddenly calm.

Her next stop was the secret meeting-place of the Dionysians. Crossing her fingers and hoping that the members would be there, she arrived at nine o'clock in the evening on a weekend day. She remembered the way. She was rather coldly received. Robert was the most hostile: "It's your fault he's dead."

"Have you spoken to any journalists? Have they asked you questions about Theo's death?"

"No," replied Marcel. "No one knows of our acquaintance with Theo."

She begged and begged: "Will you please keep quiet about it? Please, I've suffered enough, losing the one and only man I've ever cared for, that I ever will love. Don't tell them, Marcel ... don't tell them ... promise me!"

"That it was your fault?" exclaimed Robert. "We'll shut up ... for the right price."

Without hesitation, she bribed them all. All except Marcel. He refused her money. They swore to uphold their promise. No one would

The Forbidden

know the truth as long as she lived. Thus, the cause of Theo's death was described in the newspapers as undisclosed, inconclusive. And the matter was dropped.

Epilogue

The first thing Juliette went about doing was getting the best treatment for her syphilis that her dead husband's money could buy. She spent vast sums first on conventional treatments. And when those didn't work, she turned to crack-pot 'experimental' ones, which only made her worse, if anything. Before too long, she was undergoing a rapid physical deterioration. Her health was the first to go. Then her good looks. Her disease was so far along at the tertiary stage, that there was no hope for recovery. All she could pray for was a painless death. In time, only a very small portion of her husband's once large fortune remained.

After the war had ended, she suffered from paresis and then her first fit of madness, and was taken as a patient into Le Jean Renard Mental Asylum.

Both directly *and* indirectly, she had wiped out the whole Bidault family. "I've ruined everything," she would mutter, straitjacketed in a chair in a large vacant room filled with other lunatics. "It's all my fault. I've ruined his whole family. I'm the cause of it all. I'm the cause of his parents' deaths. I'm the reason Theo's mother's dead! I'm the reason for Theo's father's death! I'm the reason for Theo's death!" No one knew what she was talking about and they mistook it as nothing more than mindless raving.

She wept and wept. But tears only prolonged the agony, the guilt, the pain. Death came relatively quickly. A complete cure for syphilis was not discovered until the 1930's.

Ironic as it may seem, her daughter Celeste was left without parents just like Juliette had been left parentless when she was a young girl. Marcel adopted her. He felt it was the least he could have done. So typical of him. A friend to the end.

The Forbidden

From the Peasant Life to Paris

The Forbidden

Part 1

Romilly was a crude little provincial village in the heart of the Norman countryside and looked no different than many others just like it in France's rural regions. Entirely inhabited by peasants, most of whom worked the land which proudly belonged to them for centuries, passed down from generation to generation, the village was a place where no secrets existed. Everybody knew everybody else, what they were up to, what good they had done, what sins they were guilty of, and that was that, since scandal was the only interesting thing that ever happened in such dreary parts. Of course, the country definitely had its charm as well. Nothing, especially not the stuffy, noisy, over-populated cities, could compare with the vast, open, beautiful and peaceful spaces of the rural environment. Romilly was one such space, home to only a few hundred. There was one church, but it was in terrible shape and the village elders refused to pay for repairs, reasoning that poor people were starving on the streets, homeless, and that the money must be used to build an almshouse where the unfortunates could freely find the necessities.

"But surely spiritual food is more important than material food!" argued the village's one and only priest, Father Villot, who went to the townhall to petition his case.

"More important, perhaps. But not as physically nourishing!" the leading village official, Mayor Monsieur Argot, flared.

From there a violent verbal confrontation ensued where absolutely nothing was resolved.

Only making things worse by trying to lighten the mood, one of the elders, Monsieur Henri Catillon, a stout and jolly sort of man, laughed:

"Bugger the church! And bugger the almshouse! Why not build a new brothel? Surely you'd have more people going there than the other two places combined!"

In holy rage, the priest pounded his fist on the table so hard, it

The Forbidden

shook and spilled a cup of coffee on the stout (but suddenly not very jolly) elder. He leaped from his seat, his fat belly burning from the extreme heat of the beverage. "Shit!"

"Ha!" spat the priest. "There, do you see what God has done to you?"

Monsieur Catillon didn't even heed him, too wound up in his own discomfort.

The priest left in disgust. "Heathens!"

The season was spring and everybody in Romilly was in a good mood, it seemed. It was something in that time of year, perhaps something in the air, that brought out the good in the otherwise world-weary peasant soul. The winter was behind them and only summer awaited. Ah, yes. Sweet summer. God's promise of great sunshine. Of laughter, recreation and long lazy days. Of lovers' strolls along the river which flowed just outside of the little village. Yes, summer. The season of nature's glory.

It was at this blessed time of the year that a child was born to the Joyeux family. A girl. They named her Isabelle. She was a very pretty infant, pampered by all the young and nubile maidens as well as the old and barren matrons. Marie, her mother, was praised for producing such an adorable creature. Why all the attention? Because it had taken her until age thirty-five to give birth. Nobody believed, after her first ten years of childless marriage, that she would ever bear a child. And her humiliation had been heartbreaking, especially when she saw all the other women with their children, laughing, playing, hugging. It had crushed her. For so long, her husband and she were semi-outcasts in the world of the married with children. But finally, at long last, she delivered--and in such style! All the women admitted that hers was the cutest baby of all. She's the baby Jesus himself if he were a girl, they chuckled.

At age six, Isabelle's parents were separated. And she would never see her spendthrift womanizing drunkard of a father again. She cried for days, but her tears were wasted for nothing. The break-up was an irreparable one.

Because the land badly needed tending to and her father was no longer around to maintain it, Isabelle had to help out in anyway she could and was unable to start her education until age twelve. The school was not

The Forbidden

far from the church and a short walk from her house. Her first day was a little frightening, but she learned quickly and soon proved that there was indeed a brain behind those soft and mesmerizing eyes of hers.

She was placed beside another girl named Jeanne, a fifteen-year-old almost as attractive as her, and the two of them instantly became friends despite the few years' age difference. Jeanne was nice, but she was also a crude girl (in more ways than one). She was very outgoing and liked joking around. But her speech and manner were sometimes rude and 'indecent', and that got her into trouble from time to time. She didn't care, though. Those prissy, old, hypocritical bourgeois could spew their venom all they liked. She wasn't intimidated. She assumed that she was only saying and doing publicly what they were saying and doing privately--or at least thinking it.

One day, as the lessons were being handed out, the class was as still and silent as an evening in the woods. The teacher, Madame Daigle, a tall, freakishly thin and ugly-faced hag who was strict and never allowed any misbehavior in her class, wrote on the chalkboard in her fast, nervous hand-writing. The slightest offence, no matter whose fault, merited a thrashing in front of the class from her. It was the accepted brand of discipline which every respectable parent believed in, peasant or not.

"She's a Lesbian, you know," whispered Jeanne, smothering a giggle with her hand.

"A what?" the clueless Isabelle inquired. "What's that?"

"She likes women."

Isabelle gave it some deep thought, still not comprehending. It's not that she wasn't bright. On the contrary, she was very clever. But she was also quite young and naive, knowing very little about sexuality.

"Don't you know what I'm getting at?"

"No."

Frustrated, Jeanne broke the perfect quiet of the room with a booming voice:

"She makes love to women!"

Madame Daigle broke her chalk, dropping it to the floor. She briskly swung around, knowing full well that the remark was made about her, as the whole village had been spreading the rumor. Whether it was true or not, she was lucky she still had her job.

Grabbing Jeanne firmly and rather harshly by the forearm, she dragged her to the front of the class, making her bend over and lift her

The Forbidden

skirts so that the horrified gaze of the entire class was centered in on her cotton knickers.

"I'll teach you to disrupt my class!" the mean spinster roared. "You're a bad seed. A rotten apple. And when Providence catches up with you, you'll get just what's been waiting for you. Now don't bend your legs--keep 'em straight and fairly apart."

Whap! Whap! Whap!

"Have you had enough?" Madame Daigle cruelly gasped.

Jeanne turned her head back, defiantly giving the older woman the ugliest grimace.

"No, I didn't think so!" the crone answered her own question. "Three whacks can't be enough. Let's make it a round number--eight--and be done with it."

This teacher truly was a sadist, going beyond the call of discipline. This was physical abuse under the guise of 'discipline.'

Isabelle looked on in complete amazement and disgust. She had never seen anything like it before. Aside from seeing her father slap her mother once, this was her first exposure to violence. Little did she know that it was sexual violence.

Even after the last strike, Jeanne made not one peep. No tears on her face either, though it was red. She wasn't afraid of pain. She bore it well.

When the beating was over, Jeanne hid her pain well, gave her teacher a final mischievous grin merely as a form of revenge, knowing how it would enrage her, knowing how it would take the power away from her and make her feel like the little misfit had won.

After school, the two new girl friends decided to go for a swim. The river was always nearby. It wasn't the Danube and it wasn't the Seine, but it was good enough. A clean fast-moving crystal blue stream of water bordered by strips of tall, marshy grass.

Isabelle thought about what her friend had told her in class earlier that day and she asked:

"Is it really true what you said? Is she really what you say?"

"Yes. Everyone knows, you ninny," Jeanne chuckled.

"Did she hurt you? Those blows must have left their mark."

The Forbidden

"I don't know. It stings though. Can't wait to get into the cool water. It'll take away some of the hurt."

They arrived at a rocky part of the riverside secluded from both directions by high towering cliffs. Between them was a small private sandy beach.

"Let's go down here," suggested Jeanne, taking Isabelle by the hand and running so fast, Isabelle almost fell face-first. Her hat was swept by the breeze and she almost failed to notice, concentrating so hard on trying to keep up with the sprinting Jeanne.

"But wait," said Isabelle, peeved off when they got to the sand. "I have no swimming-clothes with me."

"Don't need them. We'll go in the nude," her friend replied in such a casual manner that dissolved any inhibitions the unworldly Isabelle might have had.

In no time at all, the modest twelve-year-old Isabelle was standing in front of the prematurely buxom and beautiful naked body of her slightly older friend, whose skin was a white color, but a healthy white, like ivory; fleshy oval thighs like one sees on sculptures; a large but well-shaped behind; slender, oblong breasts capped with fat and reddish-pink nipples; hips and a waist that were a little heavier and broader than what was considered fashionable even in those days. However, she had the long legs of a model, and best of all, the incredible charm of her face--very graceful features. Gorgeous. Especially the orange hair, eyes and lips. They were Perfection itself. And in the valley between Jeanne's upper-thigh, Isabelle caught her first sight of pussy. She was surprised to find such an abundance of hair there, since her own growth so far amounted to little more than a few short wisps.

Jeanne giggled as she was apt to do, very conscious of her companion's eyes roaming the terrain that was her ripe young frame.

"Don't just stand there glaring! Undress!"

Isabelle obeyed, and within seconds they were both running into the water, splashing each other.

Many birds flew by, and they could be heard all around. There were no clouds overhead, just a deep expanse of blue, like the one they were swimming in. They swam and swam until exhaustion seized their limbs.

"Want to tan for awhile?" asked Jeanne.

Isabelle agreed.

The Forbidden

"Last one out kisses frogs!" shouted Jeanne, getting quite a head-start.

She made it first upon the scorching pale-gray sand and fell on her back, laying down on her elbows, gasping, but with her unending smile intact. She got a very good view of the blonde-haired Isabelle coming out of the water. A much more petite physique. She truly was a frail little thing, half a foot shorter than Jeanne. But she certainly was the prettiest near-adolescent Venus of them all. A face like something out of a Leonardo or Botticelli painting; crooked moderate breasts, slender and loopy. Jeanne delighted in what she beheld--physically, it was everything she wanted to be. But she harbored no envy or resentment. Rather, she was allured by her friend's body.

Isabelle collapsed beside her, equally out of breath. Breathing deeply, hotly, they stared at each other, mouths only a short distance apart. They could feel each others' breaths, the emanating heat from each others' flesh. The tension grew after every moment. For once, Jeanne's boldness failed her--the courage of a kiss was not in her.

Isabelle bowed her head, escaping Jeanne's eyes whose blatant lewdness could be read so easily.

"Wow! Look!" gasped Isabelle, pointing to Jeanne's backside. The paddle had left its marks. Purple-blue bruises bulged from her flesh.

Jeanne sat up and had a good look, touching them. "Ou!"

"It hurts, eh?" Isabelle managed to stupidly say.

"That Madame Daigle's a fucking bitch! See if I let that dirty bitch lay a hand on me again! She's a filthy dog."

Jeanne abruptly stood up and yelled: "Hear that, Madame Daigle? You're nothing but a filthy, good-for-nothing she-bitch!" And she imitated barking sounds.

Isabelle thought it pretty funny. She laughed and realized that there was this irresistible childish streak that attracted her to Jeanne. In the same way that Jeanne had admired Isabelle's body coming out of the waves, Isabelle now realized how much she admired Jeanne's personality.

"Wanna go back in the water?" asked Isabelle.

"Sure," said the still-weary Jeanne, slouching and jogging after her friend, who was the first one in just as Jeanne had been the first one out.

Almost immediately, Isabelle started getting into some swimming difficulties, for the currents where she found herself were rough and turbulent and dragged her away downstream. She was swallowing water,

The Forbidden

drowning.

"Help!" A half-subdued cry came from her lungs.

It was loud enough for Jeanne to hear and she swam towards her in a flurry of haste. However, the tide was fast taking her away--faster than Jeanne could swim. The distance between them doubled after every few seconds.

"Jeanne!" cried the drowning girl, barely able to keep her head above water. There was something enticing about her desperation, about the way she seemed to be looking Death in the face.

Jeanne, meanwhile, was too busy trying to swim as quick as she could to bother with a verbal response.

Suddenly, out of nowhere appeared Leon, a fellow classmate of theirs. He was a strong, charming youth who had his eye on Isabelle since the first time she stepped into the classroom. He had followed them to their private little beach, and hidden away, had been spying on them the whole time.

He dove into the water and somehow managed to get a hold of Isabelle, and with much effort, he led her out of the current and to shore. Isabelle held on to him for dear life the whole time, like a lover. When he laid her down on the ground, she was reluctant to let go (was it fear or something else?), and he fell on top of her ... accidentally, of course.

After the heroic feat he had just accomplished, his courage was not lacking, as Jeanne's had earlier been, and he kissed her, then and there, picking Isabelle at her most vulnerable and grateful. Isabelle didn't mind. She reveled in the moment as much as he did.

When Jeanne got out of the water and saw what was happening, a pang of jealousy pierced her soul and she rushed over all the faster.

"Let her go, you brute!" she spat. "You can't just go around raping girls!" And her fists pounded his back. But to no avail.

Leon and Isabelle only laughed.

"It's alright, Jeanne. He's not hurting me."

"Oh, isn't he! The brute!" She backed off reluctantly, still agitated.

Leon asked to walk Isabelle home, to Jeanne's great displeasure. He even got her to agree to be his girlfriend.

Finally, Jeanne really put her foot down. In her usual rude fashion, she said:

"But you don't even know him!"

"Well good, that leaves a lot of room for discovery," Isabelle

The Forbidden

retorted.

    Leon smiled.

    All of the villagers came to church on Sunday. That included Isabelle and her very religious prude of a mother, Madame Joyeux. Most of the peasants were more superstitious than religious. They believed that so long as they went to the old, decrepit church once a week and survived one morning of sermons they half-understood, their souls were saved. The church really was seriously in need of repairs. Parts of its structure were rotting away. It dated back to when Romilly first came to be, which was some time in the late seventeenth century.

    The priest was passionately in the middle of a sermon that started out being an enlightening and organized lesson on greed and lechery, and deteriorated into a heated attack on what he called Mr. Argot's stubborn apathy for spiritual values, and Monsieur Catillon's unclean sexual habits. Of course, the two men were present. Monsieur Catillon was too much of a coward to challenge the priest, and was afraid of the people around him and their righteous indignation as they murmured among themselves, spitefully whispering, "shame" into his ears. He preferred to cower down, taking it as something he deserved and would have to live through. Under normal circumstances, the villagers' moral outrage would not have been nearly as pronounced, but the sensationalistic sermon had strongly awakened their deep puritanical side, and because they were in church, eager to show one another how offended and enraged they were in the name of decency, they treated the two men like outcasts, even though a good number of them in attendance were just as blame-worthy. But Monsieur Argot, on the other hand, wasn't about to take any of it. Being the feisty, hot-headed character that he was, Monsieur Argot stood up, interrupting the black-robed, self-righteous bigot on his soapbox with these words:

    "And you pretend to care about the poor! You give a sou here, a sou there, and you're so, so satisfied with yourself. You think you've done so much! And you pat yourself on the back and get a real nice warm and tingly feeling in your belly, and with a big broad smile, say, 'I'm a good person. I give to the poor.' What you give isn't worth one small heap of shit!"

The Forbidden

With a satanic hatred, the priest replied, "and I suppose you have fed all of the mouths that cry from hunger! I suppose you have the perfect answer, Monsieur Argot!" His mockery and sarcasm were obvious.

"As a matter of *fact*, I do! I want to build an almshouse!"

Diverting his attention from the priest, who was so angry he looked like he had fire coming out of his nose, Monsieur Argot directed his speech to the congregation. In a sensible tone, he began:

"I'm sure we have many in this room who barely made it through last winter. As I look around at these pews, I see spots that aren't occupied when last spring they were. Yes, we have all lost somebody we knew to starvation. We always have the Word of God with us--the Bible. It doesn't require a church to teach its teachings. And it certainly doesn't require a priest. What we do need now, urgently, is a house for the poor who would otherwise perish. Warm meals for their aching bellies. It's that simple--the difference between life and death. You can't teach dead people the Word of God!"

Everyone started nodding in agreement. To his benefit, Monsieur Argot proved a very persuasive orator. People muttered approvingly amongst themselves.

"Blasphemy! Blasphemy!" repeated the priest.

Monsieur Catillon, like the playful idiot he was, stood up and clapped. Everyone laughed. Thus encouraged, he would have spoken and made a big fool of himself, but he was stopped by his wife, who had the good sense to sit his arse back down on their pew by yanking on his coat.

But by the time the Blessed Sacrament was about to be handed out, Monsieur Catillon stood up again to his wife's great dismay and this time he went too far:

"Father Villot, I shit on your sacrament! I've turned Protestant! What do you say about that!"

He was kicked out of the church and that was all the reply he got.

In no time at all, Isabelle had become teacher's pet. Madame Daigle had always had more than a teacher's eye on her and now it was evident to the whole class. Isabelle did nothing to attract this treatment and certainly didn't want it. It made her feel like an 'outsider' among her classmates, and she was disliked by all the other students (except Jeanne, of course)

The Forbidden

because of the favoritism. This resentment was increased by the fact that she was an excellent student, the best of them all, with or without Madame Daigle's special attentions.

One day, these special attentions towards Isabelle became a tad too evident--for Jeanne, anyway. It had bothered Jeanne quite enough the way Madame Daigle patted (more like caressed) Isabelle on the shoulder or the head whenever she was satisfied with a written assignment of hers. Or the way she regularly complimented her on her good looks or appearance. But one Monday afternoon, Madame Daigle definitely crossed the line. The class had returned from the outdoors, as every student had been asked to pick something out of nature, whether it be a flower, acorn, etc ... and draw it at their desk. Isabelle chose just a common leaf, that's all. Not very ambitious. When Madame Daigle saw her hard at work, she came over to see the young girl's progress.

"What artistic ability," she said flatteringly. Only when around Isabelle did she let a soft, sweet and tender side shine through. With most everyone else, she was often a mean and irritable cat. So enchanted was she by this young beauty that even she, herself, failed to notice how foolish and giddy some of her behavior around Isabelle could be. Jeanne saw it better than anyone, and was disgusted.

"Thank you. I'm trying to put in a lot of detail. You know, there's a lot more to a leaf than just its shape and color."

"Uhu," replied Madame Daigle with a girlish giggle.

Jeanne noticed how the teacher was furtively looking down Isabelle's blouse. There was more of the usual and familiar petting, or rather, caressing. However, this time there was something a little more: Madame Daigle reached down sneakily and gave Isabelle's breast a quick and gentle squeeze with the palm of her hand. Jeanne saw what happened, and knowing that Isabelle was too much the timid sort to stand up for herself, she shouted in a fury:

"I saw that, Madame Daigle! Don't think I didn't!"

In the most spiteful, yet low tone, the teacher whispered, "you saw nothing ... and if you want a diploma at the end of the school year, you'll keep quiet ..."

Jeanne didn't respond, only folded her arms and puckered her lips in contempt.

Isabelle, too, made no response. She merely kept on drawing, trying to forget the whole thing.

The Forbidden

After school, Isabelle and Jeanne walked fast away from the school-yard.

"Hurry," said Jeanne, "I don't want Leon to follow us."

They ran into an isolated opening in the woods, falling down on top of each other on the sun-kissed grass. Jeanne sat on top of Isabelle with her legs sprawled, laughing, her dress hiked-up to her thighs.

"Get off," laughed Isabelle, trying to breathe. "You're smothering me!"

She managed to push her friend's plump body off.

They lay there on the ground, side by side, silent, staring off at the blinding light of the sun. It was comfortable.

"What audacity! What abuse of power!" spat Jeanne.

"What do you mean?"

"What do you think I mean! That woman touched your tit!"

"I know," Isabelle said rather stupidly. She said nothing more.

"I know? ... I know? ... Is that all you have to say? Who does that skunk think she is, taking advantage of young girls like that. In the very least, it's unprofessional, not to mention improper."

"I know, I know. Let's not talk about it anymore. Let's just forget it." Isabelle seemed tired of the incident and didn't think it was a big deal.

"It seems everybody wants a piece of you," Jeanne mused. She was jealous of Leon's attraction to Isabelle and now there was the "perverted" teacher's conduct to be jealous about. Jeanne wanted Isabelle all to herself. She didn't know it, but deep down inside she was forming a "crush" on Isabelle. "You'll need me to look out for you."

"You're a great friend," Isabelle admitted, taking her hand warmly.

There was another relaxing pause, as their clasped hands began to sweat.

"I'm going up to the crag to watch the lunar eclipse tonight. I've always been curious what one looks like," said Jeanne. "Would you like to come?"

"That would be really nice, only I've already promised Leon a rendezvous," Isabelle confessed. "After all, we *are* seeing each other now, him and I, as you know. I'm sorry. I'll do something with you tomorrow night."

"Slave to love. That's what you are. A slave to love," frowned Jeanne.

The Forbidden

Five years passed by and the love-birds, Leon and Isabelle, were still together. It was evening. Seventeen-year-old Isabelle put on her nicest clothes and set out to their meeting-place. Leon was now twenty-one years of age, but he looked and behaved younger than that. They were to meet at the landing-docks at seven o'clock and then have a stroll along the beach, maybe have a bite to eat and drink at one of the local popular riverside cafes.

She arrived five minutes early. No sign of him. Then ten minutes passed. Still no sign. Then, twenty minutes. Isabelle started to worry.

"Maybe it's the wrong hour ... or? He did say the landing-docks, didn't he?" she said to herself.

The moon was full and many stars crowded the sky. A slight wind swept the surface of the water, causing tiny ripples. The silence was creepy. It was unbearable. Isabelle began to feel depressed and an unbearable feeling of rejection gripped her.

"Where is he!"

Meanwhile, Jeanne was on her way to the brothel. All her life, she'd heard wild stories about that shabby, ill-kept 'house' and how many of the men complained that its state of disrepair was a disgrace to the profession of prostitution. The stingy, elderly madam who ran the establishment, a certain lady of Polish descent by the name of Madame Odette Pontiatowska, refused to make any changes. She had been in business for over thirty years, and for just as many years the brothel was a mess--bad hygiene observed by the whores; untidy rooms; high prices; and a number of other things that are better left unsaid. Surprisingly, with all these faults, the 'house' still made rather good business, as was evident by its thirty years in operation. Why? might one ask. Because of one major reason: it was the only bawdy-house in Romilly and the only one for miles.

Jeanne came up to it and stared at the windows, which were alight but shuddered. The sound of music could be heard coming from within, as well as the loud and unrestrained voices of merry-makers.

"There must be dancing going on, and drinking ... and who knows what else," she whispered to herself.

Suddenly, the front door opened, so Jeanne jumped behind a shrub to avoid being seen. There appeared Madame Pontiatowska, holding a man

The Forbidden

by the collar, and tossing him out the door. He was drunk, wobbling along, and the force of the push had him flying down the front-steps and into the dirt below. There were only four wooden steps, but it was still a harsh fall, leaving the poor man vomiting on the ground between inaudible mutterings of "you old bitch!"

"Don't think, Monsieur Yonne, that you can mistreat one of my girls without consequence! What you did was inexcusable!" the old matron roared, and swiftly slammed the door behind her.

Monsieur Yonne passed out, his face swimming in a yellow, foul-smelling puddle of his own puke.

After what she'd just seen, Jeanne's senses were stirred-up. She was curious and wanted to see more. Opening the small, wooden gate, she sneaked onto the property and made her way to one of the windows which happened to be open. She pulled back the shudders, looked inside, and was shocked. In what appeared to be the salon, some kind of orgy was going on. Each male customer was swarming with two or three girls. They sat on luxurious sofas or sang and danced obscenely. Some of the women were half-dressed, while a few had on almost nothing at all, with only their thick pubic beards to veil the contours of their cunt-folds. Jeanne was never to forget a portion of the song that was being played on the piano and sung:

With a slut like you, every day is a stroll through heaven
With a slut like you, I don't need my other seven
Won't you show me that charm of yours
From which secret honey pours?

Jeanne started studying the clients individually. She recognized at least half of the people. They were well-respected pillars of the community (or thought to be so). Then her eyes caught sight of something that almost made her faint--it was Leon! He was there in the company of some of his dirty, no-good friends. Two poxy-looking, much-rouged whores were kissing and fondling him. He just stood there, laughing and spilling half of his drink in his drunken attempt to bring the glass up to his liquor-stained lips.

Poor Isabelle! thought Jeanne. She was so angry, so full of disbelief, that she felt like running in there and giving him a piece of her

The Forbidden

mind, but someone yelled:

"Hey, who's that girl at the window?"

When Jeanne heard this, she took fright and ran for dear life, never looking back.

The next day, Jeanne told Isabelle everything she saw, embellishing quite a few things in her eagerness to make Leon into a villain.

Isabelle could hardly believe what she was hearing. "That's it, I'm breaking off my engagement!" she cried. They had been secretly planning to wed after she had turned eighteen. "I never want to see that bastard again!"

"Yeah, that's it," cheered Jeanne. "Tell him to fuck off! That shitface doesn't deserve a girl like you."

"Did he really sleep with those girls?" She sighed and sobbed.

"Yes," lied Jeanne, letting her licentious imagination take over. "With two of them at once. I'd bet anything they have the clap, too."

"What's that?"

"Why, syphilis of course."

They talked for hours and hours about it, until Isabelle's gentle voice grew tired.

"I know! Let's go to a play! That'll get your mind off all this unpleasantness," Jeanne suggested enthusiastically.

"No, I can't. I don't feel like doing anything. I just want to lie here."

"Nonsense! Is one failed romance going to be the end of you? You're like some cripple that could walk, but is too afraid to try."

Isabelle chuckled. "Alright, I'll go. Maybe it'll lift my spirits somehow."

"Now you're making sense. Tonight we'll have a good time!"

Strindberg's controversial play *Miss Julie* was playing at the Theatre de la Fleur. Isabelle and Jeanne prepared to take a ride to the nearest town, Saint-Sevigne, where the performance was to be staged. They got dressed up in their tight, plain-made bodices of wool and even stuffed them with handkerchiefs for a more 'ample' appearance. Isabelle stuffed her small backside as well while she was at it. It was fashionable for women to have a big, round and firm arse.

The Forbidden

"Not me, though," giggled Jeanne. "My buttocks are ample enough as it is!"

When their carriage arrived, they were off. The weather was nothing to rejoice in--stormy, windy and cold. Thunder exploded like dynamite in the dark, and lightning frightened the horses.

"Dreadful night," sighed Isabelle, huddling close to Jeanne for warmth and a sense of feeling safe.

Suddenly, Jeanne noticed that there was someone inside the spacious carriage with them on the seat opposite--an old man. They hadn't noticed him before because of the pitch dark and because he had been as still and silent as wood the whole time. The man was sleeping, perhaps returning somewhere from a long and strenuous day.

Jeanne was startled at first at the discovery of his presence and then found it amusing how funny he looked, snoozing with his mouth gaping wide open, like someone who was having his soul sucked right out of him. His eyes were closed by heavy lids and his large head leaned against the far side. His hair was grizzled and messy, and his nose was so odd-looking that the only thing to indicate it was a nose was its location on his face. But by his dress, one could tell he was a rich dandy.

"Look at him," Jeanne chuckled quietly. "He looks like a clown without make-up."

Isabelle chuckled.

Jeanne snickered. "I'll bet if I wobbled my tits in his face all night, that still wouldn't wake him up."

They giggled a little louder and he moved, but didn't awaken.

Jeanne was in a wonderful mood, especially feeling that the relationship between Leon and her best-friend was finally over. She couldn't help making another coarse joke:

"He's so old. Can you imagine how lifeless he is below the belt?"

The thunder struck closer than ever and the man jolted, giving out a faint "whoa" before returning to his dreams. His flabby mouth was now closed, but he started snoring like a wild boar.

"Will we be listening to this for the rest of the way?" Jeanne rolled her eyes, referring to the snores. "What music."

All of a sudden, the carriage went over a bump that shook it so fiercely, Isabelle thought her head would go flying through the roof.

Almost falling to the floor, the man cried aloud on the fringe of waking up:

The Forbidden

"I don't want to die yet! I'm only seventy-three!"

When he was fully awake, he sat up calmly, very surprised to be in the company of two young ladies, especially such pretty ones, and he was embarrassed by his outburst.

Jeanne wittily said to him, "don't worry, sir. You haven't met your Maker yet. Although, you still might, if the catastrophic weather conditions around us are any indication."

Then they realized that the carriage hadn't been moving for awhile.

"I wonder what's the matter," the old gentleman pondered.

The driver knocked on the door and Jeanne opened.

"I'm sorry, Miss, but we went over a rather sharp piece of rock. It's impossible to see anything in this God-forsaken dark! Anyway, one of the wheels broke. I can't go on."

Jeanne's positive mood abruptly turned to irritation. "Damn buffoon! Can't even steer right! ... How far are we from Saint-Sevigne?"

"Only half a kilometer," replied the sorry man. "However, if you will permit me, I would suggest that you not venture forth anywhere, but stay in the carriage until morning. It's too dangerous."

"Oh, bugger off," she said. Turning to Isabelle:

"Come on. The play doesn't start for some time yet. I'm making it to that performance tonight if I die trying!"

"Are you sure that's wise?" the more sensible Isabelle asked.

"Who cares. Are you coming or not!"

Isabelle, afraid to spend the night alone with a strange man and quite a ways from home, decided she had no choice but to go.

"If you will allow me, ladies," said the elderly dandy, "I will happily escort you to where you are going."

Jeanne was about to protest, but he cut her short. "Please," he said sweetly, "two young girls like you, unaccompanied at night, particularly a night like this? I simply must insist. Otherwise, you could be assaulted by tramps on a desolate road like this. Besides, you'll find I am the perfect gentleman."

They nodded and hurried away with him under his umbrella, leaving the driver behind. Fearful of theft, the driver wouldn't have left his horses and carriage behind for the world.

As they walked in a hurry, Jeanne started talking:

"Thank you so very much, Monsieur--"

"Jean-Francoise Lafayette," he interrupted.

The Forbidden

"Yes, Monsieur Lafayette ...You're right, who knows what kinds of rogues and despicable types could be lurking off in the woods or on the road. We are indeed grateful for your company. Who would we have to save us from thieves? Who would we have to safeguard our chastity, if you weren't here to chaperon and protect it?"

The Monsieur grinned widely at this. What real protection could an old fart like him be anyway?

"And what's more," added Jeanne, "without your umbrella, we would look a perfect mess, unfit for appearance in public ... especially at the theater!"

The old dandy started off being a very charming, kind and talkative sort. "Say, you girls don't know who I am, do you?" he then asked out of the blue.

"No," they replied. "But we can see that you're a good Samaritan."

After awhile he turned completely silent and stiff. No more sweetness. No more smiles decorated his broad, flabby lips.

Without a second's notice, he grabbed Isabelle by the shoulders and forced her to the ground, spreading her kneecaps far apart with his old, yet still surprisingly powerful enough limbs.

"Get off her, you dirty old brute!" screamed Jeanne, jumping on top of him, trying to wrestle him away as he violently fondled Isabelle's breasts.

"You get off me, you fat cow!" he hissed at Jeanne, spraying Isabelle's face with spittle as he spoke.

Isabelle struggled, but the weight of the two bodies was too much. She could barely move.

Jeanne had muscular, rugged peasant arms and yanked on the half-bald man's hair with a force that refused to be ignored.

He finally let go of Isabelle and turned his attention to Jeanne, as Isabelle lay recovering, the front of her bodice ripped open and some of her handkerchiefs lying all over the place. Her molested breasts hung in indecent disarray, heaving bare with her every breath.

"If you prefer that I poke your cunt instead, then let's have it your way!" he bellowed at Jeanne, raising up her dress and running his fingers up her crotch. As he was about to attempt to rape her, Isabelle came up from behind with his cane and cracked him over the back of the head with it as hard as she could.

He fell unconscious like a tonne of bricks, his pants at half-mast

The Forbidden

and genitals drooping like a gigantic earthworm.

Isabelle looked away in repulsion at the sight of that ancient, quickly shrinking penis. She was flooded with remorse. "Is he dead?"

"God I hope so!" Jeanne got to her feet, brushing off her clothes. "Look at us, we're a complete mess!"

They stared at each other seriously for a moment before bursting out in relieving laughter, which was immediately replaced by tears.

"This has been the strangest night I have ever experienced," sighed Isabelle.

"Yeah. I guess we won't be going to the play, huh?"

They returned to the carriage where they stayed until they found another ride home the following morning.

Isabelle confronted Leon about 'the brothel incident.' "You slept with a pack of whores! My friend saw you, so don't try to deny it! It's over between us!"

Pathetically, he begged for another chance, swearing that he didn't actually sleep with them, he was only playfully amusing himself with them, which was actually true.

"Why were you there, then!"

"Because my friends pressed me into going with them."

"No, I don't trust you anymore. Besides, I'm too angry to love you. You'll have to find another girl, a girl who won't mind her man sleeping around on her. That shouldn't be a problem for you."

"But I don't want another girl. I only want you. Please. You've got to believe me. It was just harmless amusement and meaningless flirting. I ... I--"

"Love me? Is that what you were about to say? If that were true, you would have showed up! I sat waiting and waiting for you and ..."

Isabelle abruptly turned around and walked away quickly and angrily. "I simply never want to see you again."

"There, see?" said Jeanne to Leon with a smug look on her face tinged with malice, "that's what you get for bleeding a girl's heart," and she ran over to join and comfort her weeping friend.

It looked hopeless. No matter how hard he would try, no matter how sorry he was, Leon felt he would never get her back again.

The Forbidden

"Oh my God!" gasped Jeanne the next morning after skimming through a newspaper.

From an article on the front page, they learned that the old man, Monsieur Jean-Francoise Lafayette, who had been in the carriage with them on the night of the storm, was an aristocrat, but not just any aristocrat: one of the most famous and wealthy men in France, a high-ranking government minister! The article said all about how he was found dead by the roadside and that he had last been seen boarding a carriage after having attended an important day-long political conference. Investigators stated that his body was found in an 'obscene state,' like someone who had been ravished. The editors would not go into further detail for fear of offending their readers (Isabelle and Jeanne knew full well what these editors weren't revealing). The article added that there was no sign of theft.

Isabelle read one of the crucial sentences aloud:

"'Authorities say that it is *not* known what person or persons were responsible for this most appalling murder.'"

The newspaper also went on to explain how police detectives and investigators could not call in for questioning the man who had driven the carriage in which Monsieur Lafayette had been traveling because he died of pneumonia the following day. Due to Isabelle and Jeanne's return to the carriage that night, the driver had been forced to spend the whole freezing storm on the driver's seat of the carriage, out in the open, with only an umbrella to fend off the rain. His death, therefore, was no great surprise.

When they'd finished the last paragraph, they stood motionless, in shock.

"I had no idea who he was," muttered Isabelle with a blank expression, referring to Monsieur Lafayette.

"Well, I don't care who he was. He had no right assaulting us the way he did. Those aristocrats think they can get away with anything. He got just what was comin' to him." That was Jeanne's firm attitude.

They decided that to avoid a lot of unpleasantness and scandal, they would tell no one what happened. Besides, their intent hadn't been to kill the old rake. The whole terrible affair would be their secret, so help them God. And nobody would know.

The Forbidden

The building of the almshouse had taken all of three years and many problems had sprung up during the construction, but in the end it was a success. And no one was more pleased than Mayor Argot. Likewise, no one could have been more displeased than Father Villot.

Confronting Monsieur Argot one day on the street, the priest said:

"So you think you've won? Christ said that we will always have the poor."

"Does that mean we should neglect them altogether?" retorted Mayor Argot.

"No, of course not. But we must accept their plight as the order of things. There are certain things that we as human beings are powerless to change. And we must accept that fact, instead of deceiving ourselves by believing we can become Gods ourselves and make the world a perfect place. As you obviously may have forgotten, there is such a thing as evil. And it's rampant in our world whether we like it or not."

"My, those are cynical words for a supposed man of God. Listen here, you naysayer: I think we can make a change--a substantial change. The divine nature spoken of in the Scripture can defeat the bad sides of human nature. Surely you, a priest, would not dispute that. And you, sir, have obviously forgotten that there is such a things as good. And it's rampant in the world whether *you* like it or not. 'Do not be overcome by evil, but overcome evil with good' (Romans 12:21). That's Bible authority for you."

Feeling humiliated and put in his place, the priest clenched his fists. He lost control over his emotions in a thoughtless and idiotic outburst:

"Your almshouse is a triumph of public vulgarity! An excuse for idleness! That money could have been put to good use, like the church repairs which I suggested. Now Romilly will be known as the filth-infested, disease-swarming cesspool of the poor! ... Look! They're flooding in from all over. Word of your cursed almshouse has reached the ears of every damned wretch north of the Seine."

"Good," Mayor Argot said with a smile. "I hope we help many lives." As he said this, his heart became troubled by a main concern: with the coming of winter, which was just around the corner, would they have

The Forbidden

enough food for everybody coming in through their doors?
"You can't feed the whole world," the priest spat, walking away. "You'll soon realize that. You may have a good heart and good intentions, but what you lack is a realistic outlook and practicality!"

A horrible drought and famine took an iron-clad hold on the land. The clouds refused to rain and the land, too, refused to produce. The wheat harvest was the poorest, which meant that bread would be in scarce supply and expensive to buy in the towns of the region. Even those with up to fifty acres of land found that their former prosperity had run dry and that they were in need of outside help to make ends meet. Everyone, at one time or another, was forced to find some good, old-fashioned charity at the almshouse. Even the proudest of fools humbled themselves for a loaf of bread. The priest himself was made to eat his words by having to go to the almshouse or face the bleak consequences--near-starvation.

Monsieur Argot saw the father receiving his meal, and said to him:
"I think that now, finally, you understand."

However, in a relatively short time, the almshouse, too, ran out of resources. There were just too many people touched by the tribulation of failed crops. Some people became so desperate, they ate rats after the livestock they had no choice but to slaughter and eat. Many left the village, and even their property, to find better luck in the towns and cities.

Perhaps most shocking of all, Jeanne became a whore, selling her body to survive. Isabelle refused to join her. Not only because she was a Christian, but also because she didn't want to become a hypocrite in Leon's eyes and in her own eyes. It was prostitution that destroyed her love for him and she wasn't about to make friends with it.

"It's immoral. I don't feel right about it," confessed Isabelle. "I don't want you to be a cheap little whore."

"I won't be," explained Jeanne. "I won't be doing it for pleasure. It's all in the name of survival. I need money to take care of my family and myself. You know that."

"But won't they wonder where the money's coming from?"

"Dear Isabelle," paused Jeanne, with a look of nonchalance, "there isn't a family in all of Normandy more indifferent about morals than mine. My father's wanted to have a go at me all his life. Probably did when I was

The Forbidden

little, for all I know. As for my mother, she lost her virginity before she started growing hair between her legs, she told me. She never recovered emotionally and her life's been a living hell ever since."

"Wow, I never knew all these things about your family."

"Well now you know. It hasn't been easy being raised in such an environment of immorality, drunkenness, and even abuse. But it has toughened me up. Made me numb. And in some ways, for that I'm thankful. It'll make my job as a prostitute a lot easier. I'll play dead, emotionally. That's what I'll do. Those repulsive scoundrels will get their fifteen-minute fuck, but that's all. I won't allow myself to feel lust, and I'll sure as hell refuse love. I'll just lie there and let them do their business."

Finally, the village whoremongers of Romilly and the surrounding countryside were given a new choice in a fine, young pretty girl named Jeanne, and in no time at all, she stole a noticeable portion of Madam Pontiatowska's business away from her. It was no surprise. While the madam's wenches were unclean, disheveled, often haggard and in most cases approaching middle-age, Jeanne was clean, fresh, beautiful, and young. She became every wife's worst nightmare and many a husband's most pleasant dream. Isabelle continued to disapprove strongly but she knew she couldn't dominate her friend and make her decisions for her. All she could do was to give her opinion and plead with her. Each time, Jeanne assured Isabelle that the whoring would only be temporary and these persuasions usually managed to ease Isabelle's apprehensions. However, Jeanne seemed to be descending deeper and deeper into the abyss of whoredom. Her number of customers grew steadily and before long, she was no longer in need of money. Had more than enough. She began to feel a bond with her regulars and often shared whole-heartedly in their lasciviousness. Monsieur Catillon was her most frequent customer. Isabelle came quickly to realize that her friend was no longer motivated by necessity, but greed and sexual need. She'd always been aware of Jeanne's coquettish and pleasure-loving side; in fact, ever since they became close, Isabelle worried that her friend would end up on the wrong side of the tracks. Now her worries were confirmed. And if that wasn't bad enough, even Leon showed up one day to try to get a slice of her. Heck, everyone else was doing so!

"Have you no shame?" Jeanne said. "Isabelle was right about you. Do you always have to let your cock do your thinking for you?"

"If she had confessed to having a beau behind my back, I would

The Forbidden

have forgiven her. It was she who left me, not I her."

"The only right thing she could have done!" snapped Jeanne.

Leon came close to her, grabbing both her wrists tightly. He had a stern and suspicious expression on his face. "It was your doing, wasn't it? You did it, didn't you? It's because of you that she left me."

"I don't know what you're talking about!"

He released his grip, taking a step back. "It matters little now anyway."

He realized that Jeanne wouldn't sleep with him. She may have been greedy and promiscuous--a tart of easy virtue--but she valued her friendships, and Isabelle's friendship she valued the most. For Isabelle's sake, she wouldn't have fucked him for any price. Her maliciously narrowed eyes said it best.

Leon got the picture. He turned around and left without saying another word.

Jeanne wasn't interested in upsetting Isabelle, so she wisely didn't bother to tell her about her little confrontation with Leon.

The village was rife with its latest scandal--this time its most outrageous and unbelievable one to date, which was resulting in the upcoming trial of a woman named Michele Beraud accused of practicing unnatural relations with animals. Two German Shepherds were put to death and burned, along with one billy goat. She confessed to the crimes, but swore under police examination that she was put up to it by her so-called depraved husband, Andre, under whose dominance she was allegedly kept prisoner. Furthermore, her lawyers were going for the insanity plea.

When Father Villot heard of the story, he shook his head in disbelief, commenting in casual conversation to one of his more pious confessors:

"I've heard of the homosexuality and incest that goes on in Romilly ... but this? This is something else!" And he recalled an obscure verse in the Old Testament that forbid bestiality.

"It reminds me," said the confessor, "of another shocking incident I recall back in 1872 when I was living on the outskirts of Paris. A few devotees of some magician or sorcerer or other, I believe his name was Levi ... well, anyway, the peasants, superstitious as they are, poor souls,

The Forbidden

attributed the practices of these few harmless dabblers to the unexplainable deaths of their cattle and disease among the locals. There was even a ghastly witch-hunt; of course, all that nonsense was put to an end in a trial that was quite well-known for some time simply as: the Black Magic Trial. Any reasonable man, be he religious or not, can see the good in Science and the wonders it does for Progress. But for the Christian, the supernatural is also a reality. These young men, looking for power and knowledge in the occult, may very well have conjured the Devil, or at least one of his many demons. And directly through these powers, they worked their evil."

The priest didn't reply straightaway, but when he did, it was unjustly condescending:

"I don't believe in the existence of a 'devil'. It's pure myth. In the Bible, I think he's only a metaphor for evil incarnate. I believe in the existence of evil, though. One needs only look around him and be fully satisfied with the evidence. What troubles me and what I'm afraid of is that evil will one day outweigh good. For every good deed, two, three, or four evil ones. God help us so that doesn't happen! It would mean the end of Humanity."

The confessor said:

"As an ordained priest, aren't you obliged to believe in the existence of the Devil? The Devil *does* exist. And so do demons. Now understand, I don't mean the paganized version of the Devil as that red, hairy, goat-horned boogeyman we were taught to fear as children. That's ridiculous. But I disagree with you: Evil is more than a force. It's source is an entity. And that entity is the Devil."

People at the bar and brothel made fun of Monsieur Catillon because he was known to have had an illicit affair with Michele Beraud, the confessed zoophile.

He denied it vehemently, but was not believed.

"'Fess up now, Henri," his cronies teased, "how many chickens did she make you stuff, ha, ha, ha."

"Fuck off!" he would feebly reply, too dim-witted to think of a clever or biting response.

But once his humorous side got the better of him and when one of them, an aging harridan, asked him what it was like to fuck a cunt polluted

The Forbidden

by a dog's sperm, he looked the sneering bitch in the eye and replied, "that I don't know. But this I do know: it feels fantastic blowing off in your daughter's womb. She's a great bit o' cunt. You've taught her well!"

The woman, giving free rein to her easily excitable personality, jumped at him viciously, scratching and punching. Even when they pried her away, she was still able to kick him a few times.

"Liar! My daughter's virtuous!"

"Yeah," replied Monsieur Catillon, wiping a bleeding lip. "About as virtuous as a Parisian trollop! And you!--you'd sell your soul to Satan and then fuck him too, just to get drunk as a fly at a urinal, you worthless drunk cunt. Look at you. It's taken only five years of hard drinking to kill your looks. You were once a good-looking woman ... in your youth."

By the end of the night, they made up, like old friends sick of fighting. Ironically, like the old satyr he was, Catillon persuaded her back to his bed ... where another quarrel exploded.

The procuress Madam Pontiatowska and her brothel-women were looking for Jeanne, otherwise known as the village slut. They spotted her at the marketplace. Just the very sight of her fueled up their aggression and they hurried to confront her. This would be no peaceful confrontation! The madam was less than pleased that Jeanne had taken much of her 'business' away from her. Even lowering the price of her unappealing hussies did relatively little to boost her earnings.

Jeanne was busy picking and buying tomatoes.

The madam, pretending to be shopping also, started talking to Jeanne:

"Funny to see you here, child. Didn't you used to work the land with your family? What are you doing buying food? You're a peasant. Don't you grow it?"

Jeanne forced a false smile:

"No, madame. I guess I've found an easier way."

"I'll say!" the elderly woman gasped. Trying a friendly approach, the madam added:

"Listen, girl. You've had your fun. Now how 'bout you leave the grown up stuff to us grown-ups. Find yourself a husband, start a family, and leave all the whoring to my regulars, the real professionals. You're

The Forbidden

only a novice. A young girl. You don't know what you're getting yourself into. Once a whore always a whore. But there's hope for you, child. Get out of this abominable trade while you still can. You don't know how capricious men can be. One minute they're kissing you all over, swearing eternal love, the next they're knocking your teeth loose with bare knuckles."

Jeanne didn't seem the least scared or intimidated by these warnings. Nor did she fall for the find-yourself-a-husband routine. Coolly, she replied:

"I see jealousy knows no bounds. I'm sorry if your customers prefer fucking me than any of your dirty bunch. It goes to show that they have taste. Obviously, you're doing something wrong and should fix it before your last and most devoted customers bid you an eternal adieu as well."

This infuriated Madame Pontiatowska so much that she blew up in Jeanne's face:

"Stupid wench! You haven't heard the last of me! I'll make you so sorry!"

"Oh, really? I already am. I'm sorry that I've disturbed my pleasant afternoon arguing with an old bag like you!" Jeanne started walking away.

The madam realized she'd accomplished nothing, so she cleverly changed her tune and cried out, "Stop! Oh please stop for a moment!"

Jeanne turned around to face her.

The madam started pleading, "join me and my brood. You'll be taken care of. You'll have everything you need."

Knowing how ill-paid Madame Pontiatowska's prostitutes were, and the squalor they were forced to live in, she very wisely declined, which infuriated the madam some more.

"Ungrateful slut! You haven't heard the last of me!" And she started throwing tomatoes at Jeanne, hitting her square in the face and staining her new dress.

Jeanne ran away, cursing.

The trial of Michele Beraud began after a brief hearing and the story became an even bigger local sensation. Reporters filled the courtroom, all armed and ready with their paper and pencils. If convicted, Madame

The Forbidden

Beraud would be facing a maximum of fifteen years behind bars. The prosecution tried to convince the jury that the defendant was perfectly capable of rational thought and was of sound mind. The trial idled on rather slowly and nothing much of note was determined until Madame Beraud, herself, took the stand. By all accounts, she was a fairly unusual-looking woman of twenty-six years, but looked ten or twelve years older than her age, like many rough, hard-boned rustics. She had a white china-doll face, small, green beady eyes, very delicate, thin lips and a long sharp nose. Her hair was strawberry-blonde, with a crown of ringlets pendulating from the edges of her eyes. Her dress was somewhat out of fashion, but exquisite and quite new-looking. Obviously, she wasn't insane enough to show up in rags, if insane enough to copulate with God's lesser creatures. The cross-examination was boldly direct, explicit and certainly not for the squeamish or easily offended.

"Was your mind disturbed when you committed these sexual offenses allegedly under the express instruction of your husband?" the prosecution asked.

"Yes," Madame Beraud replied. For the first time, she looked worried, and as if fearing that she wouldn't be believed, she added, "I've been twice committed in the past."

Realizing that they might have her cornered, the prosecution dug deeper. "Where were you committed?"

"At the St. Philippe Hospital in ... in ... Le Havre."

"When?"

"In my youth."

"How old were you?"

"I don't recall."

The following day, the prosecution introduced documents of proof that Madame Beraud had never once been treated at the St. Philippe Hospital in Le Havre. And another crushing blow to the defense was that a trained specialist was brought in to determine if Madame Beraud was mentally unbalanced. He evaluated her and in his objective and professional opinion, she was not mad but feigning. Lucky for Michele Beraud and her lawyers that she still had her spouse mind-control story to fall back on--that she was only carrying out her husband's sexual orders under the threat of physical abuse. She raved on and on about how he frequently beat and raped her. The husband denied the charges. And when her body was examined, not a mark was found. She also made some rather sexually

The Forbidden

graphic and detailed allegations that husband Andre Beraud forced her into sodomy, analingus and coprophilia. The prosecution convinced the courtroom that these were lies. By this time, the jury were growing quite displeased with the defendant.

But perhaps the most damaging evidence came from the eyewitnesses themselves--fellow neighbors of Michele Beraud and her husband--who once or twice saw the perverse activity with their very eyes. According to them, Madame Beraud acted out alone, unaided by her husband. This information had been attained by the police on the night of Michele Beraud's arrest, and a doctor verified that traces of animal semen were found in her vagina.

In their closing arguments, the prosecution summed it up best:

"It's clear for the court to see that among other things, Madame Beraud is a pathological liar. Not only has she tried to deceive you, the jury--and very poorly, I might add. She has also tried to put the blame on her husband for a perversion so unspeakable, it dare not speak its name, a perversion she practiced, in secret, and on her own, until she was found out. Though she may not be a lunatic in the strict sense of the word, she must be 'sick' and diseased in the mind to have engaged in such abominable acts. Such a woman is certainly not fit for civilized society. I ask the jury to find the defendant guilty on three counts of sexual bestiality, though who knows how many others there have been over the years! and I ask the court to do the only responsible thing--hand out the strictest penalty possible ... fifteen years behind bars. This woman with her corrupting influence must not be allowed into the society of normal people."

No one, not even Madame Bernaud, was surprised by the quick verdict: a sentence of fifteen years in a women's correctional facility.

When she heard the jury's decision, she stood up, knocking her chair over and growling:

"You know I didn't do it, but you want to believe I did, you stupid perverted pigs! May you rot in Hell for putting an innocent victim in prison!"

Isabelle was more than ever starting to feel the strain that her friendship with Jeanne was having on her life. People knew of their friendship (since

The Forbidden

they were often seen together) and they couldn't figure out why such a good, chaste girl like Isabelle could be so close with her complete opposite in the form of Jeanne. But, as the saying goes: opposites attract. Isabelle ignored the whispers and dirty looks of the women and the wry smiles of the men. She disagreed with the lifestyle that Jeanne had chosen for herself, but that didn't mean that she would be any less fond of her. As long as Jeanne stayed a great and loyal friend to her, as she had been up to that point, Isabelle would try to do the same in return.

Jeanne and her family, the Audrans, invited her to dinner. She accepted, not telling her mother, who she knew would not have approved. They'd had several fights over her close relationship with Jeanne, and telling her about her acceptance of the dinner invitation could only have provoked the most explosive of them all.

"They're a rotten lot, the Audran family," her mother would always say. "Everyone thinks so. Godless, slovenly, immoral ... a real pack o' sinners."

"But didn't Jesus dine with sinners?" Isabelle retorted.

That evening, Isabelle arrived at the Audran residence. They were very glad to see her--one of the few people actually not too embarrassed to associate with them.

Jeanne had two brothers--one an imbecile, and the other lacking as much in social graces. The first one's name was Jules and the other was Joseph, both were in their teens. They were harmless enough--and disgusting enough, too. Jeanne's mother was Henrietta, a chubby woman, and very prone to laughter. Isabelle noticed that Jeanne got not only her physical form from her mother, but also her personality. Her father was Georges, a man of average build. He was strikingly handsome and Isabelle saw that it was from him that Jeanne got her great looks.

They all sat down at the dinner table, while Henrietta prepared the food--rice with pork. Isabelle wasn't surprised when the family didn't say grace at the table, nor when she observed their dinner-table manners as they ate their food like savages.

"Is that all you're eating?" Jeanne giggled, looking at Isabelle's plate. "What's wrong with the food?"

"Yeah, you skeleton," Joseph rudely remarked. "Get some meat on

The Forbidden

them bones."

"Ignore him," said Jeanne, giving her foul-smelling brother a dirty look. "He's just jealous of your nice figure. He needs two chairs just to sit down--one for each butt-cheek."

They laughed.

"You should talk!" he exclaimed, glaring at his sister. "Your stomach's the girth of the oldest oak tree in all the land! No, actually, you're not quite that slim!"

Henrietta held her sides, bubbling with laughter. "Please ..." She smiled. "You children really are cruel. Apologize to each other."

"I'd rather kiss a dead toad." Jeanne glanced away.

"Well I'd rather kiss manure-drenched boots!" Joseph hissed.

"Good, what's stopping you! Go out and do it then!" Jeanne hissed back louder.

Isabelle was starting to feel uncomfortable with all this senseless quarreling going on. But that wasn't the only thing making her uneasy. Georges' eye was on her the whole time. He said nothing. Not even to his wife. But he stared incessantly. Georges was shameless. Isabelle pretended not to notice. That only encouraged his lecherous stare. Isabelle was eighteen by then and could have passed for twenty-one. Her adorable, teenage prettiness had been replaced by a fuller, more mature beauty. She was truly a woman.

"Ill-bred beast!" shouted Jeanne at her other brother, Jules, the imbecile, who was picking his nose and flinging snots at her. "Watch it! You'll get it in my food, you degenerate! ... Swine!"

Not comprehending what she was saying, he only laughed because he saw what a strong reaction his behavior was getting out of her and it amused him. Technically, he wasn't even an imbecile, since an imbecile could have the I.Q. of an eight-year-old. He was an idiot, literally. Couldn't think beyond the scope of a four-year-old.

'Stop it, I said!"

"Jules, behave," said Georges with weak, almost murmuring authority. He was a man who couldn't even control his own household, let alone his robust sexual desires. Henrietta was the man of the house. She was the head of the family. Unfortunately, she didn't mind anything that the two brothers did. She even seemed to find their pranks and dirty habits perversely appealing in some way. Thus, Jeanne was outnumbered and alone.

The Forbidden

Just as Georges was putting a forkful of rice into his mouth, Jules spit right on it (a perfect hit!), and before Georges could react otherwise, he put it in his mouth.

"Ugh!" he sighed. "Dirty trick!"

But that was all he did. He didn't yank the belt off of his trousers and give the idiot a good and proper thrashing like most other fathers would have done. Not even a rebuke. Nothing.

Joseph, inspired by his brother, started burping. Each time, he tried to burp louder and longer. He was a real virtuoso. After about a dozen very impressive burps, Joseph was in the mood for displaying his other talent--unequaled farting skills. After each resounding burp came an even more resounding fart. The one and then the other, over and over again.

Georges must have gotten pretty irritated at last, for he actually spoke out:

"Stop it!"

Joseph chuckled and kept on going, which made his mother howl with uncontrollable laughter.

Even Jeanne and Isabelle were laughing at this point. Jeanne wanted for her family to make a good impression on Isabelle, so that's why she had been treating anything inappropriate with absolute scorn. But now that she realized Isabelle was no longer ill at ease and was having a good time, Jeanne too loosened up.

"Not only are they like the sound of thunder," boasted Joseph, "but they're completely odourless."

He raised a butt-cheek each time he went to fart.

"My, my," started Henrietta, "hasn't your bum-hole just about been blown to bits by now?"

Even Georges chuckled when he heard this.

In the meantime, nobody, least of all Jeanne, noticed Jules come up to her from behind and stab her breast with his fork.

"AAAaaaaWwwww!" She went from giggles to a horrendous shriek of pain.

The blade went half an inch into her flesh.

Jules looked at the blood on the fork, and apparently mistaking it for something tasty, he lapped it off.

For once, Henrietta was not amused. "To your room! The both of you!"

As Georges just sat there and held his head in both hands in a

The Forbidden

gesture of despair, Henrietta removed her daughter's chemise. Blood ran down Jeanne's belly from the wound.

"Stop the bleeding!" Jeanne sobbed.

They got a handkerchief and put it over the wound. It was just above her nipple.

Jeanne was trembling in a fit of hysterics.

Isabelle tried to comfort her friend as best as she could. The bleeding stopped after a while, sponged away with water and then covered by a dry rag.

"Will you be alright?" asked her mother after the mood was more calm.

"I guess I'll have to be, won't I?"

Thus concluded the lively and bizarre dinner. Isabelle didn't know what to think, except that it had been a very 'unusual' experience.

"Would you like me to drive you back home, Isabelle?" asked Jeanne's father, giving her that same suggestive look.

"No!" she quickly exclaimed. "I mean, no thank you. I like the breezy night air. I think I'll walk."

Pretending not to hear her reply, he grinned:

"I wouldn't hear of it. Wait here. I'll tie the horses to the cart. It won't take but a moment."

And he ran for the barn like a man chasing after a thief.

Isabelle had it in mind, then and there, to make a run for it. But she was far too timid and polite to do such a thing, especially since Georges happened to be her best friend's father. However, he did make her feel nervous.

One of the windows from the upper floor of the house opened and she could see the miserable brothers, Joseph and Jules.

"What are you doing down there?" Joseph hollered from above.

"Waiting ..." she paused, not knowing why.

"Waiting for your lover ... to lift up your skirts?" He laughed. "If he's not coming, may I? I know how to stuff a girl real good, honest."

Isabelle ignored him.

"Hey, answer me! You wanna have a tumble in the hay? Huh? I know you do!"

Isabelle was appalled but kept her composure. "Like father, like son," she whispered to herself.

While Isabelle was too busy ignoring them, Jules left momentarily

The Forbidden

and returned to the window with his chamber-pot. Smiling stupidly, the idiot emptied it, aiming for Isabelle. He missed, and Isabelle lept when she heard the putrid contents hit the ground, coming within inches of splashing and smearing her.

"That's what you get for treating us like a snob!" yelled Joseph, slamming the window shut.

Georges appeared with the cart drawn by two horses. "Hop in."

She climbed up beside him. The time was ten o'clock and darker than pitch, except for a few lonely stars and a dim and distant half-moon. Autumn nights were often chilly, and this one was in particular.

Georges could see she was shaking. "I should have brought a wool blanket. I can see you're cold. Would you like me to put my arm around you for warmth?"

Isabelle gave only a vague nod, her nose running and limbs rattling. It was the lesser of two evils, she thought.

"Hmm, you certainly are cold. Cold as ice." And he wrapped his broad muscular arm tightly around her. "There, that better?"

She gave no response.

Georges tried to start up a conversation as the horses galloped along. "You know, you really are a very pretty girl." His breath came even closer.

As Isabelle glanced up at him, she could see his moist and gaping lips closing in on her. She turned her head away right when he was about to kiss her.

This offended him. He grabbed her chin and forcefully tilted her face towards his. "What's wrong? Have I been unkind?"

"If you don't mind, I'd rather walk the rest of the way, if it's all the same to you. My home's nearby. I know the way from here."

"But I do mind," he said in the tone of a lecher used to getting his way. In his younger days he had been quite the lover and well-admired by women. "I didn't offer to take you half-way. I offered to take you all the way. If I put myself to the trouble of taking you in the first place, I might as well deliver you right to your doorstep. It doesn't make sense otherwise."

Isabelle knew there was no persuading him. And who knows what he'd try next? she thought.

"Can you stop? I have to pee."

"Fine," Georges groaned. "But don't take your time. I hope to get

The Forbidden

back home sometime before sunrise!"

Isabelle took off into the bushes. When convinced that she was out of his sights, she took a path through the woods to get home.

As late as ten minutes later, Georges was still there yelling out:

"Hurry up! What are you doing in there, diddling yourself? I have to get up bright 'n' early tomorrow, in case you didn't know!"

"Fire!" echoed a cry in the middle of the night, as many villagers got out of bed, and upon looking out their windows, saw a great ball of flame somewhere in the distance. A few (being regular brothel-hounds) knew exactly what the disturbance was about as soon as they peered outside: the brothel was burning to the ground.

Fleeing their wives, they ran with almost a religious fervor to save the establishment from total destruction. But why all the bother? It wasn't as though many of them went there any more (they were getting their services elsewhere, namely from Jeanne). Nevertheless, it appears they realized that it was the least they could do for a whorehouse that had served them all those years when Jeanne was still in her crib, or not even yet born, for that matter! Perhaps it was a sentimental attachment, a loyalty they felt for all the good times it had given them.

Monsieur Catillon, of all people, still sentimentally drunk from the night before, wept like a mother who'd just lost her son:

"Save our palace of pleasure," he wailed poetically, stupidly.

While everyone was trying to stop the fast-spreading flames, the priest, Father Villot, was being arrested for setting the fire.

"There it is, your blessed bordello!" he yelled as the policemen dragged him away. "Engulfed in a hell of flames as you shall soon be--ye of the damned!"

Nobody noticed him. They were too busy with their feeble attempts to put out the flames. The problem was that they didn't have the proper equipment. And buckets of water filled by a nearby well did very little to extinguish the raging red fury.

Pretty soon, every last bit of the structure was ablaze. They stopped trying. They knew it was too late. The villagers present, most of whom were men, and many of whom had enjoyed the forbidden delights stored for generations within that house's yellow walls, stood in

The Forbidden

amazement. They couldn't believe their eyes. Bowing their heads and perhaps letting out an unmanly tear or two, they said a prayer for Madame Pontiatowska and her whores, all of whom perished in their beds in the merciless flames.

A few wives, staring from their bedroom windows, cheered. One of them even declared, "It's about time this happened!"

Isabelle was leading a cow into the pastures the next morning. Along the path, she had to go relieve herself. Squatting down under a tree behind some shrubs, she lifted her gray skirt over her haunches, revealing hips and thighs that once skinny and shapeless, were now plump and well-formed. Her smooth buttocks were as round as oranges, and just as firm, no longer scrawny.

She pushed and pushed, and it took a few seconds for the reluctant turd to see the light of being. But as with all turds, his birth was inevitable. And what an interesting little creature he was, this shy specimen of darkest brown. This was no peewee, but a monstrously thick and large piece of mother nature's handiwork.

"Aaahhh," sighed Isabelle, as if extracting pleasure from the procedure, when she heard a stifled laugh from somewhere around her. Startled and opening her eyes, she let her dress fall, with the hard turd still lodged half-way up her well-stretched anus.

"Those gotta feel good comin' out!" laughed a voice she easily recognized. It was her old boyfriend, Leon. He was spying on her, which was no surprise.

"Get lost, pervert!"

"I will," he replied, "just as soon as you shit out that big cigar stickin' out so good between those cheeks!"

"You're just as bad as the rest of them! I never liked you! The only reason I went with you was because you saved my life!"

Leon was deeply hurt by her comments because he really did love her. Loved her still. Without another word, he left.

Isabelle didn't see him leave, all she heard were footsteps running away, becoming fainter and fainter. The coast was clear. Lifting up her dress, she finished the job and wiped herself with some freshly-fallen foliage.

The Forbidden

Isabelle smiled, having a quick glance at the massive and impressive product of her bowels before leaving, as if she were proud that her body could produce a sizable turd any big, burly wood-cutter would find a challenge to better. The sun shone intensely on the giant, brown lump; and the following spring, a clan of daisies would grow from that very spot.

Nobody was happier about Father Villot's arrest than Mayor Argot. "That fanatical bigot! Ha, ha, now let's see him meddle in our affairs."

But many of the villagers were also afraid, for they strongly depended on their priest for matters of the soul, like children depend on their parents for matters of the body. "We have no priest! Brilliant! Now we shall all become heathens!"

Some didn't care one way or the other, and others were even relieved. "Nothing but good can come of it ... the church butting out of our lives."

Realizing that he now had an excuse to tear down the old church, Monsieur Argot didn't waste time. "What use is it without a priest anyhow!" he argued.

At nightfall, he and a couple of his cronies came to the place with torches. But they came secretly and furtively, hiding in the shadows, careful not to be seen. They didn't want the blame to fall on them.

Isabelle and her mother happened to be inside the church, praying long and hard for their priest; for his well-being; praying that he would be able to return to them soon. Suddenly, they could smell wood burning. Raising their heads, they could see black smoke coming from the front corner of the church, and little by little, the encroachment of orange-yellow flame. They could hear the voices of men outside.

"Oh my God, mother! What's happening!"

Isabelle's mother didn't answer. She looked startled. "Hurry, we've got to get out of here."

But as they ran for the entrance doors, they saw that they were burning. Isabelle and her mother's escape route was obstructed.

The two women fell to their knees, daughter holding mother, mother holding daughter, crying out at the top of their voices, "help! help us!"

The Forbidden

As the arsonists were about to flee, Monsieur Argot paused. "Wait. I think there's somebody inside." He could vaguely hear the desperate pleas.

"Come on, there's no time to lose!" the others urged him. "We have to flee now, or it'll be too late. Do you want to go to prison!"

"I'm sure there's somebody inside! We must go back!"

In the distance, people were already coming to the scene. When they saw them, the other men took fright and fled, leaving Argot alone.

Monsieur Argot kicked the flaming entrance doors in and rushes inside. There he could see Isabelle and her mother through the smoke and fire embracing each other in panic.

Leaping through the flames, he grabbed Isabelle first and carried her out unharmed. But by the time he came in the second time for her mother, the fire had spread further and the barrier between the victim and himself was wider. Knowing that there wasn't any time to lose, and that it was now or never, he took the dangerous risk of leaping in for her, this time catching his leg on fire. He lifted the woman up in his arms and hurried her out. But by the time they were safely away, Monsieur Argot's entire leg was on fire and he screamed like a man locked in some horrendous medieval torture device.

He tried rolling around on the ground, but the fire spread faster than he could smother it and before anyone could do anything, his whole body was like a bunch of dry twigs in a well-lit fireplace. By the time they put him out, he was charred and dead.

None of the witnesses to the burning knew the whole story, and Monsieur Argot was declared a hero, believed to have been the first one on the scene, who gave his life for the lives of these good, pious women. Everyone called him a saint, even those who held grudges against him, formerly believing him to be an ungodly and spiritually indifferent man. The name of Mayor Argot was not soon forgotten in the village of Romilly. Nor was the truth of the whole incident ever uncovered.

The sun beat down hard, making Monsieur Catillon sweat profusely. In no time, he was down to his undershirt. "Damn heat!"

He was sitting in front of his cottage on a doorstep, enjoying his second bottle of brandy. His malnourished dog sat loyally by his side, even

The Forbidden

though his master didn't give a hill o' beans for him. The dog was filthy, flea-bitten and thin as a flagpole. His ribs stuck out from his sides, tightly pressing against the skin. Just about the only time Monsieur Catillon paid any attention to the animal was either to abuse him or to play cruel jokes on him.

Knowing how thirsty his dog must be, Monsieur Catillon poured almost half of his bottle into the dog's bowl for fun. The animal ran over, wagging his saliva-soaked tongue stupidly and gulped it all up in seconds.

Monsieur Catillon couldn't stop from laughing when he saw the dog stumbling around, falling over and getting up with difficulty.

"Poor lad! Is this your first time getting sloshed?" And he laughed until his stomach felt like it would rip open.

Isabelle's mother saw this from her backyard and made her indignation felt. "Monsieur, you are a fiend! What you are doing is criminal! Are you aware of that fact?"

"Bugger off, woman! I'm not afraid of women's tongues!" he grumbled back in a half-drunk, half-coherent voice.

Jules and Joseph were walking down a dirt road, looking for some trouble to get into, when they spotted a peasant-girl named Lise, who everybody at school called Stink Breath. She was sowing seeds in a field. The winter had just passed and people were getting ready to work the land again, which was slowly starting to soften up after an unusually cold and frosty February.

"Hey, Stink Breath!" yelled Joseph. "How many people have you killed so far with your breath, hee-hee."

"At least I don't have a retard for a brother!"

"Yeah, I know," replied Joseph. "You have a slut for a sister, which is much better," he added sarcastically.

"Take that back!" she roared.

"Yes, alright ... if you let me feel you all over." He laughed.

She took a fistful of seeds and threw it in their faces. "There, you pigs! I hope I stung your eyes!"

Jules sensed the girls' animosity and he retaliated in the only way he could think of--by spitting. Mustering up a big ball of spit between his gums, he let it fly, landing it right on the tip of her nose. Jules was known

The Forbidden

for his accuracy. And it was definitely a direct hit.

Joseph let out an ear-splitting guffaw, pointing at Lise's nose. "It looks like slime hanging out of your nose!"

She wiped it off right-away, burning with fury.

"That's what you get for mistreating an idiot!" Joseph grinned.

Then began one of the most stupid and childish verbal fist-fights in history.

"You're so pathetic," said Lise, "that your enemies are the closest things to being your friends!"

"Well, you're so stupid," replied Joseph, "you can't even wipe your ass without getting shit-stains on your fingers!"

"You're so ugly, even circus freaks make fun of you!"

"You're so worthless, that on the day you were born, your parents were already scheduling your funeral!"

"Oh yeah? You're so disgusting, you vomit at the sight of your own reflection in the mirror!"

"You're so weak that little street-urchins pick fights with you ... and win!"

"Reeking cunt!" he exclaimed.

"Limp-prick!"

"Maggot!"

"Worm!"

They went at it until it started getting dark out and Lise was called back inside by her parents. Otherwise, by all indications, it may have lasted till the rooster crowed the next morning.

As their relationship continued, Jeanne made her infatuation with her best friend felt, but Isabelle didn't feel uneasy about it. That near-kiss back at the beach was still fresh in both their minds. Jeanne dreamt about it often.

They went to the bar together one evening. Jeanne was a frequent goer. It was where a lot of her clients went. Isabelle wasn't really enthusiastic about it, but she was persuaded to go with her. Jeanne was drawn by the sense of comradery, warmth, the drinking, the ribaldry and rollicking good fun the place inspired in every heart. The tavern was a big enough place, stuffed to the ceiling with smoke and smelling strongly of beer, full of the flavor of rowdiness and loud banter. The bar-keeper was

The Forbidden

Suzanne, a good-naturedly vulgar and bawdy woman with one front tooth missing. People called her Pirate Lady because of it and she made a great physical impression of one!

"Hi, girl," Suzanne greeted Jeanne as soon as she sat up at the bar. Isabelle followed her.

"Give us your cheapest liqueur. Me and my girl friend here are gonna lose ourselves tonight, and where it leads us? Well, we shall see."

Suzanne gave a smile. "That's the spirit!"

The band was playing and people had cleared the tables and chairs to make room for dancing. And did they ever! It was like the Moulin de la Galette... or Moulin Rouge!

One of Jeanne's customers came up beside her, chugging his beer. "Who's this princess by your side?"

Usually she treated her men kindly. But this time her jealous annoyance got the better of her, and she said, "hands off. This one's pure and innocent. She doesn't let herself get stuffed, especially by the likes of you." Leon was the only man Isabelle had ever slept with.

"What do you say about the burning of the brothel?" he quickly changed the subject.

With a tactless non-chalance that was all her own, Jeanne replied, "I guess it means I'll have to be fucking more of you old farts from now on, doesn't it?"

"But eight women died in there. Surely you can sympathize."

"Have you lost any tears over those awful tramps? And what about the burning of the church? Our dear mayor lost his life in that one. But I see you care little about that... " Her words were masterfully cold, casual, and cruel. What a femme fatale! thought Isabelle. "At least I won't be pestered anymore by them." Then, turning to Isabelle, she excitedly gasped:

"Let's dance!"

They swung round and round the floor in a frenzy, bumping into people, laughing, absorbed in the rhythms and melodies of the fast and lively music. Husbands and wives, boyfriends and girlfriends--they all stomped their feet, whistled and hollered, warming the room with their body heat and sweat. The wooden floor trembled beneath them threatening to collapse, there were so many people dancing the polka.

When they were finally exhausted and wet under the arm-pits, Jeanne and Isabelle gobbled up a few glasses of really sour-tasting liqueur

The Forbidden

which they made each other drink for laughs because it was so disgusting.

Isabelle wasn't used to drinking and she was already sloshed early on. No matter how mature and womanish she looked on the outside, she was still, in some ways, the fragile young girl she had been at age fourteen, while Jeanne was the tough and rugged, well-built peasant, adaptable to anything.

Isabelle passed out, giggling as she hit the floor.

"That's gonna leave a bump!" somebody shouted when he saw her fall down.

In her tipsy state, Jeanne was having trouble controlling her own movements, and for once she felt weak as a feather, as she tried to pick her friend back up. "Will somebody help me?"

The men, who were all staring like dumbfounded fools, finally got a grain of common sense and helped put Isabelle in a chair, fanning her.

"She bumped her head pretty hard," one of them said. "I hope there's no damage."

A little blood leaked from the wound.

It took another half-hour before Isabelle came around, and when they saw her open her eyes and rub her head, they all cheered:

"She's all right!"

A Jewish woman in about her mid-twenties moved in alone next door to Isabelle. Her family was well-to-do and they allowed her a place of her own. The house was a fine one--spacious, aesthetically decorated and lacking nothing in the way of modern conveniences like indoor plumbing. Isabelle saw her moving in and she was curious. What was her new neighbor like? It took less than a week to find out. Isabelle started talking with her one day when she met her leaving her house and they hit it off marvelously. Jeanne, too, came to like her. She was Sarah Harowitz, a bright and charming young lady with pretty dark features, sensitive like Isabelle and yet strong, like Jeanne.

The three of them enjoyed themselves paddling around on the river, going swimming, going to the bar, taking walks, chatting and doing all the other regular girlish things, including eyeing members of the opposite sex. They didn't resent Sarah for her wealth and privilege. Nor were they envious.

The Forbidden

"You're so lucky, Sarah. I'll bet you could live just about anywhere. Why Romilly of all places?" asked Jeanne.

"Well, my father wants to keep me away from the dangers and decadence of the cities and towns. His parents grew up in Romilly, amongst the peasantry, and he has a real respect for it. It was his idea ... but I didn't mind a bit, so long as it meant I'd be completely independent, on my own."

"Your father must be very liberal!" nodded Jeanne approvingly.

On the nicest Saturday afternoon in weeks, they took a stroll along the riverside, gathering flowers to comically place in each others' hair. Sarah had on an exquisite and stylish, new gossamer dress. Her hat was the latest fashion, with its peacock feathers, frills and ribbons.

"Jeanne!" rang out a voice from across the river some fifteen meters away. It was Paul Delorme, a former and once-wealthy tobacco company owner whose business and finances were destroyed in the Franco-Prussian War of 1870 and he was forced back to working the land. "I say, your new friend looks stunning! What's her name?" He was grinning.

"Sarah. Sarah Harowitz," she replied, glad to be associated with her.

"Is that Jewish?" he asked rather solemnly.

"Yes, it is," Jeanne answered without a thought.

His grin faded. "Well, what is she doing in France. Surely she should join her own kind in Israel. Anyhow, I thought Jews were all business-owners, lawyers and bankers. She doesn't look like either. What is she doing in Romilly?"

"Her grandparents were raised here."

Paul wasn't afraid to make his anti-Semitism felt. He hated Jews because he was jealous of what he perceived as their financial success (a success which he lost), and because they were a minority, a race which was 'different' from his own.

"Tell me, do you have something against our Sarah?" Jeanne was starting to get a little annoyed.

"Aside from the fact that she's a dirty rotten stinkin' Jew, no!"

"Ha, ha, very funny!" Jeanne gasped back. "You know what you are? You're a failure who wants to blame anyone and anything for your situation! You're just looking for a scapegoat! You make me sick!"

Breaking eye contact and pretending not to hear Jeanne's logic, he

The Forbidden

turned his attention to Isabelle:

"And there's Isabelle, the celibate who loves the disreputable company of a shameless prostitute ... and rat-faced Jew!"

"Fuck off!" Isabelle miraculously got the brazen courage to stand up to him. "You aren't worthy even to wipe her shoes!"

Jeanne was shocked. She didn't know that her timid little mouse of a friend had it in her to speak that way.

Paul was outnumbered. And intimidated. "I'm leaving, you bitches!"

"Well it's about time!" yelled Sarah.

"Yeah!" Jeanne hollered. "Go back to your pig sty, farmer-boy!"

And they laughed at his crooked body tortured and broken by toil.

Jules and Joseph, that mischief-making pair of brothers, were up to no good again. They were chasing each other. Joseph was the one being chased, as Jules scurried hot on his trail.

There was a ladder outside standing up against their bedroom window because earlier that day their father had been painting the wall. Joseph ran up the ladder and got in through the window. Jules followed. By the time Jules was up near the window, his brother sprang out of nowhere with a loud, "boo!"

Jules wasn't startled, concentrating on making it to the window. When his hands were close enough to reach the window-sill, he reached for it but Joseph started tickling him, trying to get him to let go of the ladder.

"Heehee-haha-heehee!" laughed the poor idiot, trying to get a good grip to pull himself in throw the open window.

But Joseph kept tickling, and finally, Jules could hold on no longer, losing his hold entirely.

"Jules!" yelled his brother, reaching to grab him as he started falling.

But the tips of Jules' fingers slipped through Joseph's hands and there was a sound like a bag of potatoes being dropped from a roof. Jules was dead on impact with the cobblestones below.

The Forbidden

Jules' funeral was an unusual one. People didn't mourn that he had died, since as a personality he meant nothing to them; instead, they mourned that an unfortunate idiot died in an unfortunate way, that a person who was born cursed by nature should also die ... and die at such an early age. It was almost comical to see all these people express so much emotion for somebody who meant nothing to their lives. But that's what funerals are all about to some people. A chance to become sentimental. A chance to weep and snivel, not necessarily about the deceased, but about broken love affairs, squandered finances, distant and painful memories, etc ... without the fear of looking foolish. A chance to confront one's own inner pain, the pain of living ... not just the pain of loss affiliated with someone's death.

But Henrietta realized that she would miss his playful little idiot ways, though it wasn't enough to yank a tear out of her. Joseph, on the other hand, felt very saddened and extremely depressed, guilty. Not only did he lose a brother, he lost a best friend. And it was all his fault!

In the middle of the service, the rain started falling like crazy. It was as if fate wanted the priest (who was actually from a nearby village) to hurry it up. He did. There was no tombstone, only a cross was hammered into the ground, uninscribed. Jules wasn't even given the simple luxury of a coffin. A shroud was deemed good enough for him.

Monsieur Catillon was walking with his blindly devoted dog when he came across a beggar-woman in rags sitting outside of the bank. Her presence irritated him and he immediately felt like bothering her, especially when he noticed she had three francs in her cup. Three francs! All unearned!

"How 'bout tossin' some of those riches my way. Some of us aren't so fortunate," he snickered. "But, seriously speaking, why not work like the rest если us? What's wrong with ya?"

"Drop dead!" she replied humorlessly.

Monsieur Catillon threw her a sou. "Don't become a careless spender now." He chuckled.

"You can take your bleedin' coin and shove it where the sun don't

The Forbidden

shine!" And she threw it back at him.

"Ingrate!" he exclaimed, red-faced. "If you were a man, I'd ... I'd ... oh you know what!"

"Ha, you couldn't throttle a mouse!" She laughed in his face and he walked away like someone humiliated.

For the rest of the evening, Monsieur Catillon was miserable over the incident with the beggar-woman. He felt his pride bruised. "That little nobody. Who does she think she is. That bitch ain't worth the shit I shit." And he told his wife what happened so many times that she was tempted to say, "well maybe you deserved it!" But she was wise enough to control her emotions and kept quiet.

Bored and eager to find a release for his heaped-up aggression, Monsieur Catillon chose his wife to be the outlet of his negative energy, since she was the only one around.

"So, who was that fellow I saw you talking to today down by the post office?" he lied, knowing that she had been to church. "Are you seeing somebody?"

"I didn't talk to any man there!"

Her husband was happy to see her losing her cool. That gave him an excuse to lose his as well.

"Are you calling me a liar? Tell me, what are you hiding!"

He grabbed her by the wrist and squeezed.

"Aw! Stop hurting me ... let go!"

"Not until you confess, slut! You slept with him, didn't you! Didn't you! You've made me a cuckold!"

"No!" she whimpered truthfully.

"I'm not letting go until you confess!"

Tight in the clutches of unbearable pain, knowing that he wouldn't let go until she did as he told, she screamed, "Yesssss!" and fell to her knees, crying. "You beast!" she spat, wondering how he could have gotten these false ideas about her into his mind.

"On your knees is where you belong, adulterous woman! You better pray your God forgives you!"

"Oh, I'm the adulterous one?" she sighed to herself, thinking he wouldn't hear. Well, he did. And a new fury was born in him.

The Forbidden

"What?"

Bravely, without considering the consequences, she shouted:

"Everyone says so! Not only do I suffer from knowing that you surrender to the embraces of other women, but I'm the laughingstock of the village! 'There's Madame Catillon,' they say, 'the woman who gives her poor husband none between the sheets, so he's forced to find it elsewhere!'"

Instead of becoming more enraged, Monsieur Catillon began to feel guilty about the pointless fight he'd started. His foolish aggression was now worked off.

Walking away in disgust and remorse, Monsieur Catillon tried to avoid his wife, looking feverishly for some money. He desperately wanted to get away from her for awhile. He wanted to join his cronies at the bar.

His wife, still angry about the false accusations and the way she'd been treated, refused to tell him where she kept it hidden.

"Where's the money, you Christ-fucked bitch!"

"I won't let you squander it on booze!"

"Give it here!"

He started getting violent again, shaking her harshly. In her attempt to break free, she elbowed him in the eye. He let go immediately, holding both hands over the eye.

"You've blinded me!" he hissed.

When he removed his hands, she could see a puffed-up black eye closed-shut.

"I can't open my eye! I can't open my eye!" he repeated over and over pitifully.

Now he was even more miserable than he had been after the incident with the beggar-woman. He managed to beg some money out of his forgiving wife and ran off to the local tavern, where he found Delorme.

"I saw Jeanne a few days ago," said Monsieur Delorme. "At the river."

"She's a good fuck, that one. Has love-making down to an art-form," mused Monsieur Catillon, gulping down his second beer.

"She was with her pretty friend, Isabelle, and a Jewish girl ... So there I am, friendly as a pup, when those stupid rude bitches start barking at me. So I showed 'em. Yeah, I showed 'em."

"Haa, haa, whaddya do?" Monsieur Catillon asked, beginning to feel the happy effects of drunkenness coming on.

"I ... I ..." he tried to think of something impressive to say. "I

The Forbidden

showed 'em my horsewhip and you know how the rest of the story goes!"

"Haa, haa! Good stuff. A man must always make his authority felt and the woman's role is to be submissive. Hell, I didn't make this up, it's the law of nature."

"How true!" Monsieur Delorme gasped, adding with equal stupidity: "And the same goes for that scourge of humanity, the Jews!"

They tapped glasses and drank to each other's health.

"How'd you get it?" Monsieur Delorme asked him about the black-eye, pointing to it while they ordered another round of frothy beers.

"One of my horses kicked me with his hind legs," Monsieur Catillon nervously replied. He was an even bigger liar and woman-hater than his friend. He would have rather died than admit that he'd been beaten up by his own frail wife--a short and slight weakling of a woman who weighed no more than fifty kilograms.

Monsieur Delorme wasn't one to forget, or forgive. When Jeanne began to refuse him as a customer, he really lost control.

"It's because of that fucking Jew that she's turned against me!" he muttered to himself.

He had always been in trouble with the law and even in his childhood, the gendarmes had been on his trail more than once. Eccentric, vengeful, alcoholic, bragging--those were the words to describe him.

A hunter since early youth, he knew well how to fire a gun.

Loading his pistol and concealing a knife in its sheath, he stuffed them under his belt, whistling a tune as he left his house and proceeded down the street.

Glad to see a light on in Sarah's house, he first made sure that he wasn't being watched before he went up and knocked on her door.

A sleepy Sarah opened the door, shocked to see who it was.

"May I come in?" said Monsieur Delorme. "I'd like to speak to you. I've come to apologize for that day at the river ... there's no excuse for my prejudicial remarks."

She took the bait and let him enter.

As soon as her back was turned, Monsieur Delorme grabbed his knife. So cautious as not to be heard, he walked up right behind her, and covering her mouth with one hand, he slit her throat with the other. The cut

The Forbidden

was very wide and blood poured down the entire front of her chest. She was instantly dead. Holding her suspended corpse up by the hair, he marveled at the half-decapitated head and the puddle of crimson red gushing out of her. The only thing he regretted was not having a change of clothes for himself.

"Well, at least I didn't have to use the pistol," he sighed, dropping the lifeless mass of flesh.

Frantically, he looked for a back door and found one in the kitchen. He slipped out without a sound, smeared in the blood which branded him 'murderer.'

Sarah's dead and mutilated body was found the next morning by Jeanne, with whom she had plans to go shopping. The astonishment was so great that she fainted on the spot, and by the time police got there, they thought they had two victims on their hands. Isabelle was just as shocked and grieved by the catastrophe. Not only was Sarah dead, but she was murdered. And murdered so heinously!

The first and only person Monsieur Delorme revealed his crime to was Monsieur Catillon. He trusted no one else. The revelation was made at the bar the following evening.

"Well I'll be buggered! You evil rascal, you!" replied Monsieur Catillon after hearing the whole story.

"It was her fault. Jeanne wouldn't be treating me like shit if it hadn't been for that Yiddish bitch!"

Jeanne eyed the two men from across the room. She was already strongly suspecting that Paul Delorme was responsible for the murder, but she said nothing for lack of proof. How could I get him to confess? she asked herself, searching the corridors of her mind for a clever plan.

Finding him beside his crony Monsieur Catillon as usual, she came up to Monsieur Delorme, pretending to make light of Sarah's death and pretending to feel great respect for the man who could pull off such a perfectly flawless crime.

Paul was confused by her behavior but at the same time very happy that she was apparently now on good terms with him again.

"But I thought you were close with her."

"No, she was Isabelle's friend," Jeanne lied, keeping to her

The Forbidden

cunning scheme. "I only pretended because Isabelle liked her. No, she wasn't very pleasant, I won't miss her."

Paul couldn't believe his ears. "Yes, exactly," he agreed, giving her a drink out of his tall glass.

She came on quite strong and offered to sleep with him, free of charge. How could he refuse? It would be just like before, except no money involved.

They went back to his house. She lay down on the filthy bedsheets in a dingy room with a lamp-light dimly lit. And when the kissing and fondling began, so did the interrogation. "Was it you who killed her?"

Lost in his lust, and feeling completely at ease since they were alone, he confessed, "actually, it was."

Jeanne faked being impressed:

"Hmm, hearing you say that excites me so much." But instead, she was enraged. The rage she felt towards him was so great that it took all of her self-control to prevent her from leaping at him like a wild cat and clawing his eyes out. "I'm so intrigued. Show me what you used."

Trying to thrust his cock into her, he replied, "oh, it was just some knife."

"I want to see it."

But all that the unassuming Monsieur Delorme wanted was sexual intercourse, and he stopped paying attention to her request. "Sweetheart, I'll need you to spread those thighs a little more if you want me to fuck ya."

Pulling her skirt down over her crotch, Jeanne repeated herself:

"I want to see the knife. Just one peek. Then we'll do it for as long as you like."

Irritated, he got up and she walked into the kitchen with him.

"Here it is! But I don't see how anyone could prove it was the murder weapon anyway." He pulled a butcher knife out of one of the drawers. "Satisfied?"

"Yes."

Then she feigned a headache and ran off without giving him what he had so craved. He couldn't believe it, standing there gawking.

The next morning, Jeanne summoned the police, explaining to them how she knew where the murder weapon was and giving them the identity of

The Forbidden

the murderer.

They went to Monsieur Delorme's house and Jeanne led them to where the knife was. Medical examiners conceded that the size and brand of the knife was perfectly consistent with Sarah Harowitz's fatal wound. In their search for evidence, investigators also uncovered the bloodied clothing worn during the crime. Paul Delorme suffered not only the humiliation of being arrested, but also the greater humiliation of being dubbed the key murder suspect on the front page of all the newspapers.

The trial was even shorter than the sensational earlier trial of Madame Beraud had been.

Monsieur Delorme was found guilty of first-degree murder and was executed outside of Goudacet Prison, Romilly's jail, only three weeks later.

Jeanne's master-plan worked out masterfully, to her credit.

"Sarah would have been grateful to you," said Isabelle, squeezing Jeanne's hand. "We will never have her back ... but at least justice was done."

With the public execution and death of his only true friend, Monsieur Catillon got into the habit of beating his wife more and more. Now friendless, he had a lot more time on his hands. His wife was used to the abuse and she submitted without flinching. If she had to suffer, she wouldn't give him the satisfaction of showing him the emotional effects of his mistreatment.

Monsieur Catillon also acquired some unspeakable habits which, particularly for a man in his mid-forties, were disgusting and disgraceful.

Once, seeing a little girl coming home alone from Sunday school (taught by Isabelle's mother), Monsieur Catillon walked up to her and said, "would you like to lick my lollipop?"

The girl, no older than eight, became all excited about an adult offering her what she thought would be a tasty treat. Frantically, she nodded her tiny head, wild-eyed.

"Alright, here it is," smiled the Monsieur, pulling his dirty trousers down to his knees and fumbling out a penis that stood half-erect, like a giant earthworm.

"That's not a lollipop!" she gasped in disappointment.

The Forbidden

"I know," he replied, "I lied. It's a cobra. Are you afraid? Touch him. He doesn't bite. I promise. See? No fangs. He does spit though, but it ain't venom." He laughed.

Suddenly, he could hear the child's mother in the distance running and screaming, shaking her fists at him. Before he even had his pants buckled back up, she was pounding his head with her knuckles and pounding his ass with the tips of her shoes. Everyone who saw him laughed at this fool holding up his undone pants with both hands while being chased by what looked like a raving madwoman.

"There he goes, Monsieur Catillon, our most dignified, most reputable citizen!" they mocked in jest, flexing their jaws in laughter.

It didn't take long before Paul Catillon was back behind bars.

Famine had killed a quarter of the village population, and people were still recovering from it when in came the plague of 1899. This time, the killer was cholera, and it came from out of nowhere. A few inhabitants of Romilly swore it spread from one of the towns, where an epidemic had broken out. In their attempt to escape it, some townsfolk migrated to the local villages, one of which, of course, was Romilly. Unbeknownst to them, some of them were already afflicted with the terrible illness and therefore spread it to the villagers.

Hysteria struck the heart of every peasant and townsperson. People panicked in the streets, festering with red ugly sores counting them among the doomed--among those struck by the plague. Whole communities and parts of the countryside were utterly decimated.

"God is bringing the wrath of judgment and pouring it on our heads!" some people believed.

"No, it's the Devil that's to blame!" others insisted.

The number of casualties in Romilly steadily rose every week until there wasn't one family that had not been affected, whether by the death of a family member, friend or relation.

News quickly spread into the big cities and the government took all precautions necessary to keep the epidemic out of urban centers. Doctors and physicians were sent off into the towns and villages to do all they could--some even died while doing it.

As strange as it may seem, out of this turmoil was born the worst

The Forbidden

kinds of violence and perversion. Afflicted victims took out revenge on neighboring enemies by giving them the virus; people who knew they were doomed gave up their final days on earth to bouts of promiscuity and drunkenness, in order to forget the inevitable and perhaps escape it, if only for a little while before the dreaded and unwelcome arrival of Death. Fear and paranoia often ended in brutality. It was an awful time all around.

Marie was one of the unfortunate ones. After whispering her deathbed confession in an ever-weakening voice, she turned to her daughter, Isabelle, and meaningfully said, "keep the Faith!"

Mouth agape and eyes rolled heavenward as if espying a host of heavenly seraphs, she died without a groan. Cholera's latest victim ... with more on the way.

With the tragic death of her mother, Isabelle saw no point in stayed in Romilly. There was nothing in the sordid little village for her, except, of course, Jeanne. She had never really liked it. And with her education complete, she thought it was about time that she did something exciting, something adventurous with her life.

"Jeanne, we've got to leave this dirty plague-ridden hell!" she urged her friend.

"Sure," agreed Jeanne. "Many of my customers are probably dead now anyway. I wouldn't be able to survive here much longer."

"Nor I. My mother's house has to be sold. That'll bring us some money. With it, we can go to Paris and live the exciting bohemian life! I can see it now--romance! elegant evenings! No one will know we were peasant-girls. We'll dress up like real ladies and pretend we're--"

"Cocottes?" joked Jeanne.

They laughed.

"Can you imagine me in fancy embroidery, in a tight fashionable gown, behaving refined and well-mannered and educated? What could I possibly say to those stuffy upper-class types?" Jeanne smiled.

Isabelle replied jokingly:

"You can tell the ugly ones that their wealth makes up for lack of beauty."

The Forbidden

Part 2

After selling Isabelle's house for the first reasonable price, they boarded the next train to Paris. No wrong could come to them. And they were on their own, with the uninhibited splendors of Paris awaiting them!

The two girls found themselves an apartment and settled in rather quickly. They would find no trouble adapting to the fast life--a lifestyle all too non-existent in the country provinces. This would be a chance to let their hair down and loosen their corsets. A chance to meet charming, good-looking men who knew very well how to please their women.

Weeks went by and they still weren't worried about their financial situation, nor was there cause for them to be, although they were spending freely.

One early afternoon, Isabelle was strolling the street in her finest new clothes, twirling her bright, colorful parasol in the air over her shoulder. Cafes abounded from every direction--a dozen on every boulevard. As she lingered in a daydream, she didn't pay much attention to where she was walking and tripped over a crack in the walkway, dropping her book and falling headfirst into the arms of a dirty, rough-looking man. He wasn't handsome. Nor was he young. He helped her back up to her feet as she tried hard to regain her composure.

Isabelle was about to thank him, when she noticed how dirty his filthy hands made her clothes. This infuriated her greatly. But rather than seem unthankful and ungrateful, she said nothing, simply nodded with a half-smile, and went on. Obviously, the man was a worker in some factory. Probably on his lunch break.

"Wait!" he ran up to her. "You forgot something!"

And he brought her the book she'd dropped. It was Jeanne's copy of Pierre Louys' *Aphrodite*.

"Thanks," she curtly sighed, turning away hastily and walking quickly as if fearing he would start following her.

The Forbidden

He did.

Grabbing her by the elbow, he swung her around. "Please! ... I don't even know your name."

"And why do you need to?" Isabelle asked rudely. She was truly becoming more and more like Jeanne every day.

"Because I would like you to lunch with me. I know where there's a great place. And the menu's cheap."

With a disinterested frown, Isabelle said:

"Sorry, but I don't see how that's possible just now ... good day!"

Rather desperately, he cried, "I saved you from planting your gorgeous little face on the cold hard sidewalk. Surely I deserve some small hint of thanks?"

"You ruined my dress! Thank you very much!"

"Would you rather I'd let you collapse and injure yourself? Huh?"

"Don't be foolish!"

People were starting to take notice of what they mistook to being just another lovers' quarrel. Paris was filled with them, especially in the summer-time. And the pedestrians mumbled amongst themselves, eyeing them.

Isabelle noticed this. It made her uncomfortable. She started almost jogging away. What had started out being such a pleasant day had turned into such a wretched one! And why? Only because she had lost her balance and tripped! Stupid clumsiness!

When she looked over her shoulder, there he was again.

"Please, if you'll just have lunch with me, you'll see--"

"It's out of the question!" Isabelle yelled almost on the verge of tears. "Why can't you leave me be! Get lost!"

The man grinned. "You're just playing hard to get, aren't you?"

To her tremendous relief, a policeman came up to Isabelle and asked, "ma'am, is this man harassing you?"

"Yes! Yes! I fear for my life!"

The dirty man retorted:

"The same life I saved from--"

"Alright," said the officer, dragging the man by the arm. "Isn't it time you head back to work?"

"Kindness rewarded by cruelty!" exclaimed the dirty, eccentric man, grimacing at Isabelle, as the officer took him away.

When Isabelle got home, Jeanne was at her mirror, trying on some

The Forbidden

new cosmetics recently come into fashion.

Isabelle slammed the door. "In some ways, Paris isn't what it's cracked up to be!"

Jeanne looked at her, confused and amused. "Whatever's the matter? Did some wealthy young man refuse to surrender to your seductions?"

The next half a dozen or so years passed quickly in gay ole Paree in the carefree and self-indulgent lifestyle Jeanne and Isabelle allowed themselves to lead. And Paris was still their darling. They just couldn't part with her. The year was 1906. And with the new century came a new sexual openness and amorality, a new freedom from the shackles of Victorianism. The ultra-prudery and straitlaced dullness of the 1880's were dead and buried. This was a time when the vogue was for women to be extravagant, flirtatious, bold, witty and well-schooled in the art of love. Women who could seduce very easily and just as easily be seduced. And men admired the thick-fleshed, large-breasted female. The Parisian woman was a fashion-slave, tormented by an asphyxiating corset, as she tried to cram her feet into shoes almost half their size. And no true lady was without her hat--a hat weighted with various kinds of flower-decoration and priceless feathers plucked from the senseless slaughter of tropical birds.

From 1905 to the First World War, decadence in Parisian polite society would reach its pitch. However, that didn't necessarily mean that propriety was over and done with--at least not on the surface.

Jeanne was in the habit of defying convention in a variety of ways. Firstly, she cut her hair short and wore what was then considered risque and ahead-of-its-time clothing.

Then there was the smoking incident. She was smoking one of those stylish Moroccan cigarettes on a bench next to a mother holding her infant wrapped in her arms.

"It's disgraceful for a woman to smoke," said the mother as if to herself but clearly meant for Jeanne's ears. She didn't even look at Jeanne when she spoke. "What a bad smell," she coughed, brushing her hand in front of her face as the wind blew Jeanne's smoke in her direction. "And it can't be good for the baby!" she added with some force, finally irritated enough to face Jeanne with a mean grimacing stare.

The Forbidden

"I'm sure you'd agree, madam," started Jeanne in a peeved tone, "what I do is my business."

"Not when it interferes in the lives of other people."

"Please. I'm merely enjoying a cigarette in peace. I'm not bothering anyone. If you don't like it, you're very welcome to walk away."

The mother took offense. "And why should I be the one to leave!"

"Then stay! I don't give a fuck! All I ask is to be left in peace."

The woman rose with her son in her arms. "I've never been treated so rudely in my life!" she said and strutted away.

And, of course, there was the bicycle incident. On the weekend, once when Jeanne was cycling down one of the country lanes along the Seine, she thought she heard somebody near. When she stopped to look over, there was nobody there. She rode on. And for some time there wasn't a sound until a voice not five meters behind her said:

"My, how round your buttocks are. I like how they press against the fabric of your skirt. I'm in a sweat and it ain't the ride that's done it, hee-hee!"

Jeanne was terrified. Where did this dirty old man come from? She'd never seen him in her life. Due to the length of her skirt, she knew she couldn't outrace him, and since he wasn't showing any form of aggressive behavior, Jeanne thought it best merely to ignore him.

The man was sixtyish but well-built and robust, crooked-nosed, with white, uncombed hair covering his shoulders and a hard, unshaven face marked with deep, unsightly lines and wrinkles. His old and worn clothes were as common as any farmer's, and that unforgettable face of his remained fixed in a constant grin.

"So you won't talk will ya?" he said after a pause, still grinning.

Jeanne just continued on as before, not even turning her head.

"My name's Philippe Gagnet. It would sure brighten my day to hear yours."

"Monique Le Brun," Jeanne lied.

"That sounds like a prostitute's name," the old crow ungraciously uttered.

"Why?" Jeanne exclaimed.

"Because I knew a prostitute named Monique. She stole my heart ... but then she broke it. Broke it into a million pieces."

Moved by sudden curiosity, Jeanne asked:

"Why? What happened?"

The Forbidden

"My best-friend lured her away from me. They got married and that was that. I never forgave him. Never."

By this time, he was riding alongside of Jeanne. Stopping her bike with one hand, with the other he pointed off to a shack beyond an acre or two of tall, golden, wind-swayed barley. Jeanne sensed how rough with age the man's hands felt as they gripped her soft, smooth, and tiny wrist.

"That's where the bastard lives!" he exclaimed. "It's been over fifty years and I've finally let go of my anger. I'm on my way to make my peace with him, to re-new the friendship I have so missed all these years."

Jeanne was slightly touched and stayed silent. It wasn't often that she was at a loss for what to say.

"Would you like to come along and see how everything turns out?" he asked her.

She nodded yes.

When they got to the door, he knocked but there was no answer.

"Are you sure he lives here?" asked Jeanne. "The place seems deserted."

He opened the door and guided her inside. There was no furniture. Not even a lamp or fireplace. Immediately, Jeanne saw that it wasn't a dwelling but a hayloft.

The door slammed behind her and when she turned around, she realized all too late that it was all a trick.

"Now you're mine, hee-hee, you little slut ... prepare to bare that beautiful round arse!" The old man slobbered as he spoke.

"No! Let me go!" Jeanne spat. She became as nasty as ever, clawing at him and punching as he tried to get her to fall to the ground.

"I've been through this sort of ordeal before!" she screamed in her frenzy, recalling the attempted rape she and Isabelle had gone through at the hands of Monsieur Lafayette, "and the last fucker who tried what you're doing didn't live to see the light of day!"

"Is that a fact?" he said, mockingly grinning as always. He didn't believe her.

His rough hands started removing Jeanne's black garters, mauling her soft fleshy thighs.

"I love chubby chickies," he moaned, sticking his crooked nose down her tight-corsetted, bubbling bosom.

"Dirty old bastard!" Jeanne exclaimed.

"Yes, I am old, aren't I? Old enough to be your grandpa. But, you

The Forbidden

know, even grandpas get a thrill rocking tiny little heinies on their knee. Don't you remember how nicely it tickled your infantine little cunny at that age? C'mon, think back, ha, ha, ha."

Jeanne's struggling was doing no good and the more she struggled, the more energy she lost. Pretty soon, she was exhausted, her bosomy chest heaving up and down like a tidal wave.

"I'll scream!"

"Go ahead," the man replied. "Nobody's within earshot. But, hey, maybe the sheepdog will hear you and come triumphantly to your rescue, ha, ha, ha."

He managed to yank down her underwear with one hand. He examined it:

"Hmmm, white, frilly, cotton knickers." He chuckled.

Jeanne was humiliated.

Next, the scoundrel reached under to touch her pubes. "Ah, there he is, the fuzzy little creature ... and what's this? ... well I do declare, it's a hole of some sort ... such a wide and yielding slit ... you must be more than an occasional lay; why, you must be the lay of the land!"

When Jeanne heard this, it brought back memories of her whorish life back at Romilly.

"Aaahhh!" she screamed, over and over. Nerves bulged from her bright-red face. Watery eyes, teeth clenching, and limbs tossing epileptically. Her battle to break free repeatedly proved unsuccessful. The old bastard, as she called him, was just too strong, even for a big country lass like herself.

When Jeanne finally got home that evening, Isabelle was concerned. "Where have you been?"

Jeanne was too humiliated to admit what happened to her at the hands of the old scoundrel. She didn't want to admit that she'd fallen for his phony story either.

Isabelle noticed that she appeared troubled and traumatized in some way. "Is everything alright?"

"Yes, of course," Jeanne was quick to respond. "I just fell off my bicycle today and got a few scrapes, that's all."

The suffragette movement in France was well on its way, fueled by similar

The Forbidden

movements in England and overseas. Some men saw these "wild" and "hysterical" women as a threat. How dare they stand up to male authority! Never in human history had it been challenged so strongly, so audaciously.

Jeanne was a fervent suffragette and it was at one of their rallies that she met an attractive American named Natalie Clifford Barney, a woman known for her wit and sapphic liaisons with a certain Liane de Pougy--one of the era's famed demi-mondes. Natalie was also renowned for her elegant and often decadent parties. Like a handful of other avante-garde society women, she openly paraded her female love-affairs before the hypocritical eyes of an outwardly shocked public. Madame Barney was the leading founder of a notorious literary salon which welcomed famous actresses and distinguished courtesans into its circle. She invited Jeanne to come to a soiree that evening.

"Where is it? How will I get there?"

"Here's the address." Natalie handed her a piece of paper, her calling card. "Be there by eight o'clock."

Jeanne nodded. "Wait! Can I bring a friend?"

"Of course."

Jeanne and Isabelle arrived on time, met right away by Natalie, who seemed very pleased to see them both. Most of the guests seemed to be women. And everyone was stunningly attired. The two country-girls from Romilly soon realized what an intellectual, cultivated and talented group of people they were honored to be in the midst of. Natalie introduced them to the Marquise de Morny, Lucie Delarue-Mardrus, Renee Vivien, and Anne de Noailles. Natalie, herself a poet of some caliber, was fond of gathering to her parties a whole spectrum of intellectual and outcast women. Mata Hari came often. And so did the Marquise.

Natalie Clifford Barney wasn't one tied down by narrow conventions and codes of conduct. She did as she pleased and said what she liked. Born in Cincinnati, she brought with her a carefree outlaw American charm people were drawn to. A shapely, feminine figure, golden hair, pastel-colored skin, strange steely eyes, and a biting smile were all part of her attraction, including a refined mind. Lucie Delarue-Mardrus, who resembled her in some ways, was a raven-haired seductress with the pale-est, most hairless skin. She even shaved her cunt bald. Cadaverous

The Forbidden

and ghostly, there was a lack of health and vitality to her being that strangely affected the moods of those around her. Like the Marquise de Morny, she too liked to dress in men's clothing from time to time and went out in public in her drag, never detected as female. However, she was a woman of breeding and exceptional intelligence. Then, there was the blonde Renee Vivien, a fine Lesbian poetess, who based her poems on her violent and tumultuous love-affairs. Her poems were very lovely and intense, if a little prosaic, uninspired. High-strung and sickly thin, filled with a fanatical need for erotic love--these were just a few of her traits. She was also kind-hearted and generous, with a mysterious and unpredictable side. Renee had Jeanne's naughty, puerile personality and was addicted to alcohol. She could down more glasses than a sailor five times her size. Discipline and sobriety were words she didn't understand, choosing to live in a constant state of romantic anarchy of both mind and senses. It was this state that would burn her candle out prematurely and destroy her before she even reached age thirty. Anne de Noailles was a different sort of woman altogether. Short and pudgy, she wasn't good-looking in the face either. Rumanian by birth, she was shy by nature and much preferred to express herself in her writing rather than verbally.

As she took time to look around Natalie's fine home, Jeanne was impressed by a collection of Courbet paintings decorating the walls with frank displays of sapphism.

Natalie saw her adoring the art work. She came up behind her without a sound, startling her with the words:

"Lesbian love spares no one, it affects the duchess *and* the working-girl. Gomorrah is continually extending its borders."

"Gomorrah? Is that the fashionable term for it now?"

"Yes. I call myself a true Gomorrahean woman."

"And what about Sodom, then."

"That applies only to men," Natalie explained.

They began to have a little walk together around the salon, as Natalie pointed out all the various people and told her an enticing mixture of fact and gossip about each.

Jeanne was intrigued by a certain dark-haired, sensual-looking woman in the company of Renee Vivien, who had on a slinky dress and silk stockings.

"Who's that?" she asked.

"Oh, that's Colette. She's married to the infamous publisher Henry

The Forbidden

Gauthier-Villars, a man who practically lives to draw scandal to his name. Everyone calls him Willy. By the way, are you familiar with the Claudine novels?"

"Yes, I love them. I have--"

"Well, anyway," interrupted Natalie, "Colette's the one who really wrote them. And her husband takes all the credit, signing them all under his name."

"But why?"

"He says it's because he wouldn't sell a one under Colette's name. Stupid double-standard, that a woman shouldn't read such books, let alone write them. The plagiarist! Probably all of his novels are plagiarized. Except for his articles, he's probably never written an original line in his life!"

"And the books sell?"

"Of course. All people have to hear is that the book is 'overtly scandalous, unhealthy, perverse' and well-written of course ... and you've got an instant best-seller on your hands. I mean, take my lover Liane for instance. Who would have thought that in '98 her *L'Insaissable* would have sold such a huge number of copies? And then there was her *Idylle saphique*, another notorious novel detailing my sex-life with her. Let's face it, people love the forbidden, and Lesbian love has always held a deep fascination and appeal for the sexual psyche. There's an abundance of racy books dealing with this subject today. See that man across the room there? That's Pierre Louys, a man who dislikes homosexual men but loves Lesbians; he's infamous for his collection of Lesbian poems, *The Songs of Bilitis*. And you wouldn't believe what an uproar Colette's novel *Claudine in School* made when first published, simply because it hinted at romance between the teenage Claudine and her female teacher."

"Please, introduce me to her," said Jeanne, excited by the idea of meeting one of her favorite authors.

Colette and Jeanne hit it off well. It was lust at first sight. Natalie practically had to pry Jeanne away, conscious of Renee Vivien's jealousy.

When Natalie and Jeanne were at a safe distance, Natalie revealed how Colette was taking temporary refuge with the Marquise de Morny, better known as Missy, because of troubles in her marriage with Willy. With the Marquise, Colette was finding the financial and emotional support that she needed. To Willy's credit, however, it was he who'd first introduced her to Natalie, who in turn had introduced her to the rest of the

The Forbidden

sapphic circle.

All this time, Isabelle stood awkwardly alone and apart from everyone else. Natalie noticed this. "Let's go to your friend."

Everyone was seated and a broad discussion was taking place by all those present.

"Renee," asked Anne de Noailles in her meek voice, "however do you keep that figure? I would die for that waist-line."

"That's my little secret. Why should I tell you? We never learn anything about you until we read your poems."

"Well, then, I'll make a note of it to be more open from now on."

Madame Le Roche, an older woman whose sole goal in life seemed to be to make people dislike her, said to Madame Delarue-Mardrus:

"And you too, my Lucie, should try to put a little color on that skin of yours. You remind me of an albino horse I once saw at the races."

Making the discussion a little more serious and interesting, the Marquise began talking about a discussion she'd had with her maid, arguing, "all human beings are bisexual to some extent."

"I disagree," Pierre Louys said, adding with a sneer, "you cannot imagine the horror and distaste I feel at even hearing the word 'pederast' said aloud."

"Do you really dislike male homosexuals so much?" she inquired, disturbed by what she took to be prejudice.

"Let's just say that Sodom is one of the cities I would not care to visit during my next vacation," he retorted, chuckling.

"I suppose you think that a clever remark," said Jean de Lorrain, the only male homosexual in attendance. Then, turning his attention to Colette and her profession as exotic dancer and mime, he uttered:

"My dear, you would blush if I were to tell you how clearly and blatantly your dancing shows off your exhibitionism. What delight you take in being seen by a crowded theater gawking at your nakedness."

Boldly, she replied:

"Well, I've always felt most comfortable naked. Let them gawk, if that's the reason they come. I pack the place up, earn a good living, and that's all that matters to me."

"Yet," concluded Jean, "offstage, your modesty is like a nun's. What a paradox."

Natalie joined in:

The Forbidden

"It's interesting how much more permissible in society female homosexuality is to male homosexuality. Is it because of patriarchy? Is it because men don't view women as a threat? Women like myself, women who love women, are seen as something harmless. The Lesbian is never seen as threatening, but rather, the victim of some strange psychological disorder. Her choice is not regarded as the result of freedom, but of frustration with men, rejection by men, or disillusionment with men. In the public eye, the Lesbian is not so much preferring women as she is fleeing from men. As for the bisexual woman, she is even more readily accepted by men who regard her homosexuality as a charming caprice, a sensual vice from which he too may benefit. But I believe that women who reject men and only pursue women become extra-feminine, not less so, and yet, in so doing, they are treated with contempt for having cut themselves off entirely from men."

"I completely agree with you," uttered Colette with enthusiasm, staring at Pierre Louys. "What no heterosexual will have the capacity to understand is that in Woman, I feel this tender sensation, a soft sensation of safety, this special womanly affection, this caring and motherly touch. Women who sincerely and passionately love other women possess it. It's this characteristic that gives them an indefinable appeal, one you men can seldom understand ... and never appreciate."

Pierre Louys, who as a heterosexual man was fascinated by lesbianism, said: "The reason why most men love lesbians is because it's more arousing to see two women rather than one, and furthermore, for many men there's nothing appealing about looking at another man's genitalia. Are any of you familiar with the playwright Strindberg and his marriage to his bisexual actress wife Siri von Essen? Unlike me, he found her lesbianism a problem and I think he even used it as an excuse to divorce her. I think he was pathologically obsessed and repulsed by her lesbian tendencies with her friends. He was paranoid and troubled in many ways. But I love his play *Miss Julie.* Just as a sidenote, I've realized that men who identify themselves as heterosexual but have bisexual or bi-curious tendencies find no interest in lesbianism. But completely heterosexual men, like myself, find lesbianism appealing. Also, it seems that women who are younger are more inclined towards lesbianism; maybe it's a generational thing because we now live in more liberal times and also maybe because young people are more open to experimenting sexually and have more opportunity to."

The Forbidden

Liane started talking about her lonely youth and how terrible the struggle to hide her true sexual identity had been:

"If at least I had learned to masturbate, the urges could have been subdued. The fires could have been extinguished. But I was raised a respectable, little, bourgeois school-girl in Marseille. What did I know about anything?"

After a while, Renee changed the subject to prostitution and promiscuity. She was opposed to neither.

"The fact of the matter is, the virgin is just as alluring as the whore," reasoned Pierre Louys, "and likewise, the sinner just as intriguing as the saint."

Next, the topic was beauty--every woman's favorite subject.

"I believe that beauty is the greatest curse to befall a woman of noble birth," said Lucie Delarue-Mardrus, to Anne's great delight. "Why? Because I have known many great beauties who committed suicide when their fiftieth year rolled around. In their youths--sparkling gems. But as soon as the hair had grayed, as soon as the skin turned loose, wrinkled and dry, yellow and withered, and as soon as even their jewels and make-up couldn't conceal the effects of aging, they plunged into deep and hollow despair."

Finally, after hours of discussion, the topic turned on an equally cynical note to love.

Anne spoke for the first time since her remark at the outset of the discussion. Perhaps she had been saving her eloquence for last when she said:

"From love we want nothing but love, as I've heard Colette say ... yet we fail to realize that there's much more to a relationship than merely love ... It's better not to philosophize about love, the good or the bad that comes out of it. They're both going to happen anyway. It's fate."

The conversations really lost steam when Pierre Louys started boring everybody with his beliefs of neo-Catholic liberalism. He was a man torn between his conservative religious inclination and liberal pagan impulses.

The evening came to a close after a few drinks and a few peculiar words concerning Sarah Bernhardt's one-time protege, the neurotic Maurice Rollinat, a debauched fin-de-siecle poet infatuated with Poe and Baudelaire.

The Forbidden

A week later, Madam Natalie Barney held another party. Jeanne and Isabelle were given invitations. This time round, there were a few new faces, the most noteworthy of whom were: Thomas von Pfhol, an Austrian count; the playwright Henry Bernstein; and the rebel poet Charles Swinburne, along with his friend, the gloom-and-doom novelist Thomas Hardy, among lesser illuminaries.

Joris-Karl Huysmans stumbled into the salon half-drunk, shocking everyone by reciting some of Paul Verlaine's later poems and reading from his own satanic masterpiece *La Bas* before he was politely but firmly asked to leave.

Jeanne and Isabelle arrived late, showering Natalie with apologies.

"Don't apologize," said Natalie, "it's fashionable to be late. I never arrive at the opera but fifteen minutes after it's begun."

Introductions were made, but when Jeanne came to be introduced to the Austrian Count Pfhol, she froze and nearly fainted. He gazed at her with a wide grin and those burning eyes. His white hair was combed and his nose crooked; his clothing was exquisite; indeed, he was overdressed; a man in his sixties, yet healthy and strong-looking. But that grin--that wicked grin--that unmistakable grin! Yes! It hit Jeanne like a stone!--this was the man who had raped her in the abandoned shack! Jeanne barely recognized him now, he looked like such a neat gentleman.

She drew her hand away at the last moment before he had a chance to shake or kiss it.

Natalie spotted this change in her, a sort of panic attack. "What's wrong, dear?"

Jeanne could barely speak, weak in the knees. Her vision was blurring. She wanted to tell the truth, to get it out, but couldn't.

Isabelle stood beside her, not knowing what to think.

The count began to grin even more and to laugh very nervously.

When Jeanne saw this, it somehow subconsciously gave her the strength to speak:

"It was you, sir, who raped me! You! I'd recognize your ugly face anywhere, you lecherous swine!"

Natalie was shocked. "This is a grave accusation, Jeanne. What are referring to? Are you sure this is not a case of mistaken identity? You seem

The Forbidden

ill and delusional."

"It was he! It *was* him!" she pointed frantically at the count, who stood right in front of her.

Natalie knew that under the circumstances, she had no choice but to believe her, and said:

"Count Pfhol, I don't know the circumstances of this accusation, but I must ask you to leave this house immediately. You are no longer welcome for the time being until I get to the bottom of this."

"But ..." he began, as if to form a defense. "Oh, it's useless!" And he left with subdued embarrassment and rage, only adding, "I assure you this woman is mistaken."

Natalie ushered Jeanne into a private bedroom. Isabelle came as well.

"So you're sure this was the man?" Natalie asked again, wanting to make certain.

"Yes--there's no mistake! He was disguised in common attire, but I'd recognize that face anywhere." Jeanne was quickly coming back to her normal self.

Natalie believed her. "I should've known," she said, "it's always the quiet and unsuspecting ones like him. Everyone thinks highly of this count ... Now, tell me how it all happened. Every detail."

Jeanne began recounting the whole story of how she had been taking an innocent bicycle ride on the outskirts of the city when she noticed she was being followed by the count wearing coarse and common clothing. He looked dirty and disheveled then, nothing like at the party. It sounded outlandish, incredible.

And Isabelle asked:

"Why didn't you ever tell me about this? Why?"

When she heard this last remark, Natalie's mind was decided. She did not really believe her. The seemingly so kind, polite Count Pfhol, one of the wealthiest men in Europe, dressed like a peasant? Bicycling? A man as old as him raping the strong, plump and feisty Jeanne? And she didn't tell anyone, not even her best friend? Too many things just didn't make sense to the keen-minded Natalie.

"Wait here and rest awhile," said Natalie, pulling the traumatized Jeanne under the covers of a bed. "I think it's best that you not strain yourself after what you've just been through ... and Isabelle, you stay and watch over her."

The Forbidden

Isabelle nodded.

"I'll come back in an hour or two to check up on you," said Natalie, leaving the room.

"My God, is it true?" asked Mr. Hardy when Natalie returned to her guests.

"Now listen everyone," said Natalie in a lowered voice and with the utmost seriousness:

"I don't believe any malice was meant by our dear Jeanne ... but it was all in the mind. I was willing to believe her until I heard her story. It doesn't seem credible. And we all know what the count is like. None can find any wrong in him. Now don't get me wrong--I don't doubt that she believes she was raped. However, you saw how disturbed and hysterical she was. The girl may need medical help ... I don't want a word of what happened here tonight to leave the walls of this room, understand? I'll not be responsible for tarnishing the name of such a fine, fine gentleman. It'll be hard enough apologizing to the poor fellow for how disgracefully I turned him out of doors tonight."

Everyone solemnly agreed to keep it secret.

"And what of the poor disturbed young lady?" they inquired.

"She's sleeping it off in one of the rooms."

It took some time, but before the night was over, Natalie got Jeanne to agree that it was in her best interest to keep the whole incident and her "rape story" to herself, while pretending to sympathize with and believe her.

The following day, after finding out where the count lived, Jeanne vengefully wrote him a very strongly worded and somewhat childish note:

I challenge you, you Pig, to a duel.
Never mind that I'm a woman. I'm
man enough to stomp out a weasel like
you on any given moment. Meet me
at the clearing in Bresson Woods tomorrow,
Five o'clock dawn. Tardiness will
mean cowardice. It wouldn't suit

The Forbidden

*me at all well to have to wait any
longer than I have to to blow your
brains out.*

    Jeanne

        The count knew exactly who the note was from. Grinning, the first thing he said was:

"Jeanne? I thought you said your name was Monique! Ha, so you *did* lie to me about your name," adding light-heartedly, "you'll have to pay for that tomorrow."

When his friends tried to get him to change his mind about the duel, he would reply:

"I'll show her. Those stupid suffragettes. They want no double standard? Well, I'll treat 'em the same. By God I will. Who says that a woman can't duel. New Woman indeed. I tell ya, when women discover how harsh Man's world really is, they'll be only too glad to return to their little lives of sewing and knitting. I'll teach that wench a lesson!"

Meanwhile, Isabelle tried desperately to get Jeanne to reconsider. "This is so, so foolish. Jeanne! He'll shoot you!"

Jeanne's casual reply:

"First of all, I'll be the one left standing when all the smoke has cleared. Second of all, I won't rest a wink till my vengeance has been satisfied. And third of all, my dear sweet Isabelle, I do appreciate your concern. Really I do. But it's too late even if I were to change my mind. The note is sent. He'll have read it by now. The stage is set. And the final act will see me triumphant! ... But we mustn't let Natalie or the others know of this. We've managed to keep our secrets in the past. I don't see why we can't now ... The stage is set," she repeated, "and the final act will see me triumphant!" Jeanne's face lit up as she vividly imagined what was to come.

"You *can* change your mind. Simply don't show up. You're being too selfish, not to mention stupid! Have you even once stopped to think how I'd get on without you? You mean so much to me. I ... I ... you know I love you."

Jeanne was very deeply touched, embracing her immediately. "And I love you, too, my dearest Isabelle. More than you'll ever know ...

The Forbidden

and when I send that old ball of pus into an early grave, we'll go out and celebrate!"

Isabelle knew that it was no use. Jeannne wouldn't listen to reason.

Five o'clock. A very calm and silent morning. The perfect atmosphere for suspense. The perfect atmosphere for a duel. Both parties arrived before the appointed hour, as if to prove their mutual eagerness and enthusiasm.

There were two witnesses, and one of them handed out the pistols, with the words:

"The rules are simple. You'll each have only one shot, so use it wisely. Turn your backs facing each other and take ten broad steps. You will then turn and fire. If neither party is hit, this procedure will be repeated. Any questions?"

The count and Jeanne only glanced hatefully and silently at each other before turning around and starting their paces.

The witnesses counted off:

"One, two, three, etc ... "

When the two adversaries turned to face each other, Jeanne shot without hardly even aiming, her anxiety was so great. She'd never used a firearm in her life. Panic gripped the very depths of her soul as she realized that she missed him altogether!

The count stared her down with a wide and devilish grin. He was a perfect shot. Hunting was one of his favorite hobbies. Jeanne knew that she wouldn't live to see the next second go by. Raising his pistol and aiming very carefully, with a clear and easy target before him, the count fired.

Suddenly, the most unforeseeable thing happened! When he shot, the pistol blew up in his face. Somehow, the bullet got jammed in it and the impact of the explosion was so great that it resulted in instant death for the unfortunate count, whose charred face hit the ground hard. A freak accident.

Isabelle ran up to her friend, weeping and rejoicing:

"I thought you were done for! I thought you were dead!"

"No," Jeanne said calmly with a smile, "the gods of Justice intervened just as I knew they would."

"Oh, you proud silly ass!" laughed Isabelle, hugging her all the harder, aware of how lucky Jeanne really was.

The Forbidden

The third day of January, 1907. Natalie got tickets for Jeanne and Isabelle to go with her to see Colette and the Marquise de Morny (otherwise known as Missy) in a mime called *An Egyptian Dream*. It was about a mummy who awakens from eternal sleep (played by Colette) and frees herself from her wrappings. Nearly nude, she mimes the tale of her lovers from times long past.

The Marquise's husband was also in attendance, and like the rest of his family, was less than pleased by his wife's public exhibition of herself on a theater stage. His family hired a gang of thugs who came to the performance with them to cause trouble. Willy, Colette's husband, was also there in the stage-box.

All went smoothly enough until the ending climax of the performance, when Colette and Missy exchanged a long, hot, rapturous kiss onstage. At first, the audience sat in the absolute silence of their astonishment. However, it was then that the thugs began to shout protests, insults and boo's. The audience took the bait and quickly repeated the clamour, joining in and adding their voices ever-increasingly to the noise until it became thunderous.

In a moment of stupid and inopportune bravery, Willy stood from his seat high up in his stage-box and applauded the kiss with passion and zeal. The public's indignation was diverted to him and he was forced to depart in a roar of booing. In the meantime, Missy's husband sneaked out through a side-door.

Jeanne and Isabelle seemed to be the only seated and silent people in the audience. Almost everyone else was on their feet, throwing things on stage, cursing and causing a riot.

When they got home that night, Jeanne and Isabelle talked about it until the sun came up. And then still some more. They couldn't believe that so much fuss was made of what seemed to them a rather harmless incident in the story.

The scandal that erupted from 'the kiss' was phenomenal and exaggerated.
The most popular newspaper of the day recorded it as follows:

The Forbidden

"It is almost impossible to describe to respectable readers the revolting scandal created last Saturday evening at the Theatre de l'Arts by the Marquise de Morny, dressed as a man, and Madame Gabrielle Colette, in her husband's presence. The scene was so repulsive that the audience was forced to intervene and demand the show's end. Monsieur Willy, the husband, was so amused and complacent at the pantomime, that as far as I'm concerned, to him it could just as well have been a reproduction of scenes from the private lives of the three persons involved, and it presented a spectacle of such audacious immodesty that the entire audience rose up against them."

The play was banned from any further performances by the insistence of the Morny family. Willy was fired from his job and Colette was forced to take sanctuary in a ground-floor apartment and to stop seeing Missy publicly. A campaign of denigration, caricatures and gossip was started against them. Cartoonists and humorists had a ball. And it was a satirist's dream.

In an interview, Colette surprisingly found it in her to choose a bold response, rather than an ashamed or apologetic one. When asked about the event that the whole of Paris couldn't stop yapping about, her response was frank and disgusted:

"My impressions? ... I'm incredibly upset by the cowardice of those who saw fit to hurl insults at me. You know I only avoided getting hit in the face with a chair because I was able to shield myself in time? ... Do you call that nice? Is this what society has deteriorated into?"

"Forget about it, Colette," the Marquise de Morny whispered, "forget about it," and then to their interviewer:

"My dear sir, last night we saw gentlemen, elderly distinguished gentlemen even, behaving like street slum scum!"

"So long as they leave us alone ..." Colette said. "You asked me a while ago if I had stage fright from the audience's reaction? No, that's not in my nature. I assure you that such immature and uncalled-for displays don't frighten me in the least. In fact, I don't intend to abandon my profession, even if I'm forced to leave the country to practice it."

Willy found Colette at his earliest opportunity. She was lounging with her feet stretched out on a settee in Oriental fashion. He told Colette that she had been selfish and imprudent by having agreed to take part in the controversial performance in the first place.

She merely replied, "oh, sorry!" and proceeded to change the

The Forbidden

subject.

Willy applied for legal separation two weeks after the scandal broke, pressured into it by his new love-interest, who was threatening suicide to get Willy to marry her. Willy's divorce petition stated that Colette had not been living with him since November, 1906 and that she had publicly and insultingly demonstrated her firm intention not to come back to him.

Colette launched a countersuit two weeks after that, accusing him of adultery.

Jeanne and best friend Isabelle became closer and closer with their new acquaintances. Colette, Missy and Renee asked them to accompany them on a visit to their invalid English friend, Mary Bassington. Though pretty and fun-loving, much of the time she had little to laugh about and could occasionally be quite irritable towards others, prisoner to her two-wheeled contraption and the most uneventful life imaginable.

"She's so lonely, the poor child," said Colette, "so locked away in her father's large mansion. We'll cheer her up pretty good, won't we Jeanne?"

"Yes. I can't wait to meet her."

"She paints."

"Is she good at it?" asked Isabelle.

"Yes ... As a girl she was even pen-friends with the late Guy de Maupassant. Wrote to him ... before he became insane and died. She did a funny drawing of him I must show you."

When they arrived, Mary was overjoyed to see them. They followed her to her bedroom and started chatting frenziedly like teenage girls.

Mary started entertaining her guests with lurid lies about orgies in the servants' hall of her house and other such juicy stories. Renee used the word 'cunt' out loud, and they all laughed.

"I hope my parents heard," giggled Mary.

"How old are they, seventy?"

"At least," joked Mary. Changing the subject, she gave Missy a long, thoughtful gaze. "Why do you always wear men's clothing?"

"Does it really matter what one wears?" Missy retorted

The Forbidden

defensively.

Mary whispered to Isabelle:

"It's rumored she's an androgyne."

"Who, Missy?"

"Yes."

"I don't believe that," chuckled Isabelle, eyeing Missy.

"What? ...What are you little mice muttering about?" Missy curiously inquired.

"Yeah," said Jeanne. "What are you giggling about."

Isabelle, at first hesitant, replied:

"Mary tells me Missy is not only a she, but also a he, if you catch my meaning."

Jeanne: "That's ridiculous! My God! If that isn't idiotic!"

"Touch her 'there', then. Do it!" urged Mary from the seat of her wheelchair.

Jeanne wasn't exactly the shy or timid type. Rushing over to Missy, she reached her hand under her dress, pressing her palm over her crotch.

Mary herself was a tribade, though with little experience, as opposed to the other Sapphos in the room. "Is she wearing knickers?"

"No," replied Jeanne, adding with a sense of relief, "and she most certainly *is* a female!"

Mary, who of course knew it all along, uttered, "what a surprise! ... By the way, Missy, we hope you're not offended, are you? It was all in the name of fun. Right girls?"

They nodded.

"Yes, I know," said Missy, cool and composed. "And I'm sure what your former lovers have said isn't true either, that you have smelly armpits and practice poor genital hygiene. Is it, Mary?"

Mary took the offense very hard. "You know that's an absolute lie, you bitch! No lover of mine said that!"

Angry at being called a bitch, Missy retaliated:

"That's absolutely true ... because you've *never* had any lovers!"

"And how would you know!"

"Because no one would fuck a freak like you." Immediately after saying it, Missy felt remorseful.

They stared at each other in silence. No one dared break the tension. Then a few abrupt giggles burst out of their lips.

The Forbidden

Almost at once, the two women flung themselves at each other--not in fury, but in apology.

"Please forgive my horrible remarks," gasped Missy, fervently embracing Mary. In her emotion, she even lifted her out of her wheelchair seat.

"I apologize too!" replied Mary, wiping a few tears from her eyes. "I've behaved like a real bitch towards you today. Forgive me ..."

A few days later, they paid Mary another visit.

"When was the last time you came!" complained the invalid.

"Tuesday," replied Renee.

"Well it seems like a month."

"We're taking you out for a picnic, you cranky old wasp," explained Missy. "It's time you get some fresh air circulating through those dusty, clogged-up lungs of yours. It'll rejuvenate you. You'll see."

"I can't," she said. "It worries my old folks too much. They wouldn't allow it."

"What do you mean?" said Colette. "You're thirty-one years of age. Do you still need your parents' permission?"

"It feels like it," Mary answered. "I've been pampered and taken care of all my life. In many ways, they still haven't let me grow up. No, I guess I don't need their permission, do I?" She smiled.

For once, Mary stood up to her parents' binding authority, breaking its bars forever. For once, she truly felt liberated. It wasn't only the fresh air of the outdoors she'd be breathing, but also the fresh air of personal independence.

When their carriage arrived, they got in, let down the hood, and soon were off to the countryside.

"Paris has its charms, like all beautiful women," Mary mused. "But nothing beats nature."

"Well then why don't you leave the city?" Renee asked quite logically.

"Are you mad?" spat Mary. "Not on your life!"

After an hour of riding, with Missy at the reins, the path started becoming somewhat bumpy and uneven. The strong smell of shit permeated the air.

The Forbidden

"Ugh," sighed Colette. "Where's that coming from? Isn't it a little late in the season for the fields to be covered with manure?"

"Yes, really!" hissed Mary. "Is this the fresh rustic air you spoke of? No thanks! I prefer the dark, stuffy hallways of my house to this!"

"Don't fuss," said Missy, getting the horses to go faster. "I'm sure we'll be out of this air in a while."

But the smell only got worse. And it seemed so present. So near.

Nothing more was said about it. They found a nice clearing near a sloping ravine, and Missy announced, "this seems like a fitting spot. Let's have the picnic here."

They all jumped out of the carriage ... all except Mary.

"Here, let us help you," they offered.

"But I don't have my wheelchair," she said.

"Doesn't matter. We'll carry you. You're not exactly heavy are you, little thing."

She hardly weighed ninety pounds.

"No!" she shouted frantically.

This made the others concerned. "What's wrong?"

She wouldn't say.

"There, there, quit being a little baby," Jeanne demanded, and she abruptly lifted her out of the carriage single-handedly to Mary's great and sudden dismay.

The others were in shock as they noticed a small brown puddle where Mary had sat. Not only that, but there was a wet brown stain circle on her dress around her buttocks.

Mary burst out in tears of crippling embarrassment. "I'm sorry! I'm sorry! I couldn't hold it! Please don't be disgusted! I! I! I couldn't hold it!"

"You poor creature," said Missy. "Why didn't you ask us to pull over?"

"Because by then it was too late."

There was a pause.

"So that horrid smell was really ..."

"Me," muttered Mary, mortified.

There was a pause before Mary's hysterical tears turned to hysterical laughter. From the depths of humiliation to the heights of hilarity.

Feeling that her laughter gave them permission to laugh as well, they did.

The Forbidden

"Well," said Renee, "there's no use standing around. We've got to get you back into a new change of clothes."

"Yeah ... there goes our picnic," Mary regretfully sighed.

Renee was in a state of misery. For weeks, she had been planning to appear at a costume ball dressed as Lady Jane Gray on her way to the block to be beheaded. Renee was devastated to find out just eight days before the event that she had unknowingly gained ten pounds.

"The greatest possible misfortune has consumed me," she moaned to Natalie, her favorite lover.

She set out to lose the weight in the required time, ingesting nothing but tea and alcohol. Not only would she sacrifice her health through this severe fasting, but she also forced her body to cope with long exhausting walks in the woods.

On the night of the ball, Renee had still only lost half of the weight. Somehow, she managed to cram into the very slim dress, and in a profound degree of discomfort, went to the ball. Natalie and Colette came with her.

Not a moment went by when a man didn't dance with her. The young studs were enthralled by this pretty petite blonde with the face of an angel. Natalie didn't feel threatened by all the attention her girlfriend was getting because she knew Renee had no real romantic interest in men.

In the middle of a dance, Renee collapsed.

"She's fainted!" somebody yelled aloud.

The music stopped.

Everybody tried to help but succeeded only at getting in the way.

Renee's corset and dress had been so tight on her that she hadn't been able to get enough oxygen and therefore had passed out. She was fanned and given cold water.

When Renee was okay again, Natalie muttered:

"I knew something like this would happen. You little silly, what will I ever do with you. You'd die for appearance's sake if you had to!"

It didn't take long for Colette to be back on stage. Her new production, *The*

The Forbidden

Temptress, was more salacious and even more provocative than *An Egyptian Dream* had been.

She was sharing the lead role with a fine actor by the name of Wague--a real skirt-chaser. Nothing embarrassed him, and he was always looking for a good prank to pull off. Among his hobbies was one where he would pretended he was a pervert. To begin with, he'd select his victim, usually a shy and solitary young girl, or some worn-out old maid. Next, he'd take a seat opposite her at a cafe or restaurant and stare directly and unblinkingly at her with those lascivious eyes of his. He would scrutinize her face, its every wrinkle, until she blushed and turned her head away or fled in fear of this stranger who looked like some obsessed sex maniac.

"It's an excellent acting exercise for the face," he would remark. "When they set up a class for me to teach drama at the Conservatoire, I'll make all of my students practice it."

Years later, thanks in no small part to Colette, Wague would get his class and enjoy a good living from it until his death at a ripe old age.

Colette and Wague were having a rehearsal of *The Temptress* with the theater director.

"All right, you two, let's do the scene," ordered the director. "I want to see the sequence where you, Wague, tear off her dress."

Wague was more than glad to oblige, and on Q he attacked a startled Colette who, meanwhile, resembled a weak and gasping animal caught helpless in a trap. The struggle was very dramatic, as the dress tore from top to bottom, and there stood a motionless Colette at the end of it all, half-naked, her bosom barely veiled by a thin, loose strip of fabric.

"Wait! Wait!" hollered the director in displeasure, adding mildly:

"All right, you're doing just fine ... just ... you've got the effect right ... but ... I don't know ... the scene would be even more powerful, it would be more striking, more gripping, more realistic if ... if ... the problem is, it needs more flesh! Yes, that's it! Show us more flesh, my dear!"

Colette couldn't believe her ears. She threw a fit:

"Needs more flesh? I'm naked as Eve as it is!"

"No ... no ..." he murmured to himself, caressing his chin in a deep state of thought. Then, his eyes grew with intensity, as the idea he'd been looking for struck him:

The Forbidden

"I know! I've got it! It's perfect! ... Pull a breast out of that dress!"
"No!"
"What did you say!" he growled.
"I barely survived my last scandal! This one would finish me and my stage career! ... If you're so mad about breasts, perhaps you should grow some and play the part!"
"Cheeky bitch ...You're sacked!"
"And a good thing too!" spat Colette, stomping off-stage and to her dressing-room.

Isabelle was awakened from her sleep at one o'clock in the morning by strange sounds coming from the next room, which was Jeanne's. There came a continuous moan, and a high-pitched shrill. It wasn't like the snot-nosed snoring Jeanne was usually guilty of. Isabelle sneaked over to the door. She turned the handle, but it was locked. Her curiosity was bubbling over. But so was her concern. What could be happening in there? she thought.

Noticing the key-hole, she looked through and got an eyeful of one of the biggest shocks of her life: Jeanne and Colette making love. Fiercely and hungrily, they kissed each others' mouths, breasts, bellies; frigging, sucking, licking, lapping, squirming, sighing, writhing, convulsing. Isabelle's heart beat faster than it ever had in her life. However, after a few moments, she started to feel guilty about what was turning into voyeurism and she returned to her bed, still shaking her head in disbelief. She had always guessed that Jeanne was a Lesbian ... but to see her in the act with her very own eyes? Wow! Isabelle didn't know how to react. Her first definite feeling was jealousy. She saw Colette as an intruder. An intruder on her and Jeanne's relationship. Her preoccupying thought was: would Colette steal her best friend away from her?

When Isabelle awoke the next morning, she found Colette gone and Jeanne in a very good mood.

"Hmm, you look happy," said Isabelle. "One would think you've just awakened from a sizzling night of passion."

"Absolutely," Jeanne casually replied.

"I heard some noise coming from your bedroom last night. What was it?"

The Forbidden

"Oh that. I had cramps. Kept me up half the night moaning."

"Yeah, well, I'm sure Colette helped soothe away those so-called cramps, hmm?" Isabelle said with a sharp tongue and witty boldness she'd learned from Jeanne.

"Huh?"

"I know what happened last night. Saw it with my own eyes."

"Oh, and how's that," asked Jeanne, grinning incredulously.

"That's not important ... Jeanne! You hardly know her! Besides, she's a girl! How could you do those nasty things with another woman! Did she teach you all that?"

"I admire her writing talent, alright? That's all. Mind your own business. What I do is up to me, not you. You're starting to sound like your mother."

"Leave my dead mother out of this!" Isabelle blared.

"I can't stand another moment of this," muttered Jeanne and left without even her gloves or hat. She slammed the door so hard, the walls shook.

When Jeanne wasn't back home by nightfall, Isabelle became worried and went out searching for her. The first obvious place to check was Colette's.

"She's not here," said Colette after her maid answered the door.

"I don't believe you." Isabelle barged right in, budging Colette out of her way.

"Jeanne! Jeanne!"

"Go away!" Jeanne replied.

"Ah, so you *are* here! Do you know how sick with worry you've made me?" exclaimed Isabelle, entering the lavish bedroom Jeanne was occupying. "Even husbands return home to their wives after a quarrel and make it up."

"No they don't," stated Jeanne with authority, "they go to their mistress' apartment to make love and then complain to them about their wives afterwards."

"For Christ's sake, let's just go home."

"I'm sorry, Isabelle. It's too late. I've already persuaded Colette to let me stay with her."

Pretending not to care, Isabelle sighed, "do as you like."

The Forbidden

"It's amazing how many brother and sister combinations have made a name for themselves in the Arts. There's the Bronte sisters, the Rossetti siblings, The Goncourt brothers, and the list goes on," said Henry Bernstein at Natalie Barney's latest literary party. "Or look at Alexandre Dumas and his son of the same name. Inspiration must be in the blood."

"I don't know if that's necessarily true," argued Pierre Louys. "I like to think of myself as a writer with at least some talent, yet my son hasn't creatively proven himself once to me--though, of course, he's still quite young. He's more interested in guns and military stuff."

"As far as I'm concerned," said Lucie Delarue-Mardrus, the greatest erudite of them all, "there's a complete contradiction in the way their inspiration was formed. For example, with the Bronte sisters, everything they wrote was completely made up, imagined, completely non-autobiographical. Everything that happened in their romances had to be guessed at because the sisters, themselves, lived very boring conventional mundane lives, very different from the characters in their novels. However, when you take a look at the Goncourt brothers, for instance, everything they wrote came directly from personal experience. If they were going to write a novel about a prostitute, they would go live in a brothel. Now that was super-realism! That was getting to the core of truth!"

"Yes, I agree, Madame Delarue-Mardrus," said Henry Bernstein. "My plays *La Griffe* and *La Rafale* are good examples, I believe. I cannot ever imagine how *Germinie Lacerteux*, the Goncourt book about an erotomanic and alcoholic prostitute, could have just been made up. It's too detailed with anecdote, strikes too true a note to be a product mainly of the imagination ... A writer should never guess, he should always know. If he is unsure, he should research, or in the very least, he should ask."

"Here you have defined Realism for us, Monsieur Bernstein. But pray, tell us, what is Naturalism?" asked Madame Delarue-Mardrus, as if to test his knowledge on the subject.

"Naturalism is merely a branch of Realism ... a form of realism that focuses on reality, *but* focuses almost exclusively on the dark and sordid side of reality. It's a narrower, more limiting philosophy and art. But Naturalism is dead. It died with Maupassant. It died with Zola. In the same way, Realism died earlier with Flaubert. Though, some would argue that

The Forbidden

Flaubert was more a Romanticist than anything else."

"Well-said," commented Lucie Delarue-Mardrus. "*Gil Blas* is the publication that's best represented that kind of writing. I wonder whether it's contributed to a decadence in French writing, or a renaissance."

"To be perfectly honest, both, I think," replied Monsieur Bernstein. "It's true that *Gil Blas* gives a lot of room to sex, and so on, in its pages. But I'm sure you know that its circulation is enormous. People like to read smut. That's all there is to it. People enjoy being titillated."

"Well," started Madam Delarue-Mardrus, "I, for one, prefer to be stimulated in the mind ... not the genitals."

A few chuckles filled the room. Up till then, the other guests had been silent, intently listening in on Henry Bernstein and Lucie Delarue-Mardrus' little chat.

"By the way," Natalie Barney changed the subject, "has anyone read today's front page? Three vicious whore-killings occurred last night not ten blocks from this very spot. The press has already dubbed the unknown individual responsible for the atrocities as 'The Paris Ripper.'"

"Let's hope they don't sensationalize the issue like they always do," said Madame Delarue-Mardrus. "I could never understand why these murderers are always glorified and made into heroes because they dare do what they dare do. I don't understand the fascination. It's disgusting!"

Colette, Jeanne and all the others were invited to dinner by Mary. Mary's father wasn't feeling well, so only her mother joined them. Isabelle and Jeanne didn't speak a word to each other, even though they were missing each other already. The meal was veal and mashed potatoes.

Mary's mother was a very feeble and withered-looking little thing. No color to her skin. No life in her expression except for austerity. She was the reticent sort, perhaps thinking but seldom speaking.

"So, Madame Bassington," began Natalie, "Mary tells me you like gardening."

The old woman didn't reply, sipping her coffee silently as if lost in her own little world.

"I say, Madame Bassington!" Natalie raised her voice, which made Mary giggle. "I hear you're quite the gardener in the family?"

The older woman looked at her strangely for a moment. "Oh, I'm

The Forbidden

sorry, Miss Barney, I thought I heard you say something."

Mary chuckled. "Mother's been hard of hearing for ten years now."

"What's that you say dear? Ten tears now?"

They all laughed.

"Whooh, I must have said something amusing to get such a response." She smiled, looking around at the surrounding faces.

"More meat, mother?" Mary offered.

"Yes, I do feel the heat," she replied. "Darn hot this time of season! ... oh, you meant would I like some meat? Sorry ... why, yes, I would, thank you."

They chuckled.

"What an adorable little thing she is!" Colette said, referring to Mary's mother and speaking so loud that even she could hear.

"Oh, heavens, I don't s'ppose you mean me," giggled the woman stupidly.

"No, of course not!" Colette joked, "I meant Natalie, actually!"

"Oh," sighed Mary's mother with eyes that suddenly turned sad.

The others chuckled.

"So," said Jeanne, rather impolitely, "how long have you been deaf?"

"What?" she said, enticing further giggles.

"Deaf! How long have you been deaf as a corpse?"

Mary's mother got hysterical, like someone outrageously offended, and sternly replied:

"I *was* never aware that I *was*, young lady!"

"Wow," whispered Jeanne to herself rather cruelly, "so maybe you're deaf *and* dim-witted."

Jeanne got a letter from her family. She opened it and read. They had tracked her down and wanted to pay a visit to their one and only daughter, whom they hadn't seen in years. They even complained that she didn't write to them often enough. Inviting themselves, they said that they'd be over on the following Saturday afternoon.

"Saturday? That's only two days from now!" Jeanne moaned.

Needless to say, she wasn't looking very forward to it. As Isabelle already knew, they weren't exactly the most conventional or appealing

The Forbidden

family in the world! How would her intellectual and aristocratic friends respond to such common peasants?

She told Colette the news.

"That's wonderful," said Colette. "They can stay with us. There are spare rooms." Colette was by now completely divorced from Willy and was collecting a fortune in alimony. Her house was large and lavish.

"Oh God, just the thought of it gives me a headache."

"Why, what's wrong with them? Don't you get along with your own flesh and blood?" asked Colette.

"Oh, I get on with them well enough ... but that doesn't mean I like them."

"Come on, I'm sure it'll be fine. I'd love to meet them."

"No you wouldn't!" snapped Jeanne. "Take my word for it!"

"Well, in any case, we won't force them to spend their hard-earned money on some stupid hotel when there is more than enough room for them here. Right?"

Jeanne gave a weak nod.

"Besides, how long did they want to stay for?"

"The letter says a week or so."

"A week?" said Colette. "That's nothing. They'll be gone before you know it."

Jeanne wasn't at all surprised when her family showed up at her doorstep a day early.

"I wasn't expecting you until tomorrow!"

"We were so eager to come," replied her mother. "And besides, we wanted to surprise you."

"Well that's just magnificant." Jeanne half-smiled.

Her parents, Henrietta and Georges, hadn't changed much, except for a few gray hairs. But Joseph, Jeanne's brother, had grown from a filthy, little country lad into quite a handsome young man. Jeanne spotted the change instantly and would never have recognized him if he hadn't come with their parents. She even conceded that if it wasn't for the fact that he was her brother, she would have felt an attraction to him.

Colette gave them a courteous welcome and bid them into the sitting-room. The maid was cleaning the windows.

The Forbidden

"Look Georges," said Henrietta in wonder. "They even have servants."

"Well I'll be damned," he replied.

"Would you like some champagne?" asked Colette.

"I'll have some beer, if you please," said Georges.

"This is a very impressive home, madame," said Henrietta. "You are very privileged."

"Not really," Colette replied. "There are a good many I'd rather have over this one."

Henrietta was startled by her words. It was by far the nicest residence she'd ever been in.

"Are you married, Madame Colette?" asked Henrietta.

"Divorced."

Discourteously prying into Colette's life, she asked:

"What was the problem?"

"Well, I'm not usually in the habit of discussing my private affairs with perfect strangers, but since you *are* Jeanne's parents, I suppose I don't mind too much. Truth is, he was a horrible lecher. Slept with any slut he could get his grubby, rich hands on, if you'll pardon my language. Anyway, he was old enough to be my father. He could be kind and generous, but that was only in an attempt to buy my love and affection. Fool that he was, he didn't realize that only sex, not love, can be bought. He couldn't tell the difference. Men don't feel love like we women ... I would argue whether or not they even want it."

Georges was too caught up in drinking his beer to even lend an ear. But Henrietta was listening to her hostess and looking a little startled:

"I thank you for being so open with your life. A bad marriage must be a terrible thing. I reckon Georges and I have been among the lucky few, right Georges?"

"What was that, dear?"

"I said, how's your beer?"

"Fine, fine. Good stuff, this," Georges smiled, licking his lips.

Colette: "If you're hungry, I can--"

"No, no, we ate on the train," Henrietta replied. "If you'd please just show us to our room, we're quite tired from our trip."

Colette gave them separate rooms.

"Don't worry," Georges whispered to his wife, "I'll come to you tonight."

The Forbidden

Colette returned downstairs to find Joseph talking with his sister in the parlor. They really seemed to be getting on. Colette spied on them, and as soon as Jeanne left him, Colette took him aside:

"Joseph, would you like to come to my bed tonight?" She was very much taken with this dashing youth.

Joseph was no stranger to the pleasures of women and he nodded vigorously.

"My bedroom's the third on the left, up the stairs," she told him.

Colette, like Jeanne, was bisexual, meaning that men took her fancy as well, especially good-looking, young men like Joseph. They caught her eye and awakened her lust. Still, her deeper love was for women. A little later in the day, Colette confronted Jeanne with a question:

"Your parents don't know about us, do they?"

"Of course not," replied Jeanne. "I mean, they are liberal-minded. But I don't think they would know how to handle it. It'll be far less complicated and much better if we just keep it to ourselves."

"I agree," said Colette.

"And it doesn't bother you they're so crude and common?" asked Jeanne, still feeling embarrassed about her humble background.

"Hell no. I like simple, down-to-earth folks. Though your mother is a bit nosy, isn't she?"

The night came, bringing with it no moon or stars to speak of, only a biting chill that whistled like a ghost outside of the windows.

Everyone staying in Colette's residence had retired to his or her bedroom. Joseph prepared to go to Colette's bedroom, while Georges prepared to go to Henrietta's. Henrietta, meanwhile, decided she was tired of waiting and was changing into some very showy lingerie to slip into Georges' bedroom to surprise him. Jeanne, too, got ready to head over to Colette's bedroom after she didn't come to hers.

Coincidentally, they all left their rooms at nearly just about the same time, each with his or her oil lamp, and since their rooms were all either beside or across from each other, they immediately confronted each other in the dark--all four of them!--Jeanne's whole family, including herself! Colette was the only one left in her room (expecting Joseph's arrival soon).

The Forbidden

At first, they didn't know what to say to each other in this awkward situation and there was an embarrassing silence.

"I was ... I was just going to get a drink. But I'm not thirsty anymore." Henrietta had a foolish expression on her face as she said this, turning back to her bedroom with a frown.

"Yes, yes, I was too," Georges imitated her excuse, "but I'm alright now." He went back to his room.

"And I ... I ... I have to go to the outhouse," muttered Joseph.

"But you have a chamber-pot," said Jeanne, trying to trap him. She was suspecting where he was off to.

"Oh do I?" he said, feigning surprise. "I thought I didn't ... well, I'll go use it then ... Oh, and where were *you* going?"

"Oh, me? Well," Jeanne's head looked up, as if searching the ceiling for a good lie to use, "I was starting to have a headache and thought a little walk would do me good."

"How do you feel now?"

"Much, much better. The ache is gone. Good-night," she said, returning to her own bed.

"Good-night," said her brother, returning to his.

And for the rest of the night, each one of them were so afraid that someone would see them sneaking off "disgracefully" into another person's bedroom that they didn't dare try again. As for Colette, she mistook Joseph's not showing up as a lack of interest on his part.

The following day, Henrietta decided to explore the house, admiring it as she did. She came across her daughter's room. No one was there. Making sure not to be seen, she sneaked inside and started snooping around. In one of the drawers, she discovered a photograph. But not just any photograph-- it was an erotic one! In it, both Colette and Jeanne were dressed as ancient Roman goddesses and Colette was fondling Jeanne's breasts, while Jeanne had her hand over Colette's barely-veiled and rather hairy pubis.

Henrietta wasn't shocked or outraged, but she was furious. She showed it to her husband, who laughed. Normally she shared his sense of humor, but not this time.

"Oh! And what's so amusing about it, you old crow!"

"Even an old crow can have a laugh once in awhile, can't he?" he

The Forbidden

replied like a true freethinker. "Look, I'm sure nothing was meant by it. They were probably just imitating some Renaissance painting or something."

"Yes? ... And since when do *you* know about Renaissance art!"

"I think you're over-exaggerating. I'm sure it was just modeling, a pose. Do you honestly suspect it to be something more?" Georges asked.

"Is this why you live together?" Henrietta flashed the photograph in Jeanne's face as soon as she returned with Colette from a cinematograph show. "Is this what they like in high society?"

"Where did you get that!"

"Never mind that," her mother hissed back guiltily.

Jeanne gave her an evil stare:

"I'd be much obliged to you if in the future you wouldn't go through my things!"

"I ... I ...Oh, that's beside the point! Explain this ... this ..."

"If you must know," began Jeanne, "the photograph is harmless. If you knew anything about art, you would know that classical settings and characters like the ones in the photograph are considered perfectly innocent. There's nothing obscene about it."

"But ... but ... you have your hand on her ... on her ..." She couldn't finish her sentence.

"Alright! Alright! If you must know, Colette and I are lovers! There! Are you satisfied?" yelled Jeanne.

Colette covered her face with one hand, shaking her head.

Joseph was confused. If what she says is true, he thought to himself, why would Colette have asked me to her bed? He didn't realize there was such a thing as bisexuality.

"No, I'm not satisfied!" Henrietta roared.

"What's more, young lady, we're taking you back to Romilly," added her father.

"Over my dead body!" Jeanne exclaimed. "Colette loves me! And I love her! ... besides, you didn't seem to object when I sold my body back in Romilly those years ago! Is this so much worse?"

"Yes! You were sleeping with men, not women ... and were paid for it. You were supporting yourself ... and us. How do you support

The Forbidden

yourself now?"

"Colette has money," Jeanne replied. "We do very well. We're in love, don't you understand?"

"Jeanne," said her mother more calmly, more rationally. "Please, listen to me ... it's only a passing whim. A temporary thing, this kind of love. You'll soon be over it ... especially as soon as you fall for some tall, dark, handsome soldier, or clerk, or--"

"Sorry mother, I'm not the sort to have whims. What I feel is stronger than any whim!"

In a theatrical fit of frustration, Henrietta made a brazen confession of her own:

"Do you think I don't know what you're going through? I, too, loved another girl! Yes, me! Madly and hopelessly in love! We made love five times a day! Couldn't stand to be apart! ... However, as soon as I met your father, I realized what healthy true love really is! Not till then did I know."

"No!" cried Jeanne.

That night, Jeanne realized that what her mother said was right. She didn't love Colette, she needed Colette. It wasn't love, but necessity and companionship and lust that tied her down to her. Besides, she knew that Colette was still having liaisons with Missy and perhaps even Renee.

For the rest of her parents' stay, she avoided them and they her. They were too pleased with their accommodations to leave the next morning like any other outraged parents would. A week and a half passed before Jeanne heard their carriage depart. No farewell. No wave good-bye.

Jeanne started missing Isabelle terribly. She very much regretted their stupid argument which resulted in the break-up of their friendship--a friendship that was once so unbreakable. Colette sensed the change in her and wrongly attributed it to the guilt she thought Jeanne was feeling over her parents' rejection of her and her 'forbidden love.' Withdrawing into herself was just one of the many ways Jeanne tried to cope with her feelings. No matter how hard she tried, Colette could not get to the bottom of what was troubling her lover.

Despair reached a peak in Jeanne when one day, while strolling along the Seine, she took a plunge, trying to drown herself. Some

The Forbidden

fishermen on shore saw her and immediately went to her rescue.

"Let me go!" she hollered, trying to pry her rescuers off of her as they came by in a boat and attempted to hoist her up and aboard. "Mind your own business!"

They were shocked and bewildered by her response. "Is this the thanks we get?"

She also tried to overdose on drugs, but she couldn't stop from vomiting and that saved her life.

"My God!" she would exclaim, "It must be easier to walk through the eye of a needle than to kill one's self!"

At the same time, Isabelle was missing Jeanne just as badly. Thoughts of Jeanne haunted and tormented her mind. She would go for days without eating. And although she wasn't the type of person brave enough to attempt suicide, suicidal daydreams did distract her quite often. Her wonderful former life with Jeanne came to her memory over and over, cheering her up, always followed by lonely thoughts of what life was like now without her.

Isabelle decided to make peace with Jeanne and apologize, never mind who was at fault. She left her apartment, walking the whole way to Colette's. All along the way, she thought about what she'd say to Jeanne. It was frustrating, but finally, she found the right words. When Colette's house was in sight, Isabelle's heart started pumping anxiously and her pace slowed down. Full of doubt and with little courage, she managed to make it to the front door. But when she was about to knock, she chickened out and ran the other direction, sprinting as fast as she could like an escaped convict until she was completely out of breath. Turning around, she saw the front door of the house was now only a small speck in her vision, off in the distance. Half of her felt tremendous and liberating relief, but the other half felt the exact opposite. By the time she got home, she was as miserable as before.

Paris was still filled with news of the notorious whore-killer, dubbed as the French version of Jack the Ripper who before him had terrorized the East

The Forbidden

End of London with his own series of similar killings. People, especially women, and most especially prostitutes, were in a state of alarm, as he killed a new girl almost every week, and always in a completely different part of the city, so it was hard to predict where he'd strike next. The police night patrol was increased in number, as the safety of the urban populace and the search for this depraved individual became an ever-increasing concern for the law. The only clue the police had to go on with this seemingly clever and unpredictable serial killer was that he always struck at night, according to the autopsy examinations. No one had ever actually seem him. His method was this: he would solicit a prostitute, give her money to get them a room at some cheap seedy hotel while he waited outside unseen, and when they were both together in the room, he'd use her helpless, defenseless body to perpetrate some of the most horrible, inhuman and perverted acts possible. Thus, he was never seen by anyone but his victim, and his victim never survived to tell the tale--pathologically careful attention was paid to securing a quick murder, usually in the form of a vicious overkill.

It was a Friday evening and the whore-killer hadn't killed in over eight days. 'A killing is due' was the general warning on all Parisian boulevards and streets. The trade of prostitution saw a colossal decrease in business since the first few slayings had occurred, and pimps began to complain. Jeanne, fearless and foolish as she was, couldn't beat the temptation of visiting her favorite jewelery boutique as she so often liked to do. She didn't even notice that the streets were far more empty than usual and that the policeman seemed to outnumber the average citizen.

After leaving the boutique with a beautiful necklace she'd bought just at closing time, Jeanne continued happily on her way down one of the less fashionable side-streets, trying to get a cab. None seemed to be available, so she walked on.

Suddenly, sharp footsteps could be heard some ten or fifteen paces behind her. Jeanne quickened her pace. The footsteps behind her also quickened to the same pace. And as her pace increased, so did the pace of those other footsteps. But she didn't dare look over her shoulder. Before long, her fear was on the verge of panic. She started jogging and when her stalker did the same, she ran as fast as she could. But it wasn't fast enough, as she could feel the callous and icy flesh of a hand grab her shoulder, tighten around her throat and another hand firmly cover her mouth.

"Not a sound!" His putrid breath kept whispering in her ear. "Not

The Forbidden

one sound!"

Nobody came to Jeanne's aid, which led her to believe that no one saw what was happening, and her oppressor dragged her into a dank, old alley filled with all kinds of rubbish and the pestilent rats that fed on it.

He opened a door and tossed her into a tiny dwelling, locking the door behind him. There was a dim lamp-light and it flickered on her kidnapper's face.

"Who are you?" Jeanne said, cowering.

"Ask the press. I'm in their newspapers all the time."

"You're ... that ... that ...!"

"Yes. I'm that ... that ... monster! ... And what may I do for you ... or rather, what may I do *to* you, ha, ha, ha!"

"Just let me go. Please. I can't see what you look like, really. In fact, I even like you," Jeanne lied. "What an exciting adventurous life you lead. It must be a real thrill."

The whore-killer laughed aloud. "Well, wha'd'ya know! A real admirer!"

"Yes! I read up on you like a fanatic!"

"Really? Well then, if you're telling the truth, you should have no trouble answering a simple question: how many days ago did I last strike?"

Jeanne was too frivolous to read newspapers. She barely even kept up with current events. "Uh ... uh ... two days ago!"

"Wrong!" he hissed. "You lying bitch! You're no admirer! You hardly know who I am!" He felt extremely disrespected. His ego was deeply affected. "What kind of moron are you, not to know who I am! I'm the greatest criminal of all time! Got that?" he added idiotically.

Jeanne nodded out of fear.

The media attention was the first attention he'd ever gotten in his whole life and he loved it, reveled in it, was addicted to it. In that sense, the press was his unknowing accomplice! Having grown up in a broken home, he had always been ill-treated or ignored. And the same trend continued when he hit adulthood. He was desperate for attention and if it meant going out on a killing spree, so be it. Negative attention to him was better than no attention. At least he would be making a big impact on the world around him, never minding that it was such a horrible impact. Maybe not a positive impact, but an impact nonetheless--and a powerful one at that. People would remember him. He would matter. He would no longer be insignificant in the whole spectrum of things. Nothing gave him

The Forbidden

greater joy than to see and read the front pages of newspapers record his infamies. He cut out and kept copies of them all in a scrapbook.

"But I do know ... you're a whore-killer, right? ... I'm no whore!"

"Do you think I'm that discriminating that I kill whores exclusively? ... I've also slaughtered a few little virtuous girls like you when I had the opportunity, just to suit my good side, see? ... Now enough talk! Let's get down to the ... preliminaries, shall we?"

"The preliminaries to what?" said Jeanne.

"Why, murder, of course ... I can't just kill you right-away. That would be too simple, too anti-climactic. I like to think that after the amount of times I've been through this, I like to be a bit more creative."

Making Jeanne lie on her stomach and gagging her, he tied each limb to a bedpost and got out a whip, lashing the living daylights out of her. He stopped to masturbate after every flurry of lashes, rejuvenated by the sight of the bruises or a rip in the skin. Whenever blood began to show, he licked the wound like old Count Dracula or Lestat. After that, he poured salt on the wounds. At the arrival of an orgasm, he pointed his penis at the wounds and ejaculated into the largest one of them.

"More salt in the way of sperm, ha, ha!" he exclaimed.

The suffering Jeanne experienced was horrible. Her blood splattered her back, the walls, even the villain in whose scorching grip the whip held tight.

Then, he stopped and Jeanne could hear him having a drink. "Torturing you wenches is first of all fun," he gasped to her, "but it can also be mighty exhausting."

About ten minutes passed before the horror was resumed with these words:

"Ah, now I feel as fresh as the day I was born!"

Untying her wrists and ankles, he got a rope, tied the noose around his own neck, tied the other end around a hook hanging from the ceiling, and stood up on a chair. In his right hand, he held a knife.

"Alright, this is what you do," he explained, eager to involve her in a new perversion. "When I tell you, I want you to kick the chair away from under me."

Jeanne was in a sad injured state but did as she was told on his instruction and he started choking from the rope, frigging off with one hand and holding the knife with the other.

She thought of making an escape through the door, but she knew it

The Forbidden

was locked from the inside. And as for windows, there were none.

This Ripper's body went through violent convulsions and when his orgasm came and he ejaculated, he started cutting the rope. The knife was very sharp and it cut easily, but in his frantic state of mind, it somehow slipped and he accidentally dropped it.

Panic struck. "Give it here!" he gnashed through clenched teeth, his face beet-red, with an expression of total urgency.

Jeanne realized this was her salvation and that the only trial left to her would be to watch this wretch die in misery.

"Please! ... Help me!" he rasped unintelligibly. "Cut ... the ... rope!"

Jeanne turned around. She didn't want to watch him suffering, whether he deserved it or not. The knife lay beside her. She stared at it with empty eyes. She knew that this man would have killed her.

Soon, the nightmare was over. He was dead.

The biggest media frenzy that Paris had ever seen arose. Jeanne told the police her story of what happened. It was so incredible, so hard to believe, that some of the investigators had their doubts ... until she showed them her ghastly wounds and led them to the serial killer's shabby little dwelling where he still hung lifeless from the rope.

Jeanne was hailed a kind of heroine. The suffragettes used her as their perfect feminine ideal. The religious community saw her victory as a victory over evil. Her story was told and retold. And the general public never seemed to have enough of this lurid tale. Even novels and plays, retelling her story, were written and staged with considerable success.

It cheered her up, all of the positive attention. But she still wasn't happy. Without Isabelle there to share in the spotlight with her, there was a void, a void that neither Colette, nor Natalie, nor any one of her other fine friends could fill.

Eventually, she became sick of the recognition and avoided everyone until things settled down. She wasn't interested in being in the public eye. She preferred to be anonymous, unknown, significant only to herself and the few people precious to her life.

The Forbidden

Isabelle had been very concerned when first she heard of Jeanne's kidnapping and all the rest. It almost drove her to Jeanne's doorstep once again. But when she heard that Jeanne was recovering and was alright, she changed her mind about making an urgent visit.

"If she likes, she can come and see me," was Isabelle's stubborn remark.

After a month, Jeanne was perfectly well again. She even started going to Natalie's parties regularly. There, one entertaining evening, Natalie introduced her to Kevin Ridgeway, an English singer.

"I just love music," admitted Jeanne. "Unlike a painting or photograph, music is ever-changing, ever-moving, like dance."

"There's a beautiful and insightful truth to the way you speak," he flattered her.

"It's your songs--your words, your melodies ... they inspire me to speak this way."

Her whole life, she had been a fervent admirer of this celebrated tenor from Brighton, England. Even when she lived in Romilly as a girl, she would take the long ride to the city just to see his performances.

Gradually, she seemed to forget her romantic affections for Colette and re-discovered them in Kevin. Colette wasn't unduly hurt and they still remained good friends.

One morning, after an unforgettable night of sex, Kevin asked her the question that had been on his mind a long time, but he had always been looking for the right moment:

"Please don't say no ...Will you go back to England with me after my singing tour here is over?"

Jeanne was stunned. She didn't answer right away. She couldn't. The question was far too unexpected. "You would marry me?"

"In time." He smiled.

"I ... I don't know, I ...," she paused. Then her eyes lit up. "Yes! Yes! I'll go live with you!"

That night, Jeanne couldn't sleep. Was she doing the right thing by

The Forbidden

agreeing to go off with a man she was still in the faze of getting to know? Was she over-idealizing him because of his god-like entertainment idol status? After giving it some very deep thought, she saw that perhaps she had been a little hasty with her decision, especially when she considered how much more she'd miss Isabelle. Now, at least, she could still see her at Natalie's parties, even if she didn't approach her. But if she was to move to England, there would be no chance even for that. Jeanne couldn't bear that the distance between them would be so great. They'd be almost worlds apart.

Meanwhile, Isabelle had also started a relationship with another man, hoping it would fill the void in her life. It didn't. And the more she saw her new boyfriend, Maurice, the more she came to see how much in love with Jeanne she had been all along without even knowing it, and that was why she was so miserable without her. Maurice had looks, but little else to recommend him. He was tall and beautifully blonde and blue-eyed, but uninteresting and unexciting. She couldn't stop thinking about Jeanne. She was amazed that a stupid, trivial little argument had so severed a bond that had been so strong. Isabelle realized that what she had thought was her concern for her best friend had really been a subconscious jealousy of Colette for stealing Jeanne away from her.

Sad news afflicted the whole circle of friends. Renee Vivien, their gorgeous blonde poetess, with her dimpled cheeks, her soft laughing mouth and gentle eyes, died. The funeral was a very mournful affair, particularly for Natalie, her lover. What was particularly striking about it was that Natalie was normally quite a stoical person, and never went to funerals, yet she was there, and showed much grief. She emptied enough tears to fill a bucket. But the others were also deeply shocked and grieved. At the grave, Jeanne and Isabelle stood closer to each other, physically, than they had in a long time.

"She was so young," Natalie whimpered through her handkerchief.

Lucie Delarue-Mardrus made a striking observation:

"Poor Renee burned herself out. She was the fragile, creative, high-strung type which are the most susceptible to destruction--in her case, through an excess combination of alcoholism and erotomania."

"It's true, Renee was an alcoholic," said Natalie. "She even

The Forbidden

developed a little system that made it possible to drink in public without being caught."

"She was such a sweet tender thing," reminisced Jeanne, "still like a little girl."

Isabelle spoke out:

"She once said something that I haven't been able to forget since. She said, 'there are fewer ways of making love than they say, and more than they think. But the most important thing of all is to follow your heart and find true love.'"

Jeanne glanced at Isabelle when she uttered this. She shed an extra tear, but it wasn't for Renee.

After the funeral, Natalie Barney found that she couldn't stay on at Neilly, where she and Renee had lived together, because the place was just too full of memories now. She moved elsewhere.

Maurice and Isabelle were returning home from an annual fair they had gone to. They were alone together in their carriage and the body warmth between them as they cuddled against each other made Maurice feel very aroused. He wrapped his hard, well-shaped muscles around her feminine body. In a way, it reminded her of that night Jeanne's father was driving her home and the advances he had made to her before she managed to get away by faking that she had to go off behind some bush to pee. Maurice didn't know this memory was on her mind, nor did he care. Through his trousers his sex pressed hard against her thigh and she immediately knew what he wanted.

"Oh God, I love you ..." he whispered in gasps, unbuttoning his pants.

When he hiked his hands up her skirts and started sliding Isabelle's knickers off, she tried to stop him.

"What's wrong? Don't you love me too? ... Say it."

There was a pause.

"Say it!"

Isabelle just sat there as if in a coma, still and emotionless. The only time she moved was when Maurice tried to touch her. She cringed away from him.

Near the end of the journey, Maurice threw a tantrum:

The Forbidden

"You're just wasting my time! All along, you've just been wasting my time! What's wrong with you, for Christ's sake! What's the matter with you! I've been seeing you for more than three months and we haven't fucked once! You don't even let me touch your cunt or fondle your breasts! With the greatest of reluctance, you showed me your tits ... and that wasn't even long enough for me to appreciate them!"

"They're scrawny!" she retorted. "What's there to appreciate!"

"They're perfect! ...Why won't you give yourself to me?"

"Oh, I have to pee. It will only take a moment. Get the driver to stop," said Isabelle.

Maurice did.

Isabelle got out and immediately made a run for it. She didn't care anymore. She would get Jeanne back in her life if she had to die trying.

Maurice saw her scurrying away. "Isabelle! Where the hell are you going, you fool! Come back here! Come back!"

Meanwhile, at that very hour Jeanne was waiting for Kevin to come pick her up for their voyage to England. His concert season was over and they were to travel first-class upon the luxurious French liner *Normandie* back to his country.

The longer she prepared and waited, the more doubts surfaced in Jeanne's soul about leaving. And there was always the nagging revelation her heart had made to her: she wasn't truly in love with Kevin, she only loved his voice, his talent. In the same way, she hadn't been in love with Colette, she only loved her novel-writing talent, and liked her companionship and financial support.

"No, I can't do it!" she shrieked aloud and ran out of the house, heading for Isabelle's apartment.

She ran and ran down the gray, worn-out road. The darkness couldn't have been more peaceful. As she passed certain houses, the muffled sounds of speech could be heard within and occasionally the smell of freshly cooked meals tempted her nostrils. But nothing could distract her from her purpose.

Finally, Jeanne could run no more. She stopped and bent forward, exhausted, putting her hands on her knees. Her face was greasy and glistened with sweat. She wiped it. When she looked up again, she could see a figure in the distance, a silhouette. As it came closer, Jeanne could tell that the person was a girl and that she was running. She looked familiar. When her face came into view, there was no mistake. It was

The Forbidden

Isabelle.

Recognizing Jeanne, Isabelle stopped dead in her tracks. Isabelle was now realizing that from the very beginning without even knowing it, she had been just as much in love with Jeanne as Jeanne had been with her; at the same time, Jeanne was feeling how very much her romantic love for Isabelle really meant to her. Both women stared at each other for what seemed an eternity. Then, at the same time, they flung into each others' arms, embracing and kissing like lovers being reunited after the longest time apart. And everything that so badly needed to be said between them, was said through those frantic embraces.

The Forbidden

Sisters In Love

The Forbidden

Part 1

"Will you marry me, Clotilde? ... Unfortunately, I have no fancy, verbose declarations of love in which I could envelope you. I'm no poet ... but what I feel, I feel. I know only this one clear and simple truth: Jacques loves you, loves you more than anyone or anything he's ever known in this world. Will you ... have me?"

It was the question she had been waiting for since she and Jacques first became lovers. She could see the sheer sincerity of love burning on the tip of his quivering lips and nervous expectation glowing in his eyes. Those clear, gray-blue eyes of his.

"Of course! Yes! *Yes!*" her lungs resonated, as an ecstatic relief filled her soul. Finally! Finally he asked her! And luckily, she didn't faint before answering ... or after, by some strange miracle!

They embraced tightly, fervently, bubbling over with pure love and, gradually, the tinglings of lust. They kissed with a desperate hunger, devouring each other mindlessly, locked in a timeless, sweetly intense, almost subconscious world of their own.

"But my darling," said Jacques, suddenly breathlessly breaking away from her lips. He was holding her forearms with force. "You know we'll have to elope, seeing as you're already engaged to the man of your father's choosing, that ghastly beast of a man, Duc Norbert de Marelle. That stupid cad who doesn't deserve one sou of his inherited wealth!"

"He's ugly as a bat! I would rather be sent to Hell than live with that gargoyle!"

"Don't worry. I'll never leave your side. That's my eternal promise to you. Even if you should choose, one day, to reject me for--"

"As if that were possible!" She laughed.

"But dearest, look. I don't want you to make a decision you would regret for the rest of your life and make me regret as well. Both my parents are penniless and of meager middle-class background. Not one spot of

The Forbidden

gentry in them. You'll go down in social station. You'll be as common as they come ... as common as me. Are you prepared to make this sacrifice? You do understand what this elopement will mean for you ... for us?"

"I don't care! I don't care a fig!" she kept repeating frantically, unthinkingly.

"You'll be an outcast forever. Your rich father will strike you forever from his will. You won't become the blue-blooded duchess that your family expects you to--"

"Stop it! Stop it! Titles, money, property, it all means nothing to me! All I know, all I care about, all I feel, is this incredible love for you, and all the joy it holds in store for me. I don't care about all the rest. Don't you see? Don't you hear me? I really don't care!" the seventeen-year-old Clotilde exclaimed at her loudest, most heartfelt.

Jacques gave her the brightest smile, rubbing her soft, rosy cheek. "That's all I needed to hear," he sighed.

Clotilde d'Arleux was a pretty, fresh-faced, fragile beauty, light as a pussywillow, delicate and graceful in every way. Though slight, she had a nice, mature pair of very soft and bursting breasts held tight and snug in her corset. Her skin was fashionably white, with a touch of pink to give it that wholesome appearance. But that wasn't all there was to Clotilde. Her mother saw to it that she received a good education growing up, and that wit, the art of seduction, and charm were incorporated into her personality. Lessons on religion and respectability were rather neglected.

Jacques Savant, her suitor, was twenty-three years old; he was the adventurous, enterprising sort of gent. But he was no rake like many men his age who did nothing but chase beautiful society women and lead them to their ruin through all manner of plotting treachery, lies and deceit. Jacques had once served as gamekeeper at the d'Arleux family estate, until Clotilde's father dismissed him when he started to suspect that he and his daughter were becoming a little too close for his liking.

That evening, after the servants had gone to bed, Clotilde came down and said good-night to her parents. Her father, Henri, was a very fat man, with brown, bushy whiskers and a nose that always seemed red. Rarely was his face not in a grimace, and even when amused, he seemed to find smiling irritating. He was a most austere individual, completely emotionless, except where anger was concerned, and a real pompous ass. His wife was Claudine, a witty, audacious blonde who found him hard to tolerate. She was a woman of sophistication, class, full of energy and fond

The Forbidden

of talking, but about 'male' subjects like science and literature, not the light, frivolous and foolish things the women of her generation were expected to chatter about. She was self-schooled (having through the years read every volume in her husband's vast library which had been in his family for generations and which he himself never used); in her middle age she found herself immensely learned. Moreover, she was certainly attractive, with her head of delightful, fashionable curls; long, lazy eye-lashes; and bright, blue eyes; her slim, curvy figure; and great, arching bosom. Her daughter had certainly inherited her looks.

"And a good-night to you," replied her mother. Her father only glanced up at his daughter in his usual disgusted manner before lowering his gaze back upon the flames in the fireplace. He sat hunched in such a comical manner, caricaturists would have had a ball sketching him like that. He slowly chewed on his pipe, hands folded. The only reason on earth why Claudine had even married her husband was because her family were well-to-do land-owners of the upper bourgeois eager to marry her into the aristocracy. With an amorous woman's cunning, she managed to entice the gullible and unsuspecting Henri, who promised to marry her just to stop her from pestering him. It goes without saying that his parents were less than pleased by the marriage. They felt he married beneath himself, when there was absolutely no need, since his family was every bit as wealthy as Claudine's; so, for the first few years, Claudine received callous treatment from his family. But in time, through her beauty, wit, charm, and erudition, she found acceptance. The men were flattered and enchanted by her free, coquettish ways, and the women were amused by her witty, chatty, charming, bawdily funny and jovial nature, as well as being impressed by the knowledge she had attained from books.

Leaving her parents with the impression that she was going to bed, Clotilde left the room and entered the dark, vacant hallway leading to the front door. She had on her nightgown. When she got to the front door, she put on her shoes, put her hand on the knob, and turned her head furtively to see if she was being watched. There was no one in sight. Chuckling quietly to herself, she quickly opened the door and closed it cautiously behind her without a sound. Once outside in the chill of the night, her breath became visible, like the smoke of a chimney. Excitement coursed through her veins. She ran down the stone steps leading up to the estate, pulling off her nightgown as she ran. Underneath, she had on her finest dress. She opened the iron gate and stood there patiently. Not half a minute later, she saw a

The Forbidden

carriage tossing along the gravel road. It was the carriage she had been waiting for.

"Whoa!" exclaimed the driver, pulling on the reins as he stopped right in front of Clotilde. The carriage door swung open violently, almost scaring her half to death. And there was Jacques, smiling as always, holding his hat off to her. He got out and gallantly offered his hand to assist her into the carriage. Her tiny, gentle fingers curled around his strong hand as she hopped aboard. And they were off.

She started kissing him rapidly with short, hard pecks, sighing, "I love you."

Jacques, overwhelmed, wrapped his arms around her and laughed jokingly: "If you waste all of your love on me now, there won't be any left over for later tonight."

"Where are we going?"

"Your parents will likely send out search parties first thing in the morning, so the only truly safe place is Paris. Nobody could find us there. The place is huge ... I know of a good hotel where we can spend the night."

"But when will we be married?" she said anxiously, tapping her foot, as if fearing that she had been tricked and that he might try to talk his way out of it.

"Worry not, my angel ... We'll find a church as soon as we awake tomorrow morning. We'll be man and wife before the bells strike noon!"

Jacques started kissing Clotilde's neck, biting its tender flesh gingerly; he yanked her dress down over her shoulders and down to her waist, untying her corset and letting loose two large and heavy, though firm and well-elevated globes of flesh; the areolas were wrinkled, light-brown and the nipples were fat, engorged, sticking out. Rummaging under her skirts, Jacques put his hand over the material of her knickers at the crotch area. He felt she was warm down there, with her cunt resonating heat and throbbing; as soon as his palm was skin-to-skin with the thick-fleshed vulva, he could feel its damp condition. He pressed two fingers to her clitoris and was pleasantly startled by its size and hardness. Clotilde began rubbing her cunt lustfully against his hand, and Jacques cupped and squeezed the moist, swollen, round mons as he caressed it up and down with growing urgency.

"Poke it with your finger now!" she exclaimed.

Jacques obeyed. He fingered her cunt-hole mercilessly, hardly aware of what he was doing, he was so excited.

The Forbidden

"You like that do you not, you delightful wench!"

"Yes! Yes, speak lewdly to me! ... Use obscene language! I'm your whore forever, my love!" She, too, hardly knew what she was saying and she didn't care.

Clotilde dug her nails into him so hard, he thought he was going to bleed. But his pleasure was such that the pain almost added to the euphoria. He pulled down his breeches to expose a somewhat thin but long and upright member standing tall and hard with desire.

"Now fuck me, you great fucking-john!" she shrieked, already having cum three times. Now she wanted her orgasm. She wanted it desperately.

Without tenderness, without hesitation, he thrust it in firm and fast. Clotilde's was a long-lipped pussy, and by that time she was so soft with lust that the penis slipped in without the slightest of difficulty. But she was deliciously tight inside. Tight, hot and slimy. It made for a wonderfully snug and stimulating fuck. And as they fucked, Clotilde would stiffen her cunt-muscles down on his penis, only increasing his pleasure. The sex was a very pleasant forty-five-minute affair which, when it was over, left them both perfectly satisfied and with smiles aglow.

In a matter of hours they were in Paris. The city of lasciviousness and crime, poverty and dubious dealings. A haven for all the scum of the earth, as well as the seat of government and home to many of the most prominent business people in France.

It was a starless night, and the moon looked rather lonely up there all alone, banana-shaped and white as winter. Jacques gazed out of the carriage window, listening to the confused chorus of voices outside, where every class and every kind of person walked the same streets. He was appalled by how squalid and pathetic were some of the bodies and faces he beheld, and it infuriated him to see, from time to time, an extravagantly attired gentleman step out of his carriage or exit the opera-house or some such place, and completely ignore the horror of poverty around, as though he had somehow, through the years, learned to build up a blind immunity to it.

"Is this how demoralized is our age?" Jacques muttered to himself in disgust, watching everything that passed by outside.

"What was that you say?" came the drowsy voice of his true love as she slowly roused herself from sleep.

"Hush now, darling. We'll soon be at the hotel. Then you may

The Forbidden

return to your dreams undisturbed."

She cuddled up against him, warming herself against the cold night.

"Stop here!" shouted Jacques when they had arrived.

They carried their things in, which wasn't much, since all they had was Jacques' belongings.

"We'd like a room for the night," he told the hotel manager, a thickset, shabby man with an untidy beard and fierce, red-tinted eyes.

"You would now, would ya? And is this fine piece of meat your lass, then?"

"She is my ... " and he paused, not able to think of anything morally irreproachable to say, but finally said, "my wife."

"Oh, I see," grinned the hotel manager disbelievingly.

He named his price, which was reasonable, and Jacques agreed.

"Here she is," said the hotel manager in his hoarse, loud, bass voice after taking them up to the upper floor and opening one of the rooms. "It's one of our finest. Even the bed and bedcovers are brand new, you'll be pleased to note, heehee. Enjoy, heehee."

He left and went back downstairs, his mind already filled with racy images of what he pictured would soon be going on behind that door. The room was indeed spacious and clean, even elegant in a sort of rustic sense.

Jacques sat at the edge of the bed. He looked worried.

"What is it?" asked Clotilde.

"It's ... it's ..."

"What? Is it me? ... Are you regretting what we've done?" she asked anxiously.

He embraced her. "No, no! Of course not. That isn't it at all. I was just thinking, how will we get by for the next month or so? We'll need to stay in hiding, you understand. I can't take you back to where I live because your parents know where that is. That's the first place they'll search. What will we do for money? Did you bring any, as I requested?"

"Oh, damn it!" she gasped. "My mind was full of so many things ... I forgot."

"Well that's perfect. All we have to go on is fifty measly francs."

"That's enough for now," she meekly and stupidly said.

"Oh shut up, what do you know!" he shouted. "You're still a little girl who doesn't know a thing about the world ... cloistered up in your

The Forbidden

father's decrepit, old estate since birth ... locked away in a pretty fantasy!"

Suddenly, she broke down in tears, jumping on the bed and covering her face in the pillow.

Jacques began to regret what he said. "You don't need to cry," he whispered. "You know I didn't mean it like that ... honestly."

She sat up, turning to face him.

"It's just that we're in a bit of a fix, that's all," he added.

"I've thrown everything away for you ... for our love. Please, Jacques, never be cross with me again. It hurts me too much. Much more than it should. My heart is sensitive to your every gesture, your every word. Please remember that."

They hugged lovingly for a long while.

"You're absolutely right, we'll find a way to get by," he sighed optimistically at the end of it all.

When the maid came into Clotilde's room back at her father's estate to do her bed the next morning, she found no one had slept in it, and Clotilde was nowhere to be seen.

"Madame!" she yelled. "Madame!"

Both Monsieur and Madame d'Arleux rushed into the bedroom.

"Where is she?" asked the mistress of the house.

"There was nobody here when I first came in," replied the maid.

"Scour the house! I want all of the servants looking! I want the house searched inside out! The outside property too! You hear me?"

"Yes ma'am, right away ma'am," the maid barely had enough breath to say. She was shaking nervously, fearing that her mistress would take her temper out on her.

"What's this!" exclaimed Madame d'Arleux, marching over to the writing desk. There was a note on it in Clotilde's handwriting. She read it aloud:

I've left with Jacques. He and I are to be
married shortly. I could not ever see myself
marrying the man you had chosen for me.
I know I have disappointed you and I hope

The Forbidden

*you and father will find it in your hearts
one day to forgive me.*

Clotilde

    Her father was deeply upset. "Quickly! We must organize a search party for her! I'll see that girl in hell before I ever let this bugger of a marriage go through! Damn that Jacques! Damn him into hell!"
    When one of the maids retrieved Clotilde's nightgown from the front-yard, Henri snatched it and muttered: "That clever little devil!"
    The gendarmes were summoned and after the circumstances were explained, the search, consisting of some thirty armed men, began. Jacques' family was visited first and foremost.
    "We ain't seen him since he left last night," his father candidly said. "He never told us where he was going."
    Nothing, not a single clue was uncovered in the small town, or the towns surrounding it, for that matter.
    Henri: "Have you found them?"
    "Not yet, sir," was time and again the reply.
    Frustration set in. Claudine promised never to forgive her daughter. "She has destroyed my love for her. It is her own doing!"
    "If she is not found by today, I disown her forever!" flamed Henri. "If there is a scandal, I will never let her set foot in this house again. You're right, my wife--she leaves us no choice."

"My word! It's already half past twelve!" gasped Clotilde after waking.
    Jacques was still asleep. "Your lovemaking last night was more divine than ever," he murmured.
    "Well, you know you always bring me to new heights," she returned the compliment. "But now to another matter: marriage. Let's go and tie the knot of matrimony before they find us and ruin everything."
    "Oh, you worry too much. Let me do the worrying for the both of us. Don't trouble your pretty little head about anything. Fill it only with nice thoughts. I don't want a nervous or sullen mate to spend all of eternity with." He smiled.

The Forbidden

"My disposition is neither nervous nor sullen. I rather think myself cheerful. And I seldom worry."

"Indeed. In your privileged life, you've had nothing to worry *about*."

She gave him a frown. "You know," she said, "sometimes I think you almost begrudge me my beginnings, the easy, carefree life I've been fortunate enough to have led. But let me tell you, was not all fun and frivolity."

"Oh no?" he gave her a mocking glance. "Then what else was it?"

Now she was angered by his snide skepticism, and gave no response.

Jacques eased off, kneeling submissively at her feet. "I know what you're trying to say. And believe me, I understand. I was just having a little fun ... Hurry up and get dressed, or we'll be late for our wedding!"

Her face suddenly lit up in a smile.

"How much do you suppose it will cost?" she said.

"Not much, I would guess." It would be a very private and modest wedding indeed.

When they came into the church, the priest had just finished hearing an old woman's confession.

Jacques: "Hello Father, my name is Jacques Savant, and this is my fiancee, Clotilde d'Arleux. We've come to be married, if we may trouble you briefly to undertake the ceremony ..."

"Oh, certainly, certainly ... But you'll have to wait. You see, it is now one o'clock, and I'm hearing confessions until three."

"We have money ..."

"Oh, I assure you, my boy, that is not the problem."

"But you have no confessors at the moment," persisted Jacques. "I know of no other church where ..."

"People are coming and going all the time ... I must be available for them. Besides, there's a Protestant church just down the road, my son."

"I'm a fervent Catholic, Father. I'd never suffer myself to set foot in a Protestant church. The very idea is sacrilegious!"

Moved by Jacques' last remark, the priest compromised: "Well ... there are no confessors at the moment ... I suppose it can be done now if we make haste. Come," he motioned them to follow.

He led them to the altar. The priest raced through the whole ceremony in the most apathetic fashion, he didn't even bother to ask why

The Forbidden

no one was attending the ceremony, why there were no witnesses. Jacques and Clotilde sensed this, but from them there certainly came no complaint. They wanted it over just as badly as the priest did.

In the end, the priest was relieved to declare: "On this October 14th, in the year of our Lord 1669, I hereby now pronounce you man and wife!"

The passionate kiss came just as someone exited the confession-box.

"Excuse me, Father Le Brun," said the person annoyedly, "but I have been waiting here for half the day it seems! Do you suppose you could spare a moment to lift this burden of iniquity off my soul!"

"C-certainly, certainly," repeated the priest, feeling like someone does when they sense they've been neglecting their duties. "I shall be with you promptly, my son."

The marriage certificate was hastely signed and stamped.

Jacques and Clotilde snickered as they watched the priest clumsily scamper on over to the confession-box, apologizing profusely.

In the days and weeks that followed, they found their money supply almost completely exhausted, even though they'd confined themselves to very careful and meager spending. They were almost penniless.

"I think it's finally time we leave this filthy gutter of a city," said Jacques.

"But where will we go?"

"Why, to my family, of course."

"But is it safe?"

"Well, it's either that or stay and starve!"

"Your point is well-taken. When would you like for us to leave?"

"Well ... now. We can leave now," he replied.

They called for a carriage and were soon on their way.

"What's your town called? There are so many in the vicinity." Clotilde knew very little about where and how the peasantry and middle classes lived. She had never been exposed to any of that lifestyle. She would quickly learn just what she'd gotten herself into.

"It's Torque; it is not really a town, but you cannot rightly call it a village either."

The Forbidden

In the days that followed, life with Jacques and his family was nothing like she'd expected. She couldn't believe the drudgery, the sheer hardship of simply making sure there was enough food on the table. On top of that, she and Jacques were constantly bickering over stupid and serious things alike. As the weeks turned into months, Clotilde really began to regret having run away with him. She realized she had been too young and naive to make such a huge, life-changing decision.

"I do not know how I ever agreed to this in the first place!" she shouted one day as she and Jacques were carrying buckets to the well.

"Well we need to get water..."

"Not that, you ass," she rudely hissed, like someone undergoing a lot of frustration and strain.

"What's it now, then!"

"You took advantage ... took advantage of me. An innocent girl. Shame! Shame on you! What a life I had waiting for me! What a comfortable, extravagant life! And look at me now! Look what you have turned me into! Filth! Poverty! Struggle after struggle after struggle! All we do is toil! Like slaves! Like domestic farm animals!"

"Now listen here!" Jacques grabbed her elbow, squeezing hard. "Let me remind you of something ... let me refresh your memory ...What did I say to you before we eloped? What did I say? I warned you this would happen! I told you to weigh the consequences! Hell and damnation!--I feared this would happen! An aristocrat belongs not among commoners just as a commoner does not belong among aristocrats. But you're one of us now."

She dropped the buckets. "I'm going home."

"This is your home."

"No, I mean my *real* home," she replied coldly. "I shall beg forgiveness ... on hands and knees if necessary, if only they will have it in their hearts to take me back."

"After they know you've married me? It's useless."

"But how would they know?" she said with a smug expression, which suddenly turned pale and grim: "... Begorry, you're right! I left a letter on my desk ... it clearly stated that I ... that we were to be married. Aaaaarrrhhh!"

"Now pick up that bucket, you useless woman."

When he said that, something in Clotilde snapped in her mind. How dare he treat me this way! How dare he, a mere farmer's son, treat me

The Forbidden

like some cheap scullery-slut!

"Ah, there's still hope yet! And you know it! That's why you're trying to dissuade me! My, you must take me for quite a fool. And I don't blame you. I was fool enough to marry you, now wasn't I."

"Then go! Go, and never come back!"

"I won't! I won't need to ... ever!"

Clotilde began to run. She found and raced down the country path leading to her father's grand estate. It was a good ten kilometres at least. But after the life she'd been getting used to leading, her body had grown quite well-conditioned.

It was the beginning of December but rain had melted all the snow, causing floods. It was a dark afternoon. Chilly and overcast. What had once been Clotilde's prettiest dress looked now almost like the rags of a tramp-woman. Nothing about her bespoke of her true background and birth anymore.

All of a sudden, through the semi-darkness, after a long time walking, she could hear the wheels of a carriage. She hardly got out of the way fast enough, as it swooshed past her.

"Stop here, driver!" said the voice of a man. He sounded young. The carriage stopped a few paces ahead of her.

Out came a well-dressed man looking very regal. He walked up to Clotilde, who just stood there frightened.

"Ah, you fresh country wenches are all so pretty," he said, running his fingers through her curls, adding in a patronizing tone: "'Tis a pity indeed that underneath such a pretty exterior, all you are is ... a lowly peasant."

Stung by the remark, Clotilde for the first time felt real pride in her nobility:

"For your information, sir, I am of noble birth!"

He chuckled mockingly. "Oh, I see. Clearly you are. Of course."

She hissed: "I am the daughter of Henri d'Arleux!"

"My, that *is* something." He smiled. "Tell me, then, mademoiselle ... why are you dressed this way?"

"Because ... because I've been living with," then she stopped herself short. "Listen, you don't believe a word I'm saying, do you."

"Oh, on the contrary, I find your tale most interesting." He put his hand on her breast: "Perhaps you can tell me the whole story in my carriage."

The Forbidden

"Pig!" she spat. "I see your game! I'm no trollop!"
And she stepped back.
"Oh, come, come. All your kind ... you're all trollops! Never met one that wasn't."
"Well I'm not!"
"Well, then," he said with a smile, adding mockingly: "I'm sorry to have offended you, a woman of such noble lineage, ha, ha, ha!"
"Bastard," she said between clenched teeth.
The man knew he wouldn't get anywhere with her, and he left.
After another half-hour of walking, Clotilde sighed a big sigh of relief. And she had good reason to. There it was in the distance. She'd made it to the estate at last! Soon she would be back in her cozy bedroom, waited on by servants, living the good life as before. Her parents would be so glad to see her back after such an absence that they'd be only too willing to forget the past if only to have their beloved daughter back once and for all. These comforting thoughts circled round her head.
She came to the black gates leading up to the estate. They were locked from the inside. The whole estate was surrounded by a thick stone wall.
"Shit!" she gasped, shaking the gates in frustration.
Having grown up on the estate, she knew the property well, so she was aware of how to sneak onto it with little difficulty. Clotilde found a little opening through the ivy-covered west side of the wall. The area around it was so thickly-wooded that no one from the outside could know it was there. It was a tiny entrance, which once had a door, but the wood had become so soft and rotten that as a little girl, she one day managed to kick it down without a soul finding out about it.
As she sneaked through the small entrance and onto the property, the yard was silent. No one and no thing in sight. But as she came over to the front of the house, two rottweiler dogs lay, unchained, by the doorstep. Clotilde froze. She gulped a loud gulp. Apparently her father had purchased a pair of watchdogs! Black, sleek, vicious watchdogs with foaming mouths and razor-sharp teeth. One of them slept, but the other one spotted her. He started to growl. This awoke the other. Both dogs stood up. Their growls became more constant, more hostile. They slowly came closer towards her. She knew they took her for a trespasser. Clotilde knew better than to run. They could sense her fear, but she was like a statue--didn't move a muscle. The growls quickly turned to barks. Now the dogs were

The Forbidden

closer than ever. Clotilde was so scared, she wanted to scream. She was so scared that she lost her footing and fell backwards on the ground.

The dogs saw their chance, and they seized upon their helpless prey.

"Help! Someone!" screamed Clotilde as one of the dogs bit into her throat, while the other dug his teeth firmly into her leg. "Aaaaahhhhh!"

Suddenly, the front door opened, and there appeared her father, with musket in hand.

She saw him. "Help! Help, me!"

He fired the musket in the air, and the dogs scurried away, leaving a bloodied and wounded Clotilde moaning and trembling on the cold, damp ground.

"How dare you come here! What business have you coming here? How did you get past the gate!"

Clotilde was too traumatized to reply. And she was shocked by his callousness.

"Answer me! Answer me! ... Do you know what scandal we have had to endure? We've been shun by all good society! All high society has snubbed us on account of you! Well, you shall have all of your life to think about your selfish recklessness!"

It turned out that she wasn't terribly injured. A bit of flesh, mostly skin, was ripped from her calf and there were some marks on her neck, but that was the extent of the damage.

Clotilde managed to get up on her feet. "I've come to beg your forgiveness, father. I want to be back with you and mother."

His response was quick and biting: "Your mother and I have disowned you forever--now be off! ... I would rather not let the dogs finish what they've started."

Servants appeared at the front door, awoken by all the commotion.

"Take this girl to the gate and show her out," Henri said to one of them. "And never let her in."

"Father!" She wept. "How could you!"

He just turned his back. Where compassion and forgiveness are concerned, he was as impotent as they come.

Her mother, Claudine, watched from her bedroom window, hardly able to keep back her tears. She covered her mouth in grief, trying to control her sobs. She had a change of heart, and if it hadn't been for fear of her husband, she would have rushed out to her daughter's defense and

The Forbidden

rescue.

"My dear child ..." she muttered.

By evening, just as Jacques was getting ready for bed, Clotilde burst in through the door. She was exhausted, wet and feverish, coughing and sneezing all over the place.

"Where the devil have you been!" he exclaimed. He wanted to become angry with her, but when he saw what a sorry state she was in, he realized she needed some quick attention instead.

"Here, I have still got some soup left over from dinner. I will heat it up for you," he said, helping her get out of her drenched clothes.

She started to doze off in her weary state, but then she became hysterical, apologizing pitifully: "Please don't abandon me, Jacques! Please! I need you so much! I'm sorry, Jacques, I am sorry for what I said."

"Have you forgotten already?" he began, "I promised I would be with you always; I meant to keep that promise. And I still do."

She smiled back, squeezing his fingers.

Two months later, Clotilde realized she was pregnant.

"How long have you known?" asked Jacques, overwhelmed by the news.

"Not until now," she said. "I think it must be twins."

"Are you speaking in jest? This is marvellous; this is ... phenomenal!" Jacques rejoiced. "We will be a real family. It's a blessing from Heaven, oh yes. I'm certain."

At the final stages of her pregnancy, Clotilde started developing back problems and was bedridden. This put an added strain on Jacques' shoulders. But their love and optimism saw them safely through everything that came their way. Clotilde learned to be reconciled to her modest new life and every challenge was overcome.

Labour pains came late one night.

"What's wrong, Clotilde? Is it the babies?" Jacques looked concerned.

She shook her head. "Oh Jesus, it's time!"

His eyes were heavy with slumber, but Jacques managed to roll out of bed. "I'll get you to the doctor."

"No, there's no ... ah! God Almighty that hurts! ... There's no

The Forbidden

time!"

"What? Well, I don't know what to do!" He was right. He was ill-prepared to cope with the situation. Clotilde started screaming. The pain was unbearable.

"Just push!" he managed to say. "Flex your muscles down and thrust it through ... as hard as you can. Take a deep breathe and push!" Jacques didn't know how it was possible, but he was actually giving her the right instructions. He'd never seen a birth before, aside from that of livestock.

The first baby popped out rather easily, all at once. All wet and bloody, so very little and fragile, weeping madly.

The second one decided it didn't want to come out quite so easily.

"Come on, now, one more!" gasped Jacques. "Just push! Push it out!"

"I ... I can't!" Clotilde shrieked. "I can't!"

"Come on, now, darling. Push it out like a turd!"

Minutes passed. No progress. After several hours, both Clotilde *and* Jacques were thoroughly exhausted, both physically and mentally.

"Come on, try. Just once more," begged Jacques.

Somehow, Clotilde found the strength to, and out of the stretching opening of the vagina appeared a head and one arm and shoulder.

"Ha-ha!" gasped Jacques. "That's it, my princess! The little bugger's half-way out! One more big push will do it!"

The rest of the tiny body squirted out, and suddenly, Clotilde's pain-ridden, shaking, screaming body stopped moving completely. Her head rolled to one side, mouth gaping open. Her bulging eyes went lifeless.

Jacques was too busy rejoicing in the birth of the second twin to notice his wife had just breathed the last breath in her body.

"Clotilde! Clotilde, you did it! It's over! It is accomplished!"

Having wrapped the babies (both girls) up in cloth, he got on top of Clotilde, kissing her face fanatically with wild joy. "Did you not hear what I said, you silly goose?" He laughed.

Abruptly, he shook in disgust, receeding in horror when he saw she was lifeless. He tapped her cheek. He shook her violently. She didn't become any less dead.

"No!" he roared, his tears of joy instantly turning to tears of sorrow. His cries mingled with those of the newborns. Outside, the thundering rainstorm was none too quiet either.

The Forbidden

From the very beginning of his new wifeless life, Jacques found it impossible to tend the fields and all his other daily chores and duties while simultaneously caring for the needs of the twin infants. He offered them to various neighbors and relatives, hoping to somehow get them off his hands and in proper care. But it seemed most families had more than their fair share of mouths to feed and could do without two more.

"I am so poor and busy as it is. I cannot afford to look after *two* babes alone. It is not possible. What do I do?" he asked a friend. "Drown them? Smother them? It would be so quick and effortless. But no! I'm Catholic--I believe it would damn me."

"There exists a very simple solution," said his friend. "Pack them off to a convent."

"Capital!" exclaimed Jacques. "How could I not have thought of that!"

Both twin sisters grew to be copper-blonde after their mother, with eyes the color of light brown. Even their physiques were nearly identical--slightly plump but firm-fleshed, somewhat short of stature, strong and sturdy, with ruddy complexions. As teenagers they looked mature for their age. However, psychologically they were quite different from one another. While Marie was the humble, sensitive and shy type, Gabrielle was as bold, reckless and uninhibited as her mother had been. Neither of them was particularly religious. The nuns found this disheartening, but they'd grown to love the two girls so much that their indifference to the religious and spiritual was often overlooked, or at least conveniently ignored and tolerated. As long as Marie and Gabrielle gave the appearance of, and behaved like good little Catholic girls, that was good enough.

Although most of the nuns were very kind on the surface, Marie and Gabrielle occasionally found their behavior a little surprising to say the least. A small group of the nuns would sometimes be found reading aloud to each other a pornographic work about licentious nuns in Renaissance Italy known as the *Ragionamenti* by Pietro Aretino. Furthermore, every morning on the Sabbath, for instance, all of the nuns would walk around

The Forbidden

the convent, singing hymns and self-flagellating as a means of purging themselves of sin and sinful thoughts. They struck themselves across the back and shoulders as they walked, almost entranced and seemingly immune to the pain. A more disturbing spectacle, though somewhat less common, was when the nuns all gathered round in the pews of the chapel and one of their fellow sisters was flogged by the Mother Superior at the altar in front of the others, who looked on with either placid or intrigued expressions on their faces.

One day, Gabrielle was left with nothing to do. There were no more chores or religious duties. She had a whole hour to kill. Her life had been so routine, every day the same, that she was at a loss. What could she possibly do other than just sit there daydreaming? She lay down on her bed.

"Ahhhh," she sighed, overwhelmed by the pleasant, acute sensation the body feels when its tense or over-worked muscles suddenly get to stretch comfortably. The sun flashing in through the window felt soothing, like the warm hand of God. Gabrielle giggled as she remembered when once at age six she was caught touching herself, and the nun slapped her hand for it; for several years, that same nun, Sister Martha, a very straitlaced, unsightly and humorless woman, would smell Gabrielle's fingers every day to see if she had been frigging herself off. The memory of it made her feel erotic urges, and she started mildly rubbing her pubes through her clothing, slowly. But the erotic 'itch' became more and more unbearable. Soon, she was rubbing harder and harder, eventually sneaking her fingers right into her knickers. Her clitoris stuck out like a miniature thumb, like a pinkish-brown, tiny tongue sizzling between a crevice of folded flesh. Gabrielle was in a frenzy, pulling the knickers down to her ankles, letting them dangle there at her feet as her dress was rolled up to her waist and her pubic muff fully exposed. And what a sparse growth of light-brown hair it was, with more than just a hint of the bright-colored red labia showing through. Just after she climaxed, she heard a voice:

"Gabrielle!"

It was Martha! She marched into the room, grabbing her by the arm. "Caught you right in the act!" she hollered. "You shall surely do penance for this, girl! Just you wait!"

Gabrielle just laughed, like it was all some big joke to her.

"Oh, so this is funny, is it?" said the nun, roughly jerking her arm.

"Where are you taking me?" said Gabrielle.

The Forbidden

The nun dragged her to the altar before the wooden image of Christ.

"Now thrash yourself! We must beat out the sexual lust churning around in your flesh!"

"Sister, leave me be," replied Gabrielle rather calmly but peevishly, like someone beginning to get fed up.

"Hear me, you disobedient imp! If you will not humble yourself before the Cross, then I shall do it for you!"

Sister Martha started whipping her frenziedly but not very hard. To her amazement, Gabrielle didn't cry. This excited her.

"What, no tears? You enjoy it, do you not! You Jezebel! Sinner! The demons of licentiousness have you by the throat, do you not understand? They must be exorcized! I will teach you to think only pure thoughts! Pure thoughts!"

In defiance, Gabrielle started to masturbate.

"Oh, you little harlot!" gasped the nun. "You like doing that, don't you? If it were up to you, you would lie there fingering yourself morning, afternoon and night! Admit it. Admit it!"

"Yes!" shrieked Gabrielle.

She raised her skirts up over her waist as before, rubbing her naked cunt on hands and knees, with her ass sticking out cheekily at Martha.

Martha could bear the sexual tension no longer. She dropped the whip, reaching down to fondle the large, sturdy buttocks, so tight and round.

"You like when I do this, don't you, tribade!" hissed Martha. "You think you've tempted me, don't you, proud bitch! You think I'm smitten with you, don't you? Don't you! Spawn of Satan! You would like to lead me away from righteousness, wouldn't you, you tempting little whore. You would like me to suck your cunt, would you not?"

Gabrielle pinched her own nipples, squeezing the breasts. She'd never heard of cunnilingus before, but the thought of having it done to her enticed her.

"Yes," she sighed.

Sister Martha got her head between the girl's thighs and started giving her a tongue-lashing she would never forget. Driblets of sticky, sappy cum fluid were leaking all over her mouth, nose, cheeks, face and chin as Gabrielle shuttered and writhed in an onslaught of lust, letting the

The Forbidden

middle-aged nun freely gorge herself on delicious, virgin cunt-meat, the inner-lips pendulating like loose, flabby strips of lard.

"The smell and taste together are something divine!" the nun groaned, as Gabrielle cooed with eyes closed and lips smiling.

Gabrielle acknowledged to herself that being cunt-sucked was even more enjoyable than masturbating, and her cunt couldn't stop shaking from the stimulation of Martha's lips and tongue. She could hardly take it! Her clit was so sensitized, she felt like jumping up and down! How much longer could she endure the onslaught of Martha's constant, unrelenting licking? Somehow they ended up in the sixty-nine position and made the cunt-pleasing mutual. Gabrielle was at first overwhelmed by cunt. She couldn't believe she was doing what she was doing. But, imitating her partner well, she quickly acquired a taste for it, and soon buried her face in.

When it was over, instead of fleeing in shame, Martha took Gabrielle to her breast and explained that almost half the sisters there had Lesbian tendencies. It had been going on for centuries. The older sisters usually secretly initiated or seduced the younger noviates who had just joined the order, and the cycle was repeated over and over, generationally. Of course, however, the majority of the nuns found such behavior morally repugnant, and it was never openly encouraged. Officially at least, it was strictly forbidden.

"You must keep what we have done a secret," Martha said.

"I won't tell ...When can we do it again?"

Four years passed.

"Your sister was absent from Mass today, Gabrielle," said Martha. "She'll be flogged. Come to think of it, I cannot remember the last time she went."

When they came downstairs to the chapel, the flogging of Marie was already underway. Martha came upon the spectacle completely spellbound as she crossed herself and knelt down amid the echo of Marie's cries. Martha joined the other sisters. For the first time, the sisters became so restless in their pews, so excited and stirred up, that they yelled out remarks, almost gleeful in their enjoyment of poor little Marie's punishment. They demanded harsher strikes. The sound and fury of the lashes mesmerized them. The Mother Superior was so enthused by the

The Forbidden

reaction she saw that she fell back in exhaustion, having given Marie the harshest flogging she had ever administered to even the most seasoned disciple of the leather. The welts and bruises upon her broken flesh were not a pretty sight. Martha was the most stirred-up of them all. She clapped her hands and cheered, screaming out obscene and sadistic suggestions.

Meanwhile, Gabrielle had to run outside. She couldn't bear what she was seeing. She wanted time to think. She was afraid for her sister's well-being, afraid that her body wouldn't take too kindly to the same sorts of beatings that were regularly inflicted on the other life-long flagellants, all of whom were quite used to it. She was afraid her sister wouldn't know how to enjoy it, or how to learn to. She didn't want her to suffer.

Walking around all alone finally got to Gabrielle, and she ran back inside, eager to see how the flogging was coming along.

"I will stop them if I must," she whispered to herself.

When she came back into the chapel, Gabrielle was awe-struck. What in God's name was going on! The nuns were actually taking turns whipping Marie, who tried very desperately to get away. But she was far too weak and abused to do much. And whipping wasn't all they were doing. Some of them twisted and wrenched her breasts, slapping her cunt and clitoris, face and sides. They went mad, absolutely amok.

Gabrielle's first reaction was shock and disgust, but because she had already previously been perverted by Martha, the spectacle somehow appeared to her a strangely enticing one, and for some horrible reason, she forgot all about saving her sister from the clutches of the nuns. She watched spellbound as they acted purely on primitive impulse, pulling on Marie's nipples hard. It looked like they didn't even realize what they were doing, completely out of control, throwing Marie to the ground and stomping and treading on her stomach. One nun even kicked her in the head for good measure, and grabbing a fistful of her pubic hair, she yanked until fuzzy handfuls came out. The Mother Superior struck the whip over Marie's buttocks until they burned like fire. The welts, cuts and bruises all over Marie's body now looked really ghastly. She was barely conscious, her body convulsing. Blood came from her every orifice, including nose and ears. She even seemed to cry tears of blood!

After some time had passed and all their energy was spent, in their blase the sisters looked aback clear-headedly at what they'd done, and they couldn't believe it. It was all truly like a dream. Like something out of a bad dream! It didn't seem real. It couldn't have happened. But it did.

The Forbidden

"We've all become the Devil's madwomen," Martha broke the silence.

Marie finally came to, and she murmured desperately and incoherently, like a dying person trying to divulge a lifelong secret. The murmur came louder, and easier to make out:

"Ga ... Gabr ... Ga ... Gabrielle ..."

Gabrielle leaped over to her sister at last, embracing her lovingly, burning with guilt for lacking the initiative to come to her rescue.

"I'm here, Marie, I'm here." She embraced her piteously, tears in her eyes.

The other nuns swarmed around to comfort her as well, extending only the most loving sentiments. What a hypocritical paradox!

"My dear sister," cried Gabrielle. "My dear precious Marie. I ..."

Fortunately for Gabrielle, by the time she had come upon the frenzied scene, Marie had been almost totally unconscious, so she was unaware that her sister had done nothing to try to save her.

The incident was never mentioned again, either by Gabrielle, Marie, or the other sisters. Marie recouperated. There was no permanent damage but she did need to heal up. Since the incident with her sister, Gabrielle involved herself deeper and deeper into the sadomasochistic practices of the nuns. It turned into a compulsion.

"Are you certain that you don't want to do it?" asked Gabrielle some time after Marie's full recovery. "It would be only very mild this time ... and only open-hand spankings. That's all."

"No. I don't want to be inflicted with wounds. It's mad." Marie easily refused, still haunted by her terrifying experience.

"I understand completely." Gabrielle sympathized and didn't insist on it.

It was the Sabbath, and Gabrielle joined the others out on the convent grounds, chanting prayers and hymns as she lashed herself over the back and shoulder blades like some Medieval penitent.

Marie watched high up from the belfry. Her sister had become one of *them*. She feared that soon she would be alone. The singing voices of Gabrielle and the nuns rose right up to where she was. She could see her

The Forbidden

sister pass by as she circled around the convent with the others over and over. She could scarcely understand how the women could degrade themselves in such a demeaning manner while at the same time angelically singing such beautiful, poetic, uplifting verses.

As usual, nothing eventful happened all day. But in the evening, after dinner, as the nuns retired to bed, Marie overheard Martha admitting to one of the nuns, Therese, that she and Gabrielle were lovers, and that their affair had been going on for many years. She confessed it because the other nun had suspected it, and she implored her not to tell the others.

"Please, no one must know," whispered Martha sternly.

"You've nothing to fear, my lips are sealed," the elderly nun said with a grin; she was a white-haired, wrinkle-faced and kindly woman. She seemed to have no problem with the idea of Lesbian love.

However, Marie herself was stunned. Her sister? Loving another nun? Marie didn't even *like* them! And here was her sister, not only enjoying their company ... but something worse!

"I need to speak to you." She found Gabrielle in the hallway.

"What's wrong?"

The nuns had all gone to bed. No one was around.

Marie: "I know about you and Martha."

Gabrielle, not surprised: "I suppose you were bound to sooner or later."

"With another woman? That's so ... so ..."

"Martha and I love each other. What is so bad about it?"

"Sh! Keep your voice down!" hissed Marie.

"Do you not know that several of the sisters are guilty of the same thing? It's perfectly common."

"That's beside the point."

"Do you hate me now, then?"

"No, Gabrielle. I still love you. I shall always love you. You are my near and dear sister! My own flesh and blood."

Marie gave her sister a tight hug.

Then, breaking free, Gabrielle said: "But I refuse to be treated with patronage. Or reluctant tolerance."

"No," replied Marie. "Your choices are your own. You will live with them, and die having made them, like the rest of us. If you truly love Martha, then there's nothing I could say or do that would make any difference. I can disapprove, but ultimately, your decisions are yours to

The Forbidden

make."

"Hey!" gasped the Mother Superior, sticking her head out of a doorway. "What's the chatter all about?"

Gabrielle: "Oh nothing, Reverend Mother. Marie and I have just come to an understanding."

"Well, off to bed, girls. I do not want you up so late."

It was nine o'clock in the evening.

In the wee hours of the morning, the nuns were awakened by somebody bellowing madly at the top of his voice outside of their bedroom windows.

"Oh my God!" gasped Martha. "It's a man! How did he get here? There probably isn't a dwelling within leagues of here!"

"There's no carriage. He must have walked," said Gabrielle, gazing out the window.

"What's he saying?" asked Martha.

"Open the window," ordered the Mother Superior. "We might as well see what the vagrant wants."

"Yes," agreed Martha, "if only to have him back on his way all the sooner."

The Mother Superior opened the window, sticking her huge head out:

"What in the Lord's name do you want? Do you know the hour, sir? Do you know the time? We are women who toil for every hour of the day. We need our sleep! I think you understand!"

And just as she was about to slam the window shut, the man cried out: "Please, madame. Please! I need shelter! I beg of you! How could a bride of Christ refuse a fellow servant of the Lord--"

"Oh, if you would only be on your way, sir. We have no spare beds."

But the stranger never relented for a moment, begging for a roof over his head, if only for the night. The Mother Superior saw there would be no way of getting rid of him, so she succumbed to his pleas: "Yes, yes, all right ... If you are a proper, decent, and well-behaved Christian."

She took him to a spare bed reserved only for esteemed visitors like rectors and bishops.

"You can sleep here. But I want you out come morning. I don't

The Forbidden

mean to sound hard, but this isn't a charity, you know. I cannot put my girls under any risk by letting in just any poor wandering traveler, least of all a perfect stranger."

"But I am no ordinary traveler, my lady ... I am Apostle Paul. I have recently arrived from Ephesus. My journeys have been many. I've come to bring Good News! The day of the Lord approaches! The hour draws nigh!"

The Mother Superior closed the door behind him without a word. "Oh my word, I've let in a lunatic," she muttered to herself.

She locked the door to the nuns' sleeping quarters for safety.

All the sisters slept in the same spacious room, with the beds beside and opposite one another from both sides of the room, like in a hospital.

"Where is he?" the other nuns asked, pestering her relentlessly until she lost her temper: "He's in the guest-room, of course. But I fear we made a terrible mistake. He seems harmless enough, but I insist that none of you come near him. The man is mad, in the literal sense. He thinks he's St. Paul, poor fool. His behavior may be unpredictable, dangerous. Stay clear of him!"

When they got up at sunrise, the nuns seemed to completely forget their Mother Superior's warning. A group of them snuck out into the hallway, edging towards the room in which the man slept. They had wanted to knock, but found the door slightly ajar, so they looked in.

"My word!" Sister Therese sighed, swooning backwards, startled.

"What?" asked the others, finally so eager that they accidentally flung the door open after bumping into each other in their attempt to have a look through the door opening.

The man was lying in bed, on top of his covers, completely naked. His clothing was on the floor. The round bulb of his half-erect penis rested against his concave belly. He was still asleep. The nuns just stood in stunned silence, their eyes soaking in this lewd image. So that was what the opposite sex really looked like underneath! they thought to themselves, half-marveling in and half-repulsed by the sight. The stranger looked to be in his late twenties, wholesome and handsome, with reddish-brown hair and a rather Herculean build.

The Forbidden

Suddenly, he stirred from his slumber, shaking out the cobwebs as he got up on his elbows. When they saw him getting up, the nuns took fright, as well as blushing from their shameful voyeurism. They started to flee down the hall, their shoes making such a noise over the hardwood floor.

"Wait!" shouted the man. He ran after them, still with no clothes on. "Have you any idea who I am? Wait! Wait, I say!"

Luckily, the Mother Surperior intervened after being summoned from her private chamber.

"Stop, sir! And get a hold of yourself!" She spoke with a courage that surprised even herself.

The man suddenly became afraid, speechless. Submissively, he responded: "But my lady, I was merely trying to tell these women who I am."

"Your identity to them is of no consequence."

"But my good lady, do you not know? ... I am the Apostle Paul, great and devoted servant of our Lord Jesus Christ!"

"You are nothing of the kind!" she quickly and sharply spat. "Now, I kindly ask you to return to your room. And for heaven's sake! clothe thyself!"

"Yes, ma'am." There was a pause. "Then I am not Apostle Paul?"

The nuns, hiding behind the forbidding figure of their Reverend Mother, couldn't help but see he was no threat, and started to find the whole thing rather amusing, rather funny. A snicker or two escaped the Reverend Mother's notice.

"Hell's bells! No indeed not! Now will you put something on? You could hardly have forgotten that this is a nunnery! We don't allow persons to run about bare as a newborn!"

"Yes, I q-quite understand," he stuttered, scampering back to the guest bedroom. "But I *am* Apostle Paul, I *am* St. Paul," he repeated to himself in whispers. "... Am I not?"

"Whatever will we do with him?" Martha asked. "He's a strong man, I doubt we can make him do anything."

The Mother Superior: "Strong in body but weak in mind."

Gabrielle: "I think you're mistaking insanity for imbecility. The man is deranged, not dim-witted."

The Mother Superior: "Yes, you're right. I'll pack him off shortly, sisters. That I will ... Now, to your duties, off you go."

The Forbidden

When all the nuns, as well as Gabrielle and Marie, had dispersed, the Mother Superior went up to the guest bedroom. She knocked on the door. "Sir, may I come in?"

"Go away!" came the voice from within.

"Please, sir." She turned the knob. The door was locked.

"Please go away! Don't you see? I'm under a tremendous test of faith! I don't know who I am! If not Apostle Paul, then who?"

"If you would only open the door, we can discuss it."

"No! You want to deceive me! You ... you liar!"

The man became more and more agitated by the minute and the Mother Superior saw she wouldn't get anywhere, so she let him be.

When the Mother Superior later passed his room in the middle of the afternoon, he still had not come out. There had been no sound from within the room for hours. Then finally by evening she heard his voice. He was stomping his feet rhythmically, marching up and down the room, saying things like: "Hut, two, three, four, company halt!"

The Mother Superior chose to ignore it.

While everyone was sitting down and enjoying a pleasant dinner, Gabrielle inquired: "What's our madman been doing all this time?"

All of a sudden, moments later the man rushed in.

"Pardon my intrusion, ladies! But I bring you urgent tidings! I am a courier and I bring word from the King's court. France is under attack by the English! Hurry! We must flee! We'll soon be under attack!"

The nuns all started to grumble among themselves, disturbed by his mad ramblings.

The Mother Superior shook her head: "Alright now, that's enough."

"Don't you people know anything? Saxon knights from the north are approaching! They'll slit our throats! Oh, imagine the bloodshed!" He broke down weeping, falling to his knees. "Imminent destruction for all! No time for escape!"

"Saxon knights? That's Germany! I thought you said it's England that's attacking! ... Martha," said the Mother Superior, "help me drag him back to his room."

After they laid him out on the bed, he quickly fell asleep.

"I wonder what he'll decide to be tomorrow," chuckled Martha.

The Forbidden

The nuns came to his room the next morning, only to find it vacant. He was gone. No trace of him. Not even his clothes.

"I suppose he fled to escape the onslaught of the Saxon army," chuckled Martha. "Or did he mean the English navy? Ha, ha, ha!"

Some of the nuns were secretly and perversely somewhat sad to see him go. His presence brought some sense of excitement to the monotony of their otherwise boring and uneventful lives.

That day was as demanding as most others. Marie picked berries from the crack of dawn all morning until her fingers ached. She was sick of it.

"Let's take a walk," she said to her sister Gabrielle after accidentally spilling one of her buckets as it slipped from her grasp.

"You need to pay more attention to what you do!" said Martha. "Pay attention to what you're doing for once. You can't just always sleepwalk through the daylight hours the way you do."

Marie gasped. "Can I help it? Really, I don't understand how you and the others can bear it all, living here like this ... without the slightest complaint."

Martha, sticking her nose up in the air: "Because we love the simple, modest, hard-working, holy life. You don't! We love God and *that* makes all the difference in the world."

Marie stood up angrily: "You don't love God! You know nothing about love! None of you even behave like true Christians!"

Martha: "Ha! This coming from an infidel like you!"

Marie, grabbing her sister by the arm: "Come along, Gabrielle. Let's have that walk now."

Marie pulled on Gabrielle's sleeve, forcing her to run with her.

"And leave me to do all the work? Oh no you don't!" came Martha's voice from behind them.

The sky was clear. Not a cloud in sight. The sun blazed with such warmth. It was like the most delightful day of summer. Any summer.

Once they were on the rough path leading away from the convent, Marie couldn't help but ask, "what do you see in that horrible woman? I mean, she's not pretty ... or likeable. And she's *at least* twice your age."

"The way she treats me is not the way she treats you. Besides, love

The Forbidden

is more than skin-deep ... When you find the right gentleman, you will know what I mean," Gabrielle answered soberly.

"I'll probably wind up a dried up old spinster if I stay here much longer," whined Marie. A pause. "Gabrielle, does it never bother you, knowing you're an orphan?"

"No, not at all. Does it bother you?"

"Yes, sometimes. I want to know who our mother and father were. I really do."

"I don't know," said Gabrielle. "It makes little difference to me. They didn't want us, so why should I care about them or who they are ... So here *we* are. It's not so bad, convent life."

"I hate it. So dreary and dull. I hate the nuns too. Mean, strict, hypocritical, narrow-minded ...Underneath, they are not the kind, pleasant people they would have the outside world believe. That is all pretense."

"Maybe so, but never forget, you owe your life to them. It was they who took us in, remember. Without them, we would have been starving in the streets. Who knows where two abandoned babes like us would have ended up."

Marie: "Why do the nuns not tell us who our parents are?"

"You asked them once when we were little, remember? They don't remember. How can you expect them to? It was such a long time ago when we were brought here."

"It bothered me growing up that we were the only orphans. No other children. No other companions. It's been so lonely. You're the only one I can confide in. You are the only one I have. That is why it bothers me to see these depraved nuns maintain so much influence over your life. I fear they'll somehow turn you against me in the end."

Gabrielle giggled. "My, how silly you sometimes sound."

They strolled for a very long time.

"Shouldn't we turn back?" said Gabrielle.

"Why, are your feet getting sore?"

"Sore and tired."

"Uhu, very well. Mine are also starting to ache."

Just as they turned, they heard the shouting, cursing voice of a woman and the loud, pleading voice of a man.

"Where's that coming from?"

They looked around.

"Up the road," said Marie, pointing.

The Forbidden

They came to a peasant hut of medium size, very pastoral and plain, with a thatched roof. Like the home of a shepherd. A hot family dispute was underway. A tall, thin, clumsy-looking man had just been caught by his short, pudgy wife committing incest with his daughter. The wife was furious, chasing him.

"Come here, you coward! Afraid to face your own wife!"

Meanwhile, the comely, sweet-faced but dowdy-looking daughter chased after her mother, swearing that she'd been coerced, playing the innocent one.

"And you! I'll deal with you later!" roared the wife at the teenage daughter.

The girl was struck with such fright that she ran off into the woods.

It didn't take long for the wife to catch up to her wretched husband. "How long has this been going on, you stinking reprobate!" She struck him awkwardly with her fists, over and over. But, by then, she was so fatigued and short of breath that her weak and awkward blows did him no real harm. The husband put his arms over his face, fending off the angry blows. "How long have you been stuffing her!"

He ignored the question: "Is it my fault that your slut of a daughter will fuck anything that moves? Is it my fault you taught her no decency growing up?"

The wife: "Did you have to roger her in our own house, God A'mighty! What if my mother had come round like she often does this time o' day! Fine mess that would've been!"

"Would you prefer I'd have taken her out in the fields? Or would you rather that I had found some village wench instead? Would've brought home the pox if I'd a' done that! So I chose the lesser of two evils; so why don't you just crucify me then!"

"Oh, I'll do worse than that! I'll castrate you! ... Just shut up, you mongrel. The longer you speak, the stupider you sound!"

"*You* shut up!"

"O Heaven help us! With his own daughter, Christ sakes! She'll get it from me, she will. With his own daughter, Christ sakes! You've still the mind of a fool child ... and a thoroughly wicked one at that! Imagine the kind of imbecile you'd give your daughter! Oh God, I pray she's not with child! ... I'll show her!"

"Don't you dare lay a hand on her."

The Forbidden

"Where is the little harlot? ... Nowhere in sight, eh? Well I don't blame 'er. She knows what's comin' to her, by God."

Gabrielle and Marie could hardly believe their eyes. They said nothing, until prudish Marie remarked: "People of peasant stock are such vitiated, such perverted creatures. How could they? With their own kin! I fail to understand how--"

"Now, now, Marie," said Gabrielle, "we mustn't judge. Judge not lest ye be judged, remember?"

"I know. But still."

For the next few days, Martha had been feeling quite unwell. She was bedridden, and her condition didn't improve. On the sixth day, her symptoms became more visible than ever: high fever, eruptions of reddish spots on the skin, and severe headache. She even showed signs of serious nervous symptoms.

"Oh Lord, what do we do?" said the Mother Superior. "I'm no doctor. It's obvious if we don't act quickly, her days are numbered."

"No!" spat Gabrielle. "She can't die, she mustn't!"

None of them knew that Martha had caught the acute infectious disease known as typhus. It had been transmitted to her by lice. The nuns were at a loss, they didn't know what to do.

"You'll pull through this, Martha," Gabrielle tried to reassure her.

"Maybe not," replied Martha. "I know I'm not a good woman. Maybe this is God punishing me, a punishment of divine wrath. I will die soon."

"No," said Gabrielle. "Don't give up prematurely. You've got to fight the illness! Fight it with your mind! You must have the will to live. Otherwise, you're already dead. The Lord doesn't punish just for the sake of punishing. He's too compassionate and clever for that. If God punishes us, it's to teach us a meaningful lesson. It's constructive punishment, you could say."

"Such wisdom," said Martha weakly, "in such a young mind."

"But I feel sure God is punishing us for giving shelter to that madman!" said the Reverend Mother stupidly. "If this is a plague, then we're all dead!"

All throughout, Gabrielle was the only one who sat by Martha's

The Forbidden

bedside, showing true compassion. The others were afraid of being infected.

"Tend to her, but be careful, do not touch her ... you may catch her sickness," they warned.

The fever became so overpowering by nightfall that Martha started shivering compulsively.

"Martha! Speak to me! Speak to me!" yelled Gabrielle.

Martha started moaning, rattling her teeth. "C-cold," she sighed. "Cold ..."

She was hotter than ever, drenched to the bone with sweat. Death came abruptly. Her convulsing body went motionless like a trembling leaf when it hits the ground. She simply lost consciousness ... forever.

Gabrielle moped around for days, mourning the loss of her lover. She now seemed as dead as Martha, at least in her soul.

"Did you really love her that much?" asked Marie, deeply empathizing with her.

"Up to this point, I have never loved anybody more ... except you. But that's a different kind of love."

"There will be another. You'll love again, worry not. We won't be cooped up in this place forever."

"I hope you're right ... But it's impossible. Will I experience again what I experienced with Martha? Will it be as good? I do not think so. I do not feel that way. I cannot."

A year went by. Gradually, Gabrielle got over the tragedy of Martha's death, and in her desire to find new love, in her carnal eagerness to fall in lust again and to feel the euphoria of loving and being loved, she flung herself into many arms. Even Marie started to be alarmed.

"Word of your promiscuity is getting round," complained Marie.

"Oh, you worry overmuch. I'm sure Reverend Mother would like a sampling of me herself. It's perfectly acceptable here."

"Yes, but only when kept hidden behind a thick veil. If you are not more careful, those hypocrites will have no choice but to make you their next scapegoat and condemn you. You can't fling it in their faces and expect to--"

"I'm not flinging anything. It's love. I'm sharing my love with all,"

The Forbidden

she giggled.

"How many of the nuns have you taken as lovers?"

"Hmm, well, I cannot tell you exactly. I've lost count."

"Stop playing games. How many?"

"If you absolutely must know ... seven, I think."

"Holy Mary!--seven?"

"What? Is that a lot? It may be seventeen."

"You know I do not condemn you for loving women. I believe that it's wrong to judge human beings and their beliefs, although I do think it's right to judge their behavior, because the behavior of people rubs off on those around them. But I don't condemn you as a person. And yet ... even *you* must see that this behavior is not proper in the cloister, by any standard, by any morality."

"Oh, and do you know what morality is? It's a tool the ruling classes have used since the dawn of time to keep the poor and lowly in their place! Damn morality! There is no right or wrong, things just happen. Sometimes you like them, sometimes you don't."

"How can you talk that way? If you fail to recognize evil, then what you are saying in effect is that all behavior is permissible because there is no such thing as a wrong or bad deed. That would make the most horrible acts lawful!"

"But who's to say something is a 'bad' deed? A priest? Who decides what's acceptable or appropriate and what is not? For example, a crime benefits the criminal, so it's good for him. War and disease benefit the human race because they keep overpopulation at bay. Our cities and towns are far too overcrowded these days, would you not agree?"

"Then the solution is not to murder people or watch them die ... the towns and cities need to expand and improve to accommodate all."

"I am sure that is easier said than done."

Marie gave her sister a meaningful stare. "What's got into you?"

Gabrielle rushed over to her sister. "I'm sorry. I know I'm talking nonsense. I do believe in one lover at a time, and I know I'm tempting these women to break their vow of chastity ... but I'm having such a good time with the situation as it is."

"Does each of them know you're seeing seven in all?"

"Oh, I think most of them wouldn't much care. Or maybe they would, I don't know. But I'm sure most of them have other partners also. Still, each one thinks I am only with her."

The Forbidden

"But is that not a recipe for disaster? What if they discover the truth? Wouldn't each feel betrayed? Deceived? And what if they were to seek revenge? Rumors are going round about you. The cat will be out of the bag soon enough."

"I doubt anything will happen. Besides, the sisters have sworn to keep our intimacy a secret. Anything even remotely carnal here is considered a strictly private matter that concerns only those involved."

"I just ... I don't understand how something like this can go on ... in a convent, of all places!"

"Things sometimes happen where you least expect them to."

"I guess that is so."

"Tell me, honestly: have you never ever felt love? Is there no sense of romance in that tiny heart of yours?"

"No, not in the least," replied Marie. "I don't feel at all drawn to women, and--"

"But what about that strange man. You remember him. We saw him naked. Even down to his genitals!"

"Yes, so ...?"

"You know what I'm getting at. I'm sure you were aroused by it."

"I don't recall. Although, I thought he was very nice-looking."

"You don't recall?" snickered Gabrielle. "Surely, you will at least admit he was a gorgeous specimen of manhood."

"He was nice-looking ... and his body was very well sculpted."

"I'll say! It was like the statue of an Olympian discus-thrower. His arms were massive and well-toned. And his chest was--"

"Yes, I get the point."

"So you'll never love? Is that what you're telling me?" said Gabrielle.

"I don't know. How can I know, having lived as isolated as this all my life."

"You'll find somebody alright. You will fall in love. It shall catch you by surprise. You won't be looking for it. It will come to you."

"Oh, so you're a fortune-teller now."

"That remains to be seen, whether or not I am right in my prediction."

The Forbidden

"I found her lying a little ways along down the path near the creek," said the Mother Superior to the nuns the following morning, helping a young girl into the dining quarters where everyone had just been eating breakfast.

"She looks like she hasn't eaten anything in days! Go into the kitchen and bring some food out for her, will you?"

One of the nuns obeyed.

"Come and sit here by me, my pretty," said the Reverend Mother sweetly. She was seldom that sweet. Gabrielle and Marie sat in stunned silence. The girl! They recognized her! She was the very same one who had committed incest with her father!

"Now, tell me, dear, what were you doing in the middle of nowhere? You looked like a lame horse left by its owner to die at the side of the road."

The girl paused before answering. "I ran away from my wicked mother. She beat me for no reason whatever. The mad cow."

"Oh, poor dear," said the Reverend Mother, hugging the girl tightly against her own body. "Why did she mistreat you?"

No response. This gave Gabrielle a wry grin.

Marie and Gabrielle knew why she couldn't answer. They knew she could consider herself lucky that she escaped her mother's fury unscathed.

"You have nothing to fear anymore, poor adorable thing," the Mother Superior continued to baby her, kissing her forehead as if she were a mere child instead of the buxom, robust fifteen-year-old that she was.

"You can hide out here. We shall be very pleased to accommodate you, won't we sisters?"

They all nodded in agreement, including Gabrielle and Marie.

"Well it's settled then. You get the guest room."

There was an uncomfortable pause. Nobody spoke.

"You don't speak very much, do you, my girl?" said the Mother Superior, breaking the silence.

"I have nothing to say," she replied, adding, "except for 'thank you.' Thank you for providing me with sanctuary."

"Well, is that not one of the functions of a nunnery? You will be safe and taken care of. Mark my words."

The Forbidden

"If it hadn't been for you, I ..."

The Mother Superior: "Oh, come now, we're nuns, it is in our nature to harbour souls in need ...Will you at least tell us your name?"

"It's Josephine."

"And where do you live--or *did* you live, I mean."

"Less than a league south of here. My family, we're peasants. The land provides for us. We live in seclusion, just my father, mother and I. I've never even been to a town, let alone a city. But it has not bothered me overmuch. You cannot long for what you hardly know exists, right?"

Gabrielle: "My sister here," she pointed to Marie, "and I have grown up in similar circumstances. The nuns took us in when we were only babes. They've raised us. We have not a clue who our parents are. Literally, not a clue."

Later in the day when Gabrielle and Marie were alone tending to the sheep, Marie couldn't help but note: "What a discrepancy between the way Reverend Mother treated this girl, as opposed to the way she treated the strange man who came for shelter those many months ago. Don't you think?"

Gabrielle pondered for a moment. "But it's not exactly the same circumstance. For one thing, he was deranged and delusional. For another thing, he came in the middle of the night like some thief, practically barging his way in. And he was a man! What are a pack of helpless nuns supposed to think? Reverend Mother took a dangerous risk that night. And, incidentally, I am sure you will recall how threatening the man looked."

"But he could not hurt a fly."

"That may be true, but who can tell when you have a disturbed mind on your hands?"

Marie: "Whatever you say. But I was still troubled by the double standard. Women complain about patriarchy, but a matriarchy like ours practices the same prejudices."

"I think you may be over-exaggerating. There was good reason why the man didn't get the same warm treatment. It is not all a matter of showing favor for one over another."

Marie: "Should we keep quiet about Josephine's ... you know, the whole incest incident?"

"Of course," said Gabrielle. "Say nothing about it. Who knows what kind of flagellation the nuns would submit her to."

"Please don't remind me," said Marie. "One can forgive, but one

The Forbidden

can never forget, as they say."

Gabrielle looked back at her guiltily.

Mid-morning the next day: Marie was planting seeds in the fields near the path that went in two directions, south and west, from the convent. A very coarse, stoutly built sort of man came along the path from the southern direction. From where Marie was, she saw him perfectly. It was Josephine's father! Marie recognized him right-away. He looked very tired, slouching and idling along slowly. When he saw Marie, he became more animated and came towards her.

"Keep away!" exclaimed Marie when he was but a few yards away. "Don't come near me."

"Please, Miss. I mean you no harm. I'm looking for my daughter. I thought perhaps you might know--"

"Your daughter you say?"

"Yes."

From where he stood, the convent was in clear view.

"Ah, it's been many years since I seen this sacred place. How glorious it still looks!"

Marie gave him a grim look, as if to say, "sacred? This place is a den of debauchery and violence. Glorious? More like ugly and old!" But she said nothing.

"I've searched for her everywhere. I've lost complete hope! Oh, how wretched life is without my dear girl, the most virtuous, prayerful, devout child any father can wish for."

"What's her name?" asked Marie, just to hear him say it so that she could laugh at his false assessment of her, his incestuous slut of a daughter.

"Josephine."

"Yes, as a matter of fact, she is staying with us at the convent," said Marie, grinning.

Finally, thought Marie, there would be no more pampering, no more adoring Josephine. She would have to go home!

"Who's this?" asked the Mother Superior as Marie obligingly led the man inside.

"This is Josephine's father. He's come to claim her ... to take her home." Marie said the last phrase with some relish.

The Forbidden

The Mother Superior looked displeased. "Are you really and truly her father? What is your name?"

"Gerard," he curtly replied, saying nothing more. He was just as reticent as his daughter.

"We've been keeping her here, away from her mother, whom she fears like the Devil. If it hadn't been for me, she's dead starved off to the side of the road path now as we speak."

"Is she well?" he gasped.

"Certainly. *Now* she is."

"I thank you all very much, and I thank Providence for bringing her here. I owe everything to you. But now I'd like to take her home with me. Where is she?"

"I'm sorry, sir. But I can't allow it. To put her at risk again ... to be beaten? Impossible. She would just run away again ... She told us all about how her mother thrashes her." The Mother Superior cleverly hid the real reason she didn't want to let Josephine go. The real reason was that she was infatuated with her, absolutely loved her. It was a twisted mixture of platonic and erotic love. Secretly, perhaps subconsciously, she wanted to be both mother and lover to Josephine.

"She told you that's the reason for her running away?"

The Mother Superior: "Why, yes. Is it not true?"

He didn't reply.

The Mother Superior: "So you can see why it is best that she stay here."

"But that's just it! She's dead! Her mother is dead! She died of apoplexy not long ago. "

"Really?" She paused. "Oh, you poor man," said the Reverend Mother in mock-sympathy.

He looked at her like the death of his wife was no big deal to him. "Now please, let me speak to my daughter. I need to speak to her in private."

"Right this way," said the Reverend Mother, taking him to the guest bedroom.

"Father!" Josephine leapt to her feet at her first sight of him.

They embraced, and would have kissed like lovers if the Reverend Mother had not been standing there.

"I will leave you two now," she said, hastily walking away to hide her silent tears. She knew she would soon be saying good-bye to her

The Forbidden

beloved Josephine--this angel of a beautiful body but perverted mind and soul.

When they were alone, Gerard muttered to her the truth: "I murdered her."

"Mother?"

"Yes, who else ... She's buried in the woods not far from the house. No one knows a thing. No one will."

"How did you do it?"

"I'd rather not say ..."

"Tell me!" she urged him.

"I chopped her head with an axe while she slept. My God, you can't begin to imagine the mess."

"Holy Christ!" whispered Josephine, at first in gloomy awe, then hugging him ecstatically and tonguing him deep in the mouth with a kiss of joy and relief.

"You can come home now," he said. "Nothing will ever stand in the way of our happiness anymore ... ever."

Josephine had grown to like the strange mix of reclusive and gregarious aspects of convent life. She knew she would miss all the friends she'd made among the nuns. Somewhat reluctantly, she broke the news to them all.

"But I'll surely come and visit from time to time," she promised.

The Mother Superior, who'd always treated the girl like her own daughter in her attempt to fulfill those motherly urges she so needed to express, couldn't stop talking about Josephine for days to come. Josephine this, Josephine that. It drove everybody a little frantic. Especially Marie.

A fortnight later, everyone in the convent was awakened just after eleven o'clock at night.

"Sisters! Sisters! Quick! Let me in! I bring Good News, except a different kind of good news this time, ha, ha!"

The Mother Superior, startled: "Oh Lord, it's ... it's ..."

"The madman again!" Marie almost cheered. She was glad. She'd always liked him. "Should I let him in?"

"Oh," grumbled the Mother Superior, "you may as well."

He rushed in as soon as the door was opened and stomped his way

The Forbidden

up the flight of stairs to the nuns' sleeping quarters. He lunged in through the doorway and gasping like never before, he said in his booming voice: "The war is over! It's all over!"

"And what war would that be?" asked the Mother Superior in her nightgown, hands folded, with placid expression on her face. She did not look amused.

"The Saxon invasion! It's been halted! Hundreds of Frenchmen lie dead, but thousands more of Saxony's sons! I've just returned from the carnage ... it's both awful and spectacular a sight to see. The enemy's defeat is so fresh that cannon smoke still mingles with the clouds!"

The Mother Superior chuckled. "Yes, well that's all very nice," she said. "Now I'm sure you will want to be on your way to celebrate such a monumental victory."

"Yes, you're right, but I've got to spread the news! I have a horse, you know."

"Splendid. Now please go ride off and spread the good news ... So long and Godspeed!"

"God be with you all," he replied, bowing to her before pretending to get upon a horse and ride away. He looked hilarious and ridiculous, riding the thin air with his legs drawn apart and his arms and hands extended, doing as though they were holding on to reins.

"Magnificent steed you have there!" hollered the Reverend Mother, bursting with laughter.

"Thank you, Abbess!" he took his hat off to her, full of pride at the thought that she was so impressed with his horse.

A new nun came to the convent. She was very young--only eighteen. She had previously been excommunicated for mysterious reasons, but she dared not reveal that fact. Her name was Chantel, and she had the most beautiful, light-orange hair, which came down over her shoulders in curls; eyes green with just a touch of gray; medium-sized and very perky breasts; she was tall, with dense thighs and hips; a firm, curvaceous bottom.

"I think I'm in love," said Gabrielle.

"Oh, you're always in love," replied her sister.

"In lust, yes ... but this time I'm in love. Love at first sight. You have seen that new sister, Chantel, haven't you?"

The Forbidden

"Yes, why, she has joined up with us just today."

"She'll be with us permanently."

"If this is just another one of your silly infatuations--"

Gabrielle: "No! This time I really mean it. It's true, I have felt strongly before, about certain women, but ... never like this. I want her so badly. So badly. It's the most excruciating feeling of longing. You cannot imagine it. It's so pleasurable and yet painful at the same time, because I don't have her yet."

"Yes, pleasurable yet painful, like something you know very well--flagellation."

"That wasn't amusing."

"Oh, I'm sorry," said Marie cheekily.

Gabrielle, urgently: "This is serious. I am in earnest. It is hard to rein in my emotions. You know how impulsive and sensual I am."

"And bold and reckless."

"Yes ... Now, how will I get her to notice me? To really notice me ... I know! I'll sit beside her at the dinner-table. I will start asking her about herself, and the conversation will liven up from there. I'm sure we will be like sisters by the end of the evening."

Marie looked at her with raised eyebrows. Like sisters?

After the long, strict and tedious daily routine, everyone was pleased to sit down for dinner at six-thirty in the evening. They were going to have plum dumplings.

Gabrielle put her scheme in effect as soon as she saw Chantel enter the dining-room.

"Come sit by me," she offered.

"No thank you," she replied, sitting beside Marie.

Gabrielle gave her sister that dumbfounded expression, as if to inquire, "why is she with you?"

Marie's body language and facial expression replied: "I have no idea."

By the middle of the meal, Gabrielle had forgotten all about Chantel, temporarily. Gabrielle was a real glutton; she had a real gourmande taste for food, almost as strong as her taste for lesbian sex. To Marie's great horror, Chantel started touching her under the table. Starting at the knee, she worked her way up the inner thigh. Marie looked around awkwardly. No one had noticed. They were all absorbed in their meals. Chantel stared at her the whole time, but Marie didn't dare make eye

The Forbidden

contact. She hoped it would all quickly end. It didn't. Finally, Marie became so embarrassed and fed up that she swatted Chantel's hand away.

Chantel took the hint and quickly started eating again.

On their way to bed, Marie was still distraught. "The sooner we leave this place, the better," she whispered to Gabrielle.

"Did something happen?" Gabrielle had noticed during dinner that Marie didn't look very comfortable.

Marie of course knew Gabrielle's feelings for Chantel, so she kept quiet about the incident.

The next morning, Chantel asked Gabrielle if she could have a private talk with her. The conversation went as follows:

Chantel: "I know you're Marie's sister, so I wanted to talk to you alone. The truth is, I like Marie. I really like her ... very much. I want you to talk to her, reveal to her my true feelings, and I want to know precisely what she feels. I feel I scared her today by being too forward. I apologize deeply. Will you tell her I really ... I would really like to know her better ... and to apologize to her for my audacity at the dinner table."

Gabrielle, shocked but concealing it well: "I, I, I shall let her know ..." Gabrielle was completely heartbroken. She didn't sleep the whole night. Jealousy seemed to eat her heart out.

The next day, Gabrielle just blurted it out casually, almost coldly: "Chantel has intimate feelings towards you ..."

"But I don't understand," said Marie. "We're twins. Why me and not you?"

"Oh, what I wouldn't give to know the answer to that. But, you know even twins aren't completely identical. Some are fat, some thin, some intelligent, some ignorant, some--"

"Yes, I understand."

In the days to come, Gabrielle treated Marie in a cold, somewhat unfriendly manner. She acted as though it was her fault that Chantel liked her instead.

Marie meanwhile continued to repulse the girl's advances. "Who taught you to behave this way!" Marie once rebuked her.

After her every attempt failed, Chantel simply gave up.

"Ah, at last," said Marie to herself with relief after some time had

The Forbidden

passed and she realized that the little ordeal was over.

Tragically, one morning soon afterwards, Chantel's body was found at the foot of the belfry. She was dead. She had lunged herself from the very top. There was a brief note. It said only:

My death is no accident, my friends. Marie will know why I chose it.

Yours,
Chantel

Chantel's unrequited love had caused her to commit suicide. Gabrielle was genuinely grief-stricken, but a part of her was secretly, revengefully, perversely pleased that Chantel had never won the love of her sister. Marie, on the other hand, secretly felt like it was her fault that Chantel had killed herself, and that she was to blame. When the nuns asked her what the note meant concerning her, she simply pretended not to know.

The Mother Superior confronted Marie privately. "What did Chantel mean by 'Marie will know why I chose it?'"

"Must I repeat myself over and over?"

"Yes! Until you tell me the truth. You are concealing something ... and I want to know what. Say, what are you hiding?"

"Just leave me alone."

"Do you want me to send you packing? I *can*, you know."

"Fine! To think that I've survived this long with you and your odious kind in this shit-hole."

"Oh, you've really done it this time!" spat the Mother Superior, feeling the full sting of the insult. "I want you out—*now*!"

Marie scampered to the bedroom, getting her things from the closet and drawers beside her bed. She then rushed to find Gabrielle, who was in the kitchen baking bread.

"I just quarreled with Reverend Mother ... she's thrown me out!" gasped Marie hysterically. "Hurry, let's leave!"

"Are you sure?"

The Forbidden

"We must! We must! ... If you'd rather stay, that's--"

"Don't be ridiculous," replied Gabrielle, trying hard to hide the fact that she would desperately miss the nuns if she were to leave the convent.

"But you really like it here," said Marie.

"I'd hate it here if *you* left," retorted Gabrielle. "I'll get my things as well ... Should I say good-bye to everyone? I have to, don't I?"

"No, don't! They'd never let you go!" exclaimed Marie.

Before they knew it, Gabrielle and Marie were on the road. No one saw them depart. They were saying good-bye to the only home they had ever know. It was not without a feeling of regret.

Several hours later the madman came back. This time, he wasn't riding a make-believe horse, though. It was one of those dim autumn days, with a lot of dead leaves swishing around in the breeze. The sun was nowhere to be seen. But no rain either. It was however very windy.

"Oh, here he comes again!" said the Mother Superior to herself, spotting him through the big bedroom window.

The man was waving his arms hysterically, yelling things out.

Most of the nuns were assembled in the chapel for prayer and took no heed.

The Mother Superior answered the door.

"And who are you this time?" she said irritatedly.

"You don't recognize me, abbess? It is I! Aye! You remember!"

"I wasn't sure for a moment," she replied, "I thought perhaps you'd changed identities for the hundredth time."

Not comprehending the sarcasm, he stared at her in bewilderment for a second before speaking in a wild and excited way: "You and the others will have to evacuate ... quickly!"

"Oh? And why is that," she said more than asked in the same callously calm tone she always took with him.

"Don't you know? There's a fire! A forest fire! The wind is spreading it eastward. It's a wild one, this one is. Hurry! Away! Before it is too late!" He shook her frantically.

"Listen, madman ... I mean, *sir*. We don't have time for this. Go bother somebody else with your tall tales. They were funny for the first few

The Forbidden

times, but enough is enough."

She slammed the door in his face, locking it. He hollered and banged on it for a few minutes, but to no avail. He finally stopped.

"Oh, thank God he's left, if only for awhile."

The Mother Superior watched him sprinting southward down the road path.

Two quiet hours passed before one of the nuns ran up to the Reverend Mother in her private study, gasping: "There's a black smoke on the horizon ... We can see orange flames. They surround us from the east and north. It seems to be encroaching this way!"

The Mother Superior gulped, covering her face with her hand. "The madman warned me! Oh, God ... I didn't listen, I did not heed. It's like *The Boy Who Cried Wolf*... He told me, yet I didn't pay any attention."

"Told you what? Here, we must hurry. The other sisters are quickly packing up a few of their precious belongings. We have no time to lose."

"Of course! Let's away from this place!"

Naturally, they took the southern path towards safety, and didn't stick around to watch the convent under threat of burning down.

"My Lord, what can we possibly have done to deserve this?" the Mother Superior despaired, beating her breast.

They were forty-eight nuns in all, including the Reverend Mother, and they followed the path for what seemed like ages until they came upon the only dwelling in sight. It was where Josephine and her father lived.

"Mother of God!" exclaimed one of the nuns. "Look!" she pointed to the front of the house. "It's Josephine ... engaged in the act of copulation!"

It was indeed Josephine, rolling around in the tall grass with her father, who was fucking her fast and fierce.

When the Mother Superior saw what was going on, she nearly fainted. "Saints above! What are you doing, my daughter!" she exclaimed. She raced up to where they lay. "And I took you for an innocent, virtuous girl! Ugh! Disgraceful!"

"But he ... he is not really my father!" lied Josephine.

The Reverend Mother wasn't listening: "You ... you ...! You can't fool me, crafty trollop! Fornicating with your own ... your own ...! Oh, I can't even say it! I'm so ashamed of you, I know not where to begin! What an abomination!"

The Forbidden

The Mother Superior had gotten herself so worked up, she looked to be on the verge of a heart attack. She looked like she was suffering from vertigo, and almost collapsed, placing her hand over her chest and gasping for air. "... Josephine, you've disappointed me greatly. I adored you so. I loved you like as though you were my own!"

"I think your love was of an altogether different kind," retorted Josephine.

"What are you insinuating!" the Reverend Mother looked at her, appalled. She began to feel very faint. "Oh, I must sit down ... and rest. I feel so weak and light-headed. It's all this walking ... I am not as young as I once was."

Father and daughter saw their chance for escape and they took it.

"Come along, Reverend Mother," the others insisted. "Leave them be. We must find safe shelter."

The Mother Superior looked at them, nodding submissively. Then suddenly she said in a frown: "Where's Gabrielle ... and where is Marie?"

The Forbidden

Part 2

The year was 1691. Gabrielle and Marie were now twenty-one years of age. The convent had burned to the ground, and so did Gerard and Josephine's hut. The flames took them by surprise and claimed the lives of both father and daughter. The nuns however managed to get to safety in time and were accommodated at another convent not far from Dieppe, where the sisters were a lot more conventional, chaste and holy, where there was no practice of lesbianism and flagellation and worship was very austere.

Marie started feeling a bit guilty for dragging her sister away from the nuns. "You weren't going to become a nun ... were you?"

"No, of course not," replied Gabrielle.

"But you do miss them, don't you?"

"Not nearly as much as you think. Really, it matters not. Besides, the nunnery burned down."

"Yes, what a strange coincidence ... right on the day we left. Gabrielle, where do we go from here?" said Marie with a questioning expression.

"Neither of us wants to be a nun. Where do we go? What do we do? That all depends on what you are looking for, what you seek," answered Gabrielle. "I, for one, want to marry rich, then leave the man with all his money." She laughed. "What about you?"

Marie thought about it for a moment: "I just want to find employment ... lead a modest working life. Like a plain and sensible human being."

Gabrielle: "You cannot mean that."

Marie: "I do."

"You cannot go far with such low ambitions, I tell you that much."

"Neither will you, with criminal schemes."

"Oh, it happens so often, people have probably stopped calling it

The Forbidden

criminal."

"Well, I don't want a castle, or a count with fortunes stashed away ... All I want is a good, honest man ... one who shall take care of me and I him, one who will love and cherish me. One who will make me happy. He doesn't even have to be handsome or young. Just kind. A simple country life would suit me nicely."

"Marie! With your looks, you can do much better! Find yourself a rich libertine and be his mistress ... then suck him dry to the last franc. Those scoundrels deserve no less."

"Is that what you're going to do? Just take advantage of men? Use them?" asked Marie, startled.

"Yes ... until they have no more money. Then they'll have no more use for me. I'll pass on to the next in line. And thus it will continue. I'll be as crafty as a devil, and as cautious as a ... as a ..."

"Thief in the night."

"Precisely."

"I wouldn't be able to live that way," confessed Marie. "My conscience is too keen. I'd probably die of remorse."

Gabrielle: "Oh, I know guilt. I understand guilt. But how can you feel guilty taking from a bunch of rogues who abuse and belittle women everyday? They think they're so clever, they think they're so powerful, the greatest thing since oven-baked bread!"

"You can't say that about *all* men."

"But you *can* say that about *all* libertines. They think they have all the power? They think they can dupe any woman and stuff her under their belt. Let's see about that, sister, let us see about that!"

"I'm just worried about you, that's all. Who knows where you could end up after tricking a few immensely wealthy or influential gentlemen--"

"Oh, don't be silly. Those sorts of men are out of my league, I wager. You have to have a name, you have to be a renowned demi-monde to snatch one of those prime steaks. Or am I mistaken? At least, I think that is how it usually goes. No, I think I shall have to aim my sights a little lower. The higher bourgeois or perhaps even lower aristocracy may be within my range, I wager."

"Where will you meet the men?"

"In Paris, of course. Oh, taverns, public places, such as theatres, the opera ... perhaps even church. Perhaps I shall make a name for myself

The Forbidden

as a courtesan."

"Gabrielle! You will never cease to shock and surprise me."

"I'm glad. I want the men to say the same, completely unsuspecting of my true motives."

"You are evil!" giggled Marie. "But what if you truly do fall in love with one of them? What then?"

Gabrielle paused. "I don't know... I'll cross that bridge when I get to it."

:Well, one thing's for certain, it will be a fast and risky life. I'll worry about you."

Gabrielle mused: "And here's another certainty ... we each have dramatically different plans for our lives in this world, we've each chosen dramatically different paths."

"Yes; and this calls for a toast," said Marie. "Here's to your future, as mistress to every scoundrel in Paris."

"And here's to yours, as a country lad's wench, ha, ha, ha!"

They both laughed and drank.

When they awoke after noon the next morning, Gabrielle and Marie were in much lower spirits. Yes, they knew it was time. It was time that they would have to part, each to seek her separate destiny. Their ambitions were radically different from one another, as were their personalities. There was nothing they could do about that. Who knows, perhaps fate would unite them again somehow, someday.

"It will be hard living without you," said Gabrielle, holding Marie's hand firmly. "You're my sister, the one I love most. The only one I care about. We've never been apart."

"Let us face it, my sister," said Marie, "we may look similar on the exterior, but within, we are like black is to white ... And yet, we completely understand and love each other. I shall miss you just as much, you can count on that."

They embraced emotionally.

Marie: "So you're off to Paris? Look out for yourself ... Oh, what do I have to worry about. You've the mind to take care of yourself, and your good looks can only count towards added benefits."

"I hope a future lover pays me a compliment as sweet as that one,"

The Forbidden

said Gabrielle with a smile.

"I hope both of us find what we're looking for. What a blessing if things turn out that way."

So, you're going to try Orleans? To find work."

"As a servant-maid, yes."

"Oh, tell me you'll reconsider." Gabrielle shook her frantically in a semi-jovial kind of way, laughing but pleading at the same time.

"I'm sorry, Gabrielle. It's a difficult decision, but it's one I can at least live with ... I know I would hardly be able to live as a courtesan or something of that sort ..."

"Not another word," said Gabrielle, patting the back of her sister's hand, "I understand perfectly. And I respect your decision. I wish I were capable to making it. But, alas, the promise of wealth, and perhaps repute, or even disrepute, tempts me muchly. I want the high life. I feel I was always destined to become an aristocrat, or at least a rich criminal. I have always sensed as though I were destined for the high life; does that not strike you as strange coming from one raised by nuns?"

From a tiny sack of coins which she had pick-pocketed, Gabrielle gave Marie half of the money and immediately took a coach to Paris. She certainly wasn't one to waste time, especially with a disposition as determined as hers was.

The ride to the capital was a smooth but tiresome one. Three other people shared the coach with her--a friar, a rake, and a prostitute. The friar was a pot-bellied man, fond of drunkenness. He had a full beard, flabby, contorted lips, and two small tufts above each ear was all he had for hair. The rake beside him was dressed superbly well, as if he were off to some highly elegant engagement. Golden, looped locks of hair came down to his neck, and when he smiled, his thin rouged lips made a wide V. His head was rather small, but every feature, from his dark-blue eyes to his glistening white teeth, was flawless, even the fashionably powdered skin of his face. His build was rather light and lean but well-muscled. The prostitute across from him, sitting beside the friar, was an old and weary one, no newcomer to the sex trade. She was thirty-six going on fifty-six by the look of her. The gray hairs were slowly sneaking up on her, the skin on her face clearly aged and worn, which no amount of make-up could mask. Furthermore, she'd gone fat, like so many whores well past their prime. But she had fabulously large, gargantuan tits trailing down to her belly, and those alone on occasion stole her customers away from those fresh, young,

The Forbidden

pretty, small-breasted tarts she worked with.

"So you're off to Paris as well, my dear?" asked the friar with inquisitive eyes.

"Y-yes, I am," Gabrielle replied nervously, not expecting to be spoken to after such a long silence in the coach.

"And you are alone?"

"Afraid so."

The friar frowned. "Pray, forgive me for prying, and please do not think me one to exaggerate, but I hope I will be forgiven for saying that Paris is no place for a young lady ... most especially a handsome one like yourself, unchaperoned ... I would not be surprised if you wound up in a brothel, Mademoiselle. That's how things are there. The streets stink like refuse, but the stink of moral degeneracy behind closed doors in that city is twice as bad."

Gabrielle looked at him silently, but intently, with a pouty expression.

"I'm sorry," he apologized, "I didn't mean to ..."

Gabrielle: "Oh, that's quite alright, really ... I knew all of this before ... well, I suspected it ..."

"Don't listen to him," said the prostitute. "The man probably thinks hanging one's knickers out to dry is moral degeneracy, ha, ha, ha!"

"Yes," agreed the rake. "This so-called man of the cloth talks of moral degeneracy, how evil it is, and then he gets excited reading about Lot seduced by his two daughters in the Bible, ha, ha, ha!"

The friar, angrily: "See, my lady! We have proof positive of what I say! These two typical Parisians with us here! ... just a sample of the immorality you will be facing as soon as you step off of this contraption. But I will pray for you, little one, I will pray that--"

"Pray that she loses her virginity to a gentleman rather than a tramp, ha, ha, ha!" laughed the rake.

"Pay them no heed, my child. They can't help it. That city is the modern-day Babylon. Not one vice is lacking. And whom-so-ever enters, cannot help but be affected and afflicted by the transgressions therein."

"If you will pardon my saying so," said Gabrielle, "but I don't see how a modern city like Paris can exist if all such things happen there ... how is it that the government doesn't--"

"The government? Ha!" said the friar. "The government doesn't know a thing, or rather, it does, but pretends not to, turning a blind eye.

The Forbidden

These things don't happen so much on the surface as under it, my dear. You'll know what I mean soon enough. Then you shall do one of three things: either join in, turn a blind eye to it yourself, or leave."

Gabrielle didn't dare tell the friar of her intent to become some mighty man's mistress, and to swindle or marry some dissolute roue.

"Why *are* you going to Paris?" asked the whore.

Gabrielle didn't reply. She was caught speechless.

"Perhaps you're visiting someone?" the friar helped her out.

"Yes ... that's it."

"Oh, that's nice." He smiled. "Who is it you are visiting?"

Again, Gabrielle couldn't think of anything to say. The whore sensed victory, and took full advantage: "Ha, ha! You're off to make your fortune! You're off to latch yourself onto some well-to-do bugger and suck him dry. A money vampire. That's what you are! And you're surely not the first I've seen!"

Gabrielle didn't realize that she could have defended herself by denying the charge. After all, the whore had no proof what-so-ever of her allegation and it could just as easily have been denied. However, Gabrielle's silence gave her away.

The friar gave her a disagreeable glance and then refused any more communication when first he had been only too happy to talk to her. Even the whore and rake now gazed upon her with scorn: "Look at the bitch, pretending to be something she ain't ...Well, we have removed the mask."

Once in Paris, Gabrielle was only too pleased to part with her traveling companions. All she had with her was a small bag of things. Clothing mostly. But as soon as she started walking down the boulevard, searching for inexpensive shelter, a small urchin boy no more than eleven or twelve years of age ran by grabbing onto her bag and tugging. He yanked so hard that she lost her grip, and in stunned shock, before she had fully grasped what happened, he had disappeared into the crowded streets behind a maze of city-folk.

"Stop him! Thief!" she yelled.

But no one came to her aid. Absolutely no one. She couldn't believe it. She thanked her lucky stars that she'd put the money she had in her shoe. She took off her shoe and squeezed the money in a tight fist. Without it, she knew she would have been a goner. Gabrielle looked around her, the hem of her skirts dirtied by mud, but she was still nicely

The Forbidden

dressed. Just a few buildings ahead, there was a tavern. Her eyes lit up. A tavern--that was a good place to start with her scheme. There were bound to be many men, all kinds. It was getting late, and she knew the place would be packed.

She proceeded into the establishment with caution. It was very spacious, dim-lit, and the atmosphere was merry and frolicsome. Of course there were many loose women with painted faces and gaudy attire, and the room had its fair share of womanizing, well-dressed gentlemen. As soon as Gabrielle took her seat, a gentleman approached her.

"May I buy you a brandy?"

She could scarcely see him in the dark. "Yes, please."

He sat down by the flickering candle-light. She saw his face for the first time. Her heart skipped a beat. It was the rake she's met in the coach!

She got up quickly to leave, but he grabbed her wrist. "No, don't go."

"I would prefer to ... I, I thought you were someone else."

"Nonsense. Don't be such a child. Sit down, I only want to talk to you."

"I have nothing to say to you," she said.

"But I have something to say to you," he retorted.

Gabrielle didn't even dare look upon his face again.

"Let's stop playing games, alright? You have something I want, I have something you want. Let's quit the nonsense and get down to business."

"What are you saying?"

"I'm saying I want you ... to be my mistress."

"Out of the question!" hissed Gabrielle, regretting her remark the moment after she had made it, realizing that that had been her goal after all. But in a way she just couldn't bear the thought of being *his* mistress, even if he was good-looking. She'd never had much of a taste for men anyway. She would far rather have preferred being a moneyed matron's or young countess' mistress than his. But she knew she had no choice for the time being. She needed a conquest, quick. It was a question of survival.

"Alright," she said. "I accept ... But wait!" she added, realizing that maybe she'd agreed too hastily "What do I get out of the deal? I tell you one thing, I don't come cheap."

"Certainly not," he replied. "How does ten francs a week sound?"

The Forbidden

"That's all?" complained Gabrielle. "Surely you jest."

"Is that a 'no'?"

She changed her tune. "Alright, I accept, you stingy sod. But you won't keep me long at that rate."

"That's fine, I don't intend to." He laughed.

That last remark really cut her to the bone. She was very annoyed but kept it all in. She would show him! She would get the last laugh!

They started drinking. Brandy wine. The rake didn't notice that while he gulped, Gabrielle sipped. He got inebriated as fast as any homeless drunkard off the street corner. He was all smiles, hiccupping and muttering incoherent remarks, most of them foolish and obscene. After an hour or so, he said, "enough. I'll not want to be drunk tonight, no my dear," he snickered, "now that I have you ... Come, let's leave this den."

He tried to stand, but couldn't. "Ha, ha," he laughed; and the next thing Gabrielle knew, he was on the floor, having collapsed. Unconscious.

Quickly, Gabrielle robbed him blind, even pulling the rings right off of his fingers. Few people seemed to notice, and those that did, didn't care. Many of them were guilty of worse crimes.

She found lodgings at a shabby inn. The rent was very reasonable, but accommodations were untidy and filthy; even the bedsheets bore stains and the foul odor of bad hygiene. The proprietress was a dwarfish hag with a rasping voice, tiny beady eyes, and an abnormally long chin which curved like that of an old witch; every part of her body seemed round--her head, her torso, even her chubby arms and legs. She was elderly and worn out and didn't take much pride in her inn; the place wasn't looked-after at all, it seemed--not since the death of her husband years earlier. It had once been a reputable, fashionable inn when first built by her husband almost three decades earlier. Since his death, however, his mean, lazy, stingy wife, who by the look of her didn't care about personal appearance let alone the appearance of the inn, took over. All she cared about was hounding her tenants and even scaring them to death into paying her the rent due when she suspected that they were experiencing financial difficulties.

"Inn-keeper, this room's a mess," said Gabrielle, as she paid for the first week's lodgings.

"Well see if you shan't soon get used to it, Miss High and Mighty. What'd you expect, a palace chamber in Varsailles?"

"Well no, but ... Oh, never mind. I'll tidy it up myself."

"Do what you like. But I'll expect your rent money on my desk the

The Forbidden

beginning of every Monday morn, got that straight?"

"Yes, yes."

The proprietress was about to close the door behind her when she was tempted to ask: "You're new to Paris, ain't you? I can tell it on ya. What can a village lass like you want in this God-forsaken hell-hole? I'd advise you get out soon. You won't last long. Not alone you won't. There'll be only one place for ya, and it ain't the prince's palace, I'll tell ya that, missy."

Gabrielle insolently pretended to ignore her, but when she saw that the woman still had not closed the door behind her, she rudely said: "Yes, thank you, I understand and appreciate your kind concern," and practically went over and kicked her out.

The proprietress took offense. "Well I never! ... And you'd better have the rent money for next week, or you're out on your arse!"

Marie had never felt more alone. She felt Gabrielle's absence like the presence of an itch that never goes away. In some ways she regretted not joining her.

"We should have stuck together," she whispered to herself, freezing to death, and with no place to go.

She had spent the entire day looking for employment. No experience, no references. No luck. No one wanted her. No one needed her. The emptiness and gloom she saw around her built up inside of her as well. She believed her days were numbered. She felt she would soon die. And the world wouldn't even notice. Even her corpse would be overlooked. She'd wind up a nobody in death as in life. All her days had been spent living isolated like a nun. The outside world was far different. How would she cope? How would she adjust herself to its ways? She lacked the determination and survival instinct of her sister. What would she do? Where would she end up? These questions circled around her mind so many times, she became dizzy with anxiety. The snow started falling very heavily. It was like a fog. One couldn't see. Her face was numb in a matter of minutes. Fatigue set in. A mesmerizing drowsiness. She wanted to stop and lay down. The temptation was incredible. Marie wobbled over into a narrow and vacant alley, falling down against the wall. Her head fell forward, limp; her legs stretched out; she let her muscles go loose and

The Forbidden

relax. Very quickly, she was almost asleep. Dreams seemed to intermingle with semi-consciousness as her body wanted to sleep, but a part of her said: "no, this might not be a good idea."

Suddenly, crackling footsteps in the snow came her way. She didn't hear. They came closer.

"Mommy, this lady is almost a snowman," a child said.

"Oh my! Let's help her up. She'll catch her death if she falls asleep in this weather," said the woman with the child.

"She will never wake up if we don't help her," the childish voice remarked.

The woman with the child was a big, sturdy figure, and she lifted Marie up, helping her to her feet.

"Stand up," she said. "You must try to stand on your feet and find some warm shelter."

Marie, half-comprehending, half-nodding, got to her feet, only to slide back down into a hunch.

When the woman tried to help her back up, Marie said: "No, leave me here." Her voice was so faint.

"Under no condition, my dear," replied the woman, practically carrying her down the street to a poorhouse.

"You haven't eaten anything," said the woman, "no wonder you have no energy."

"I have been on my feet all day," said Marie, still gradually waking up from her weariness.

"We'll get some nice, hot soup into you. That should do the trick."

The woman was a pauper, and the little, thin, sad-eyed girl with her was her daughter. They had dirty faces. They knew poverty. They knew it well.

"How long have you been ... like this?" asked the woman.

Marie glanced at her momentarily before sneezing. "You mean on the streets? ... Only since today."

"Is that so?"

"Yes. I've lived in a convent all my life. My sister and I left. But we parted ways--a dreadful decision. Now we are both on our own, alone."

Marie became very talkative, which wasn't in her nature, and it brought her back to herself, combined with the hot, nourishing soup she started slurping down. She told the mother and daughter the whole story of her life with the nuns, detailing many of her good and not-so-good

The Forbidden

experiences, and so on. She explained how she'd been orphaned since infancy, and how the desire to know her father and mother haunted her. The woman sympathized with Marie, often shaking her head as if to say that she understood.

"What's your name, by the way?" Marie asked.

"That's incredible. I know every single thing about you, and you don't even know *my* name!" the woman laughed. "I'm Evangeline. My daughter here is Christine."

"She's so lovely. They're always so adorable at that age. All children."

"Uhu, well, this one's blessed with her mother's fabulous looks," laughed Evangeline, jokingly.

Marie started asking her about herself, what she was doing in Paris without her husband, and where she lived.

"I don't have a husband," said Evangeline.

Marie didn't understand right away. "What do you mean?"

"Surely I need not spell it out." Then, lowering her voice: "The child's out of wedlock. Illegitimate."

"Oh, how difficult that must be!"

"You said it!"

"But you love her."

"More than my own self," replied the woman. "I'd sell my body if it meant saving hers."

"Have you?"

"I haven't been pushed quite to that point yet ... but I know there may come a time. The poorhouses are fuller and fuller every year, fewer people are able to fend for themselves ... even intelligent and able folk."

"Hunger and poverty is a horrible thing," Marie mused gloomily.

"But you live with it. You forget about complaining, and the greatest struggles become commonplace. Survival from day to day is the one and only predominating thing on your mind. Everything else is secondary. I, personally, have an added burden--my daughter here. I have to make sure she has all she needs. It scares me to death to think what would happen to her if I were to pass on."

"Perish the thought," uttered Marie, comforting her.

Then, something made her say: "God's looking over you, I know it."

"Is he? Do you feel he is?"

The Forbidden

"Yes."

Marie suddenly had an overpowering desire to know that God was there, and that he knew Man's sufferings. She wanted desperately to believe that he cared. Then out of nowhere, supernaturally, through a personal revelation that could only be termed mystical in nature, she was convinced that it was God who had saved her! It was God who sent Evangeline her way and to her rescue! She felt that God really does work in mysterious ways.

While Marie was given rest and shelter, Gabrielle was busy trying to snare men. She wore her finest dress, of course, and made quite an attempt to look upper-class and elegant.

"There she goes, Miss High-and-Mighty," said her inn-keeper landlady as she spied through the window on Gabrielle strutting her stuff. Her eyes went tight with malice as she saw Gabrielle stop an older gentleman on the street as if to ask directions. "The sly temptress! She's already got her eyes on his money-bag, I wouldn't wonder. My, she sure works fast."

Gabrielle and the gentleman talked for a very long time. Finally, they started coming towards the inn. The spying inn-keeper tried to make herself scarce. She didn't want them to notice her prying eye. But it was too late. Gabrielle marched over to her like a queen, proudly proclaiming: "Well, proprietress, I'm to be married. I leave here tonight. And good riddance!"

"You hussy! I saw how you operate! Shameless! A common street whore has more discretion!"

"Oh, quit pretending you believe in manners and morals. And don't judge me, woman. Don't forget, sloth is one of the Seven Deadly Sins. Get that in your skull, lazybones."

"Better a sloth than a slut! ... Harlot!" the woman shook her fist.

"Ha, ha! Well, if you will excuse me, I must be off to my new home, a grandiose mansion in the south of France, in a fashionable vicinity of Avignon. Adieu ... forever!"

"I wouldn't count on that!" spat the old woman with a wry smile.

"I would," retorted Gabrielle, leaving to join the elderly gentleman in his carriage.

The Forbidden

The man was the Comte de Vanier, a very tall and skinny man with bad teeth and a crooked nose. But he had gentle eyes, and still had most of his hair, even after sixty-seven years of life. When he spoke, his tone was always mellow and mild. He seemed to Gabrielle like the type of human being who gave often to charity and believed strongly in the supremacy and necessity of virtue over vice.

In the carriage, Gabrielle didn't know what to say to him, though she wanted to say things that she hoped would make him think very well of her. But he was already smitten with her anyway.

"Have you ever been married?" she finally ended up asking.

"No ... never. Never in all my life. This would be a first for me."

"And for myself as well."

"I should hope so," he chuckled, but the joke eluded Gabrielle. "You are so beautiful. I know we shall lead a wonderful life together. I know you want me for the money and life of leisure and luxury, and I do not condemn you for it. In return, you will make me very happy."

Suddenly, Gabrielle started troubling herself with doubts. What if this man wasn't what he claimed to be? What if he wasn't what he appeared to be? What if it was all an act? What if he wasn't wealthy and prosperous? What if he didn't own a grand chateau up on a hill? What if he never intended to marry her? What if he only intended to use her? What if he was a violent and dissolute brute? It was a risk she knew she would have to take. It was too late to turn back to her old lodgings, especially after her last encounter with the inn-keeper.

In the days and weeks that followed after their wedding, Gabrielle was indeed pleased and relieved to discover that the man was very rich and very kind. She was surprised, however, to see more and more that this man wasn't at all like what she had led herself to believe her 'conquest' would be. This was no libertine; this was a deeply moral and spiritually inclined individual, and she wished that he were a rogue because that way there would be no guilt over wronging him should the time come.

Every evening, the comte read his Descartres, or lectured her with one of his many religiously philosophical sermons, all of them written at his leisure (something he had much of). On occasion, she even enjoyed listening, and she was especially struck by one of them, a part of which went:

The Forbidden

The incredibly complex make-up and function of the body and mind--this alone!--is enough to convince one of God's existence ... Even the rational nature of the Universe is proof there is a Creator God, or in the very least, some form of unfathomable, highly sophisticated, supernatural Intelligence behind it all. How can there not be? My dear, science's greatest failure is that it has not and can not detect God. And science is proud-- whatever it cannot detect through the five senses, it ignores or denies the existence of. What science will never understand is that, although its laws can be applied to and effectively used to explain the physical world, its laws lack the tools to explain the supernatural world. So, since we live only in the physical realm, and since we know only what we can experience through the physical realm, things beyond this realm cannot be known, though we may presume to know them. Questions about the existence of God and life after death cannot be answered by scientific means, and thus cannot be proved or disproved. But, their existence must be presumed for--if nothing else--the sake of maintaining ethics and as a means of discouraging and warding off cynicism, debauchery, and crime. Without morality and a sense of right-and-wrong, there is no such thing as civilization because all there can be is the law of the jungle and barbarism, where behavior is controlled only by human instinct, not human conscience. Everything becomes permissible--the perfect breeding ground for violence, devastation, and every form of excess. The result of this anarchy is not peace or freedom as is sometimes argued, but the exact opposite of both those things--disorder and slavery.

Under his influence, Gabrielle couldn't help but become more like her new husband, whom she even became fond of; he was like the parental figure she had never had. In time, though, she became less and less satisfied with her sheltered, traditional role as his wife. She became bored with it. Furthermore, she missed the company of women. One night, while he slept, Gabrielle snuck into her husband's private study, taking out all of his savings from a chest. Quickly changing into some formal attire, she left without so much as a trace.

When the Comte de Vanier woke up at noon the next day (as was his custom), he found a folded piece of paper on his wife's side of the bed. He bolted when he noticed that she wasn't there. Snatching the letter into his hands, he read:

The Forbidden

I am so sorry, my beloved husband. Through absolutely no fault of your own, for you have been a most kind and faithful husband, I have decided that the single life is the only life for me. The shame I feel in doing this to you is unbearable even as I write this. You are such a good, decent man, you deserve much better than me. I have never known a more angelic human being than you, and it would break my heart eternally to think that you will never find it in yourself to forgive me for this unforgivable act.

Assuring you of my eternal love,
Good-bye,
Gabrielle.

After he read the last sentence, the comte wept tears of blood; he forgave her immediately.

Gabrielle was now very comfortable--twenty-thousand-seven-hundred francs comfortable. She knew that if she had shuffled around some more she would have found even more money in the mansion, but there was the looming fear of being discovered, and besides, she had a conscience and just couldn't think of sucking dry a man who had been so good and generous to her.

By daybreak, she was almost back in Paris.

"Stand and deliver!" was the charge Gabrielle suddenly heard loud and clear.

The coach stopped.

Gabrielle glanced out of the window. There were two men, highwaymen of course--one, the young rake she had herself robbed at the tavern after he passed out drunk! and the other a pus-faced, red-haired man dressed like a valet.

"Ah, so we meet again," said the rake, his grin tinged with malice.

Gabrielle said nothing.

"Out you come!" He dragged her out of the carriage not very

The Forbidden

gallantly and stood her beside the coachman.

"You thought you'd get away with it, eh? You bitch. What goes around comes around."

"I thought you were only playing games ..." she lied.

"Playing games? Playing games! It was you who plotted to deceive me, not the other way around ... and you did!"

"But I--"

"Silence! Did I say you could speak? By God, I should shoot you on the spot. And may God damn my soul, I will."

"Donatien!" said his companion.

"What?" replied the rake.

The other man brought out the small chest full of coins. Gabrielle had neglected to lock it back up.

"Ah, splendid find!" rejoiced the rake. "Put it in the bag. All of it."

They got back up on their horses and rode off into the distance with their newfound riches.

"Damn! Damn! Damn!" Gabrielle cursed. "I'm ruined!"

She thought of turning back, but realized it was too late. She couldn't go back to the comte. He would have read her farewell letter by now. She knew she wouldn't be able to face him ever again. She felt her betrayal was too fresh and didn't comprehend that he would have been only too glad to take her back and forget it happened altogether.

The coachman, who was in her husband's employment, was made to continue on the road to Paris as before. He had wanted to return to the mansion after what had just occurred, but Gabrielle sternly demanded that they keep on. She had no idea where she would go or what she would do as soon as she was back in the city. But she knew she'd have to think of something--fast. Suddenly penniless, she certainly no longer had to worry about thieves and bandits for the remainder of the journey.

Before the sun had even crept up over the horizon, Gabrielle was once again on the unpleasantly familiar, dirty, crowded streets of gay, old Paris. The odors, the sounds, the sights--it could only be Paris! It was an atmosphere, an identity all its own. She walked from place to place all day, by the end of it just about ready to sit down and beg for a meager sou when just hours earlier she had been twenty-thousand-seven-hundred francs rich! All those gold pieces stolen! Oh! She could kill that rake! Like a hypocrite, she cursed him to hell for his crime, not giving it one iota of thought that she had been guilty of the exact same thing, and more than once.

The Forbidden

Right when her despair was at its peak and she was ready to give up and just crawl into some dark corner and into oblivion, a woman came up to her. "Hey, I remember you!" she said.

Gabrielle vaguely recognized that voice. Wait a second! It was the voice of that whore she'd met in the coach on her first trip to Paris!--the coach she had shared with the friar, the rake, and her! Gabrielle looked up. Yes, it was that woman, the prostitute. She stood a few paces away.

"I knew it," the whore muttered to herself with glee. "I knew you would come to this end."

"What end is that!" spat Gabrielle.

"Donatien told me ... He had you followed. He sent me to you to look after you."

"Donatien? Who's ...?" Then she realized. She recognized the name. It was the name the valet had used to address the rake! The whore knew that he had robbed her!

"You know him well? That bastard? Are you friends?" Gabrielle's indignation grew.

"Sorry, but you deserved it after what you did to him. There is one cardinal rule among criminals: thieves don't steal from thieves. Or didn't you know that?"

Gabrielle kept quiet. Then: "You can get my money back from him, can't you?"

"Surely not! It would be easier to survive a beheading." She laughed.

Gabrielle hung her head low in gloom.

"Listen, lass, I'm here to give you a break. I know of a good, clean 'maison' just across the street from here. I'll persuade the bawd to take you on. You'll make ten francs a night easy. What do you say?"

Gabrielle was startled. Should she accept? Did she have a choice? She nodded, "yes."

"Alright, it's settled. Come with me and meet the other girls. You'll make a lot of friends there, I guarantee it."

From the outside, the brothel looked a little run-down and low-class, decrepit, but big, with three floors.

Gabrielle: "By the way, I don't even know your name."

"It's Alexandra," she answered, leading Gabrielle inside.

The inside was just as dim and seedy as the tavern Gabrielle had been in before. Certainly not clean and well-maintained like she had been

The Forbidden

led to believe it would be. The women outnumbered the men two to one; the women pranced about in dishabille, behaving in stereotypically flirty, playful, shameless ways.

"Where did you grow up?"

"In a convent, near Dieppe."

Gabrielle didn't have to wait long before meeting the bawd, a monstrously obese, rough, manly, foul-breathed brunette with a prominent wart on her oily chin.

"Who's this?"

"This is Gabrielle," said Alexandra. "She wants to join up with us."

"She does, does she?" The bawd seemed to study her with something like an old man's lasciviousness. She was like a satyr who knew every whoremaster's excess, though she was indisputably female, with pendulous tits as heavy as sandbags and half-deflated.

"Good to have you aboard," said the bawd with a smile, taking Gabrielle's hand and kissing it like a true gallant. "Ha, ha, ha!"

Alexandra started taking Gabrielle through a bit of a tour of the establishment, getting her acquainted with her new home and workplace. There were many rooms.

"Remember, Gabrielle, you have nothing to be ashamed of. The whore's profession is a noble trade, as hard and time-consuming as any other. And it *is* a job like any other; those who disagree are either ignorant, bigoted, or hateful to begin with. Such people one cannot reason with. Puritanism is a madness ... How experienced are you in ... sexual matters?" Alexandra asked, not expecting to get much of a reply at all. "I'm sorry, what am I asking? I mean, how could you possibly have any experience, after living your whole life among a pack of stuffy, old nuns, ha-ha."

"Well, I have never been with a man, that is sure and true, but ..."

"But?"

"I have made love to plenty of women."

"Capital! That will really come in handy here. So you have no reservations when it comes to Sapphic love?"

"No ... none. I daresay it's the only kind I like, it's the only kind I know."

"Well, I shall take you from room to room to give you a taste of the kinds of customers we get on a daily basis. You will get a feel for the sorts of things you shall be expected to do. Understand?"

The Forbidden

"Yes. But first, tell me, what will I get from all this?"

"Free lodgings, three square meals, and of course some money for clothing, amusement, that sort of thing. It's very reasonable. Trust me, I've been working here for three years now, and the bawd, Madame Tonneau, has always taken care of all my needs and kept me safe and treated me right as far as pay. If I were a street-whore, you can't imagine how beat-up I'd be by now, and cheated and ravished. I'd be a goner by now. But as soon as you work in a place like this, you know you're protected, and customers are easier to come by, and the men know they can't get away with nothin' vicious."

The first room Alexandra opened on the ground floor was occupied by two men. They were fucking a petite redhead from both front and rear simultaneously, while a second whore dildoed one of the men up the asshole. Gabrielle couldn't believe her eyes, and she gazed on in wonder. The second room: a young, barely-adult male finger-fucked a whore's small, wiggling ass as she sucked his crinkly, hairy, red ball of sacked testicles and tossed him off. The third room: a middle-aged man ran a large, light feather over a pair of nipples to erect their lust and over a mammoth pudenda which was getting wet. He playfully smeared the whore's secretions over her face and she inhaled and licked them joyfully. She smiled and smelled good, clean, sweet. He buried his face in her cunt and gave her hidden clitoris a sucking it would never forget. Inspired by such oro-genital intensity, she then milked his cock for all it was worth, gobbling up his spunk blasts as they hurled upwards like a small fountain all over her face. The fourth room: a man and his wife played voyeur to a woman lying on the bed masturbating and fully exposing her pink inner-lips protruded out over the brownish outer-lips. The wife strapped on a dildo and fucked the whore while pinching and pressing her glossy, smooth nipples. This really got the husband excited. He pushed his wife aside, and coming up from behind the whore, he snuggled his nose in her anus while tongue-savoring her cunt in a way that sent her convulsing wildly. Her clitoris doubled in size, becoming more visible, more rigid. The fifth room: a frail, imp-like man with a goat-beard spat hot, thick, salty sperm onto one whore's low-slung ball of pussy-pork. Her breasts were long and slender, with stiff nipples that faced away from each other. Still not done, he gave her a nervous nudge of his pale, feeble, half-erect penis, delicately piercing her flower with only the round head, wiggling his way inside of her and rocking back and forth in the hope of getting completely hard again. Sixth

The Forbidden

room: a man released a hot riverlet of piss at his whore's sensitized clit. Bull's eye! It made her cum after minimal frigging. She had the most elegant head of bouffant hair and was never short of requests by men asking her to let them ejaculate into it after fellatio. The seventh room: Gabrielle listened as a man within screamed, "If I don't get a fuck this minute, my tadger will shrivel up and turn into a cunt!" His exposed rod, with its blue, bulging veins, stood slightly bent, and four whores took turns deep-throating it. One of them had big, bouncy, udder-like breasts, and she wrapped them around it, smothering and squeezing their pillowy softness over his towering hardness. The eighth room: a young-looking whore, still in her teens, fresh from the country, fucked a man three times her age; back home she had had an affair with her grandfather, and had a strange proclivity for enjoying sex with older men (sometimes much older). The ninth room: a man was fucking the fattest whore in the brothel. He liked them big, and he didn't even care how big, as long as they had pretty faces. The tenth room: a man was fucking a whore from behind, shoving and rocking his cock in up to the balls. His cock was all of nine inches long, and while he fucked her, she recited verses from the Bible, especially passages filled with seething sexual condemnations. This kept them both in the mood. And in the eleventh room was a man who enjoyed fucking only criminal women and those with venereal diseases. He also had a preference for crippled women and those otherwise deformed, deranged or handicapped, physically or mentally. The twelfth room had an orgy. As for the other remaining rooms, there was everything from first-time cunnilinguists who feared cunt would taste bad (and were pleasantly surprised), to sadomasochistic initiations, sexual rituals of bondage, domination and humiliation, lesbian peep-shows for the amusement of both sexes, and bisexual romps of every stripe. Although Gabrielle didn't know, in one of the closed rooms even bestiality was enacted and a big German Shepherd dog was forced to fuck a willing whore to the accompaniment of the jeers, jokes and laughter of rowdy on-lookers who no doubt paid more than the average sum for such a rare treat. Once the dog found his groove, he was pumping in and out of her with such unrelenting speed and skill, the humiliated whore couldn't hide her enjoyment, and certainly wasn't chaste enough to fend off the climax that shot her to the stars!

"How do you like your new home?" Alexandra grinned.

Gabrielle paused. "... It seems like a very ... a very ... festive place."

The Forbidden

Alexandra laughed.

Marie had started living with Evangeline and Christine in their squalid, rundown one-room dwelling right in the thick of the slums. Still unable to find work, she had taken to begging. She was tempted to whore herself every time she saw how happy and well-off were those well-fed hussies she saw walk by her from time to time. But no. There was no way she would sink that low. Begging was as low as she would go. It was humiliating, but at least it wasn't immoral. It wasn't immoral to be in need. I would rather commit suicide than become a prostitute, she thought to herself, disliking those women with a resentment for what they had and she didn't, and for daring to do what she wouldn't. The poorhouse was so overcrowded and overused, one was truly lucky to get more than a single meal each day. Christine had grown ill due to malnourishment. She looked weak and bloodless. Evangeline, fortunately, had a job as a laundress. But the wages were laughable. Things were not looking good for either one of them. Finally, Marie had reached a low point. She knew she couldn't continue down her path much longer. She would need to take action-- drastic action. This realization made her restless. She didn't know what to do, where to begin.

A fortyish man, opulently dressed and very stately, came up to her and handed her some money one dark, cloudy afternoon. "I hope this can do you some good," he said in that refined, mild-mannered, sympathetic speech of his, squeezing her cold, dirty hand with his warm, clean one.

She thanked him politely.

"My, you're trembling," he observed. "Do you work? Have you employment?"

"No. No one hires."

He paused. "Well, I'm in need of a maid-servant. Do you think you could handle such a position? If so--"

"Yes, yes!" she exclaimed, her eyes instantly crammed with tears of hope. "I shall prove a most loyal and hard-working servant! You can count on that, oh yes!"

She started hugging him madly. He told her to stop, but she couldn't.

The Forbidden

"Please, people will see ... This is most undignified." His blushing embarrassment was, however, tinged with delight that she was so truly thankful.

"When can I begin?"

"Now, if you like."

Marie paused for a moment. "But wait. What about Evangeline ... and her daughter, Christine."

"Who?"

"A mother and daughter I've been living with."

"What about them?" he said.

"Could you ... I mean ... could you possibly find positions for them in your home as well? Please! The mother works at the most god-awful job and her little girl, poor thing, is deathly ill and half-starved. We adults can do without proper food ... children cannot."

"But if the child is ill, unfortunately she's no use to me," he said. But when she looked at him with those pitiful eyes, he had to give in. "Alright. I shall hire them as well--as scullery maids, on trial. That's all I can offer them, that is all I can promise. I will pay them as one, seeing as the other is only a child and probably of little use. Working in the kitchens, I assure you they'll both have enough to eat, and a fair wage one can live on."

Again, Marie flooded him with thanks.

"Very well, here is my address," he said, handing her a card. "Tell your friend that the three of you are hired. If you are still interested, come before noon. I will want to have a look at the woman and her child. I shall be glad to receive you, and you can start work immediately. Do not worry yourself about references, for I shall soon enough know if you and she are what I want. I have indeed been meaning to hire more servants for some time. You will be working alongside Julie, a chamber maid who has been in my employ for some time. Your friend and her daughter will join our cook Brigette in the scullery. Any questions before I go?"

"No, you have well explained everything. We will be glad to see you tomorrow."

Although there was a twenty year age different between them, Gabrielle and Alexandra were soon on sexually intimate terms. They flaunted their

The Forbidden

sexuality like the temple harlots of ancient Persia, making love wherever, whenever, and however they wanted. The other whores didn't mind. In fact, some of them liked to watch. But gradually, Gabrielle was growing tired of prostitution. It was certainly no fun fucking a bunch of sleazy men every day, and then having to hand over most of her earnings to the bawd. She had absolutely no interest in men to begin with, especially the types that frequented low-class brothels. One night in particular proved to be a turning point.

It had been a very slow day. The bawd was restless. She was taking out her frustration on her girls. Finally, a customer barged in through the door. He was a familiar face, a real nasty wretch who enjoyed all sorts of coprophiliac extravagances, including being shit upon by the whore of his choice. He paid upfront for an night's worth of revelry, and as soon as he spotted Gabriel, she was his.

"Hey, lass, come here."

Gabrielle obeyed. He led her into a room where Alexandra lay in bed, reclining in a voluptuous pose.

"You, there," he said to her. "I want you as well."

Alexandra opened her eyes. "Yes, sir!" she said in a rude tone.

He shoved Gabrielle to the floor; to Alexandra: "I want to see you suck her."

He sat down on a chair as Alexandra approached Gabrielle and proceeded to take her to the bed.

"No! On the floor! I want you on the floor ... like a dog, ha!"

Gabrielle leaned down on the ground, lifting up her skirts to give Alexandra access to the narrow, gaping slit. Alexandra applied her tongue to the fleshy hole.

"Come on! Put a bit more into it! I wanna see you lick it, I wanna see you like it!" he spat.

Suddenly, he pulled down his breeches and joined in, mouthing their bodies and slobbering all over them. He was as foul and disgusting as a grave-robber. His love-making was selfish, sloppy, clumsy, cold and rough.

Alexandra and Gabrielle endured everything without complaint as they were conditioned to do. But as soon as he described his desire to see them rub his feces all over each others' bodies, Gabrielle finally lost her cool. She couldn't take it anymore.

"Enough! I've had it!" She pushed him off of her. "Get off me,

The Forbidden

pig!"

Alexandra tried to stop her: "Gabrielle, we must do this," adding in a mutter, "Don't worry, it's almost over."

"No! This is the last straw!"

"What do you mean?"

Gabrielle's lips quivered, as if afraid to answer.

"Madame Tonneau!" the wretch exclaimed.

The bawd rushed into the room several moments later.

"This bitch refuses my advances!" he whined like a child used to getting his way, pointing furiously at Gabriel.

"Is this true?" asked the bawd.

"Yes."

"Why?"

"He's a filthy brute! His request is beyond perverse! I would rather die than fulfill it!"

"That's it, I've had it with you, get back in that room, girl, and give the man what he wants!" demanded the bawd. "Give him what he paid for. And beg he forgives your insulting behavior!"

"No! I refuse! What he desires is so abhorrent, it cannot be done! No, I say again, I refuse!"

"For Christ's sake, child, do as I say!"

"No!"

The bawd came up and struck her across the face for what she took for blatant and disrespectful disobedience. There was a loud sigh, as all the other on-looking whores couldn't believe their eyes.

"Strike me again; I still won't debase myself with that animal," Gabrielle said insolently, with contempt.

"You're sacked! Now get out of my sight!"

Huffing and puffing like a dragon, the bawd stomped away to her private chamber and slammed the door, cursing aloud even after the door was shut.

Alexandra quickly joined her in the room and tried pleading for Gabrielle, apologizing for her. It was no use. The bawd was a hard, stubborn woman. Her mind could not be changed.

"Are you leaving with me or not," said Gabrielle when Alexandra next appeared. "... Or is this where we say good-bye?"

"Of course I'm coming with you ..."

The Forbidden

So, Gabrielle and Alexandra were on their way to something new. Prostitution was now a thing of the past. A certain relief came from their contemplation of this fact. But the relief was mingled with uncertainty. How would they proceed? After all, they would need to make ends meet.

Gabrielle started dressing in men's clothing and even cut her hair short. Her idol became the great conqueress Joan of Arc. She felt naturally drawn to her own inner masculinity far more than to her femininity. Alexandra, however, was all woman, from the way she felt to the way she looked and dressed.

"We will stay with my mother," said Alexandra. "She's a feisty old woman. In her sixties and still lives alone, runs her farm alone, makes her own food, everything. I doubt she has ever been ill in her life."

"Sure we won't be a bother?"

"To the contrary, she'll be only too pleased to accommodate us."

They arrived at the nice, snug little cottage on the outskirts of Rouen. It certainly looked roomy and comfortable enough for three.

"Mother, it's Alexandra!" she cried out, knocking on the wooden door.

The door opened. A long-nosed, long-haired woman with a toothless smile appeared. She was dressed warm in cotton clothing, with a black shawl over her head. One could smell the burning wood of the fireplace from within. And the heat generated within seemed to draw one inside.

The old woman swung her arms around Alexandra immediately, crying. "Oh, child, it's been so long since I've seen you! You can't begin to understand a mother's love for her firstborn!"

"Oh, I've been working these last few years."

"Working? Where?"

Alexandra didn't answer.

"Well hurry up and get inside," said her mother.

"You're letting the cold in."

The yellow flames of the fireplace were the only light. The wood crackled, and every few seconds, a spark flew harmlessly. The rest of the room was dark, spooky, with flickering shadows. The old woman got them to sit down in rocking-chairs and smothered them in thick, cozy blankets.

The Forbidden

"You women are freezing!" she remarked.

"I hate this part of France in the cold months," said Alexandra, hugging herself tightly. "Mother, we will need to stay with you. At least for the time being."

"Of course you may. There are three beds. Yours, mine, and your father's, who of course is no longer with us. Your friend here can sleep in your father's old bed ...What's your name, dear?"

"Gabrielle."

"Last name?"

"I don't know ... I was an orphan."

"Oh, you poor dear."

Things were going well for Gabrielle and Alexandra. They managed to resume their former intimacy behind the old woman's back, though they had to be careful. They liked their new atmosphere--homey, comfortable, and semi-reclusive.

One day, however, everything changed. It had been a nice spring day. Alexandra was taking a stroll alone in town, browsing through the shops. She sat down at a bench after a long time on her feet. A man she didn't know soon took a seat beside her. He watched her from the corner of his eye. Alexandra pretended not to notice him. The man was about her age, with wavy brown hair and a handsome complexion.

"What wonderful weather this is," he said aloud, grinning rakishly.

Alexandra nodded, "Yes it is."

The man turned to face her, and cutting right to the chase, he said: "How do you do? My name's Arthur Gagnon ... And you are ...?"

"Alexandra La Roche."

"You're very beautiful, Alexandra."

There was a pause.

"I'm sorry, I'm afraid I don't know how to put this discretely. Come closer, I'll whisper it ..." He put his hand on hers and came closer to her as if to share some awful secret that she must never reveal. Just as he did this, Alexandra's mother was in the vicinity. Her eyes caught them holding hands. And she couldn't believe when--oh, yes!--he kissed her full on the lips without warning or reason! Just like that! In public! How disgraceful! And it wasn't just any kiss, no! This kiss possessed such ferocity, such

The Forbidden

indelicacy, that those who saw it had to first marvel at it before being overtaken by their moralistic sensibilities. Now the whole town would think that her daughter was a loose woman! In the middle of the rather long and sensuous kiss, before it was even over, her mother wanted to walk right up to her and vent her rage, but she realized that that would only have caused an even bigger scene and made things that much worse.

The old woman hurried home. "Oh, she'll get it from me! A nigh middle-aged woman like that, behaving like an adolescent slut!"

Her mother was the first to get home, and she told Gabrielle everything she'd espied. She could think or talk of nothing else. She was a very prim woman, holding all her life to a set of very strict and traditional middle-class values and mores. Gabrielle was just as outraged--but for a far different reason. She's been unfaithful to me! thought Gabrielle. What deceit! She's been unfaithful me all along! And with a man!

As soon as Alexandra rushed in through the doorway, her cheek was met by the slap of her mother's hand.

"My God, what was that for!"

"Don't think I didn't see you kissing that stranger in public just now! ... He is a rogue well-known with a very bad reputation! ... And right in the middle of the park grounds! Half the town saw! Imagine the gossip! How will I ever face the busybodies ever again! I shall never live this down!"

"But I ..."

"How long have you known him?"

"But that's just it; I don't know him!"

Her mother thought she was going to faint. "My Lord, she doesn't even know him ... and behaves like some wanton woman."

"His kiss caught me completely off-guard! I didn't want to!"

Gabrielle had already been cheating on Alexandra with a girl her own age, and yet she was angrier than ever to hear what Alexandra had supposedly done. "How could you?" Gabrielle spat self-righteously.

"Oh don't give me that!" shouted Alexandra. "You hypocrite! Don't think I don't know that you sneak about with other ... girls! But do I ever say anything? No! So don't give me that! I've tolerated you because I knew that the others were just amusements, erotic playthings, and that I'm the one you really love."

Her mother almost dropped dead after what she just heard. The secret was out! Her daughter was Gabrielle's lover! And Gabrielle was

The Forbidden

promiscuously sleeping around with other local girls! A big verbal fight ensued involving all three women. It lasted for hours. The bitter result was that both Gabrielle and Alexandra left the cottage and went in opposite directions. The newly born animosity between them broke them apart.

Meanwhile, Marie, Evangeline and her daughter had gone to see the gentleman at his giant, lavish mansion estate. His name, they soon learned, was Jacques Savant; he was a widower who lost his wife many years earlier when she died in childbirth. Though poor at the time, he had a brilliant mind and quickly turned to national politics, first as an exceptional public speaker, earning a name for himself, and then gradually and eventually accumulating a fortune as one of King Louis XIV's key political advisors and diplomats, a position he had acquired by his excellent abilities and much perseverance, not to mention a very timely stroke of luck here and there.

Jacques was warm and cordial, and received them with much enthusiasm as soon as the footman led them to the parlor-room, where they were received in the most extravagant and elaborate setting.

They began working that very day, and Evangeline appeared just as grateful as Marie for the opportunity Jacques had given them to make a decent living. Julie the chamber maid showed Marie what her duties were. The maid was relieved that finally someone would be sharing the work load with her. Marie was a fast learner and proved to be an efficient worker. She was eager to prove to her employer that he'd made no mistake in hiring her.

As time went on, Marie felt romantically drawn to Jacques. There was a maturity, an inner beauty to the man that she couldn't resist. Moreover, for a man in the latter half of his life, he was still dashing, with his adorable smile, his sparkling blue eyes and blonde hair, all of which suggested that he had been a very handsome man in his youth. His conduct towards her seemed to display the same affectionate feelings. He would pay her compliments, flirt innocently, and generally treated her with greater regard than was common between master and servant, with far more courtesy than most masters showed their servants. One evening, he called her to his private bedchamber.

"The master would like a word with you," said Julie.

The Forbidden

Gabrielle had no idea what he could want from her, but she went to him immediately. She knocked.

"Enter!"

Gabrielle tiptoed into the room. "You called for me, sir?"

"Yes, yes I did," he replied, getting up from his desk. "Something's been on my mind for quite some time and I ... I couldn't think of a way to approach you with it ... until now."

Gabrielle nodded, but said nothing.

"I called you here tonight because I ..." but then he stopped. Words failed him. He didn't know how to proceed. "My dear, you must forgive me... although I can make a rousing political speech, I'm not very good with ... intimate speech. Never have been. Even when I proposed to my dead wife, even then I was at a loss," he chuckled.

"I understand, sir. Please just tell me what you mean simply and directly."

Suddenly, Jacques sprung from his seat: "Marie! My heart is on fire!" He grabbed her forearms, drawing her to him. "Is it not apparent? I love you. Do you suppose for a moment that I hired you out of pity for your plight? If only I could say with honesty that that were so. But no--the true reason is that I felt very fond of you, then and there, because I knew that behind all those rags, I knew that hidden behind all that filth and squalor, that there was a gem! Yes, a true gem! I had to have you! Oh God I adore you! If you do not feel the same, I don't know what I shall do!"

Marie embraced him lovingly. "I'm very fond of you too, sir."

"Oh my Lord, you can't possibly imagine what bliss I feel at this moment! I'm walking on clouds!"

They started kissing fervently. Hot, starving kisses that dug themselves into each others' lips. Jacques swooped Marie off of her feet and carried her across the room over to his bed. He buried his face in her full, ripe bosom, whose flesh was so smooth, wholesome and fresh, yet soft as a dove. As it was quite late, Marie was in her nightgown. His mind was full of remembrances of his late wife-to-be on the night of their elopement so many years ago. He started ravaging through every bit of Marie's nakedness with his groaning, sighing mouth and caressing hands.

"But wait," she said. "I must be sure that you love me. I must know--"

"Marie, oh God! I love you more than anything! Truly! I'll marry you!" He was sincere.

The Forbidden

"Oh Jacques!" she cried out, embracing him passionately, as if terrified to let go. She no longer had to refer to him as "master."

She gave him her virginity as he drove in his manhood right up to the hilt, overwhelming her with powerful, lust-tingling thrusts that sent her soaring. She bit his neck, gingerly digging her nails into his back and scratching gently, as his deceased wife had done those many years ago. This mingling of mild pain and acute pleasure excited Jacques. The lovemaking was exquisite, so sensual, and yet so ethereal at the same time. It was real deep love, deliciously spiced up by the hunger of the sex organs. But all throughout, Jacques couldn't get away from thoughts of his Clotilde, and how Marie reminded him of her so much.

However, he didn't want it to be that he was obsessed with this idea or that he loved her only because she was a sort-of copy of Clotilde. After the sex, Marie and Jacques snuggled up together under the sheets, cuddling. They got to talking. Jacques started giving her an account of his life's story, about his dead wife, everything, even the elopement, and the extreme loneliness and despair he experienced after her unexpected death in childbirth.

"My wife's been dead over twenty years now. I haven't known a women in all that time ... until now."

"You have not made love to a woman in over twenty years?"

"Twenty-one, to be exact. When she died, something died in me as well--the capacity for love. I was afraid to love again. It's something you have revived in me." Then, he couldn't help but confess: "You're so much like her, when we made love I could almost swear it was as though you were her. You have her look, in body; you think and behave as she does; you even make love like her! It's most extraordinary."

"But I'm not her. Please, you must get beyond that. I'm Marie. Marie! Not Clotilde!"

"Oh Lord, I knew I should have kept my mouth shut ... I should have known my words could not help but be misinterpreted. It is true, I loved her then, more than my life ... But it's *you* I love now ... Am I making sense?"

"Yes, I'm sorry. I didn't mean to make a fuss."

Thus began Marie's affair with Jacques, and soon an engagement was announced.

The Forbidden

Forced to take to the shabby streets once again, in a few short hours Gabrielle regretted the drastic split that had separated her from Alexandra. But she wasn't about to go back on hands and knees begging for a reconciliation. She had too much pride for that. She knew she had looks and brains, both of which counted for much, and all she needed to do, she thought, was to catch another prize fish in the sea, figuratively speaking. There were always plenty of wealthy, eligible (not to mention gullible) men just waiting for an opportunity to take the bait. But she was still dressed in men's clothing, and her hair was still short. She looked every bit like a man, with her slightly plump form exhibiting no sign of feminine frailty. Only the features of her face betrayed her slightly, which were like those of an effeminate but charming-looking boy; but they certainly weren't enough to make people swear she was a woman.

One day, while on her way to buy a new dress and start her game of seduction all over again, Gabrielle suddenly froze when she saw the most gorgeous woman her eyes had ever beheld. She recognized her immediately as Lexie de Mauriac, the most sought-after debutante in fashionable Paris. She was the daughter of a prominent, high-ranking nobleman and was being courted by at least a half-dozen very worthy suitors, but had still not made up her mind. She had the title of Marquise, and this young Marquise was a true specimen of beauty, with her hair done up so elegantly; eyes so alive and flirtatious and blue-blooded; nose and lips as pretty and delicate as a flower; hair of the richest and shiniest black; her slender and very shapely figure, curving at just the right places; her petite but well-rounded breasts that bubbled up were so tightly enhanced underneath the black corset. She was stunning!

Gabrielle's heart burned with the emptiness of yearning when she saw her disappear into the opera-house in the company of a strikingly handsome gentleman. Then it came to her--why seduce men when she could just as well seduce women! She knew she'd enjoy that a hell of a lot more!

Gabrielle crossed the street to the entrance of the opera-house, but as soon as she did, she realized that she couldn't afford a seat, so she decided to wait outside. She waited for over two hours. By the time the opera was over, it was dark out, and as soon as Mademoiselle de Mauriac

The Forbidden

and her gentleman got into their carriage, Gabrielle furtively jumped onto the back of it and held on for dear life. She had an idea--a wild, eccentric and risky scheme that she planned to execute.

When the carriage entered through the tall gates of the Marquise's father's estate, Gabrielle jumped off and into the bushes to hide. She watched as the Marquise and the gentleman said their good-byes for the evening. Then the Mademoiselle de Mauriac went towards the entrance of the mansion estate where she was received by her father, mother and servants.

"Did you have a good time?" said her father. "This one's the man for you. Better than all the rest."

Her mother nodded in agreement. "Now let's get you inside."

"What was the opera?" her father's loud voice could be heard in the distance.

"I don't know," replied his eighteen-year-old daughter, "a faery story ... something German."

"Oh dreadful! Who can stand such wild, barbaric racket?" he replied. "German symphonies, now German operas--what's next!"

Gabrielle waited until everyone was inside before she snuck out of the shadows. When she came closer to the mansion estate and her eyes really took it in, its size and grandeur took her breath away. It was incredible! Like a castle fortress! At least six or seven stories high. Windows everywhere. The architecture was classic baroque, very detailed and symmetrical, very artistic, as well as highly aesthetic. The foundation alone covered almost half an acre. Gabrielle tried hard to figure out which was Lexie's bedroom. Hiding behind some well-manicured shrubbery, she watched the windows. A servant appeared in the candlelight here and there. Even her father. But still, not her! Then, suddenly, through an upper window to the far right on the second floor, because the white, thin curtain was drawn, she could espy the unmistakable silhouette of the beautiful Marquise. She appeared to be changing for bed. Or rather, one of her maid-servants was changing her. Gabrielle became excited when she saw this. She watched intently. The lights in the house soon went out in most, then eventually in all, of the rooms.

"But how will I get up to her room," Gabrielle mused to herself. She wasn't afraid to be insanely daring, to take people by surprise.

She rushed for the front doors. They were of course locked. "Pshaw!"

The Forbidden

Then she got another one of her wild ideas. There was a thick, tall oak tree standing almost right against the house from the right corner. She started climbing. It was quite an easy climb for Gabrielle, as there was a branch to step on wherever one was needed. She got to the now-dark window of Lexie's bedroom. Anxiety didn't bother her at all; in fact, she felt like her old, bold self more than ever, as she realized that nothing but mere glass separated her from her obsession. The window wasn't locked, and she managed to open it with little effort. Still of course dressed as a man in very ordinary clothing, she leaped into the room without a sound. The Marquise was fast asleep. She was as still as a corpse. But slumber only added to that already profound beauty of hers. Gabrielle came over to the side of her bed and bending down close to the sleeping girl's face, close enough to kiss her, she covered her mouth firmly, at which point Lexie jumped from her bed, wild-eyed.

"Sh! Shhh!" whispered Gabrielle. "I mean you no harm!"

Gabrielle looked convincingly like a man in men's clothing but her calming demeanor put the Marquise at ease. After the initial shock, the girl calmed down. "Who are you? What do you want?"

"I came to see you ... I came to see you because ... because you've stolen my heart," Gabrielle said frankly, with as few words as necessary. "What should I do about it?" Gabrielle then smiled sweetly.

The girl didn't know what to say. She was no longer afraid or anxious in any way, only confused.

"But who are you? You do not even know me. And I've never seen you in my life!"

"I'd like to know you, though. I would like to very much."

"How did you get in here?"

"I climbed the tree," chuckled Gabrielle.

The tension of the atmosphere suddenly eased considerably.

The Marquise smiled. "My name's Lexie de Mauriac. What's yours?"

"Gabrielle ... I mean, Guy," she lied.

"Guy what?"

"I don't have a last name."

"What do you mean?"

"I was orphaned at birth ..."

"Oh, how sad."

There was a pause.

The Forbidden

"Come out with me," said Gabrielle.
"Outside? ... at this hour?"
"Yes, come on."
"But I ... How?"
"I'm sure you can make it down the tree."
"I am sure I could not."
"If I stay here much longer, there's the danger of my getting caught."
"There's an even greater danger of that if I go roaming about with you in the middle of the night," said the Marquise with a chuckle.
"Who was that man you were with tonight?"
"Hey, how do you know about--"
"Who was he?" interrupted Gabrielle jealously.
"Nobody I'm interested in. I don't find any of those men interesting, but my father wants me married off ... and there it is. It's funny, though. He does not seem to care as much whom I marry, just as long as I do. And of course it must be a good match."
"You don't like men, do you? You're an admirer of women."
"No, not at all," she replied, to Gabrielle's chagrin. "I simply haven't found the right one ...What did you mean, an admirer of women?" asked the Marquise, somewhat perplexed.
"Never mind. I'm sure I don't know." Gabrielle momentarily hung her head low, as if embarrassed. "Lexie, when can I see you again? I want it to be in private ... in the daytime."
Lexie hesitated to speak.
"What is it? You know I'm harmless, don't you?"
"It's not that, Guy ..."
"I'd only like us to be friends," Gabrielle said desperately.
"I know ... and so would I, honestly. Nevertheless.... you're completely out of my social station. What if we got caught ..."
"Meet me at the edge of the woods near the gate tomorrow at noon. Sneak away, do whatever you can. We'll have ourselves a fun time together, I promise. Do say you'll come, oh do!"
And before Lexie had a chance to respond, Gabrielle was out the window in a flash, blowing her a kiss before she made her way back down and away.

The Forbidden

Ideal weather marked the beginning of the next day. Gabrielle had slept all night hidden in the bushes and trees of the estate grounds, out of sight. When she awoke, it was almost noon. She woke up somewhat sore.

Lexie was in the middle of her arithmetic lesson. She managed to elude her governess by pretending to go relieve herself. With no one in sight, she rushed down the hall, down the stairs, and into her room, from which she took a basket already filled with food and drink; she then scurried out the front doors.

Gabrielle saw her, signaled to her, and they met up.

"I brought a few things," said Lexie. "We can go into the woods. I know where there's a river. There's an open spot I know where the sun shines brightly. We can have our picnic there."

"Fantastic." Gabrielle was very pleased and relieved that Lexie actually showed up. She had feared that she wouldn't. It was a good sign.

"What's that in your other hand?" asked Gabrielle.

"Oh, it's a book of verse. The author isn't given."

"Why not?"

"It is quite ribald. The book has been suppressed, banned as pornography."

"Is it?"

"According to prevailing morality, yes."

"Where did you get it?"

"I bought it before copies were confiscated from bookstore shelves. My father doesn't know I have it."

"Recite something from it," said Gabrielle.

"I don't know if I should, it might corrupt you." She giggled.

"No, we men are incorruptible; it's you women who are the impressionable ones," she joked, "now read it. Read it aloud."

"I know not where to begin. Pick a page."

"Sixty."

"All right, here it goes:

Cometh the Spring on fleeting foot
To plant th' seeds of am'rous deeds,

The Forbidden

To tempt the winter-worn heart t'sing,
To ev'ry green and bright thing bring.

Gabrielle laughed. "That's pornography?"
"Hardly. But," said Lexie, "listen to this part of the poem. It's dedicated to the amorous goddess Cythera, by the way:

Copulation for the heaven-praised sake of population;
Couples, love-twined, as if round sensuous silks;
What life in tight-skinn'd cocks and lust-sodd'n cunts
For which ev'ry profligate zealously hunts
As a conqueror might war for a weak'ning nation.

Those genitals o' purple, pink, brown and red
All assemble to have savage hungers fed;
In this newborn season that's excuse for it all,
The fuck-shooting memb'rs rise exceedingly tall.

They laughed.
"Guy, do you suppose a woman could have written it?"
"No! That's impossible!" gasped Gabrielle.
"Have you heard of Aphra Behn?"
"No."
"Some of her work is very, how shall we call it, spicy stuff due to its strong sensual nature," Lexie explained. "And yet she's wildly popular. So are modern British writers of the same ilk, like John Wilmot, Earl of Rochester."

As a daughter of freethinking libertarian aristocracy, Lexie had been given a superlative education growing up. She was well-versed in all of the ancient classics and was up-to-date on the contemporary literary scene. Art was also one of her great loves. She could gaze for hours upon the paintings of Hans Baldung and Caravaggio.

When they got to the spot Lexie had mentioned they were headed for, Gabrielle was overwhelmed by its scenic quality. It was a beautiful, grassy clearing on elevated ground right beside a calm, flowing stream

The Forbidden

whose gray but lucid waters were cold and refreshing to the touch.

"The water's still cool from the thawing of winter," said Lexie after running her hand through it.

Lexie spread out a blanket and they both sat down. She pulled out the contents of her basket. There was bread, cheese, even some strawberry wine from her father's cellar. They began to eat and drink.

"Oh I'm famished," said Gabrielle, digging her teeth into the fresh, soft, white bread with its crunchy crust.

They gulped the wine without knowing any better.

"This has such a nice taste," said Gabrielle, licking her lips, the glass lingering in her grasp.

They were soon sporting half-intoxicated grins and giggles. Gabrielle started rolling on the ground stupidly, snickering. Lexie lay there leaning on her elbows, watching a frog as it sat pompously on its green pad like on some royal throne.

Suddenly, she was caught surprised by a kiss on the cheek from Gabrielle.

"What was that for?" She giggled.

"For that you are the most beautiful girl in the world," mumbled Gabrielle, with half-lidded eyes and rosy smiling cheeks.

Gabrielle went in for another kiss, and as she did so, she slipped and fell on top of Lexie, making the smaller girl lay flat on the ground.

"You know, if I were a man, I could ravish you presently if I wanted," Gabrielle joked with a goofy laugh.

Lexie rolled her eyes. "But you *are* a man."

Gabrielle was suddenly drenched in nervous sweat. The alcohol had weakened her defenses! She had forgotten she was supposed to be a man! "What I meant was, I still think of myself as a boy, ha, ha, not quite a man."

"Well, you do have a boyish face," said Lexie. "... Now get off me," she giggled.

"Not 'til you give me a kiss. Moreover, you must kiss *me*, and not the other way around."

This time taking her by surprise, Lexie landed the most explosive and energetic kiss that Gabrielle had ever experienced. She was left gasping deeply at the end of it, awe-struck. Gabrielle's chest was heaving so much that if the shape of her breasts hadn't been tied back and flattened by her to hide their appearance, Lexie may have noticed them and fled in

The Forbidden

horror, never to see her again. But Lexie couldn't notice them, she didn't know that her new lover was really a woman, and at that instant, she realized that she was falling as much in love with Gabrielle as Gabrielle was with her. After all, their personalities were very similar, and they were perfectly compatible. Gabrielle knew that the feelings she felt for Lexie ran deeper than the feelings she'd had for any one of her various previous lovers, even those for whom she'd felt the deepest love. Lost in her intense urges, Gabrielle started mauling Lexie's breasts, running her other hand up her thick and ruffled skirts.

"Wait ... don't ..." giggled Lexie.

Gabrielle didn't listen. Couldn't listen. She wanted to see some cunt, and cunt she would see. Pulling off the undergarments, she exposed the ivory-colored, little cunny with its minute slit as unyielding as a nun's. Her sight was enticed by the thin membrane of darkest pink dangling between the slightly open crack. She immediately mouthed her cunt with lips and tongue, and Lexie's initial shock was followed by great delight.

"What are you doing?" giggled the sex-ignorant eighteen-year-old.

"I'm sucking you, what does it look like I am doing?" said Gabrielle, putting to work all the expertise she had learned as a whore.

"Then you shall fuck me, shan't you?" Lexie said.

Gabrielle paused. She didn't know what to do. What excuse could she muster up for her lack of a penis? "No, are you mad? The last thing I want is to get you in trouble, with child."

They stayed for a few hours before leaving their secret spot. Lexie continued to meet with Gabrielle for months after. But their relationship had to be a clandestine one, and not a soul knew about it.

"Lexie, would you marry me if I asked you?" Gabrielle asked one day.

"Guy, you know I'd accept instantly."

"Then it's settled! Marriage--it's a wonderful idea!"

That evening, Lexie came into her father's study. She told him everything about Gabrielle, about how they had been secretly seeing each other, and especially how completely in love they were. Her idealistic father was a very jolly sort. Nothing ever seemed to bother him. He looked at everything through a comic lens. He listened to her very patiently, and then came his response: "All this has indeed come as quite a surprise to me. I wish you had told me from the very beginning that you were seeing this person. I should be flaming with rage, for there are certain people in this

The Forbidden

world that one does not trust ... Still, you cannot imagine how very moved and overjoyed I am to know you've found true love in an age when the only thing people usually find is base lust, greed, and crime. My heart is truly warmed by your confession. Are you stunned by my passivity?"

"There *is* one more thing ..." paused Lexie, "we would, that is, with your permission, papa ... we would like to marry."

"Does this gentleman have money? A title?"

"Neither."

When he saw that his question had depressed her, he relented. After all, he thought of himself as a very progressive and enlightened person. "Oh, very well, then. Marry and be done with it!" he laughed, "but first I want to meet this individual and examine him well. You know I must first approve. Are you oh so certain you truly love him like you couldn't do without him?"

"Yes, father, I do! I do!"

"And you are sure you're not mistaken about him? This is no passing whim?"

"No, absolutely not.."

"Then there's nothing more to be said." He smiled. "It's settled."

There were a few as open-minded and as libertarian as her father ... but, sadly, only a very precious few among the upper-class and almost none among the aristocracy. Lexie considered herself very lucky.

Gabrielle was ecstatic when Lexie told her her father's reaction. She couldn't believe her ears. The first thing she did was to officially acquire a last name, as it would be necessary for their marriage. The scheduled meeting between herself and Lexie's father went smoothly. She also managed to scrape up enough money to buy some very fine clothing to wear for the wedding which took place a month later. It was a very expensive and elaborate one, arranged on a very grand scale, as could be expected for someone of Lexie's background. Those in attendance were some of the wealthiest and most powerful people in the land. They were intrigued, and some even outraged, that the Marquise was marrying a commoner. It was unheard-of. Her father, rather than hang his head low in shame, reveled in the disapproval. To him it was the funniest thing. He laughed at those snobbish fools. He enjoyed the attention, the scandal.

The Forbidden

After their honeymoon, the Marquise's kind and generous father gave his daughter and her new husband one of his several large estates for a dowry.

Even after a full week of married life, Lexie still didn't know that her spouse was a woman. The servants, however, had their mild suspicions, which they were careful to keep to themselves. One morning, a maid found menstrual blood on the sheets of Gabrielle's bed. As was the custom of the day, Lexie and Gabrielle slept in separate beds. The maid told the other servants about it, and their suspicions only grew.

Eventually, their suspicions were once and for all confirmed when they spied on Gabrielle through a keyhole as she took a bath. Her feminine charms were clear for their eyes to see.

"Oh my God, we were right! The Monsieur is a she!"

Even liveried male servants had a peek to satisfy their curiosity.

That same day, the servants confronted her about it in private. As if anticipating it all along, Gabrielle spat, "all right, how much to shut you up?"

"What?" they asked, like idiots.

"Name your price. I don't have all day."

They comprehended that she intended to bribe them. After a little discussion amongst themselves, they returned asking for an exorbitant sum.

"Alright here you are ... but not a single word to *anyone*! You hear? Not *one* word! Ever!"

Meekly, they swore to her on their lives to keep the secret and quickly disappeared downstairs with more money in their hands than they had ever seen in their entire lives.

Marie and Jacques had also just started their married life together after a wedding that was every bit as flamboyant as the one Lexie and Gabrielle enjoyed; their honeymoon took them to Switzerland, a land of much awe-inspiring natural beauty, and they stayed there for two weeks.

Upon their return, Marie found a letter waiting for her. It was from Gabrielle! Eagerly, Marie ripped it open and read:

The Forbidden

My dear sister,

I was astounded lately to hear word of your marriage to the King's chief advisor, Monsieur Jacques Savant. It's so well-known, I managed to acquire your address with little effort. I knew you were destined for grand things! I felt tempted to write you, sweet Marie, if only to correspond with you. I have missed you so. It's been so long since we parted. It was foolish of us to do it. But look, everything's turned out for the best, better than either of us could have ever expected! From poverty to prominence, as they say, and in so short a space! For, yes sister, I too have been dealt a favorable hand of late. Prepare yourself for a shock-- I am husband to the Marquise de Mauriac! Yes, husband! But how, you ask? Because I wear men's clothing and behave like a man. A slightly effeminate man, of course, but there are enough of those prancing about in the society of which I am now a part, so it does not matter. I'm a noblewoman now--or rather, a nobleman! I go by the first name Guy; and since I officially had no last name, as you know neither of us know it, I had to get a new one. I chose Gilmour. So you must always refer to me as Guy de Gilmour, even when you write me back in your letters. I must end this here as I have yet to dress for a ball my new wife and I were invited to tonight. I want to hear from you post-haste.

Yours with much love,

Gabrielle.

P.S. You must burn my letters right after you read them. For now, au revoir.

The Forbidden

During dinner, Marie and Jacques got to talking.
"What do you think of children?" she asked.
"I think they're a blessing."
"Jacques, I want us to have a child."
He paused, with a blank stare.
"What, what's the matter?" She was confused
"Oh, nothing, nothing ... I was just remembering the twins my first wife birthed just before she died."
"Twins? I didn't know it was twins."
"Yes, didn't I tell you? Two girls."
"Again, how long ago was that?"
"Twenty-one years ago."
"But where are they now?"
"Oh, well, at the time, I was far less fortunate than I am now. I couldn't afford to keep them, so I handed them over to the nuns."
"Which convent?"
"It was called St. Jude's, as I recall. It's since burned to the ground, or so I heard."
Marie's face went pale.
"My dear, whatever is the matter?"
"I'm one of those infants you gave up!" Marie gasped. "My sister, Gabrielle, is the other! We are twins! We were raised in St. Jude's as orphans! We are both twenty-one years of age!"
"... But surely there could have been other twin orphans."
"No, there were no other twins, only us. In fact, there were no other orphans at all throughout all the time that we lived there!"
"But ... that would mean that ... I am your father."
Jacques was suddenly speechless. He fell back in his seat, shocked beyond belief.
"Yes! And I'm your daughter!"
He rubbed the sides of his forehead in dismay. "Give me time to contemplate this, I need to make sense of it, my mind is in a cloud."
"One thing is clear and certain, however," said Marie on the verge of weeping. "Our marriage is unlawful ... an abomination!"
She fled in tears. There was no joy in finally discovering who her

The Forbidden

parents were. Never before had Marie wanted to know the answer less! She immediately put pen to paper and frantically wrote to Gabrielle about her awful revelation:

Gabrielle,

I must first thank you for your letter which I received just this morning. This evening I have been struck a blow from which I fear I will find it impossible to recover. I have just discovered, moments ago, that my husband, Jacques Savant, is in fact my father!-- our father! His first wife, now long deceased, was our mother! She died while giving birth to us! There is no mistake to any of this, dear sister. It is the absolute truth! Oh, Gabrielle, you cannot imagine my sorrow! This is the most horrible day of my life!

Marie

    She sealed the letter and got her coachman to go deliver it that night.
    In the meantime, Gabrielle continued to cleverly deceive Lexie and her family with relative ease.
    Although smart and well-educated, Lexie was still as sexually naive as most girls her age, with little interest in sex. And as long as she didn't ask for sexual intercourse, Gabrielle had nothing to worry about exposing her true gender. As for her new lot in life, Gabrielle was more than pleased to acquire her new ties to wealth, position, prestige and nobility. She still had to pinch herself from time to time, it was so unbelievable. Never in her wildest dreams would she have guessed that she could have pulled it off. And it felt like it would last forever. However, what remained most important to her was her love for the extremely physically attractive and intellectually stimulating Lexie.
    Having bought a whole new wardrobe of men's wear, Gabrielle was dressing up for a ball she and Lexie were invited to by the Duc de Florbelle, one of the most illustrious noblemen not only in France, but in

The Forbidden

all of the civilized world.

"You look splendid," said Lexie when she walked into the room and got an eyeful of Gabrielle. "The carriage is waiting. Let's be off."

When they arrived at the ball, it was packed with people. Music played and some looked on while others danced.

"Ah, Monsieur de Florbelle," said Lexie, approaching him.

He kissed her hand. "Well if it isn't the beautiful Mademoiselle de Mauriac everyone in Paris can't stop wagging their tongues about. It's no wonder why, ha, ha."

"I'd like to introduce you to my husband, Guy."

"A pleasure," said the Duc, half-frowning with a subtle air of patronage. It was well-known that Gabrielle didn't come from the upper crust of society and that her origins were mysteriously unknown.

Lexie and Gabrielle had a few drinks. The string quartet started playing Bach.

"Come, Guy, let's dance."

"But I don't know how," Gabrielle replied nervously.

"Just follow my lead. I won't go too fast."

There, dancing with the woman she loved, Gabrielle was transported to another world. She soon found herself having the time of her life. Never had she felt happier.

"You're getting the hang of it, aren't you?" said Lexie, spinning her around, going faster and faster.

Gabrielle was going dizzy, dizzy with vertigo, dizzy with excitement, drunk with wine, drunk with love.

The noise of the music and chatter in the room filled her head. But it didn't seem real. It was like a fantasy, where time meant nothing and action had no consequence.

Suddenly, a hand roughly grabbed her shoulder.

"Ou!" she gasped aloud, drawing attention to herself.

The music stopped moments later. The room went quiet. All eyes were on Gabrielle.

"Gabrielle! It's you! It's you!"

She swung around. Oh my God! she thought. She couldn't believe it! It was her other husband, the old Comte de Vanier from Provence! The past had come back to haunt her in a big way! What a nightmare!

"What are you doing dressed as a man!" he spat in a half-confused, half-indignant manner. After the way she had treated him, she could not

The Forbidden

have expected the same warm treatment she had been used to from him.

There was a general sigh that circled around the room. The Duc was flabbergasted. Lexie was ready to faint.

"Ladies and gentlemen!" said the Comte, "this gentleman here is none other than a young woman I married, named Gabrielle; a girl who grew up an orphan, who did not even have a surname when I married her! And how did she repay me for freeing her of a life of destitution and suffering? By robbing me blind!--this ungrateful wench! She sucked me dry and then disappeared, never to be heard from again!" Though at first forgiving, the Comte had in time grown very bitter over what Gabrielle had done when he discovered that she had run away with half of the hidden family treasure.

The spectacle was most dramatic and humiliating for Gabrielle. She fell to her knees, sobbing. Lexie only stood frozen, bewildered. The initial startled sighs in the room soon turned to rapid chatter, growing louder and louder. Angry and bitter phrases were hurled at Gabrielle. She managed to get back to her feet and fled desperately. When she got home, Marie's letter was there waiting for her. She read it.

"Oh my God!" she gasped, dropping the letter. "Poor Marie!"

Wasting no time, she wrote in reply:

My dearest Marie,

I have just read your letter and my heart bleeds for you. What a horrible misfortune! I, myself, have just been struck an equally dreadful blow. I've been exposed! Yes, my true identity is known! By practically all of society! I have no time to go into detail, but you can't begin to understand the embarrassment I went through tonight! Ugh! I cannot believe it. I never imagined it would happen! And I have no idea what happens now! Surely I'm doomed!

Love,

Gabrielle

The Forbidden

P.S. I know I deserve this fate; but Marie, you surely don't deserve yours! My crimes have been wilful deception, among others, but your sin was committed unwittingly, unknowingly. You cannot be held responsible for that!

She gave the letter over to be deliver. And a short time after, the gendarmes showed up at her door to arrest her. She went willingly.

Meanwhile, back at the ball, Lexie's emotions were alternating between astonishment and anger while everyone around her consoled her, filling her ears with:

"Oh you poor dear," or, "worry not, that fraud will get just what's coming to her."

"I don't care what happens to her," muttered Lexie, "it is nothing to me." She felt nothing but pure dislike verging on hatred for Gabrielle now. "That deceiving, perverted creature. I never want to see him--*her*--ever again!"

Marie received her sister's letter right around the time that Gabrielle was put in a cell to await her trial. Shaken by what she read, her hands trembling, Marie mused: "It's incredible how circumstances can turn completely around in so short a space."

Hours later, Jacques came up to her bedroom. "I've given it much thought. Since no one knows that you *are* my daughter, and since a public revelation would jeopardize and indeed ruin my professional career, not to mention shame us both forever, we *must* keep it a secret. If you prefer, we will cease carnal relations and privately we shall behave towards one another as father and daughter. In public, we continue to play the part of husband and wife. Is it a deal?"

At first hesitant, Marie finally agreed, arguing, "we knew nought of the fact that we are so closely related. It wasn't our fault, but the fault of mad ill luck. I mean, what are the chances of such a thing happening? The Devil be blamed."

Then she told him of her sister's situation, emphasizing how uncertain her future looked. "What should I do for her? What can I do?"

"At the moment, there's little you *can* do," he replied.

The Forbidden

Gabrielle's trial began almost immediately. The charges laid against her were theft, bigamy, and impersonation fraud. There was much hissing when she entered the courtroom to sit beside a lawyer who wasn't even of her own choosing. He was a greasy-haired, sloppy-looking, inept type who slouched when he walked, like a drunkard. He was a novice trial attorney with mediocre talent and no experience in the field of criminal law; he was actually trained in civil law instead. The judge presiding was a small, tired-looking man with bushy sideburns and a badly fitting wig. He sat there in a languid expression, gazing through scrawny, little spectacles that gave some sight to his otherwise near-blind eyes.

Right from the beginning, things started going downhill for Gabrielle, as her servants--six in all!--admitted on the stand to having been bribed by her to keep quiet. They explained all of the particulars, and all Gabrielle could do was shake her head in disgust, muttering, "traitors!" Those witnesses were followed by the Comte de Vanier, whose testimony was just as solid and damaging as the rest, but whose compassion really shone through at the end when he expressed his wish that mercy to be extended to the defendant, and that if guilty, his recommendation was that she not be hung but instead be placed in a prison or asylum. Some in the court-room shared his sentiment.

Only a mere four hours passed between the opening and closing arguments. At their conclusion, Gabrielle was afforded the opportunity to stand and make a statement before the court. She sensed that her chances of winning her case were slim to none. Spontaneously, she stood up before everyone, with tears in her eyes so copious that they blurred her vision. For the first time in her life gripped by deep religious feeling, she boldly shouted her last plea for mercy in impressively exalted and moving language, making clear that whatever she felt was necessary to say: "Gentlemen, you learned in the law, do me justice! Love led me to take the step I took. All my deeds were conditioned by it. God put it in my heart. If he created me so and not otherwise, am I then guilty; or is it the eternal, incomprehensible way of fate? I relied on God that one day my emancipation would come; for my thought was only love itself, which is the foundation, the guiding principle of his teaching ... Oh God, Thou All-pitying, Almighty One! Thou seest my distress; Thou knowest how I suffer. Incline thyself to me; extend Thy helping hand to me, deserted by all the world!"

Commotion spread in the room. Some spectators cried for

The Forbidden

leniency; others shouted for her to be condemned.

"Order!" exclaimed the judge, repeatedly hitting the gavel and letting its bang resonate through every corner of the room until there wasn't a whisper. "You are in contempt! You are in contempt of court all of you! Pray, be seated and be silent!"

After some deliberation, the judge returned with his verdict twenty minutes later. He took his seat, gazing at the poor defendant with his typical indifferent expression.

The judge: "defendant Gabrielle Gilmour, the court finds you guilty on all charges. The sentence of the court is death by hanging. You are to be executed tomorrow at the strike of noon. You shall hang until dead. May God have mercy on your soul."

According to the law of the times, almost all offenses merited hanging until the 1740s when more lenient reforms would be implemented.

As soon as they put her in prison to await execution with all the other local convicts, Gabrielle put herself to work writing Marie. It was her very last and dying hope. Her pleading letter read as follows:

Dear Marie,

You cannot imagine my predicament! I have been sentenced by a court of law to death! My execution is set for noon tomorrow! Oh my God, I'm so afraid! If only I had known things were going to turn out this way! What a fool I was! And here is the result of my foolishness! I should have followed your path! In my worldliness and naivete, I failed to realize that my way could only lead to my undoing. But I have all night to feel remorseful. The reason I write you now is because I need your help! It's my last, desperate grasp for salvation. I need our father to secure for me signed pardon from His Majesty. It need not be known that he is my father, or even that we are sisters. But it must be stressed that I am a close friend of yours

The Forbidden

*and his. Our father must also say that I was innocent,
and that the trial was not a fair one. With his high rank
and close connections to the sovereign, he can procure
this pardon for me and save me. Oh, Marie, I know
I deserve retribution, I know I deserve punishment.
But death? Is that not a fate more harsh than I deserve?*

Gabrielle

      Heartbreak was all that Marie felt after reading the letter, which she receive late in the evening from a messenger on horseback.
      "We must come to her rescue!" she gasped to Jacques.
      "Don't fret, Marie, with any luck it's not too late ... I shall speak it over with the King early tomorrow morning, for I am scheduled to have a conference with him on foreign affairs, these stupid and ruinous wars which seem to obsess him so much and cost our nation so dearly. But I wager the pardon's as good as ours."

The conference concerned military news about the King's latest war of expansion. It began at eight o'clock the following morning, with Jacques attempting everything he could to conclude it as early as possible.
      "I'm glad this business is resolved," sighed King Louis at the end of it, standing up to leave, "I don't want it said of me that I'm a war-monger bent on gravely weakening my nation's financial position in Europe."
      "Not at all, Sire. Oh, Your Majesty, one more thing, if I may trouble you for just one more moment ..."
      "What is it?"
      "A very close friend of my wife and myself has been most wrongly condemned to death. Furthermore, she is, or rather was, of the nobility. Such a person cannot be executed by some commoner's arbitrary sentence. I most humbly ask for--"
      "A death pardon," said the King. "You know, you're the third one that's asked me for one this week. Damn-it, when will my blue-blooded Aristocracy ever set an example ... They spend their days in sin and

The Forbidden

infamy, and then they wonder why the bourgeois have such bourgeois attitudes!"

Jacques despaired he would not get the pardon.

"Ah, but since you have been of such very fine service to me over the years, your friend can be eternally thankful to you that I grant you this pardon for him."

The King dug into a drawer, pulling out a sheet of paper.

"What is the person's name?"

"Gabrielle Gilmour."

"Any relation to the newly infamous Guy de Gilmour, who was recently exposed as a woman?"

Jacques froze. He didn't dare say anything.

"Here you are, Monsieur Savant ..." said the King, rolling the document into a scroll and tying it with a red ribbon. "When's the execution scheduled for?"

"Noon today, your Highness."

"Well you had better get moving!" exclaimed the King. "You only have a few precious hours."

"Precisely," said Jacques. "And I cannot thank you enough," he knelt and kissed the King's hand before dashing off.

Marie had been waiting for him in their carriage outside of the palace. When she saw her father coming, waving the pardon, she had tears of joy and relief in her eyes and knew that now it would only be a race against Time. Would they succeed? This question haunted her to the deepest part of her being.

When Jacques was back in the carriage, he looked at the time. "It's already half past nine."

"Drive on!" exclaimed Marie. "To Ronet Prison!"

The carriage sped away.

"Faster! Faster!" yelled Jacques.

"I can't go any faster!" the driver hollered. "It's too dangerous!"

They arrived at the prison at five minutes past noon.

"We're too late!" exclaimed Marie in agony.

"There may still be time!" exclaimed Jacques. "Hurry!" He handed his daughter the pardon, knowing that her young legs could run much faster than his, while he tagged along from behind. And run she did, sprinting right into the building aimlessly.

"Hey, I say, what are you doing here?" said the prison governor

The Forbidden

when he saw Marie rush in. He was a bald, big-headed man, with reddish skin and a dark mustachio like a Spaniard.

"It's alright, she's with me," said Jacques.

"And who might you be, sir," he said with contempt.

"Chief political advisor to the King."

The man suddenly took on a respectful demeanor.

Jacques: "Now, pray, we have little time. I have His Majesty's signed pardon for the release of the prisoner Gabrielle Gilmour."

"Is her name specified on the pardon?"

"Of course."

"This had better not be a forged document ... It must have the King's royal seal."

The prison governor examined it and seemed to find nothing at fault with it. "Ah, well I'm afraid your trip has anyhow been a needless one. That prisoner has just been taken to be executed. I'm afraid your pardon has arrived too late. She's already been taken from her cell. I'm sure she must be dead by now. The gallows are not that far of a walk."

"Which way to the gallows!" Jacques said urgently.

"They're only about a hundred yards that way," he pointed north.

Jacques and Marie scurried back outside. In the distance, the gallows could be seen.

"There, do you see?" said Marie.

"Yes! My God! Four people are hanging!"

Jacques and Marie hurried towards the executioner and two accompanying prison wardens.

It was a frightful sight--Gabrielle had already been hanging from a rope for over a minute. Jacques easily recognized which was Marie's twin, and he shot at the thick line of rope. The first was a miss that just grazed it. But the second shot snapped the rope completely, and Gabrielle fell, tugging to loosen the rope around her neck, coughing and choking. Marie ran up to her, pulling it off and embracing her. She was alive!

There was a big explanation from Jacques as he showed the executioner the death pardon. Gabrielle was saved!

Marie and Jacques took Gabrielle back to their estate.

"My beautiful daughters!" gasped Jacques, hugging them both

The Forbidden

intensely. "You will forgive me for giving you up those many years ago, won't you? I had to do it ... but all that's now in the past. Ah, my darlings, your mother is smiling down on you from Heaven. It's a pity that she is no longer with us, but I feel quite sure she's rejoicing now from wherever she may be. The important thing is that God has looked over you and has brought you back to me at last. My gratitude cannot be measured!"

"Neither can ours!" retorted Marie.

"But if you hadn't come ... I'd be hanging lifeless and limp this very moment, with my eyes gouged out by crows," Gabrielle mused.

Marie: "I still cannot believe we got to you in time."

"But truly, how could things have ended any other way!" Jacques chuckled. "It was destiny, simply fate."

Thus ended an unpleasant ordeal. Gabrielle was offered a home with her sister Marie and newfound father Jacques. This gave birth to a whole new and happy beginning.

THE END

The Forbidden

Other published books by DAVID REHAK:

A Young Girl's Crimes (contemporary fiction)

Love and Madness (historical fiction)

Poems From My Bleeding Heart (poetry)

Crippled Dreams (historical fiction)

Did Lizzie Borden Axe For It? (true crime / historical nonfiction)

Call Me: Phone Sex with a Stranger (contemporary erotica)

Confessions and Musings of a Young Man (poetry)

Forthcoming books by DAVID REHAK:

I Was Born Dead: a memoir (contemporary autobiography / memoir)

From the Present: stories (contemporary fiction)

From the Past: stories (historical fiction)

Greatest Short Story Writer, Guy de Maupassant: His Very Best Stories (historical fiction)

Breinigsville, PA USA
08 December 2009
228855BV00001B/169/P